BEACHDAZE

BEACHDAZE

TW LAWLESS

CAMPANILE
PUBLISHING

Published by Campanile Publishing
www.twlawless.com

© 2023 TW Lawless

The moral right of the author has been asserted.

A National Library of Australia Cataloguing-in-Publication entry has been created for this title.

    ISBN 978-0-6450991-0-2 (pbk)

    ISBN 978-0-6450991-1-9 (ebook)

Cover design by Golden Orb Creative: www.goldenorbcreative.com
Cover image used under licence from iStock.com (photo ID: 532940153).

Text design and production (print and ebook) by Golden Orb Creative.

For investigative journalists everywhere,
and for those who pursue the truth

CHAPTER ONE

A deadly game

Nick Sutcliffe

I flick on the high beam, as I slow my BMW to negotiate a tight corner.

The esplanade that skirts the bay has the potential to be a driver's worst nightmare, especially at night, and especially for anyone who doesn't know the road. Fortunately for me, I know it well. Which is unsurprising, given that I've lived here since I was a child.

As I drive, my headlights dance off the tall, rendered walls that maintain the privacy in the adjacent houses, without obstructing their sea view. Perched high above the cliff road, even on a moonless night, the houses look enormous. Flat-roofed hangars, too big for the average nuclear family, they are an architect's wet dream. But my tastes have changed a lot lately; nowadays I think they're simply ugly.

I steer my way between the sheer drop to my left and the steep bank on the right, the beams of the cars coming in the opposite direction flashing in and out of view as they negotiate the twisting road. They are too far away to be of concern, and it gives me a chance to reflect on my childhood. For me, home has been a wonderland of rockpools, and seahorses, fish and chips devoured on the beach, and the stink of rotting seaweed after a summer storm. But that was before the speeding tailgaters, the reckless overtakers and the lycra cowboys on their exorbitant graphite bikes took control of the esplanade.

Over the years that followed, I've watched Serenity Bay move away from being an isolated little community of beach shacks

1

surrounded by farmland, where everyone knows everyone else's business, and gives a shit. But Melbourne's expanded into a city of almost five million people and the freeway that leads the suburban masses to the bay has changed everything. The developers have moved in, land prices have skyrocketed, and the shack owners have sold up and cashed in. I expected that infrastructure would follow growth, but it hasn't. Suddenly, there are too many people sharing the same space and, as much as the local council loves raking in the money, it hates spending it even more.

The well-heeled have acquired their summer residences, just so they can say that they spend Christmas by the sea. God's country destroyed. Money made. Lots of it.

By the time I reach about three-quarters of the way along the esplanade, I'm thinking about my future. The area has changed too much for my liking, and I'm finally doing something about it. I owe that to my family, and to the others who want a quiet life. I'm done.

The road narrows to a sharp, hairpin bend; it's caused several fatalities in recent years, mostly among the unwary. According to the council, guardrails interfere with the view, so they refuse to replace the existing ones when they rust away. More likely, they cost too much to put in. Traffic has become so heavy of late, that it's chewed up the slender verge on the bay side of the bitumen, and it's decimated the scrubby saltbushes that are meant to prevent cars from going over the cliff. The speed limit is supposed to be forty kilometres per hour, but most drivers don't do that. So, just to be extra sure, I check that nobody is following me, and slow my car to almost a crawl.

I turn out of the bend, unscathed. I'm less than three kilometres from home, although I'm already there in my mind. There is one more sweeping turn high over the bay to negotiate before the road widens and flattens out.

Just then, a light coming in the opposite direction blinds me. I feel my front left tyre leave the bitumen, but the BMW is sure-footed, and I'm able to pull it back.

'Turn off your high beam, you bloody idiot!' I say as I flick my lights at the approaching driver.

Instead of the lights dimming, they suddenly grow brighter. It is then that I realise that they aren't headlights at all. They're spotlights, and they're coming straight at me. My choice is to have a head-on collision with the approaching car, or to go over the cliff.

I can't see a thing, but I'm sure not going over that cliff. I try not to panic—after all, I know the esplanade like the back of my hand.

The lights are now nearly on top of me, and they keep coming.

I press down on the horn furiously, while I try to steer by memory.

I feel the car lurch when it departs the bitumen. I try to direct it back onto the road again, but I know that I've oversteered the moment I sense the crunch of gravel under my tyres. I hear the thud of the worn-out safety barrier and an uprooted shrub smack against my windscreen as I slam my foot on the brake. There is no traction. There is nothing.

It is too late. I feel the car going over, hurtling through the night.

My last thought before my car hits the water isn't of my wife and children, or even of all the wasted years. It is summer, and I'm in my dad's arms again, naked and afraid of the breaking surf.

And then I ask myself, why?

Chapter Two

London 2015

It was all coming to a head. It had to. Peter Clancy was about to fly off the rollercoaster, even though he wasn't aware of it. Not yet.

He'd been given enough warnings. He simply didn't expect it to happen quite this soon. Life's battles, exploits and excesses were finally about to catch up with him. Over the years he'd watched them follow him in his rear-vision mirror, accelerating behind him, narrowing the gap. Or perhaps he'd just slowed down enough for his excesses to overtake him.

It was late afternoon when he and a cool half-dozen of Fleet Street's sometime finest reporters stumbled into The Coach and Horses pub in Greek Street, Soho. It seemed that the lunchtime crowd had forgotten to move on, but Peter still found them a half-metre of the bar and shoe-horned them in. 'Drink up, ingrates and inebriates,' he announced to his friends, 'this round's mine!'

He caught the publican's attention by waving a wad of notes at him and then relayed the orders in the sequence that they were shouted out: wine, beer, spirits. He began with a scotch for himself—his favoured pathway to intoxication—trailed by a Fosters chaser.

'Here's to the best mates a journo ever had,' he shouted over the rumbling mob, raising his pint glass. After the cheers subsided, he added, 'No, no, no, I don't mean you bloody hacks, you bunch of bottom-sniffing newshounds that I'm proud to call my equals... I mean this!' He tilted his drink and slopped most of the lager over his shirt. 'Here's to the booze that makes working in this industry tolerable!'

Wahey!

From somewhere came the reply, 'And here's to you, Peter, for being nominated for the Investigation of the Year award. And may you have many, many more nominations like that, so that we can enjoy many, many more piss-ups like these!'

Wahey!

It was the perfect excuse; this time, it was his investigative story on human trafficking from the Middle East that had caught the zeitgeist. The celebration was arguably a little premature, but he didn't want to be left at the altar again. *Start the honeymoon before the marriage.* This was his third nomination over a very, very long career.

He swallowed his third Johnny Walker Green. Or was it Black? He couldn't tell; maybe his tongue was becoming colourblind. He began to say, 'You do realise that, in awards that really stand for something, I'm journalism's perpetual bridesmaid. The last time we were here, I'd...' and then he felt a pain so sharp and agonising that he dropped his glass. His knees buckled and gave out from under him. From faraway, he thought he heard his father snigger on his predicament: *It's dropped you like a stuck steer, hey?*

After that, his world became a blur of faces, of blaring lights and loud voices, of machines and tubes. No tears though. No one was that close to him. People and places from the past arrived to give him comfort through it all. He had seen the white light, but the figure at the other end had said: *Turn around; you're not wanted here.*

Once the parade ended and the fuzz cleared from his brain, a resident medical officer in the Emergency Department told him what it was: 'You've had a mild heart attack and survived, Peter. But only just.'

Then came the lecture in a Harley Street consulting room, the one about seeing it as a stroke of good luck, a wake-up call, a warning to change one's lifestyle or suffer the consequences. *Cut back, give up, live healthy.*

Good luck? Cut back, give up, live healthy?

It sounded like the cardiologist had just condemned him to a lingering death, whereas he'd always expected a quick and disgraceful yet enjoyable one.

Peter had squirmed in his chair. Yes, he would make the sacrifice—and it was going to be a great big, bloody sacrifice. *Doc, I'm a journalist not a monk.* But if it meant not dying anytime soon, he'd give it a go. He had several good reasons to live—there were still far too many stories out there to write, and too many arseholes to stitch up for him to call it quits. And a few more loves, hopefully. And maybe he'd get one of those lifetime achievements awards if he made it past seventy. Just for being an old hack. Something akin to a service medal.

So he told the cardiologist what he wanted to hear. 'Sure, I can try cutting back on the alcohol, the late nights, the missed meals and the fast food. Yes, I can even exercise and meditate. Of course, I'll take the medication you've dished out. It'll be difficult, but I've faced down hardship and danger before, no worries.

'As long as I can keep working. I must keep working. It's my life,' he implored. 'I don't have any other reason to live. You see, Doc, I eliminated every other stressor years ago. I have no wife, no kids, no family. Not even a car or a mortgage. It's the way I like it.'

Then the bombshell came from the cardiologist. 'It's not as simple as that, I'm afraid. Here you are, sat in my rooms for all of what, five, ten minutes, and you're already itching to leave. You're writing tomorrow's headline, even as we speak. The cortisol's flowing, blood pressure's rising. I'm giving you an ultimatum: you must change your lifestyle entirely, Mr Clancy, or your job will be your elegy. You must face the fact that you're not a young man anymore.

'That will, of course, require you to stop work entirely, and move out of the capital. I want you to get away from your work, and all of the bad influences that have led you astray. Find some serenity in your life. Live a healthy life. And take the bloody medication. There. Not such a terrible trade-off to secure yourself some shares in peace and longevity, is it?'

The lecture was over.

Peter left the consulting room a thoroughly changed man, determined to live a clean life. By the time he stepped out of the building and onto Harley Street, a little doubt had crept in. Somewhere between Wigmore Street and the Oxford Circus Tube station, he had begun to feel like the old Peter Clancy. A little alcohol had been scientifically proven to be beneficial and was therefore a healthier alternative to complete abstinence. It was sound enough logic, except that he hadn't run it past the doctor.

Peace and longevity were overrated.

He promptly headed to the nearest pub and got totally wasted.

CHAPTER THREE

Serenity Bay, Tyne Coast, south-east of Melbourne, Australia
Many hours' flight time from London
and all bad influences

'Well,' Peter said to himself when he first saw the bay, 'I've found serenity, just like you said, Doc. As it happens, there is such a place as Serenity. I'll send you a postcard sometime.'

After his death-defying feat, and once he'd sobered up from that one last, great piss-up, he indulged himself in a tonne of reflection and self-denial. And then he began to look ahead.

'You,' his accountant had told him, 'are my most frugal client. You rarely ask for anything. When I haven't heard from you for a while, I begin to wonder if you've passed on. And then just when I've given you up for dead, I receive an exorbitant account from an off-licence. Alcohol and rent aside, you've spent almost nothing for an entire decade: you have enough saved up to buy your own home.'

Peter was incredulous. 'My own home? I've never owned a house before. I've always thought that land ownership was too permanent and too much of a commitment for someone like me, akin to marriage… Or perhaps death. Are you sure?' he asked him.

'Absolutely certain. Not here in London, of course, but somewhere beyond the home counties would be completely doable. A little country cottage might be perfect for a man without ties. And you could retire tomorrow on your royalties—not well, mind, but if you continued to sell the odd article here and there you could live comfortably. Plus, the advance on your last book is still untouched and gathering a little interest from time to time.'

'I'll give it some thought,' he replied.

Later that day, with his accountant's blessing, he began to trawl the internet for places consistent with the concept of tranquillity.

No small country towns: I suffered through enough of them as a child. Nothing too genteel: I need real, unhomogenised life around me. And a pub. Proximity to a pub or a bar is a must, even if I only ever drink lemonade there.

He glanced momentarily at the houses listed for sale in Britain, but everywhere outside London seemed dull and grey. Besides, if he bought a place in Surrey, his mates would soon find him. Cotswold stone lost its appeal once he'd broken up with Ruby Manzanoni— his only true love—and coastal villages felt far too frigid. He yearned for warmth and kindness. But where? He wasn't the Bintang type. And Italy, Spain and Greece mandated interaction with another language, so he quickly ruled them out too.

Perhaps I should just revisit the familiar: the heat, the sand, the murderous wildlife and the flies. Perhaps I should just go back to Australia.

That notion began as a fledgling. While he contemplated his next step, the farewell parties persisted. And there were plenty of those. The parties soon turned into late-night, boozy affairs, simultaneously daring his heart to stop beating while they nurtured the fledgling into adulthood.

Leave! Go now, before it's too late!

As the days flew by, the thought of returning to Australia grew until it became too great to ignore: the greyer London became, the more he craved the blinding antipodean sun. London was turning toxic. He needed to leave there to preserve his life.

After one especially long evening, he decided: his return to Australia was imminent. He booked his ticket.

In his final email to the London crowd, he wrote: *I'm off on my next, great adventure. You'll all be pleased to know that I haven't given up drinking entirely, I'm just drinking in a different way. If you make the trip to visit me, I can promise you a lager for your efforts. Served room temperature, of course.*

Last farewells exchanged, he clambered on board the flagship of the fleet heading for Melbourne and settled back for twenty hours of sobriety punctuated by a solitary, dawn-busting hour transiting through some god-forsaken, hotter-than-hell airport. He began the journey by flicking through the menu of film and television. It was a choice of watched it / don't want to watch it, so he typed out an email or two and listened to music until his ears started to throb. Without benefit of alcohol his mind drifted to other diversions. Since any illicit substance would have killed him instantly (according to his cardiologist), he doubled up on his panic pills and slept his way through two meal services. He did the same thing once he reboarded the plane after the transit, and by the time they had reached Australian airspace, he was nursing an angry head and a grumbling stomach.

'Sorry,' said the flight attendant, 'the meal service has closed.' She looked as sour as cabin air after a long-haul flight.

'Got any peanuts?' he asked.

'No, sir, we don't offer our passengers peanuts these days. They're too full of allergens.'

'You don't have to worry about me, I'm not allergic to anything.'

'It's not you I worry about. Do you have any idea how many people die every year just from inhaling second-hand peanut breath?'

'No, I don't,' he replied, 'but what I do know is that I've missed every meal so far, so you can either bring me something to eat or I'll be expecting a refund on my ticket.'

She smiled and walked away. Awakened by the sound of digestive juices acid-etching an empty stomach, his next-seat neighbour stirred from her slumber. She took pity on him and, with a series of nods, pulled out a box of mystery snacks from her seat pocket. She offered it to him as she might to a toddler she aimed to deflect from certain tantrum. He returned her nods as a show of his appreciation.

He asked her, 'What is it?'

She raised her hand to her mouth and mimed eating.

He accepted the box and stared at the laughing Buddhas that surrounded it. There was no clue as to its contents. He read the only word he was able to decipher, *Shandong*, and decided to take a chance. The scent from the opened box was unmistakable.

'Well, whaddaya know! Peanuts!'

'Yes, peanuts,' she faltered, laughing.

The beast appeased, he fell asleep again without benefit of medication this time, and dreamt of mass human extinction linked to his consumption of peanuts. He woke just in time to sense the jolt of tyres on the tarmac.

'Home,' he whispered, although he didn't really feel it.

The first thing he did when he arrived in Melbourne was to buy himself a car. He was tempted to buy vintage—possibly a Triumph Stag as a nod to his misspent youth—until he remembered the many hours his old Stag had spent with the mechanic. Or by the side of the road. Or demanding to be filled up at great cost. At that point, he decided that a Stag was utterly inconsistent with the concept of serenity. He needed reliability. *Boring but dependable for me from this moment on. Nothing racy. Nothing phallic. Nothing red.* He bought himself a near-new Japanese car instead.

He drove past the payphone at the southern end of Serenity Bay village, and up the esplanade, wishing that he'd bought a convertible in its place, just so he could have enjoyed the sunshine and the view a little better. About a kilometre along, he turned left. From there, he pulled his car off the unsealed road, and into the gravel driveway of 65 Helga Lane.

Number sixty-five was nothing flashy, a one-storey weatherboard beach house with a basement, built in the 1970s, a bit tired and weatherworn. He first saw it advertised on the real estate website a couple of weeks after he'd spoken to his accountant. He'd followed up a week later by sending the selling agent an email from London.

'It's all about location,' the agent wrote in reply. 'Twenty years ago, houses like this were worthless. Now, they're closing in on a million dollars. Everyone wants to live near the sea these days. Imagine what you'll get for it in a few years if you decide to sell it. Make the vendors a realistic offer; you won't regret it. Wait and you'll miss out.'

Peter vacillated. He wasn't just buying a house sight unseen; he hadn't even visited Serenity Bay before. He told himself that it was a simple case of nothing ventured, nothing changed. He slept on it. Then he bought it the next day.

The agent had described it as a 'beachcomber's getaway' but, sitting in his idling car in front of it and seeing it in all its glory, he preferred to call it his 'Hermit's Hut'. It wasn't in awful condition, except for the fence and the yard, of which there was very little of the first, and far too much of the other. It was tidy enough for the undiscriminating man, a three-bedder, set high, and it came with a breathtaking view from the deck. It was the view as much as the price that sold it to him.

As long as the neighbours kept their trees trimmed, he would have a brilliant 180-degree panorama of the bay, from the horizon almost to the cliffs at the end of his road. He would even see the outline of Melbourne across the water, and the planes taking off and touching down at Tullamarine Airport. Apparently a boring, elderly couple had loved the house for decades. It was a great retirement option, the agent told him, perfect for someone without a family, like him. But, as Peter told anyone who asked, he wasn't retiring, only revitalising. He would either find himself there or lose himself entirely.

He stopped the car and stepped out. After the din of London, the silence was deafening, apart from a group of screeching white cockatoos tearing up one of his trees, and the roar of the waves two streets away. If only he'd had the sense to buy five houses the last time he was here, he would have been a multi-millionaire without a care in the world. He indulged in the idea of Peter Clancy, award-winning reporter and property tycoon, for a moment and chuckled, but that life was never for him; he lived and breathed to write.

The beach house was kind of perfect for that: kind of dull, conveniently located a walk away from the beach, a small supermarket, a coffee shop, a restaurant cum wine bar, and a liquor store. He had vowed that he would avoid the last two. He was in medical exile, a refugee of sorts, determined to maintain the pact he made with his darker side never to drink alone or socialise with anyone who'd encourage him to overdrink.

When he was last in Melbourne, he'd been a tabloid reporter living in a derelict flat over a souvlaki shop, pining after Poppy

Reynolds, a girl with an angel's face and the devil's soul. He was mates with a bloke who dressed up like a woman for a living as well as every down-and-out resident of inner-city Collingwood. He had coerced, sensationalised and maligned his way to the position of star writer for the most notorious scandal-sheet in Melbourne. Courtesy of his amazing investigative prowess and his innate ability to get under everyone's skin, he had painted a target the size of a Northern Territory cattle station on his back, that members of Melbourne's underworld were itching to take shots at. And all that just for a by-line.

But that felt like a hundred years and a thousand scars ago.

Pioneers rode horses into the wilderness to find themselves, didn't they, and I had my reasons for leaving Australia and not looking behind.

He'd needed to prove that he wasn't just a rabid reporter with a sense for a story and a complete absence of scruples. The world was beckoning: leave the colonies behind, it was saying, and come find me! And he had.

Now that he was back, he imagined that everyone he knew had died or moved on; he hadn't heard from any of them in a long time. He was unfazed: there were fewer temptations and distractions that way. He could have made an effort to contact them while he was in London, but they could have as well; perhaps Melbourne was just another bridge he'd burned.

He began the job of settling in the minute the removalists delivered the very few sentimental pieces he owned—his coffee machine, an oak desk that apparently once belonged to Colin Reith Coote (which he bought for a song in an antique shop outside Oxford), the rest of his office furniture, and his writing awards. He tried to open the garage door and failed, so he started to set up his office in a spare bedroom instead. Once the courier had delivered the rest of the furniture, homewares and bedding he had bought online, he decided to go for a walk. He needed to get a feel for his new home, and what better way than a stroll around the neighbourhood? It was something he promised himself he'd do regularly. The doctor had sown the seed and he just needed to look after it.

He couldn't remember having walked for exercise, and barely a few minutes in, he was struggling with the concept of physical exertion for pleasure. Walking was only useful if it was essential to arrive at a destination. Cycling was solely for schoolchildren and those who have been caught drink-driving. Gyms were for strange people who liked to wear lycra. His main form of exercise lately involved him either running away from trouble or running into it.

Despite its number, his house was only the second one on Helga Lane, opposite a creek and some thick bushland; protocol dictated that the house numbers related to the distance from the closest intersection rather than the number of houses in the street. A faded sign a little further along the lane informed him that he was within the Harmony Creek catchment area, and to beware of children and wildlife. He reread the sign and his brow furrowed; he couldn't be sure if the caution was meant to keep him safe, or the children and wildlife.

The houses on the opposite side to his were all on acreage, spaced out from each other. The houses on his side sat on generous blocks which weren't quite as large. As he walked, he counted another eight houses to the end of the road. It concluded as a dead-end dirt road: the way he liked it. He was assured of serenity in spades since there wouldn't be any through traffic to annoy him.

Four of those eight houses were invisible from the road, secluded behind high gates, automatic as far as he could tell, and completely hidden by the thick bush. Three of the others screamed *look at me, I've got money*. They loomed over the road, too large and too cubist for any cosy, domestic purpose. Except for a single, land-scaped garden bed, their blocks were completely cleared. They were uniform in concept: an oversized garage for the obligatory Euro RVs, a small strip of fake lawn, and a swimming pool adjoining an al fresco area for entertaining the well-heeled to the rear. He called them *home-tels*. Houses styled to look like boutique hotels. An impersonal space to stay. Built to a formula and designed with a sole purpose in mind—to impress.

The eighth house seemed to want to hide away, and because of that it stood out from all the others. Its gate was locked with a chain and padlock, and it had a *Don't Trespass* sign on it. Peter concluded that the occupiers evidently liked their privacy. Private people either wanted the world to go away, or they had something to hide: wasn't that how it always worked? He wagered with himself that these occupiers were hiding something, and that piqued his curiosity.

From the road, he counted three CCTV cameras pointing in every direction. It was enough to for him to imagine all sorts of goings-on. Or perhaps the occupants were paranoid. Or doomsday preppers. Why else would anyone care so much about the world immediately outside their gate? He peered a little harder. He could make out the roofline of a double-storey house, but that was all. The oversized fence obscured the rest of it.

He walked past it, his head on a swivel, until he was back where he started: at the entrance to his beach house. Walk and contemplation over, he decided to avoid the beach for today. *Maybe tomorrow. Too much exercise could damage you.* He looked up at his house. It was totally misaligned. The other houses looked mature, settled in their environment, respectably middle-class, like business suits and ties. His screamed long hair, body shirts, stacked heels and cheesecloth kaftans. It was his seventies bohemian rebel. He liked that. A lot.

At least his taste was consistent: he'd always found comfort in the imperfect and the slightly down-at-heel, so that was what he sought out. In most aspects of his life, close enough was good enough, and that went for his taste in women, too. Ruby had been the notable exception to his rule. She had been perfect—bohemian, to be sure—but also prosperous, a successful businesswoman and his intellectual equal. And kind and sweet and beautiful. She was an English rockstar's daughter, which had added to her allure. He'd fallen hard for her, and he'd adored her. And then he'd ruined his one chance at happiness, for a story. He still thought about her from time to time: she remained his greatest regret.

The only time he unfailingly strove for perfection was in his writing and his research. There, he could afford to be meticulous, check and recheck, cut himself a gem-quality story and then polish it until it glittered. As for everything else, perfection demanded energy he simply wasn't willing to expend.

Late in the afternoon, after a nap, he decided he'd take another stroll. By the time he went past the second house, his mind was on other things. He was enjoying the peace of Serenity Bay, mapping out his future. His mind was buzzing; he'd barely noticed that he'd drifted into the middle of the dirt road. He'd been thinking non-stop about Poppy and Ruby and others whose names he'd forgotten. No more women; from now on Serenity Bay would be his only muse. Bad relationships had been his downfall. He could never seem to find balance; he was always out of sync with the women he dated. Perhaps his new-found stability would inspire him to pursue artistic endeavours: to write more books, pick up the guitar again, learn pottery.

No, forget the last one; I'm not a retired art teacher, after all.

And if serenity ever became overly tedious, he'd turn to freelance, just to keep his hand in. Nothing too serious. Nothing that involved fast cars and angry people. He was done with investigative reporting. He'd thrown away his cunning kit; he'd never need to wear another disguise or insinuate himself into a dangerous situation ever again.

Henceforth, I'll write about nothing more demanding than angry cats and singing dogs. That's it. I'm going to look after the old ticker.

He was nearly back home and still sitting with that thought when a car horn blasted him. He was shocked by the noise, but he was even more shocked that he didn't hear the vehicle approach. By the time he realised what was bearing down on him, he could sense the warmth of the revving engine on his legs. As he dived sideways, he felt his knee collapse. Fortunately, he was still nimble enough to clear the car. A Range Rover brushed past him. The driver looked at him as if he was of no more importance than a gnat.

Peter took one peek at her and formed an immediate opinion. 'Stop blowing your stupid horn at me,' he yelled, 'or I'll insert it so far up your fat, fake arse, that it'll come out your fat, fake lips!'

The Range Rover suddenly lurched. For a moment, he thought he was going to be roadkill. *Dead like a kangaroo.* Someone like that would have driven over the top of him and not batted a false eyelash. He might have expected this behaviour in a large city, but surely not in a small beach community.

He stood up, limped slowly to the driver's window, and knocked hard. If he'd had a rock, he would have smashed it. *Heartless bitch.* Then he thought of his own heart. *Stay calm, but bite hard.*

She lowered the window slightly. It was difficult to ascertain her age, from the work she'd had done on her face. *Maybe thirty-ish? Maybe as old as Cleopatra?* She was the antipodean equivalent of a too-posh-to-push yum-mum from Chelsea, the type who constantly takes selfies of herself and her food and has a large social media following. He half expected her to say, *Welcome to the modern world of me, me, me. Excuse me, I just want to talk about me.*

Instead, she said, 'Why were you walking on the road, moron? Got a death wish? There is a footpath, you know.'

The so-called footpath was spotted with trees and covered in weeds. It was rutted, with not enough space for a cat to walk on. He began to say that, until he noticed that her lips were still moving, even though she'd long since stopped talking. Her face was otherwise as motionless and emotionless as a corpse.

'How about you ask me if I'm all right?' he bit back. 'And have you ever bothered to step out of your vehicle to see the footpath, let alone tried to walk on it? It's a fucking health hazard.'

Her eyes glazed over.

He placed his elbow against the window and leaned in. 'Thought so,' he continued. 'Too stuck-up to care about the rest of the world.'

'I'm too busy for this,' she said.

She reached for the power window switch, but Peter was still leaning.

'Then I won't keep you,' he said. 'But if you ever steer your crap car in my direction again, I'll put a fucking rock through your window.'

'How dare you intimidate me. That's called assault!' she screeched.

'No, that's called self-defence.'

The woman huffed. She closed the window and glared. As she moved away, he heard her open it again and yell, 'If you cause me or my husband any trouble, we'll be contacting the authorities. We know people.'

He yelled back, 'Good for you, love. And since you know people, can you ask them to fix up the footpath? Instead of yelling at me, how about you focus your energy on getting the authorities to fill the potholes and put grates over the open drains? Killing pedestrians is not a blood sport, you know, and it's not legal.'

A moment later, he watched her turn her Range Rover into the driveway of the house next to his.

He crossed his yard and limped to the boundary fence, just as she went to collect her mail.

'Why hello, neighbour!' he said brightly. 'Fancy seeing you again!'

The blood drained from her face when she spotted him. The woman huffed once more, and bellowed, 'So, you're the new tenant renting the old shitbox. I should have known.'

'Nup, no. Not a new tenant. I'm the new owner. Bought the place a month ago and I'm just moving in.' *Now put that on your Instagram account, Silicon Bitch!*

'Well, it's people like you ruin it for people like us! You stay far away from my family, or there'll be trouble.'

'Not a problem.' He chuckled. *I guess that means a neighbourly drink is out of the question. I'll put some bottles of bubbles laced with poison in the fridge if she pops over.*

'And since you own the place, you can clean up your yard!'

It wasn't how he had intended life in Serenity to begin. *No second thoughts. This isn't the place to have them. You're not a second-thoughts type of person.* He was more the impulsive-with-some-regrets type. He sat on the deck enjoying the warm, pleasant evening (minus an alcoholic drink), with his leg elevated on a chair and an ice pack on his knee. His only comfort was his stereo playing Etta James, a double espresso and a take-away curry. A gentle, comforting breeze was blowing in from the bay. The sea was calm, and it was having the desired effect. The music and the sea were better than pills and booze to wash away the irritants of life.

The lights from the skyscrapers flickered on the other side of the bay.

The world is calm, you're calm. Tomorrow is another day. It will be a calm one—it must be—it better fucking be. Doctor's orders.

Welcome to Serenity.

CHAPTER FOUR

Meeting and greeting

Peter was right: it turned out to be a week of calm. He unpacked boxes, finished setting up his office, and was ready to ring people for freelance work. He had even mapped out a book. Next on his list were the names of old friends and associates for him to track down. He'd start by finding out if they were alive or dead.

He began with a simple internet search of names and workplaces, and soon tracked down a couple of his old colleagues from his old stamping ground, that reviled gossip sheet *The Melbourne Truth*. He'd lost contact with most of them after the paper's demise, but a handful of old-timers had segued from writing smut for the tabloids to peddling scandal online. A few clicks, and his screen lit up with a humiliation of celebrities. The first headline read 'Singing Siren's Seedy Sex at the Seaside'. He scanned through the article and shook his head. He chuckled. *I never thought it was possible to write for a publication that was sleazier than the* Truth, *but I can see now that I was wrong. Woody Turnbull, you master baiter, you've truly outdone yourself.*

Peter paid a month's subscription and gorged himself on lewdness until it began to nauseate him. Then he turned his attention to searching for people he'd once really cared about. *Concheetah? Nothing. Sam Saturday? No better.* Past girlfriends—or at least the ones he could recall—had either vaporised or changed their names, and there were simply too many Michelle Martins and Sarah Crawfords to bother with Facebook. He had to admit that perhaps the motivation wasn't enough. He had far better things to do.

As for clearing out the garden, that could wait. The snub-nosed neighbours could bleat all they wanted. They had already put a letter in his mailbox, threatening to *take action* over his unkempt garden. It was signed *Rhiannon and Andre de Wold*. Even their names were pretentious. He had googled them instantly: hubby called himself a finance broker, and she was a 'social influencer'. *Wankers more like it. Well, you can start by staying out of my life and when the council turns up, I'll be telling them I'm trying to attract endangered wildlife.*

He sat in his office typing away, a morning view over the bay, second double espresso on the go, Spanish guitar music on the stereo. These days he'd consigned classic rock to the afternoon, and just as well he had, or else he'd have never heard the scream. Either it was Ian Gillan warming up his larynx, or it was a woman in distress; for a while, it was hard to tell which.

He put down his coffee and listened. Courtesy of his more traumatic experiences dodging gun-toting lowlifes and others bent on his destruction, he did occasionally hear noises that weren't really there, but that usually happened when he was half asleep or drunk, and usually at night. Was this in his head, or had it come from somewhere outside? He stood up and turned his left ear towards the window.

Definitely a scream. Definitely coming from outside. Definitely not in his head.

He rushed out of the front door and followed the noise. He ran up the road. Three doors away, he saw a woman arguing toe-to-toe with a man. It looked like she was trying to push him away, but his enormous girth wasn't letting her succeed. Another man lay on the ground. The big man was holding the woman's jumper with one hand, and his other fist was raised. He was getting ready to punch her.

'Oi! You!' Peter yelled.

The big man turned his head lazily, his lips curled into a snarl. The distraction was enough for the woman to break free and pull the other man away.

'You're a bully, mate,' said Peter. 'Hit her, mate, and I'll drop you on your arse.'

'Fuck off, dickhead,' replied the big man. 'This is none of your business.'

'It is my business when I see a turd-rag like you beating up defenceless people. Get away from them.'

'Okay, you nosey fuck, come here and give it your best shot.' The big man raised both his fists. The man was a mountain—not as in tall and muscular—but as in a prime candidate for bariatric surgery, an impending heart attack. He wore a grubby, torn polo shirt over dirty shorts; his ample, hairy gut hung over them like an apron. He lumbered towards Peter, and then stopped after a few steps to pull up his shorts.

Peter assumed he must have been an intruder because he didn't appear to fit the demographic of this part of the coast. As he approached, Peter could smell his greasy long hair and beard. He stank of a mixture of unwashed body and rubbish.

In the background, Peter heard a frail voice say, 'He knocked me over. Why?' It came from the old man on the ground. Then he heard the woman reply, 'Help's coming, Dad.' In the meantime, the human juggernaut kept rolling towards him. He reminded Peter of a runaway bull, except that, in his experience, runaway bulls smelled better and were a lot prettier.

'Come on, mate,' the big man laughed. 'You're gutless, aren't you?'

Peter shaped up to him. He wished he was carrying a lump of four-by-two. 'Keep coming,' he said, beckoning at him, 'keep coming. You'll probably drop dead from a heart attack before you get to me. So, keep coming.'

'That'll be the police, Dad,' said the woman, even before anyone heard the sirens.

Thankfully they were not far away. Moments later, a police car was coming up the road. The big man turned and headed back towards the woman. If he was going to try to get away, he wasn't going to get very far. Peter looked around; the police car was followed by an ambulance.

Saved by the cavalry.

The woman waved her arms and shouted, as the big man slinked away. It looked like he was heading towards the gate that Peter had passed on his walk, the one with the sign and the CCTV cameras.

The vehicles stopped near the woman, and the paramedics were out first. They started to attend to the old man, while the woman shouted at the police and pointed towards the big man. He was at his gate, tugging a set of keys from his shorts. Peter reached him just as he started to fumble with the lock.

'Piss off,' the big man said. 'Stay out of it.'

'I can't stay out of it when innocent people are assaulted.'

The big man stopped in his tracks and glared at him. 'The bitch and her dad are crazy. They came at me when I went to get my bins. If you touch me, I'll do you for assault. Now, fuck off.'

'And you can explain that to the coppers,' he replied.

The two officers were still sitting in their car, windows closed. One of them was speaking into his radio.

What had he bought into? 'Are you going to do something?' he shouted at them, 'or do I have to perform a citizen's arrest?'

'Fuck off, mate,' the big man called out to him, 'and go home. This is none of your business. They're both mad and you, well, who the fuck are you, anyway?' He grunted, pulled up his shorts again and trudged towards the police car, while Peter shadowed him.

The woman left her father with the paramedics and ran to the opposite side of the police car. 'Do something,' she yelled, 'please! He assaulted my dad and then he went for me!'

Eventually, the police officers climbed out of their car. The sergeant was clearly the alpha dog, and the constable was still a pup. The constable stood next to the woman, scribbling into his notebook, while the sergeant approached big man.

'So, what happened, Eddie?' asked the sergeant in a monotone.

'I was just outside getting my rubbish bin when her dad and her attacked me for no reason. They need to be put away: they're always harassing my wife and kids. I've rung you fellas about them before.'

'You have,' affirmed the sergeant. He turned towards Peter. 'And who are you?' He flipped open a notebook. His pencil sat uneasily between his thick fingers.

'Peter Clancy. I just moved into number 65. I heard a woman screaming for help and I ran out. I saw the old man lying on the ground, and this man,' he pointed at the big man, 'had his fist raised, ready to hit her.'

'Nah, that's bullshit,' the big man replied. 'She was trying to hit me. I was only trying to block her. She went nuts at me for no reason.'

'Well, it didn't look like that to me,' said Peter. 'You were about to assault her, and then you threatened me.'

The big man was shaking his head. The sergeant rolled his eyes. He closed his notebook. 'Did you actually witness the start of the altercation?' he asked Peter.

'Well, I heard the woman scream…'

'You don't know nothing, mate,' the big man sneered. 'You should go home and mind your own business.'

'Look,' said the sergeant, 'I think I've just about got to the bottom of this. He says, she says. You'—he pointed at Peter—'didn't really see anything. Go home. We don't need anyone inflaming the situation. If I need anything from you, I'll get in contact. You, Eddie'—he turned towards the big man and placed his hand on his shoulder—'can return to what you were doing.'

'But,' began Peter.

The sergeant sighed. He motioned to the constable to stop what he was doing and get back into the car. 'And how long exactly have you lived here? Now, you don't want to start off on the wrong foot, do you? Who knows who started it, but I'm gonna finish it right now. And just maybe you owe Mr Arnold here an apology.'

'Wow,' Peter responded, shaking his head. 'Me? Owe him an apology? And now it's Mr Arnold, hey?' *How very interesting.*

'Now you're just trying to irritate me,' said the sergeant. 'Go home before I have to charge you.'

Peter shrugged his shoulders and headed back slowly towards his house. He was pissed off at the sergeant's slight to be sure, but he picked his moments: for the time being he had decided to keep his eyes wide open and wait. He stopped in his front garden, stood under a tree, and watched the ambulance leave with the old man and his daughter on board. He observed the sergeant waggle his finger at Eddie Arnold, and Arnold look sheepish for a moment. Then he seemed to snap back, and the tables reversed. The two men walked over to the police car, Arnold slapped the sergeant on the back, and the police car pulled away.

Peter had never been a keen student of history: much like his hero, Hunter S. Thompson, he preferred being part of it over reading about it. It troubled him that he had dropped himself into a location he really knew nothing about. For Serenity Bay to feel like home—even temporarily—he needed to understand it better and, if the dispute with Eddie Arnold was going to escalate into a war, he was going to arm himself with knowledge.

Back in his office, he searched the internet. He learned that Helga Lane was named after a naturalist called Helga Schneider, whose family had bought the land when it was first subdivided. Then he searched for anything about Eddie Arnold. All he could find was that Arnold had bought his house a mere two weeks before he had bought his. Arnold had paid $1.7 million for it.

Nothing there. A bogan with money. How he got it, is anyone's guess.

He guffawed. There was a history lesson in what he'd just experienced. For eighty years, Australia had served as Britain's dumping ground for just about every minor and major villain, as well as the few who were total innocents. It had been populated by pond scum and ruled over by small fish, who refused to admit that they were only really swimming round and round in a tiny, fetid fishbowl. He had the feeling that very little had changed since. Australia was still a small town run by small-minded people; it had taken a mere couple of centuries for the country to graduate from criminals in stripes to criminals in suits. It seemed he'd sailed straight into the midst of a storm he knew nothing about and should have stayed out of.

The altercation had shaken him—he wondered if the bay was more tempest than serenity. Not that it really mattered: *keep your head down next time and let it wash over you.* He wasn't going to be there forever. A few more months and he'd sell out for a higher price. Flip it and piss off.

He was already missing the excitement and his mates in London. He might have been a country boy because that was where he was born and raised, but he thrived on the distraction of a city. London was the epicentre: he was missing the easy access to everything that mattered to him. He needed to be at the forefront of the news. He needed news in the same way that an addict needed the next fix: not for the buzz, but simply in order to live. He needed it just to feel normal.

Positioned somewhere between suburban and rural, Serenity Bay was starting to feel like Hicksville by the sea. He should have avoided doctor's advice. He didn't usually take advice. The heart attack must have scared him into listening. Peter Clancy was going to die worn out, no matter how long it took, and with no regrets. Regrets were for those who had wasted their life. *Life is short, life is shit, life is about living it to the max; make the most of it and do what you love.* Or so he thought. He didn't want another heart attack. At least not until he was in his nineties.

Chapter Five

Bellavista Farm overlooking Serenity Bay,
eight kilometres from the Hermit's Hut

For the second time that month, Jack Cunningham found his prize Charolais cattle wandering along the highway.

He rode along the boundary of his farm on his quad bike, and it took him no time to find out what the problem was. As he'd suspected, the fence had been cut again. He shook his head and asked himself what sort of mongrel dog would do that. His family had owned the farm since the end of the First World War. He was the third generation to run it. He had never seen the likes of it before. What had happened to decency, and good neighbours?

The place was never the same after the rich townies flooded the coast. Blokes he'd known all his life—good blokes, most of them— sold out to developers, until he started to feel like an intruder on his own land. The developers were paying real money—millions, in fact—and to be honest, he'd been tempted for a while. There'd be no more eighteen-hour days, and no droughts, fences or animals to worry about. But then what would he do with his time and money? Become some stuck-up townie living in a concrete box? That would be like being locked up in a jail.

There'd been farmland all around him once, as far as the eye could see, and beyond that, there'd been thick bush covering the hills. From his farmhouse, he had a clear view of the sea in the distance. To Jack Cunningham, it was God's Country, and he'd never thought it would change. Now, there were only his place and three others left. The developers were bloody vandals, pulling down the farms and ripping out the bush as fast as they could get their grubby hands on them, and then subdividing what was left into neat little squares.

So much for the green pockets that the council had promised.

The latest he'd heard was that his old schoolmate, Wally Sturgess, might be selling up. Jack himself had been getting weekly visits from real estate agents in their slick suits and flash cars, talking in their slimy, ingratiating way. Upping the price at every visit, and getting pushier too. 'Whatever you're paying, I'm not selling,' was his stock response.

But the latest business with the fence was a big concern. The first time the fence was cut, his cattle strayed onto the highway and one of them was killed by a passing truck. The council threatened to fine him, and the police did nothing at all to find the perpetrator.

That was right, they'd fine him for letting his stock stray, and never mind the arseholes who'd caused the problem in the first place. It was a fine welcome to the modern world!

Well, he let the bastards know he was going to fight it every inch of the way. What bloody choice did he have? Privately, he had his suspicions that it was either the developers, or the local hoons. Right about then, the developers were leading by a half-length.

He was more fortunate this time: he was able to move the cattle off the highway and back through the break, and then he quickly repaired the fence. His farm was a fair distance from his closest neighbour, so there was no one to keep an extra set of eyes on his place. He decided that he was going to ring someone to install a few CCTV cameras along the fence. He might even have to camp out there, to keep an eye out for whoever it was.

By the time he returned to the house, it was already mid-afternoon. He spotted a late-model black Audi A5 parked in the driveway and groaned.

They're back. Persistent bastards. He parked the quad bike in the shed and stormed into the farmhouse. There were two of them this time, shiny-suited and slicked-haired. The agents hovered over the kitchen table, which was strewn with papers. Jack's wife sat at one end. She had taken off her glasses and was wiping her eyes.

'What the hell's going on here?' he demanded. He placed his arm around his wife. 'You all right, love?'

'They said they'll get the government to throw us off, if we don't sell now,' she sobbed, 'and we'll get nothing if they have to force us out. What will happen to us then, Jack?'

'Well, they're bloody liars, love. Don't you listen to a word they say. They can't do a bloody thing.' He turned to the agents. 'So, you think you can threaten my wife now?'

One of the agents smirked.

'Think this is some sort of game? You're playing with people's lives here, you gutless little prick.'

'No need to get worked up about it, Mr Cunningham,' said the other agent. 'We're just here to help make your life more comfortable.'

'Pieces of shit. Get out of here before I throw you out.' He gathered up the papers and tossed them at the agents.

'We're making you a fantastic offer, Mr Cunningham, a lot more than the place is worth. It's the best offer we've made for farmland around here,' the agent said. 'It would be in your best interests to consider...'

'I've already told you: we're not selling. Now, get out of here before I do something I regret.'

'You need to face the fact that you and your wife aren't getting any younger. It must be getting harder each year to run this place. What happens if one of you gets sick and can't manage anymore? Your son certainly doesn't want to take over the farm.'

'You been looking into my life?' His mouth dropped open. 'You bastards have no morals.'

'Three million dollars in your pocket if you sign now. It's going to give you a wonderful retirement, and you'll still have more than enough to help all of your family.'

Jack frowned. He pressed down on the table until his knuckles blanched. 'If you know what's good for you, you'll get out of here right now! This very minute! And you'll stop cutting my fences. You'll never scare me out of here. Blokes like you, well, you'd sell your own grandmothers for a good commission and, even then, you wouldn't deliver her.'

The smirking agent began, 'But Mr Cunningham, I don't know why—'

'Right,' Jack interjected with a roar. 'Now I'm gunna start counting and you fellas are gunna start moving. Believe me, you don't want to still be here by the time I reach ten!

'One!'

The agent looked like he was about to say something else but thought better of it. Instead, he and his colleague picked up their laptop computers, and scampered towards the door.

'Two!'

After they had gone, Jack's wife was still shaking. 'Don't worry, love,' he reassured her, 'these blokes can't make us do anything we don't want to do.'

'I'm tired,' she replied. 'Sometimes, I wonder if it's worth the worry.'

He sighed. 'We have to stand together on this, Beth. Whatever happens, we need to promise each other that we won't sell out. Farming is my life, and this land is my blood. I only need two things in my life: you and this farm. Everything else can go to hell.'

'Yes all right, Jack.'

'So we're agreed then.'

She turned her head away. He wasn't sure that he'd understood what she wanted.

That afternoon, they had a visit from the local police: two officers, a sergeant and a young constable they had never met. The constable refused to look Jack in the eye.

'Well, Mr Cunningham,' said the sergeant, 'two real estate agents have been to see us.'

'Really?' he replied. 'They're always coming onto my land uninvited. They're a bloody nuisance. I've asked you fellas a dozen times to do something about them.'

'Well, that may be as may be, but here's the thing. The agents have made a complaint against you. They've told us that you threatened them.'

'Me? Threaten them?'

'Jack would never hurt a soul,' Beth Cunningham piped up. 'He might say this or that, but he'd never do anything to anyone.'

The sergeant's eyes narrowed. 'So, you're confirming that he did threaten them, then?'

'What?' She turned to Jack. 'I never said that, did I? What did I say, Jack?'

'Don't look at him, look at me,' the seargeant continued.

Jack interjected, 'You're twisting her words.'

'Be quiet! What did your husband say to the agents, Mrs Cunningham?'

'He told them to leave. That's what he said.'

'Well, that's not what they told us.'

The sergeant said that it constituted an assault, for which Jack might be charged. Consequently, in the interest of public safety, the officers would be seizing his firearms. Jack reeled. It was all too much for his wife and she had to step away.

Jack tried to reason with them. 'How can I put down stock if they become unwell?'

The sergeant shut him down. 'You should have thought about that before you go threatening people going about their lawful business.'

'But they were trespassers. Surely I have the right to protect my property?'

The sergeant sniggered. 'That sounds a lot like an admission of guilt to me, Constable.'

Jack protested his innocence while his wife wept in the next room. The police response was to order him to take them to his firearm cupboard, and to seize his firearms.

Just then, and for only a moment, he felt like crying and caving in. He felt like throwing up his arms and shouting that it was all too much. But deep down, he was made of sterner stuff: his father and grandfather made sure of that. They had faced hard times and they had come through them. This was nothing by comparison. He was determined to keep up the fight; he wasn't about to let a couple of jumped-up, slimy city-slickers in cheap suits break him.

CHAPTER SIX

The Hermit's Hut

Several days had passed since the incident on the road between Eddie Arnold and his neighbours. Peter had seen neither hide nor hair of the people involved, and the police hadn't contacted him to give a statement. He put it down to either idleness or incompetence. Deep down he suspected that they couldn't organise a piss-up in a brewery and he certainly wasn't going to go to them. Later on, he began formulating other theories.

Once again, he found himself torn between being Peter the Middle-Aged Man and Peter the Perennially Energetic Journalist. He never considered himself to be naturally addiction-prone (alcohol, reporting and romance aside). Rather, he saw himself as the champion of the voiceless and the oppressed, for which the booze, the writing and the failed relationships were mere collateral damage. He claimed that he shunned all manner of violence: he preferred to pretend that serendipity had dragged him into disagreements with members of the mob. And assorted criminals. And police officers. And celebrities and their agents. To name a few. Over the decades, the list of enemies grew ever longer.

For the sake of his peace of mind, he hoped that the street brawl was just a one-off. For the sake of his mental health, he craved for more. He had made his living off mayhem and disorder for so long, that he couldn't remember any other existence. The truth was that he had needed to surround himself with conflict and anguish his entire his professional career, simply to survive. If there was no mayhem, he created it. Wasn't that how some wars began?

Inaction was becoming tedious. How was he supposed to get rid of the adrenaline that had been pulsing through him for all those years? He couldn't wash it away in the shower. He also needed a distraction from some of his baser desires. How he yearned to immerse his psyche in a long whisky over ice.

I'll just enjoy the coffee, read the papers, hammer out some more words for my latest book, and if I'm truly desperate, I'll do the long overdue gardening. That will pass the time.

He sat down and banged out a paragraph before he lost focus. Then he checked his emails, his social media account, and his website. He only had a social media account because his publicist had said it was a good platform to broadcast his name and secure some millennial recognition. He wasn't sure any of it would translate into sales. Did millennials actually read?

He lingered over his emails. Perhaps his humour had been a little too black when he'd compared his flight home to Dante's descent into hell. Someone had ordered a wreath in the mistaken belief that he'd actually died and was wondering where to send it. Apparently, everyone else was perpetually pissed, partying, and enjoying absolutely everything that he was presently missing out on. He imagined himself in the midst of it, back in Ye Olde Cock Tavern, wallowing in red-hot disagreements and tepid pints, until he was tempted to book a ticket back to London then and there, and rent his Hermit's Hut out.

Deliverance from himself came in the form of several hard knocks on the front door. If he found Arnold on the threshold, he was prepared for a confrontation. Unfortunately, he had left his cricket bat back in London, so instead he picked up a shovel he had found in the shed, and which he had positioned next to the back door in case of future need. He peered through the window. It was the woman he'd last seen arguing with Arnold.

He put the shovel down and answered the door. 'Hello,' he said. 'Are you okay?'

'I'm fine,' she replied nervously. Her clothes looked as tired as she did. He guessed she was probably only in her forties. 'Sorry, I didn't get to thank you. I'm Mimi Connors. Lots of stuff on my mind.'

'I'm Peter Clancy. Come in, I was just about to make coffee.'

'Oh, I suppose that would be all right.' She looked around, as if she half expected something to jump out at her. He led her to the kitchen and pulled out a stool from under the bench.

'Take a pew. How do you take it?' he asked, as he flicked the switch on the coffee machine.

'Oh, milk, please. No sugar.' Her eyes circled the room.

'Admiring the mess?' he asked. 'I believe in the chaos theory. Helps me work better.'

She sniffed faintly. 'Thank you for trying to help Dad and me. And thank you for standing up to that horrible man. Eddie Arnold is nothing but a bully, you know.'

'Well, I heard you screaming, I had to do something. Isn't that what people should do?'

'Maybe in the old days. No one helps these days, especially not around here. They have their heads buried in their sandcastles around here. You'll soon work out for yourself that decency died in Serenity Bay a long time ago.' She pulled a tissue from her pocket and dabbed at her eyes. 'It's every man and woman for themselves.'

He replied, 'It's everyone for themselves everywhere these days, I'm sorry to say. How's your father, by the way?'

'Still in hospital. He's awake now, but he still doesn't know where he is. Dad has dementia, you see. He's been like that for the past two years. I'm his carer.'

He put down the coffees and took a seat at the bench. 'I hope you're okay with a latte,' he said. 'I'm not really the latte type.'

'Thank you, that's fine.' She took a sip. 'Very nice. Just what I needed.' She put her tissue away. 'So, what is it that you do, Peter?'

He was about to say 'retired journalist' but thought better of it. 'I was a…public servant. I worked for a government department.' It was nondescript enough to avoid attention, he thought; he could make up a credible history around it, and it required less effort than saying retired neurosurgeon, or retired aerospace engineer.

'I used to be an aged-care nurse, but I gave it up to look after Dad. I worked in a dementia unit as a nurse, so I thought I'd be the best person to look after him. Sometimes he's good, other days, not so good. I bought a place here, so it would be quiet for him. He lived here when he was a child, and I thought it would be better for him. You know, bring back nice memories.' She flicked a tear from her eye. 'I feel like I've let him down.'

Peter picked up a roll of kitchen towel and pushed it across the table. 'How have you let him down?' he asked.

'I keep thinking that maybe I should never have bought here. Don't get me wrong; it was really lovely here until Eddie Arnold arrived.'

'Well, you weren't to know he was going to move in next door to you.'

'That's true, but maybe we should have rented for a while. Seen what it was like, before making a commitment. Arnold has given us nothing but trouble, ever since he moved in. From the first day, he's made lots of noise. Not just a little here and there, and not just during daylight hours.' She stopped to tear off some towel and blot her eyes. 'First there were parties, and cars coming and going all hours of the day and night. Then he began cutting down the trees on his property. He's cut them all down—every single one.'

'But I didn't think you could do that. I thought this was a conservation area,' he remarked. 'That's one of the reasons I moved here.'

'Well, I thought so too,' she continued. 'So, I went to the local council and reported him. But nothing happened.'

'What? Nothing at all?'

'Nothing.'

'But if you or I did that, surely we'd get a huge fine.'

She shook her head. 'Not only was nothing done, but it got back to him somehow that I was the one who put in the complaint. The next thing we knew, he was yelling abuse over the fence. And then he really started to pick on us.' She drew her stool closer to the bench. 'He started throwing rubbish over the fence, horrible stuff, even dirty nappies,' she said. 'After Dad threw them back, Arnold threatened us, and said he'd burn down our house. His horrible brats joined in, throwing rubbish over the fence and abusing us.'

'I suppose you rang the police,' he said.

Her face fell.

'Don't tell me...'

'They did nothing, of course. In fact, I was warned about not wasting their time. The police and the council seem to be a bit like that around here, I've come to realise. Too bloody lazy to do their jobs.

'The other day was the worst, I suppose. Dad got into an argument with Arnold on the footpath, and he pushed Dad over.' She sniffed. 'He might have mild dementia, but Dad remembers what happened that day. He told the police, and he told everyone at the hospital. Of course, nobody believed him. They all thought he just lost his balance and he fell. But he didn't just lose his balance and fall, you see. They turned it onto me: why wasn't I supervising him better? Why did he talk to Arnold? The doctor went as far as to say that Dad might have to go into care, and that I may not be able to look after him. I told him point blank that that was never going to happen.'

'Can you get some help?' he asked. 'Some support?'

'We have no other family. It's just Dad and me,' she continued, 'and you're the only neighbour that came to help. One of the neighbours came over later and said they saw everything, but they weren't prepared to make a statement. They don't want to get involved because they have children.' She sniffed and wiped her nose. 'It's hard enough to take that no one will do anything,' she sobbed, 'but what is worse is that the police took Arnold's side. He told the police that Dad had tried to hit him before he fell over. He said that we had been harassing him and his stupid family. He wants to take out a restraining order against us. And he tells everyone that I'm crazy. He even told the police that I threatened to hit his children.'

Peter shook his head.

'Can you help us, please?' Her tears ran down her face and dripped onto the bench. 'I don't know where else to turn. You seem like a decent man. I'm at the end of my tether. I'm doing my best, but it's worn me down and I don't know how much longer I can fight the system. Caring for someone with dementia is hard, to say the least. Dad doesn't reason like everyone else: sometimes he can be bloody relentless. To be truthful, I've already had a nervous breakdown, and I don't want to have another one. Dad needs me to be healthy.'

'I don't know how I can help. You've already spoken to the authorities, and I offered to make a statement, but they weren't interested. All I can do is keep an eye out. My health isn't the greatest…heart condition. That's why I moved here.' He felt guilty for saying it. He knew that the incident wouldn't even make the local paper, unless there was more to it.

She nodded several times and wiped her eyes on her sleeve. 'Yes, of course. I understand, I understand.' She feigned a smile. 'I hope you get better. I won't bother you again.'

He hung his head. As he walked her to the front door, he added, 'Look, I'll try. All I can suggest is that you gather more evidence against Arnold. Photos, that sort of stuff. Maybe someone will listen then. I'm so sorry.' He brushed her arm inadvertently as he opened the door, and she started.

She said, 'It's okay, I'm used to disappointment, No one ever wants to help.'

'It's not that, Mimi, really…'

'People are scared. He's not on their doorstep. I really do understand.' She sniffed. 'Goodbye, Peter.'

'No, Mimi… Wait!' But for what exactly, he didn't know.

She walked down the stairs and quickly blended into the foliage of his overgrown garden.

He could still hear her talking to herself halfway up the road.

CHAPTER SEVEN

A wake-up call

The early-morning clang of steel was loud enough to shake Peter out of deep sleep. Moments later, it was joined by the splutter and grunt of a chainsaw starting. He had been dreaming, but his dream drowned in the hullaballoo.

What on earth was going on?

Had he overslept? He checked the clock. Five thirty-two. What the hell? He sat up and scooted to the edge of his bed. The noise persisted. What manner of dickhead was doing this?

He pulled aside the curtain and peered out of the window. His eyes followed a truck loaded with an excavator as it turned into Helga Lane and rattled past, hitting every corrugation in the road. Moments later, it pulled into Eddie Arnold's place.

What was he up to? *I know: he shat the bed and decided to wake everyone up to help clean him.* 'Not on, not on at all,' he said aloud. He slipped on jeans and a jumper, slid his phone into his pocket, grabbed his camera, and headed outside.

He strode towards the Arnold's house. The gates had been removed from their hinges, but the CCTV cameras were still there. He was halfway across the road when the next truck trundling up the road blew its horn and forced him back onto the overgrown footpath. He spun around and yelled, 'What the fuck do you think you're doing?'

The truck slowed. An unshaven man with long, matted hair leaned out of the window. 'Get off the road, you old bastard,' he yelled, 'before I run you over.' The skip bin on the back of the truck jiggled back and forth on its chains, as if to reinforce the message.

Peter couldn't decide if he was more incensed by being called old or a bastard, or by the commotion of a clattering chain before dawn. In the meantime, the truck spun its tyres. The yeti at the wheel ground the gears searching for first, and then shuddered off before Peter could reply. He watched the truck turn into Arnold's place.

Of course.

From the end of the driveway, he could see that many of the trees had been cut down, although the stumps had been left standing proud of the soil. Several trucks were parked near the house. There was the unmistakable drone coming from behind the house. What was Arnold doing with an excavator? Dredging the creek? Building a factory? Had Peter bought in an industrial zone by mistake?

Of course, he knew he hadn't. He had checked. It was all zoned residential, with a conservation overlay. He stood at the edge of the road and pointed his zoom lens down Arnold's driveway, snapping a dozen shots.

Then he approached the closest CCTV camera. 'Think you'll disturb my peace?' He lifted his middle finger at it. 'You have no idea know who I am, arsehole. Ruin my day and I'll ruin yours. Wait for the wrath, dickhead.'

He walked up to Mimi's house next, as far as the boundary she shared with Arnold. The boundary fence was listing to the left, and part of it was gone. He shook his head with disbelief and took more photos. It was clear who had removed it. Had he landed in a dystopian nightmare, where anarchy ruled and society had collapsed? Had Australia changed that much since he left?

Mimi was in her dressing gown, standing on her deck. She was watching what was happening past the fence-line, her mouth ajar. She noticed Peter looking at her, retreated hastily inside and closed the sliding door. He went to her gate and was about to enter. He thought better of it and walked away.

He had to do this dispassionately, and on his own. That way, he could control the message and focus the blowback on himself. He wasn't a martyr by anyone's definition; he just didn't want other people involved. At least, not yet.

He returned to his own house and did what any good citizen would do. Arnold's destruction could wait awhile. The police officer at the other end of the phone cut him short. It wasn't his jurisdiction, he told him, it was the council's. Peter was sure he heard him yawn. 'We don't deal with noise complaints during normal working hours.'

Peter responded with, 'Thanks, officer, you've been a great help. I won't keep you from your sleep any longer. Nightie-night,' and he ended the call.

The council officer who answered his next call offered some hope. They would send an environmental officer to investigate, but it could take several days as they were busy.

'Couldn't it be any quicker? I think I might be deaf by then. And I have a health condition that makes me nervous around loud noise. I was in the army, and it brings back...you know...bad memories. Can't you make it any sooner?'

'I'll try,' she replied, 'but I can't promise you anything.'

For a while, he sat back and waited for the noise to end. He attempted to drown it out by turning up the stereo to full volume. *Fuck the neighbours.* When his ears started to throb, he turned it down halfway. He could still hear the racket across the road, but at least his ears weren't hurting. About an hour later, someone rapped on the window of his study. He was wearing a uniform and holding a clipboard. Peter made a mental checklist: not a copper, not a Mormon, not a meter-reader or a door-to-door salesman. And definitely not Arnold. He motioned to the man to meet him at the front door.

'Peter Clancy? Steve Killian,' said the man when Peter opened the door. 'I'm an environmental control officer from the Tyne Coast Council. We've had a complaint.'

'Wow, that was quick,' said Peter. 'I was told when I rang this morning that it could take days.'

Killian frowned. 'Sorry?'

'I only got off the phone to you guys a couple of hours ago.'

This time Killian shook his head, as if he was trying to dislodge the earwax that the noise had loosened.

'The racket going on up the road? I complained about it this morning,' Peter continued. 'It's driving me nuts.'

'Can I come inside?' said Killian. 'Only, it's a little noisy out here.'

'You've just worked that out, huh?' Peter beckoned him inside and closed the door after him. 'So, I'm thinking you're not here to introduce yourself to a new resident.'

Killian was studying his clipboard. 'We've had a complaint about the state of your garden,' he said.

'So, you're also not here about the noise. Of course not. You can't hear yourself think out there, yet my garden's the biggest problem around here, huh? Well, I have a hunch I know who dobbed me in.'

Killian shifted his gaze to his pen but offered up nothing.

'What,' said Peter, 'you can't tell me?'

'Sorry, Mr Clancy, I can't disclose the details of the person who has complained.'

'Peter, please. Call me Peter. You can dispense with the formalities. So, it's a privacy thing, huh?'

'The complaint is about your garden, Mr Clancy,' he continued. 'It's overgrown. The complainant thinks it could be a breeding ground for dangerous snakes. You could be fined a thousand dollars if you don't keep your yard clean and tidy.'

'I only moved in two weeks ago: give me a break. I'm still unpacking. I'll attend to it as soon as I can.'

'Okay. I'll give you a week, and then I'll come back to check it's done. And if it isn't good enough...'

'I thought you people would be into letting nature be nature,' he retorted. 'You know, give the lizards, possums, snakes and birds a place to snuggle.'

'Not when your lawn comes up to my knees and several shrubs are hanging over fences, creating a hazard for pedestrians with an impairment. Oh, and one of your trees has died and is about to fall over. Aside from the untidiness and the snakes, your property is also a fire threat.'

Peter noted the irony in his shrubs and trees being raised as impediments to impaired walkers when the potholes and open drains obviously weren't. He realised there was no point arguing. 'Right, give me a week,' he sighed. 'Do you know any good gardeners?'

'I'll be back in a week.' Killian snapped his clipboard and opened the door. The noise from Arnold's place exploded like a runaway train.

'Are you going to do anything about that noise,' asked Peter, pointing towards Arnold's house, 'or do you think people should have to tolerate that?'

'Have you complained to the police?'

'Yes, and the police referred me to you.'

'I'm sorry, Mr Clancy, but it's their right to operate machinery during working hours.'

'Hang on a moment,' Peter replied, searching his pockets frantically. 'Would you mind terribly waiting here a little longer, while I try to locate *my* rights? Nup, not here. Not here, either. Funny that, I seem to have lost them.'

Killian looked nervous. He backed away. 'All I can suggest...' he began.

'Can you speak louder?' Peter shouted. 'Only I can't hear you.'

'All I can suggest,' Killian yelled back, 'if it is causing you so much stress, is that you go to a doctor and get a certificate, saying the noise is causing you undue mental distress and anxiety. You give that to the council, and we might impose limitations on the hours of operation.'

Peter shook his head in disbelief. 'Bugger me dead! I have to prove that noise is sending me loopy? That noise would send a deaf person loopy. Talk about an idiot state.'

'It's all I can suggest,' Killian replied, and then turned to walk down the stairs. 'And don't forget, you have a week to clean up your yard.'

'I get it. I'm the soft target and arseholes like Arnold are in the too hard basket, aren't they? I pay my taxes, but I bet he doesn't. Well, we'll see about that.'

Killian didn't reply and he didn't look back. He walked briskly to his car and backed out of the driveway.

So much for going through official channels, Peter thought. *These bludgers don't like working too hard. The hardest work they do is making up excuses and going after retirees to add to their precious stats.*

42

He made himself another coffee and tried to write over the commotion up the road. He'd written in some trying situations in the past—by the light of a candle, over the sound of nearby gunfire, and even with an angry editor breathing down his neck and a five-minute deadline—but the cacophony was doing his head in. He persevered for another two hours before admitting defeat. He felt like doing harm, losing his shit, going rogue, but most of all he felt like a drink. You know the type. A help-me-deal-with-this-shit drink. He was nearly cracking. Nearly, but not quite.

Then he had a thought. A couple of internet searches later, he closed his laptop.

Arnold seemed determined to ruin Serenity, so Peter was going to ruin Arnold's day, and possibly the rest of his life. There was more benefit in that than in getting pissed out of his head.

Your nemesis has arrived, Arnold.

He headed outside and down his driveway. He carried his long metal torch in a coat pocket; it was easier to conceal than a shovel. Sometimes the pen wasn't mightier than the sword. He had only just reached the end of his driveway, when he noticed a white sports coupe speeding up the road from the village. BMWs, Audis and Mercs were de rigueur on the coast, and sometimes even the odd Bentley, Lotus and McLaren made an appearance, so it wasn't the rarity of the Audi TT that captured his attention. It was the sound it made.

Revving loudly, the TT bottomed out on the crossover where the asphalt road met the dirt, a little further down from Peter's. The sportscar sat unusually low on the road, the shockers were almost flattened. The metal thumped loudly and scraped over the uneven ground; it was so loud that he heard it above the racket of the excavators. And then he realised why. Arnold was driving it. Peter wished he had brought his camera along to record the sight he was witnessing.

Somehow, Arnold had managed to pour himself into the Audi TT, and he was driving it like there was no tomorrow: too fast, recklessly disregarding every pothole. Peter felt sorry for the car. *Better not break the chassis, Titty Man, or you'll experience the sensation of your arse dragging along the road.*

The thought made him chuckle.

Just then, Arnold turned his head and caught him still smiling. He yelled out, 'Old cunt!' as he went past.

Peter was taken back just for a second. He wasn't old, he was more on the young side of middle-aged. The fact that he had managed to live as long as he had, in spite of everything, was a miracle. He had survived this long because he was a cunning bastard. Fifty-something wasn't old. Wasn't it the new thirty?

He tugged at his coat, feeling the body of the torch smack against his thigh. He was about to walk up to Arnold's drive when he had a change of mind. He thought of his days as a reporter for *The Melbourne Truth*. He wouldn't have walked into a fight just to make a point. When he was at the *Truth*, to get a story he was stealthy, like a hunter after prey. So he turned on his heels instead, climbed into his car, drove down to the village payphone, and made another call.

When he returned home, he sat on his deck drinking a cup of coffee.

He checked his watch. Fifteen minutes had elapsed. A few more minutes passed before he heard the wail of sirens. He watched the convoy of emergency vehicles turn off the Esplanade onto Helga Lane: the police car in the lead, a fire truck, two ambulance vehicles, and a truck from the gas company at the rear.

Sometimes you simply have to do the wrong thing for the right reasons.

One of the ambulances pulled up outside number sixty, while the others continued on to Arnold's place. The paramedic stood at the gate, frantically buzzing the console, to be let into number sixty. *Surely they'll give up soon.* He was tempted to run down and tell them that it was the Rogersons' holiday house (he'd checked), and that no one was there, but then he might well be found out.

He stood at the far end of his deck with his camera lens zoomed in on the action. He watched as emergency workers ran up Arnold's driveway, some wearing masks, hazard suits and carrying equipment. *Sorry boys,* he said to himself, *I'll make it up to you one day.* The excavating at Arnold's continued for another five minutes or so, before the noise faded away. For the first time that day, there was

44

nothing but blissful silence, and the warble of magpies. Then came the yelling and the stream of obscene language.

Arnold stood in the gateway alongside two police officers and a woman with two young children who Peter presumed were his family. Their presence didn't stop him from spraying the officers with every foul word he could summon up. The emergency workers and the gasmen were checking the property for leaks and hazards, while the excavator operators stood a little further along the driveway, looking bored and impatient.

Eventually, the officers took Arnold and his family inside, while the emergency workers continued to do what they had to do. A bit later, Peter watched him get into the back of the police car.

Yeah, take the prick to the station and throw the book at him. And then why don't you throw the furniture at him while you're at it?

Satisfied, he finally went inside and made himself a celebratory coffee. He raised his cup to the Rogerson family; victory never tasted better.

Chapter Eight

Tyne Coast 1947
Memories of home

If he stood on the granite boulder at the edge of the dirt road, Herman Schneider could just about see the full length of the coast as far as the rocky outcrop, ten miles north. There was nothing to interrupt the vast sky above him: no smoke, no trailing flak, no searchlights after dusk. Below him, the bay undulated under the summer sun, a riot of silver and topaz. It was quiet, in a way that soothed beasts and the souls of anguished men; more than anything, he wished his beloved Helga could have been there to experience it with him. At his feet, Octavia and Anastasia waited patiently until he descended the boulder and urged them on through the bush, towards the creek.

Anastasia crossed her arms. 'I don't want to go any further. I'm not going.'

'I'm scared, Papa,' said Octavia. 'Aren't there lots of snakes and spiders in the bush?'

Herman laughed. He crouched down and gently gathered them in. 'My darling little daughters, there is nothing to fear here,' he said. 'Nature is kind to those who are kind to her; always remember that. The bush is a place of wonderment and fascination. This is one of the reasons I chose for us to emigrate to Australia, *meine Lieblinge*. I wanted you to grow up with all of this: the bush and the peace and the outback. And to see it with my own eyes, if it really was as beautiful as I had been told.'

'Well, I'm not afraid of spiders, anyway. And I will scare off all the snakes,' said Anastasia. 'I will kill them and I will cut off their heads.'

'*Aber ich fürchte*, Papa,' said Octavia, shivering. 'If I go any further, a troll might get me. Or a snake.'

Herman chuckled and kissed each of them on the forehead. 'There are no trolls here, my darlings,' he replied. 'Trolls live in Germany, not here. They wouldn't find us here. And we won't be killing any snakes. A snake will only bite you if you stand on it.'

'But what if we don't see them, Papa?' Octavia cried. 'What if they hide and they sneak up on us, without us even knowing? I don't want to get sick if they bite me. I might...' She started to weep.

He stooped to wipe the tears from Octavia's face. His beautiful daughters, born only minutes apart and almost identical, yet endowed with their own personalities. Anastasia the bossy, adventurous one, and Octavia the hesitant, timid daughter.

'They are as afraid of you as we are of them, perhaps more. We're the strangers here. We just need to introduce ourselves, because we can't just barge into someone's house, can we? You wouldn't like it if a stranger opened our front door and came in, and helped themselves to our food or slept in your bed? Would you?' He watched as the wind tugged at their flaxen curls.

'You mean like *Goldlöckchen* did to the poor bears, Papa?'

He smiled and nodded. 'That's right.'

'I guess,' Octavia said slowly, 'we don't want to be rude to Mr or Mrs Snake.' She paused, deep in thought, the tears still glistening on her skin. 'All right, I'll walk a bit more, but only if Anastasia and you are beside me.'

'Of course.' He picked up a stick. 'So, here's how you do it. When you go into the bush you just beat this stick about and call out loudly, "Hello, Mr Snake, we're here. We won't hurt you. Thanks for letting us visit".'

The twins looked perplexed.

'It's true, my dears,' he continued, 'trust me. It works.'

'We trust you, Papa,' Anastasia said.

'And later on, we can visit Mama,' said Herman, as he leaned on the stick.

'Mama doesn't fear the snakes, does she?' asked Octavia. 'Perhaps we can tell her what to do.'

Anastasia added, 'But I thought she was in heaven, Papa. I haven't seen her for such a long time.'

'I miss her so much,' said Octavia. 'I wish she hadn't gone away.'

'Well, you know that Mama lives here most of the time, and these days she only goes to heaven to visit,' he said.

'But why can't we see her if she's here?' asked Anastasia.

'She is here, my darlings.' Herman wiped his eyes. 'She is, because Mama and Papa bought this bush before she…had to visit heaven. She loved it here and she loved us very, very much, you see, in the same way that I love you both. She still does. And she looks after us every day. So, you see, she can never really leave here, and she can never really leave us.' He huffed. 'You can never abandon what you truly love. It's just that sometimes we can't see things with these,' he said, pointing to his eyes, 'but we will always see Mama with this.' He placed his hand on Anastasia's heart.

'Don't cry, Papa,' said Octavia. 'We love you too, very, very much.'

Anastasia nodded. 'And we will never ever leave you or Mama. We shouldn't be sad. We should be happy that Mama lives here with us here. Shall we go and see her now?'

He swallowed his sobs. 'Yes, of course.'

The girls slid one of their tiny hands into each of his paws while they made their way through the towering eucalypts together. As they walked, he glanced down at the tops of their heads and silently thanked Helga for her legacy.

CHAPTER NINE

An industrious neighbour

The longer he spent in his office, the longer Peter spent inside his head. He didn't like being inside his head too often. It was scary there.

He pushed himself away from his desk and went outside. There was no wisdom in overgrown garden beds, so he strode across the road, climbed the steps, knocked twice on Mimi's door and waited. Her house was probably the same age as his, but it was obvious that she was finding it difficult to maintain. The yard was untidy—not as bad as his—but it still needed some tender loving care. The paint was peeling off the weatherboards and the curtains were drawn. It seemed that Mimi and her father were shutting the world out.

Her deck overlooked Arnold's yard. It should have been part of a bush conservation area, but now it looked like a scorched-earth wasteland. The sight of it made him seethe. Where were the council officers to fine him, and demand that he put it right? MIA by the look of it. What little remained of Mimi's fence had been pushed over since he last saw it, and the broken palings were lying on her side of the boundary. Parked next to Arnold's mock-Tudor mansion were the Audi TT, a LandCruiser, and a truck. Next to them stood a shipping container.

He knocked again. He didn't expect her to answer, considering he hadn't been of much assistance the other day. He waited anyway. After a while the door opened, and Mimi peered out of the gloom.

'Oh,' she said. 'What do you want? I thought you didn't want to get involved.'

'I was just wondering how your father was, and if you needed anything. Is he out of hospital?'

'Really? That's why you're here?'

He paused and dropped his head. 'And to apologise to you.'

'Well,' she said, softening, 'he's not out yet, but he's making steady improvements. Thank you for asking.' She turned away. 'I have a lot of things to do, so if there's nothing else…' She was about to close the door.

He interjected, 'I see Mr Arnold has turned his property into an industrial site.'

She snorted and turned around to face him. 'I had noticed, you know. I have to see that monstrosity every time I open my front door.'

'And you have every right to be angry about that. Have you approached anyone apart from the council?' he asked.

'Yes. I also went to the Environmental Panel, but they didn't even want to know. What's wrong with this country? We're paying people to do nothing.' She hesitated. 'Lately, I've even been thinking of going to the media. I don't know what else to do.'

'I wish I could help you. Look,' he continued, 'I didn't want to get involved, not because I didn't care, but because of my health. Earlier this year, I had a heart attack. The cardiologist warned me that I need to take it easy.'

'I'm sorry to hear that. You should have told me that the other day.' She came out onto the deck. With the daylight on her face, she looked tired and worried; she wore no makeup. 'You know that Arnold has taken over the old house next door to his, don't you? Well, now he's begun ripping it apart,' she said, 'and putting up ugly, fake, Tudorbethan timber frames everywhere. And I recently heard that he's taken over the rest of the Schneider property, too.'

'The Schneiders?' Peter asked. 'You mean the original owners?'

'So, you do know about them.'

'Well, yes, but I don't know very much about them. Do they still own some land here?'

Mimi exhaled. 'Yes, Arnold and the Schneiders share a boundary. Old Herman Schneider came here just after the war, from the Black Forest. He was into carpentry and carving—and not just animals and cuckoo clocks—but gable ends, furniture, and ornate picture frames. He hand-built a house here for himself and his twin daughters; he was a widower, you see. The house is on an acre block, and I don't know if anyone's actually bought it or leased it, but Arnold certainly seems to have moved himself into it.

'The thing is, Old Herman also owned another sixty acres which he put aside, in memory of his late wife. It stretches part of the way up that hill,' she said, pointing to her right. 'His intention was to keep it as pristine bushland, but he didn't quite get around to doing all the legalities to make it a reserve. He built his house on the edge of the bushland, and there was never a fence between it and his house, so he and the girls could come and go as they pleased. The girls never married. They lived in the house until a family member put them in a nursing home.

'I caught up with their cousin not long ago and she told me she was planning to lease the house out, but she said that nothing was going to happen for at least another three months. A week after we spoke, she put up a fence to separate the house from the land, but Arnold has taken that down now, too. It's a terrible shame; they were lovely old ladies. I can't imagine how they'd feel now if they could see this mess.'

Peter looked at the desert that surrounded Arnold's house. 'I hope you're wrong about Arnold leasing the reserve.'

She sighed. 'Well, to be honest, I'm not sure if he's leased any of it, or if he simply moved himself in when no one was looking. My guess is that it will all be sold eventually. The local greenies will have a lot to say about making sure the bushland remains as open space. Once the house is sold, who knows what will happen to the rest of it.

'I don't blame their cousin really: the poor ladies couldn't take care of themselves any longer. But it's her choice of nursing home I question. I heard that she put them in the Seaview, of all places. It's awful. I looked at it once, for Dad. It was so bad that I walked straight out of there.' As she spoke, a phone rang inside the house. 'I better go, Peter. It may be the hospital.'

'Yes, of course.'

She rushed back inside and shut the door.

He assumed she wasn't coming back, so he left. He was walking up his driveway when he spotted someone standing at the foot of the stairs, partially obscured by the overgrowth.

He chuckled. 'Why, if it isn't the Contessa of the Coast! You're looking particularly irritated today. What brings you here?'

She was dressed as if she was about to play polo, right down to the wrist band. 'You recognise me, then? From next door?'

'Of course. We met on the road. You nearly flattened me with your presence.'

She gasped. 'I did nothing of the sort!'

Peter was thinking that her accent, when she wasn't yelling at him through the open window of her Range Rover, was about as authentically British as Arnold's architecture. 'Oh, I'm afraid you did, Contessa,' he replied, purposely mispronouncing the final word, 'and then you compounded injury with insult, by sending out the troops.'

'What? I did what? And what is it you're calling me?'

'I believe it's Italian for countess. I thought it fitting, since we haven't been properly introduced, remember? I'm Peter Clancy.'

'Well, okay, let's get this out of the way,' she said, flustered. 'I'm Rhiannon de Wold. I'm here about this…this…' She waved her hand around.

He guffawed. 'I guess you're not here to have a friendly neighbourly chat and a coffee, then.'

'…this garden, or should I say this bloody jungle…'

'Yes, yes, yes,' he continued. 'The council has already spoken to me, and I'm about to go inside to ring a gardener. Okay? And thanks for dobbing me in.'

A look came over her face, but it was hard to judge what it was. She could have been surprised. Or smiling. Or scared. Who could tell?

'I need to go into my house,' he said. 'So, if you wouldn't mind moving aside.'

She replied, 'I'm glad you've seen reason. Such an eyesore!'

He shook his head. 'Oh, but I haven't seen reason. It's all such a waste of time. Beauty is subjective, but what we can agree on, is that appearance obviously means an awful lot to you, whereas I see it as a meaningless triviality. Everything grows, everything ages and everything dies, in spite of our best efforts. Evidently, appearance has taken over your whole life. To be honest, I've got more important things to do. Look, just to keep you off my back, I'll get onto the gardener ASAP.' He turned and gave her a brief backwards glance as he climbed the stairs. Her mouth was ajar. He nearly laughed aloud.

Get her a tank of oxygen, she's gasping for air again.

He was still chuckling after he went inside. *First things first.* He slipped into his office and wrote down some search keywords— *Herman Schneider, Twins, Seaview Nursing Home, Environmental Panel.* It was always good to map out a story even if it didn't pan out. He had to start connecting the dots. Circling the suspects. Developing a map.

Maybe it was time to do something constructive instead of mindlessly typing a thousand words a day, reflecting on life and growing bored and disheartened. Better for him to be an active old working dog, instead of lying around the house waiting to die. And he was going to do it without the inspiration of alcohol. Or at least he was going to try.

And to get that de Whinge woman off his case, he started ringing around for a gardener. He certainly didn't have the time or inclination to clean up a yard. For one, he was a writer, a journalist; his hands were his livelihood, the tools of his craft. Would da Vinci have gardened instead of painted? Of course not.

He went down the list of property maintenance companies who also gardened and found all of them were too busy. Then one caught his eye. Glamour Gardening Girls sounded interesting. A female crew would turn his jungle into a regency park. He called them. The voice that answered was as mellow as a plush throw rug and equally as comforting. Of course they could send someone around to take a look. Yes, they'd come today. But he'd have to wait until the end of the day. Forty minutes later, he spotted a newish Audi Q7 pulling into his driveway. He thought someone had driven in by mistake until he noticed the decal on the flank of the car. He rushed to the front door; he was impressed.

The door of the Audi swung open moments later and a stylishly attired, older woman climbed out and sidled up the driveway. She stood exceptionally tall in her Louboutins. An actress? A retired model? She looked familiar, somehow. Couldn't have been an ex-girlfriend: she didn't look angry enough. There was something about her dazzling smile, something memorable about the way she moved, as she ascended the stairs.

What? No! The woman looked like... *No, it couldn't be. Couldn't be, or...could it? Well, you could knock me over with a feather from her boa.*

'For fuck's sake, Clancy, don't just stare open-mouthed like a randy, hard-dicked, teenage boy who wants to fuck me,' she said when she reached the front door.

'Concheetah? Is it really you under all that respectability? I thought you'd dead by now. Didn't you die from cancer?' he blurted.

'That's all bullshit, Peter,' Concheetah replied with a flourish. 'News of my demise was greatly exaggerated. Concheetah may have died, but she rose again out of the ashes, like a phoenix. I am she. Or is it, she is me?'

'You always were the best drama queen I ever met,' he said with a laugh.

'And you always were the best-looking bullshit artist I ever met.'

She locked him in a tight embrace and kissed him on the lips. Their friendship had transcended the years; he had known Concheetah back when she was a transgender female, running an infamous drag queen revue in St Kilda. She had saved his life and his reputation more than once or twice. His fairy godmother of reinvention, she was the phoenix. And here he was, embracing a dear friend who, until now, he believed to be dead. It was the best gift anyone had ever given him.

'My god, Concheetah,' he said emotionally, 'it's so very bloody good to see you again.'

'Same same, Peter darling,' she purred huskily, 'but I'm not Concheetah, anymore. She really is dead. But before she died, she gave birth to Constance. Or Conni. Whichever.'

'Always full of shit.' He laughed. 'Come inside…Constance. Or Conni. Whichever. Come in for a catch-up and a coffee.'

They walked through the house and finally landed in his kitchen. 'I heard on the grapevine that Tapping Ted died,' he said once they'd sat down, 'but I never found out how. I would have loved to have gone to the funeral, if only I'd have known at the time.'

'And I would have loved to have had your support there. Yes,' she replied, tears in her eyes, 'my poor, darling Teddles died shortly before I sold out. Supposedly of a broken heart. Although that was never official. I moved to the coast not long after and established my property maintenance business. I took some of my showgirls with me.'

She sniffed back her tears. As she sipped her coffee, she told him that her business mostly looked after Tyne Coast beach houses for the Toorak parvenus, who had neither the time nor the inclination to get their manicured hands dirty. It made her a good living. She could live the same lifestyle as the clients she looked after.

'And not just that,' she blurted excitedly, 'but in these days of gender equality, I've become the must-have at every socialite's soiree. Who would have believed it? Little, old *moi*? From social pariah to gardening guru for the rich and feckless! I've been accepted into their inner circles at last!'

'And you deserve every inch of your success, plus some,' he replied. 'I remember how hard you've worked. You and Ted. I also remember the many times you were laughed at, called names and spat on. And that was just when the locals were being nice. St Kilda was a rough old place.'

'Well, I never saw it that way. It was fine. They accepted me more there than they ever did in the green leafy suburbs of Melbourne.'

'All I can say is, thank god the world's moved on,' he responded. 'It's great you've found somewhere to call home. I haven't been quite as fortunate, I guess. I worked in the States for a while and in London. But I never really found my piece of paradise.' Then he skimmed over a decade of life in a matter of minutes: how he'd succeeded and failed, and what had brought him back. 'I've had my ups and downs, but it was the heart attack that really shook me up.'

Conni smiled. 'Well, we all need to embrace the good as well as the bad and move on, don't we? That's precisely what makes us invincible.' She leaned forward and tapped him on the knee. 'My dear, dear boy!' She sighed and glanced about the room. 'I see that the look you're going for here is less shabby-chic, and more simply-shabby,' she commented. 'Why does this remind me of your horrible old place in Collingwood? Is this really the only decor that appeals to you?'

'You know I don't want to be owned by my possessions,' he replied. 'I like to travel light.'

'Light, eh? Looks like you've been living out of a shopping trolley.'

'I don't know if I'll stay yet, but I'll try to hang in there as long as my health takes to recover,' he said.

'Fuck, Clancy, you've wandered across this world for most of your life like a stray dog,' she admonished. 'One day you'll have to put down those worn-out suitcases, that worn-out body of yours. Live with someone. Let someone in.' She reached over and gave him a prod.

He nodded. 'I suppose so. I've wandered around the world for most of my life, and found violence, destruction, corruption, and misery. But not much love. Sometimes I got close. Now here's something I've never admitted to anyone else: I surrendered once.'

Her eyebrows shot up. 'To love? Well, call me old-fashioned, but I always say that you haven't really found yourself until you find Him or Her. Or Them,' she replied. 'The One. It's only with self-acceptance that you can let true love in.'

'Suddenly you've become the deep and meaningful type.'

'I've had time to reflect too, darling. We are allowed to at our age.'

He took a sip of coffee and found it too cold. He pushed it away. 'You know, I'm starting to miss London already. I miss the noise, the energy, making news and I miss my friends. In this place I have time to think. I don't know if I like it.'

'I never took you for the maudlin type. Becoming all reflective in your declining years.'

'But not depressed, never depressed,' he said, shaking his head. 'That just sounds like a waste of a life.'

Conni finished her coffee. 'So Many Women, So Little Time Clancy: that's what I called you. Hello… Did I hear right? Did you say that you fell in love for a day?'

'For longer than a day, actually. I did find her, The One, but she left for good reason. She hated me in the end. It was what…at least fifteen years ago I reckon, but I still think about her every now and then. I fucked it up, because I was worried about was getting the story at all costs. I put the story first, and she was understandably angry.'

'You can't live for a story. It'll give you success and awards, but it won't keep you warm, cuddle you and put up with your bullshit.'

'It won't. I've only just learned that. Slow learner, I guess,' he lamented.

'I thought you would never return to Melbourne; too many bad memories,' she said over her second cup of coffee. 'But you should have tried to find me. You know, I read some of your stories and all of your books, my darling. I thought of contacting you.'

'So why didn't you?' he asked. 'I think I could have done with your advice once or twice.'

'It's the man's job to contact first,' she said, laughing.

'Of course. And a woman's prerogative to say, "Piss off!".'

'Besides, I always figured that you had Stella in your corner. You still keep in touch with her, don't you?' she asked. 'She's always been such a trooper. A loyal friend—she didn't indulge your irresponsibility either. You were lucky to have an editor like her. My god, how she and I suffered to keep you together, and out of harm's way.'

'Yes, you should be both canonised,' he joked. 'And yes, I do keep in touch with her. She's in America, hosting a TV talk show out of San Francisco. Only trouble is, she does most of the talking.'

'Well, I hope you stay here for a while,' she added. 'We could do with your kind of no-nonsense reporting. We can hang out. Although I must warn you, I'll do my best to get that old booze-and-birds Peter back.'

'Still determined to kill me, aren't you?' He chuckled.

'No, I'm determined to get you to have some fun while you're here. Sitting around isn't going to make you better. You'll just die of a bored and broken heart, my dear.' She checked her phone for messages.

'Got to go?' he asked.

'No, not yet.' She put down the mobile. 'But we must arrange a dinner. Not here, of course, Silvio and I really aren't into spag bol with bottled sauce followed by supermarket dessert. So, you'll have to come to our place.'

'Thanks,' he said, laughing. 'Too posh to eat my cooking these days? How many times did I feed you and you never complained?'

'Well, I wasn't game to, my darling. I thought you'd really poison me if I complained.' It's just that an occasion such as this deserves an haute cuisine dinner. Silvio is a five-star chef, and I have to say, a five-star f—'

'Silvio? Sounds Italian. Is he the change you were talking about?'

'Yes, he is,' she replied. 'He's just one of the beautiful changes I've made.'

'So, message me with a time and a place and I'll be there.'

'Will we be expecting anyone else? A new lady fuck-friend?'

'No, I'm coming alone. I don't always need a woman in my life.'

'You really are a dead man walking,' she said. 'I'll arrange a blind date for you.'

'Please don't,' he began. 'I don't—'

'It's done, Mr Clancy,' she replied, 'Again, lucky I'm here to sort out your troubled life.'

'I know you mean well.' He sighed. 'I'm sure you won't be deterred, but if you're really determined to introduce someone new into my life, can you just make her a friend? Not a date. Someone I can talk to. Preferably someone intelligent.'

'Of course. Fine. Not a date. Someone who is your intellectual equal, and interesting to boot. I heard what you said—strictly no romance. I have somebody in mind and she's out of bounds in that department. This time I mean it!' She laughed, reapplied her lipstick, and checked her messages. 'Got to love you and leave you.' She stood up and began to make her way to the front door. 'And bring alcohol, even if you only sip at it. I can't have you without a drink in your hand. It seems totally against the laws of nature.'

'Right, you've worn me down.' He threw his hands up in mock surrender.

She air-kissed him on both cheeks.

'What about the yard?' he asked. 'In all our excitement, we didn't talk about the yard.'

'I'm sending my best crew to clean up your monstrosity of a yard ASAP. Before the toffs start thinking some crazy old recluse lives here.'

'It's really warmed my sorry old heart to see you again,' he said finally.

'Well, I certainly hope so,' she returned with a throaty chortle.

'I mean it, Conni. You and Ted always kept an eye out for me, but I never did anywhere near enough for you in return. I should have kept in touch.' His eyes turned downwards as he shook his head. 'You were never far from my heart. I missed you a lot.'

'Back at you, baby blues,' she replied tearfully. 'I just wish Ted was here to see you. He loved you like a son, you know… We both did.'

'Dear, lovable Ted… Leave it there,' Peter replied, wiping his eyes with his cuff. 'Let's leave it there.'

Conni nodded. She turned away and began to descend the stairs, her hand covering her mouth. So many years had passed, yet the loss was still raw. She had no words to add.

CHAPTER TEN

True love defaced

The bush has always welcomed me.

It was Peter's spiritual home. The sea was restorative and serene, but the bush was his first love. He was born and bred in the middle of nowhere—a cattle station located hours from the nearest town—and surrounded by wild animals that classified him either as predator or prey. They spoke a language he understood best of all.

He left the glamour gardeners to tend to his jungle, two lovely ladies who would have looked more at home on a 1980s game show. He felt sorry for them, but they appeared undaunted: the women said that they had seen worse. He allowed them free use of his coffee machine, as a way of making amends.

He was going to take a walk through the Schneider reserve, to discover its beauty.

His childhood walks alone through the bush remained close to his heart. He knew of its dangers, because his parents had drilled awareness into him, but he was also conscious of its beauty, majesty and fascination. He could fully understand why the Aboriginal people were so heart-broken and dispirited when they had been forcibly removed from it. It was their mother. It was his, too.

He could only find one overgrown path into the reserve. There was just one sign, a dilapidated one, indicating that the reserve had been established in loving memory of Helga Schneider. He swept aside a low-hanging branch and slowly made his way along the path, cheered on by a chorus of kookaburras, cockatiels, sulphur-crested cockatoos and magpies.

The bush was thick and ethereal in its shadows. As a child, he'd thought fairies lived in the bush—bush fairies, not like those in

Europe. Bush fairies were cheerful and benevolent. But this bush was infested with weeds. He recognised lantana and agapanthus, ornamental plants that had escaped local gardens to become feral pests up and down the coast. Sadly, nobody had tended it for some time.

Eventually he got to a creek that was flowing freely in some places, stagnant in others. The water looked murky and oily. Overhead, beads hung from several of the tree branches. He took a closer look. They were necklaces and bracelets, strung up with old wire; the sort of brightly coloured jewellery—chipped and bleached with age —that young girls might have played with.

He followed the beads as if they were Hansel and Gretel's trail, until he came across a cairn of rocks in a clearing beside the creek. At the foot of the cairn was a faded photograph of a young woman. It was encased in a carved frame, weatherworn, and the glass was broken. Shards of glass had scattered everywhere. He picked the frame up. It was hard to make out what the woman looked like, but he assumed it was Helga Schneider. He placed the picture at the top of the cairn and walked around it. On the other side, he found graffiti sprayed on the rocks. The crude interpretation of a phallus had been tagged, so there was no mistaking who the culprit was.

Arnold.

He continued on to a broken-down fence, and a gate lying on the ground. He stepped over the fence. Beyond it, he came upon a pile of rubbish: dirty mattresses, petrol drums and building waste. He knew whose land he had stumbled onto. He lifted his camera and took several photographs. Whether it was Arnold's personal rubbish or someone else's, dumping it so close to the creek had to be illegal.

Just then, he heard someone approaching, and he ducked behind a large gum tree.

'Yeah, it's taken care of,' he heard Arnold say into his phone. 'I took care of it, or old mate did, at least.' He stood by the rubbish pile, hands where his hips might have once been, making mental calculations. 'Yeah,' he resumed, 'no worries. Tell him I can do seventy-five cubic metres, no questions asked.'

Arnold turned away from the rubbish heap and shifted from foot to foot, his ear glued to the phone, listening to the response. Then he began to dawdle back in the direction from which he had come. Peter heard him say as he went, 'Nah, I can sort out that nosey cunt by myself. Nah, I don't need any help. Yeah, I'm sure there won't be no more trouble from him, or from that crazy bitch and her dad. Yeah, listen to what I'm fuckin' telling you, will ya? It's sorted! Tell him we'll be back operating soon.' And then his voice faded away.

Once it was silent, Peter turned and followed the trail of jewels through the reserve. Just when he thought he could walk away from journalism for a while, it was drawing him back in. Back into the action.

His words were his sword. He was back in the fight.

CHAPTER ELEVEN

Selling the dream

Rebecca Harrison delivered her pitch to the camera, kaleidoscopic beach boxes sparkling in the background, the water lapping the sand in front of her. *Perfect.* It was a glorious, warm morning. The extras in swimwear were impossibly gorgeous.

She beamed at the camera, and her well-practised smile lit up her face. 'Rebecca Harrison. I'm mayor of this little piece of heaven called the Tyne Coast.'

'Cut!'

She put her hand on her hip and bellowed, 'Could someone please bring me my wheatgrass juice?'

A tiny blonde darted forward holding a disposable cup while the crew set up the next shot.

'I'm so sorry, Ms Harrison,' she said, 'but I thought you might not want to risk...you know...spinach teeth?'

She drew the girl aside. Quietly, she snarled, 'Thinking is way above your pay-scale. You'll do whatever I ask you to do.' She took a long draught from the cup and then dropped it on the sand. 'And so now you check my teeth.'

The girl peered at Harrison's over-exaggerated grin. She wiped Harrison's central incisor with the corner of a tissue. 'You're fine.'

'Hmm.' Harrison added, 'And that's how it's done. Not exactly rocket science, is it? Now, go! Vamoose!'

The girl blushed, picked up the discarded cup and walked away. 'We're ready for you now, Ms Harrison.'

Harrison adjusted her face and continued, 'The Tyne, a world-class jewel, a tourist mecca attracting two million local and overseas visitors a year. So, how do I describe this majestic area? Quite simply, it's paradise. It's the riviera in Australia, only much, much better! The azure sea washing onto pristine, golden beaches. Little wonder people flock here year after year...'

The dolly tracked her as she walked, her white porcelain veneers twinkling every time she parted her lips. And there was a lot of lip parting. She was coming out with all gums blazing, to capture the tourist and investment dollar.

She had carelessly tossed on her prêt-à-porter white linen outfit and co-ordinating designer sun hat, her hair was braided, her makeup was courtesy of a top Melbourne artist, and her fillers and Botox by the best cosmetic surgeon money could buy. All paid for by the local ratepayer, of course. In an unofficial poll in a popular newspaper, she had been voted number one sexiest politician in Australia.

'It has a hinterland full of natural beauty, world-class vineyards and five-star restaurants. And of course, it has its fair share of celebrities like'—she leaned into a hunky male standing to the side—'our very own Jason Baneberry. You know him and love him. He's the star of Hollywood blockbusters like *Hero Squad* and *Minotaur Slayer*.'

Baneberry flashed his pearly whites and positioned his hand on the waistband of his swimming trunks. His muscles glistened in the morning sun. No surprise, then, that he was known everywhere as the Aussie Adonis.

'You've lived in some beautiful parts of the world. So, what you think of living here, Jason?' Harrison asked, her animated hands wandering close to his perfect pectorals.

'There's no place like the Tyne Coast. When I've finished a job, I can think of no other place I'd rather be than here. I can't wait to get back home. I've lived in California and Monaco but give me the Tyne anytime.'

The director cued the crowd to gather in behind Harrison and Baneberry, and then he lifted his hand above his head.

'You heard it from the Aussie Adonis,' Harrison continued, 'and now hear it from all of us.'

The director dropped his hand.

In unison, they repeated, 'It's a perfect paradise every time and anytime. Make mine the Tyne!'

'Cut,' he shouted. 'That's a wrap.'

Everyone cheered. As the crowd began to dissipate, Baneberry slid his hand down the small of Harrison's back and let it rest on her bottom.

'Thanks, Jason,' she said, pulling herself away, 'you did a great job. Thanks for agreeing to participate.'

Baneberry's personal assistant rushed up and threw a robe over his shoulders.

Harrison continued, 'Your profile will really help push the campaign along. Thanks again.' Gratitude aside, they both knew that Baneberry's fee was going to be picked up by the ratepayers.

He lowered his voice. 'I'm having a party tomorrow at my place, with a few girls. I'd love you to come. Bikini optional, and whatever goes!'

'Uh, well, I'm flattered, of course, but I'm also happily married,' she said. 'The touching thing I did before, well, that was strictly for the camera. I'm not that that sort of woman.'

'The Aussie Adonis, Becky,' he said. 'If you play your cards right, you could have him. Something to boast about.'

'Hmm, no, I don't think so. I'm flattered, but no, thank you,' she repeated.

At the click of his fingers, his assistant stepped forward and handed her a card. Baneberry added, 'My address. For when you change your mind. They all do eventually.' He winked at her and wandered off to a sapphire-blue Bentley coupe, with his personal assistant in tow. A window wound down; there were two enthusiastic blondes in the back.

The crew had all but finished packing up by the time Harrison had dismissed her makeup artist and her PA and made it back to the carpark. Someone was waiting for her there, leaning against a Lamborghini. She approached him with a smile.

'You little vixen, Becs,' he said, giving her a light kiss on the cheek. 'Flirting, no less? I saw you with that infamous shagger. Better be careful: he'll have you in bed before you can flutter those lovely lashes a couple of times.'

'He tried to invite me to his place for a pool party. The cheek of that man,' she replied, 'propositioning me, a happily married woman!'

'And you knocked back a great offer like that?' the man joked. 'You may regret it. As JFK said, a day without a lay is a day wasted.'

'And if I'd said yes to every proposition, what would that make you? Let me see, Brian Goldsmith, the coast's premier pimp and property developer?' She cracked a smile. 'You're such a bogan sometimes.'

'You know you like it. I especially like the happily married part,' he added.

'Yes, fine, laugh if you will. I didn't lie to him, although I may have exaggerated a little. To protect you—us—of course.'

'I love your loyalty,' Goldsmith responded. 'In fact, I find it exciting.'

She laughed. 'Well, if you think about it, I really am very, very happily married, aren't I? I mean, *he* couldn't care less what I do. As long as I'm discreet, Morris is unconcerned. He's got his sweet, young thang, after all.'

'He doesn't deserve you. To be honest, I couldn't bear to have you shagging that brain-dead meat rack Baneberry. Or anyone else, for that matter. I want you all to myself.' He leaned in. 'Look,' he continued, 'Adriana's out of town for a couple of days on a promotional junket, so we can shag to our hearts content in the guest house, or the pool, or even the entertainment room. Anywhere you like, my lovely.'

'Nice offer, Brian, but I want you to spoil me,' she said softly, 'and not just shag me. No more we drink a bottle of wine and I go home sex, from now on. I expect a lot more than that. You have stiff competition, you know: Adonis desires me now.'

'And you're making me insanely jealous right now. Better than that, you're making me hard,' he said, grabbing her hand. 'I can see that I'm going to have to dazzle you with a surprise.'

She snatched her hand away and looked around. She noticed her personal assistant hovering impatiently in the background and wondered why she was still there. 'Don't you have a home to go to?' she called out to her. After that, Harrison turned to Goldsmith and whispered, 'This evening, then. And you will have to dazzle me.'

His eyes followed her as she crossed the carpark, and he didn't move until her car pulled away. Then he lowered himself into his Lamborghini, made a quick call and drove off.

Chapter Twelve

Realities, big and small

Precisely as Peter had anticipated, the noise started again at seven sharp in the morning. Obviously, Arnold hadn't been deterred. The rate of Peter's swearing increased in equal proportion to the volume of the excavators. He tried to bury his head under the bedclothes, but it just became suffocating. The noise broke though anyway. He sat on the end of his bed and tried to plan his day. There were only two items on his agenda: have coffee, and then fuck Arnold over big time.

After breakfast, he slipped back into the reserve and followed the overgrown track again. He tracked the lingering smell of death to a water hole. Alongside a scatter of empty drums of various sizes, he saw a fox, a wombat, some birds and three wallabies. All dead. A murder of crows filled the tree canopy, waiting for him to leave so they could feast on the carcasses. The waterhole stunk of acetone. He flipped one of the drums over with his foot; it bore a hazardous waste symbol. The awful truth was that it wasn't the only one.

Peter had come prepared. He photographed the waterhole and the drums. Then he slipped on a pair of gloves, took a small glass jar out of his pocket, scooped in some water, and then sealed it. When he raised it to the sunlight, the surface fluoresced, and there were so many particles suspended in the water that it looked like a snow globe. The stench was searing his throat and lungs, so he didn't want to stay any longer than was absolutely necessary.

He exited the reserve at the point farthest away from Arnold's boundary. He found himself on the opposite side of the road to his own home and about a hundred metres further along. From there, he spotted two trucks approaching; the drivers were inexpertly grinding through the gears. He crouched down and waited for the trucks to pass. Both trucks carried skips loaded with building material and household rubbish, and both were heading towards Arnold's place. It needed to be recorded, so he held up his camera blindly, and snapped.

A Mercedes sedan followed moments later. It hit the crossover between the bitumen and the dirt, and then crawled past Peter. He snapped that too. *Just in case.*

He waited till the cavalcade was gone before he stood up and walked home. He took the jar out of his pocket and stashed it on a shelf in his garage. He had already contacted a friend of a friend, who had agreed to take a look at it for him. Rick Burgess special-ised in environmental science: he was arrogant, boring and useful. In short, he was the perfect contact.

The trucks coming and going had stirred up road dust, and the early morning walk had stirred up Peter's appetite. He finished the coffee and croissants he'd bought at the village and was about to get in his car to drop off the water sample, when he heard a knock at the door.

'Rhiannon de Wold,' he said even before he'd opened the door fully. 'I'd recognise your perfume anywhere. I'm very glad you douse yourself in it so liberally. You know, it acts as an advance warning system. Well, I've already done the garden, so I can't guess why you're here, but I'm pretty certain it isn't for my wit and charm, so why don't you give me a frigging break?'

'Oh?' She was taken aback. 'No, no,' she stammered, 'the garden is fine. I just wanted drop by.' She glowed from head to toe: white linen shirt left open at the navel, low-slung capri pants, bejewelled silver sandals. Even the box in her hands was white. Her mouth remained ajar. He couldn't tell if she was still stunned by his open-ing volley, or if because she simply couldn't close it.

'All right. So, what else is wrong?' he continued.

'We really did get off to a bad start, didn't we?'

Her shirt pulled tight as she held up the box. His eyes dropped to the point at which the fabric strained the most, just where her cleavage began. It unsettled him. *We men are such shallow creatures,* he thought. He said, 'I think if you hadn't tried to run me over, we might have become good neighbours.'

'Hmm.' She put the box in his hand. 'Can we start over?'

'Okay.' He was worn down. 'Would you like to come in?'

'It's a peace offering. I hope you like almond croissants.'

'Of course,' he lied.

They sat at the table. He made himself another espresso but wasn't really interested in drinking it. He made Rhiannon a herbal tea. The croissants sat in the box.

She commented vaguely about the noise from across the road, and the fact that she'd never noticed it before. Her house was soundproof, so she couldn't hear anything anyway. She looked at her hands and twisted her rings, so that the diamonds sat square. Finally, she said, 'I have a confession to make.'

Peter snorted. 'Contrary to any expectations you may have had on account of my name, I'm neither priest nor confessor. At best, I'm a lapsed Catholic. At worst, I'm…well, never mind.'

'I know what you are. I looked you up.' She continued, 'You're a famous reporter and writer.'

'Well, I can't be that famous if you had to look me up to realise who I was.'

She smiled, and this time it looked like she actually was. 'I've read some of the articles you've written, but I didn't make the connection when you introduced yourself. Forgive me for saying so, but you did look a bit like a dero the first time we met.'

'Well, thanks for the compliment. I've been mistaken for many things, but I don't think I've ever been mistaken for a dero before. What exactly led you to conclude that I was a derelict?'

'I don't know.' She sipped her tea, and continued, 'It was silly, I guess. So, I've been thinking. I thought that maybe we could help each other out. I know people who work for magazines, not that they're that much in demand these days. I checked you out with them, and they said that you have quite a reputation.'

'Right,' he said uneasily.

'Yes. As a writer…and personally.' She saw his discomfort. 'But I'm only interested in the writer part. I have a lot of contacts: I'm a social influencer, you know. I have two hundred thousand followers.'

He was unimpressed. *And how many of them are real people?*

'So, I have a duty to my followers to know things. Your moving in here could be good for both of us. That exposé on the Whitehall paedophile ring that you did, well, that was explosive. I mean, you've won awards, and everything. I like to think, we're really in the same line of work.'

He chuckled and hesitated for a moment. 'The same line of work, huh? Let me break this down for you... Once upon a time not too long ago, there was a thriving newspaper industry, not just here, but all over the world. Would-be reporters had to study journalism, suffer through their cadetships and work very, very hard, just to get a by-line. They had to tolerate second-hand smoke, first-hand bullying and unrealistic deadlines, all while resisting the temptation to drown their sorrows in bottomless barrels of VB and Vat 69.'

He continued, even though he suspected that he had lost her, 'It's interesting that you consider that we're in the same line of work. Journalists like me are accountable for every single word we write. We have editors and regulatory bodies scrutinising everything and checking it for quality control. We aren't paid particularly well, and despite what you might think, awards and accolades aren't handed out like sweets.

'From what I've seen, social influencers are regulated by little more than their conscience and the financial imperative; they peddle ill-informed opinion as the truth. You can forget education, forget research, forget hard graft, experience and talent. By virtue of something as vacuous as beauty—whatever that means, these days—social influencers have become the modern fount of all knowledge and wisdom,' he concluded. He cleared away the cups and closed the box of untouched croissants. A moment later, he added, 'Social influencers have killed my industry. I'm very flattered that you popped by, Rhiannon, and that you think a professional relationship might be mutually beneficial, but forgive me if I don't jump on the bandwagon.'

She didn't reply, but she didn't look upset. In fact, she seemed to have taken it well. *Has she even understood a word of what I said?* He escorted her to the front door.

Before she said goodbye, she said, 'Social influencers are a very important part of society. It's much harder to be a social influencer than you think, Peter.'

'I'll keep that in mind,' was all he said in return. He closed the door behind her and returned to the kitchen. Five minutes later, his mobile rang.

'Darling Peter! Bad time, good time?'

'Yes, Conni,' he replied tersely, 'what is it?'

'I take it it's a bad time. That's still no way to greet the best friend you ever had.' She laughed. 'Sounds to me like you're all blocked up. Constipated, or is it something else? Perhaps it's your monk-like devotion. It has been a while between drinks.'

'Sorry, Conni, I'm in a bit of a hurry.'

'Well, this won't take long, and you'll soon be delirious I rang. Silvio and I are having a small dinner party this Friday.'

For a moment, he wondered if he'd lost track of the days. 'But that's tomorrow. Not much warning,' he said.

'Well, you still have a day and some hours left; do you really need more than that? It's just a small, intimate dinner party with my dearest friends. And don't tell me that your dance card's full; from what I saw, you're sitting in that house fidgeting from boredom.'

'Sad but true. Only, the truth is, I'm not much in the mood for a soiree.' He didn't expand on his reasons: he didn't feel like discussing his neighbourhood problems with Conni quite yet.

'All the more reason for you to come. You never know what might arise,' she added. 'Your fairy godmother might grant you a wish or two.'

He sighed. 'But we agreed on no set-ups or blind dates, right? I'm perfectly happy as I am.'

'Really?'

She was wearing him down. 'Yes. Fine, I'll be there. I'll meet your friends and Silvio, and I'll even be the life of the party, as long as you stick to what we agreed. Just text me the details.'

'I'm doing bubbles, but if you want anything else you'll have to bring it with you. And bring lots of it: that's probably why you sound so fucked up now.'

'And I love you too,' he responded. 'Yes, all right, I'll be there, and I may bring a case of booze, just to keep you off my back. Bye.'

She was as exasperating as she was right: he needed a diversion and he needed to loosen up. He didn't dwell on it; there was work to do. He took the creek water sample from the shed and delivered it to Rick. It was going to take one week for a result, so Rick assured him. In the meantime, he would have to be patient.

Things were happening. Dots connecting.

After a lone dinner of fish and chips on the pier, he came home and watched the sunset from his deck. He read for a while, and then he went to bed, but he couldn't settle. When sheep counting didn't help, he opened the window to catch the breeze and listen to the sea. On his bedside cabinet, he kept a notepad and pen to capture his thoughts in case he found inspiration during the night. His mind was always ticking over. He was sure his mind would still be ticking over, even after he had died.

Sleep came eventually, and he drifted off at about midnight. It wasn't long after that he heard raised voices, floating in and out of his slumber. The crash of breaking glass, and he was awake and listening. *Not a dream.* It was coming from the de Wolds' place. He yawned and stretched himself out. When the noise persisted, he rose, went to the window, and looked out. The de Wolds were arguing out by the pool.

Shouldn't they be arguing inside? Isn't that one of the reasons why people install sound proofing? That way, they can argue and murder each other, and none of the neighbours would be disturbed.

He thought of ignoring it, but the argument was escalating. And becoming more interesting.

He heard Rhiannon say, 'What are you? A teenager? Sexting that little cow right under my nose, and you thought I wouldn't notice? Well? Andre! Answer me!'

Peter couldn't quite make out the reply, but he heard another glass smash, and a pool chair fell into the pool. Rhiannon turned her back and walked away. She stood in the gazebo, holding a bottle of wine and not saying a word. She looked resigned, even detached, as if she had seen this type of behaviour from Andre on too many occasions. She didn't look frightened.

Peter slipped on his tracksuit pants and a t-shirt, grabbed his phone, and went outside. He stood by the fence and watched them. Andre was in a business suit, minus a tie. He looked drunk. Rhiannon sat down on a chair in the gazebo and crossed her legs at the knees. Her impeccably shod foot jiggled, as she sipped the wine straight out of the bottle.

Andre looked like he had run out of steam. 'I'm going to bed. You fucking bore me.'

She drained the wine. 'Right back at you.'

'Bitch,' Andre hissed.

'You already called me that. Can't you think of something original to call me? Huh? Don't even think about coming to bed. Sleep in the guest room.'

'I will,' he threw back at her. 'That way, I might get some peace from all your bullshit accusations.'

'My bullshit? You know what? I really don't care what you do anymore.' She put down the bottle. 'It's a joke. All we do is play happy family twenty-four seven. This isn't a marriage, it's two people at each other's throats.'

'I'm sick of talking. And I'm sick of listening to you. Fuck you, I'm going to bed.' He staggered off.

'Fuck you, back. Fuck you!' She sat in the gazebo silently for a few minutes. Peter couldn't tell if she was crying or not. Eventually, she began to wander around the garden, stopping briefly near a bower of roses by the fence where he was standing. She buried her face in the petals.

'Rhiannon,' he said softly, turning on the torch app. 'Are you okay?'

She started and turned around.

'Who's that?'

'Sorry! It's Peter from next door. I heard you arguing with your husband, and I just wanted to check if you were all right.'

'Shit! Was it that loud? I'm so embarrassed.'

'I kind of got the gist of what you were saying to each other, so yes, you were pretty loud. You okay?'

'Well, you know... Thanks for your concern, Peter. I'm fine,' she replied. 'Same old same old.'

'All marriages have their ups and downs. Don't worry about it.'

'Yeah, right. Anyway, thanks for checking on me. I'll be okay now. He won't even remember it tomorrow. You can go back to bed. We'll be quiet, I promise.'

'Right, good. Well, goodnight, then.'

'Goodnight.'

He watched as she turned away and went back inside, and the lights extinguished one by one. Apart from the growl of a distant possum, Helga Lane fell quiet. With mosquitoes nipping at his ankles, he went back inside.

CHAPTER THIRTEEN

The Cunningham Farm

Jack nearly flipped his quad bike when he saw the devastation.

He was on his morning ride across the paddock and the sun was only barely above the horizon, so it must have happened overnight. He had been sleeping in his Land Rover out in the paddock every night, alongside the only gun the police hadn't managed to confiscate. He had been waiting for the vandals to return. But last night he had missed sleeping out, after his wife had gone to hospital with angina. Poor love was getting so stressed over what was happening. At least she was home now.

There was rubbish strewn across his best paddock. The tyre tracks that criss-crossed it belonged to a truck. A big truck, heavy enough to gouge out ruts, but still light enough not to get bogged. He rode on further to the gate that he had locked yesterday with a chain. The chain had been cut. He was pissed off, but he was glad he didn't keep the cattle in this paddock anymore.

He secured the gate and then rode back to view the rubbish. It comprised mostly of household waste and building material that, he suspected, was likely to be asbestos. That was all he needed. His paddock would be certified unusable by the council.

He returned to the farmhouse and checked on his wife. She was still in bed. He wasn't going to tell her. She didn't need any more stress. He closed the bedroom door and rang the farm neighbours. They told him the same thing: someone was dumping waste on their properties. And he knew why they did it. Dump fees had become very expensive, and there was a process involved in removing asbestos legally.

He rang the police and the environmental officer at the council, and he actually got through to them this time.

'Ah, yes, Mr Cunningham, we've noted your complaints. Yes, we're aware it's a serious problem in the community and we'll be addressing each complaint in turn.'

'And where am I on your list?' he asked.

'You're right at the top, as it happens.'

Reassured, Jack hung up the phone. The top of the listed sounded like a very good place to be. He tried to rein in his enthusiasm, watch and see what would happen first. Still, he hoped for once that they might actually catch the bastards.

Chapter Fourteen

Close encounters of the best kind

Peter was excited about going to Conni's place for dinner. He was also a little anxious: it wasn't because of the company, but the fact he hadn't ventured out socially since he'd returned home.

He went to the liquor shop and pored over the varieties. He was rivetted by the labels, from the traditional French to the irreverent Australians. He read the back of the labels assiduously: *a spectacular Beaujolais full of crisp, red fruit and light tannins*; *a cheeky Barossa Cabernet typical of the region, with a lingering palate*; blah, blah, blah...

In the end he chose a middle-of-the-range bottle of red wine and a bottle of champagne, and he threw them into the back of his car. He could tolerate both in small doses; until recent events, whisky had been his favoured companion as well as his nemesis. Conni would have to remain disappointed if she hoped to see the old Peter Clancy again in full flight, especially since he'd decided to drive himself to her house.

He left a little later than he'd intended and followed the esplanade north for about a kilometre. From there, he negotiated a steep, narrow drive at the back of the village, to the top of a hill. Once he'd reached the apex, he was rewarded by an expansive view of the bay all the way to Melbourne. It was spectacular in the early evening light. He kept going until he spotted Conni's vast, white, Long Island-style mansion. It wasn't quite Cape, yet it oozed coastal elegance, peppered with her glamorous touch.

He turned off. Once he noted only two other cars in the driveway, he loosened up. *Fewer people, more relaxed.* There was a time not all that long ago when he needed lots of people around him, even to enjoy a coffee. But not anymore. The day it changed was the day it dawned on him that he had finally matured—not aged, just matured.

He pressed the buzzer and waited. He expected to hear Conni's voice boom at the other end, or to be swept up by a gale of laughter, but there was silence. He frowned. Just as his hand was reaching again for the buzzer, she swung open the door and stooped down to kiss his cheeks, enveloping him in scent. Then she pulled him through the door.

'Darling Peter,' she said as she led him along an endless hallway, 'do come in. What a joy it is to have you here in our humble abode in the hills. Finally!' She wore a cocktail dress seamed so tightly over every curve that he wondered how she managed to walk—let alone sit—in it. Her neck dripped with jewellery. She dazzled.

He looked around. Muted tones surrounded him, giving the house a light, airy feel. 'It's gorgeous, Conni. Well done, you. You have a beautiful home,' he said.

'Don't look so surprised. You weren't expecting to still find me stuck in that awful, boudoir brothel look that I liked back in the old days?'

'Well, no, I thought you'd probably transcended black and gold tapware and crystal chandeliers by now. I'm glad you've done well, you deserve it. And may I say, not bad for a gardener.'

'A gardener? Me? With these hands?' She flashed a set of manicured nails and diamond rings on every finger. 'Entrepreneur, please. You know me,' she quipped, 'I don't do riffraff. It doesn't suit me.' She looked at his hands. 'Wine and champagne? Where's the carton of VB?' She took the bottles. 'You can't drink that rubbish. You'll die of toxic shock: your body will rebel.'

'I'm a different person,' he said, smiling.

'No, don't you dare be a different person, Peter Clancy, don't you dare! You'll just become another boring old fuck and die a miserable death. As your dear, dear friend I don't want you to end up like that. A life without passion is a slow freeze unto death, my dear, and you were never the cryogenic type.' She added, 'That's why I anticipated your move, and have graciously stocked the drinks fridge with your old choice of alcohol.'

'My liver,' he said, 'will be forever grateful.'

She waved him towards the kitchen. The smell of pork wafted past his nostrils, and he found himself salivating. It wasn't just any pork, it was porchetta. His favourite.

'Everyone,' she announced, 'this gorgeous man isn't just one of my oldest friends, he's one of the greatest journalists in the world. I present to you Peter Clancy.' There were three people perched on stools at the bench—a middle-aged, well-heeled couple and a younger woman—drinking wine and nibbling on antipasti, while a tall man with a George Hamilton suntan shaved parmesan onto a bowl of rocket leaves. Peter presumed him to be Silvio.

'Silvio darling, meet Peter,' she said. She turned to Peter, 'Silvio is a genius with food and fire. He has his own restaurant right on the water, The Pasta Master. It's spectacular. We must take you there one evening.'

Silvio looked up but didn't smile. 'Is a pleasure to meet you,' he said.

Peter was unsure whether he meant it. 'Likewise,' he replied.

'Now, no need to be jealous, Silvio, Peter and I were never more than good friends,' said Conni. 'Peter darling, these delicious people'—she gestured towards the couple—'are Harriet and Walter Bell, my business partners.'

He mumbled a pleasantry, but he didn't listen to their response. He was oblivious to them. Conni tracked his eyes across to the stunning woman in her thirties sitting alongside them.

Despite everything I said, Conni's set me up. Bloody hell!

Conni smiled. 'Oh, I see you've already spotted Misha,' she remarked. 'And no, I know what you're thinking,' she added, 'she's definitely not a set-up. You and she have something in common, but I'll let you work that out for yourself.'

Misha held out her hand and gently shook Peter's.

'You know,' continued Conni, 'Peter used to love to party back when he was interesting, but he's sworn off it. These days, he's even more dull and more celibate than Silvio was, back in the day when he was a priest at the Vatican.' She fielded Peter's quizzical look. 'But more about that another time. Our job tonight, boys and girls, is to thaw Peter out. And when that happens, be warned, he'll go off like a firecracker.'

He pulled out the stool next to Misha and sat down. Conni pushed the antipasti platter along the Carrera marble benchtop towards him. 'Now you'll have to excuse me,' she said, sashaying over to the drinks fridge, 'I'm supposed to be helping Silvio.'

She returned with a glass of wine and a VB. 'Let's test you out. A beer or a nice Nebbiolo d'Alba?'

'Leave them both,' he replied, tapping the bench.

Conni's jewellery clattered as she put down the drinks and clapped her hands. 'Bravo,' she said, 'he's already on his way back.'

'But if I die prematurely, let it be on your head!'

Misha smiled and took a sip from the glass in front of her. 'Hello,' she said. A single word placed her firmly in Eastern Europe. She had shoulder-length blonde hair, green eyes, and a light tanned skin. Slender, tall and elegant, she looked like a model.

He was enthralled. Like a bee to a flower. Perhaps he'd been rash in refusing Conni's offer of a blind date. He hoped she wasn't Russian. He always likened listening to Russian being spoken to an assault with bricks. Maybe he had a slight animosity towards Russians because they had the rare ability to outdrink him. Maybe it had more to do with his past experiences trying to avoid their wrath.

'It's a pleasure to meet you. Let me guess, you're from Eastern Europe?' He hoped that his banter would kick in once he became accustomed to her looks. Stick him with a beautiful woman and he was always a little tongue-tied.

'Well, yes. I lived in Kyiv, in Ukraine,' she replied in near perfect English, 'but I live here now. Have you been there?'

'I nearly went there on assignment once,' he said, 'but I was stopped at the last moment because of my history. I think the government thought I was a little subversive. I'd still like to see it though.'

She looked distracted and hesitantly took a sip of champagne. 'Well, Kyiv is very nice, but it is not exactly New York, you know.'

'So, what brought you here?' he asked.

Conni placed her arms around Misha and Peter. 'You were always the life of the party, Clancy: you could turn a funeral into a celebration, so please don't be dull tonight. Could Keith Richards become a Buddhist monk?' She paused for a response. 'And that thing you have something in common, any guesses?'

He replied, 'She and I are both Collingwood fans?'

'Nothing as vulgar as that,' she returned, faking a gag. 'Tell him, Misha.'

'All right,' she began nervously. 'I already know a lot about you. I have followed your stories for a while, and I have read your books.'

'See, you have a fan,' Conni teased.

'My one and only?'

'No, no, you have many,' Misha said earnestly. 'In Ukraine you are an inspiration to many journalists and others. You are a fighter for press freedom. What was it that you said in one of your books? *An investigative reporter must not be afraid to apply a blowtorch to oppression and corruption.* You see, there was little freedom for me where I grew up, and that was why I left. The blowtorch belonged only to the authorities.'

'What I do is my lifeblood and my identity; I'm lucky that way. I'm a journalist, yes, but it's not simply my job.'

'Misha always wanted to be a journalist too,' remarked Conni.

'I did, but my parents were not supportive. I finished high school and became a personal assistant to a very rich man instead, which was very boring, but it made my parents happy. Then I left that after a couple of years. But I still wanted to be a reporter.'

'You should have written to me,' he declared. 'Maybe I could have guided you. It's not too late, you know.' Just then, Silvio stamped his foot and roared something he couldn't make out.

'My cue,' declared Conni with a chuckle. 'I just love it when he dominates me.'

Misha turned to Peter. 'That's right,' she said, 'it wasn't too late. A couple of years ago I realised that it's never too late to pursue your passion. So now, at last, I am studying journalism at the university.' She added, 'And it's all because of you, Peter Clancy.'

'I seriously doubt that, but I'm honoured all the same.' He smiled.

'I'm galloping towards the end of my career, you see, and you're barely at the start of yours. Soon I'll be passing on the blowtorch to the next generation.'

'Oh, no, don't say that! You're not old and I have a long way to go. I'm only in my second year,' she said, 'and I have to do work experience and...'

Conni was following the conversation from the other side of the kitchen. She topped up the Bells' glasses, exchanged a brief conversation with them, and then returned to stand by Misha's side. She looked at her. 'Well?'

Peter looked up at Conni. 'You're hovering around like a blowfly at a barbeque. What's eating you tonight? Go away! Shoo!'

'Nothing at all, darling,' she retorted, 'and I'll go in a moment or two. It's just that she desperately wants to ask you something, but she's too embarrassed. Aren't you, beautiful?' She kissed Misha on top of her head and gave her a squeeze. 'You know, I was a father once, a hundred million years ago. I loved my children, and I always craved their love and acceptance in return, regardless of whether I was Colin or Concheetah. But they never understood me. They wanted me to live forever as Colin, and I needed to be me or die. I guess in the end it was a sacrifice none of us was willing to make, so they walked away from me. It's different with Misha. I know she came to me fully formed, but she needed a family as much as I did. Conni may have been born womb-less, but she's always harboured maternal urges. Misha is, for all intents and purposes, my and Silvio's daughter.'

Misha smiled. She sipped her champagne. 'Conni is right, there is something I need to ask. I have to arrange work experience, something like an internship at a newspaper,' she began, 'but I think I—'

He interrupted. 'I don't really know anyone here in the newspapers, only in London, and I bet you don't fancy a trip there.'

Conni sighed and rolled her eyes. 'Oh, for goodness' sake, what Misha is trying to say is that she would like to be your intern. You should be able to arrange that!'

'Aside from the fact that I'm not actually a newspaper, there wouldn't be a lot for her to do,' he replied. 'Right now, I'm developing an idea for another book and a possible article.'

'Misha asked her lecturer already if she could work with an eminent journalist. She didn't mention your name of course.'

'And?'

Misha twisted around in her seat. 'Fine, as long I am doing research, or helping you work on a story. But it is a big commitment. I can send you the details.'

'Well then, it looks like you two have it all sorted.'

'So, it's a yes?' Misha's mouth dropped open. 'Thank you, Peter, thank you. I'm honoured to have you as my mentor and I will work very, very hard.'

'I know you will. I'll get you doing something. Although, it doesn't seem fair not to pay you. To be honest, I don't have the money to do that.'

'It's all right, Peter,' Conni said, 'I already pay for Misha's fees. It's fine.' She glanced across at Silvio. 'It looks like dinner is ready.'

They sat around a limed oak table, covered in platters with enough food to feed a village.

'Before we start,' Conni began, 'I'd like to say grace.'

Peter gasped. 'You? Say grace? Since when have you been religious?'

'Shut up, Clancy. You are insufferable sometimes. I suppose, that's why I love you. Silence, all.' She bowed her head and cleared her throat. 'They come to us from far and near, to eat our grub and drink our beer. The bottles are chilled and the oysters shucked, so sit and eat, or go get f…for what we have provided, may you all be truly thankful.'

'We love you too.' Peter smiled and raised his glass. 'To Silvio and Conni!'

She continued, 'Seriously, though, Silvio and I thank you all for coming. You are all family to us. What a joy to have my dear, dear, Peter Clancy back in my bosom… I mean, the bosom of our family.'

He tipped his glass towards her.

She continued, 'It's a special celebration, not only because I have those I love most here, but because it's a decade since my change.'

'You had the…' Peter began.

'Yes,' she said with a laugh, 'I did, and it's exactly a decade today since I transformed from a chrysalis to a butterfly, from Concheetah to Conni. A decade since my rebirth. And Silvio and I have never been so happy. So, now I'll propose the toast. To change and family!'

'To change and family!' The guests raised their glasses and drank.

By eleven o'clock, Peter was starting to feel very intoxicated. The sensation was warm and pleasantly familiar. He was starting to experience the buzz, the loosening up of the tongue and the absence of inhibitions. He'd felt guilty about drinking anything at first but, by his sixth beer, he didn't care anymore.

He looked around at Conni and Silvio, the Bells, and Misha, who were all chatting excitedly as the mounds of food slowly disappeared. He was having fun, and better than that, everyone else was, too.

Chapter Fifteen

A small start

'This,' Peter announced the following afternoon, 'is my office.'

Misha said nothing. She looked around for a while, her hands on her hips. 'Peter, this is not an office, it is a pigsty. How do you get anything done in this mess?'

He thought of the many desks he'd occupied in newspaper offices over the years. There was a recurring theme: the mess and the dirty mugs went along with the deadlines. He retorted, 'Well, everything has its place, Misha, and I can locate everything instinctively. I just visualise something, and hey-presto it's there. I call it my magic trick. Let me demonstrate: I'm thinking about my latest manuscript.' He ruffled through a pile of documents. Then he retreated from his desk and shook his head. 'Well, it was here yesterday.'

'Looks like your magic is a bit rusty.' She started sorting the piles. 'How can you think in here at all? Oh Peter, there are two coffee cups under these documents.' She pushed the one that was half full in his direction. 'And this one has an insect in it. Yuk.'

'I was wondering where they were,' he said, grabbing them.

She stood back. 'I'm here to learn from you, but I can't do that in this space. I really can't think right now. I have to sort this out; can I please make cleaning your office my first job?' she asked.

'Fine, but make sure you don't throw anything out until I've checked it first.' He pointed to the whiteboard. 'And this is crucial to my investigative pieces. It's my roadmap. Please don't wipe over it, ever. I write everything important up there, and then I stand back and look at it. Eventually, I make sense of it, find the connections, and join the dots. You know, I would have felt embarrassed about the state of my office, except that this is how I've always done it. This is me. After thirty-five years as a reporter, I've come to realise that mess has always worked for me.'

'You'll get things done quicker if you're better organised,' she said, 'and you won't have to store it all in your head anymore.' She looked down at the desk and recoiled. 'Really, I'm not touching that. You're not actually using this as note paper, are you?'

Peter looked down at his desk. 'I do have a notepad, but I was in the toilet…thinking,' he replied, 'and I suddenly felt inspired. There really wasn't much choice of paper.'

'Rolls of toilet paper are not good as note paper. What if you accidentally flush away what you have written on?' She sighed. 'I'll make a list of what we need. And first on the list is a desk, for me.'

'Yes, of course.'

She looked around the room again. 'It's a disgrace, but I think that might be because you're not proud of your office. There is nothing about you in here. You don't display your awards.'

'I haven't unpacked them yet. I guess I don't really care about them, and the one I helped win for my friend, Stella, is in America.'

'You mean, the Pulitzer Prize? If it was mine, I'd wear it on a chain around my neck. I'd even sleep with it. You should be proud of your achievements.'

He shrugged. 'If you ever locate the box they're in, you can put them up. Then, once you finish creating order from disorder, I'll show you the real art of investigative journalism. We have someone we need to visit.'

She pointed to the whiteboard, and to one word in particular. 'You're writing about a sex offender?'

'What?' said Peter. 'No. Titty Man isn't a sex offender—at least, not as far as I'm aware—but he is into some heavy-duty criminal activity. I just call him that, because… Well, I'll let you work that one out for yourself. All I'll tell you is that his name is Eddie Arnold, and he's a very shady character; I'm trying to find out what exactly he's up to, and after that I'll see if it's worth my time to make it into a story. If the word offends you, I'll give him a different nickname. Does Arsehole Arnold sound better to you?'

'Oh, I'm not offended, just interested. You know, Peter, like you, my real passion is to unmask the people who do bad things in this world. By becoming a journalist, I hope that I can make them pay for the pain they inflict.'

There was something in the way she spoke that startled him. She looked as if she was reliving the past and had landed herself some-where between a scream and a weep.

He said, 'Anyone in particular? Does this person have a name?'

'No, no, never mind. Sorry.' She wiped away a tear and sniffed.

Peter wondered who the hell had hurt her, and why. He knew better than to press Misha any further, so he put it on his list of things to ask Conni.

Chapter Sixteen

Guilty pleasures

Brian Goldsmith and Rebecca Harrison met up at his house for their usual mid-week tryst.

They had seen each other this way for the last two years. It had always been hassle-free: no complications, no suspicions, and no awkward discussions with their respective partners. At a quarter to six every week, Adriana drove to Melbourne to visit family. Brian sent the help home ten minutes later and shut off the CCTV cameras. Rebecca arrived at six, and he and Rebecca retreated into the guest house with a bottle of red from the cellar. After a glass or two of wine and some lovemaking to Barry White with a porn movie running in the background, they finished the evening with a meal provided by the local Italian restaurant. Sometimes she wore red lingerie, which was his favourite colour. From arrival to orgasm took under half an hour. With the wine, food and loving out of the way, they often spent the next hour talking business and strategies, over even more red.

She lay on the couch while he poured another glass for her, and then she slipped into her bra and pants and took a sip. 'Are you going to put on any clothes?' she asked.

'Eventually.'

'You know I can't stay. Morris wouldn't like it.'

'One night you'll stay, and we'll do this all night,' he said. 'I want to have morning sex for a change, to the sound of the sea.'

She laughed. 'Getting sentimental? That's not like you. The only way that will ever happen is... Well, neither of us will be getting divorced anytime soon, so we'll just have to content our-selves with a root and a takeaway every Wednesday. Conferences excepted.' She tossed his Dolce & Gabbana's at him.

He pushed them aside and thrust his hips forward. 'Look at me,' he said. 'Look at what you've done. I want you, Becs. You make me so horny.'

She glanced at him and spluttered, 'You'll have to take care of that one yourself.' She turned away.

He sulked for a while, but she chose not to notice. Finally, he began to dress. 'You know that I love you, don't you, Becs.'

'Yes, of course,' she said. 'And I love... Well, I love all of this. I want to be with you, honestly, I do, but let's be practical. A divorce right now would ruin my political career, and it would cost both of us lots of money. We have to be patient.' She stood up. 'I have an early appointment with the hairdresser tomorrow. I must admit, I'm a little nervous. I just hope our plans come off, my love. I'm worried about Arnold and the others. We need to control them better. We don't want them going off and trying to take over. I don't want a repeat of what happened with Nick.'

'There won't be any trouble, babe. They won't cause us any grief, I promise,' he reassured her. 'Warryn and I go back a long way. Everything will be fine. I'll sort it out. I'm the MC and you're the juggler in this fucking circus; your job is to keep the balls in the air and rotating.'

'We can't afford to drop any of them.' She burrowed into his arms. 'We're close now, so close.'

'Imagine the rewards,' he said, sniffing her hair. 'And don't you go all soft and gooey on me.'

'Not a chance.'

'Once this development's completed, even after Adriana and the others get their cut, we'll still have most of it left,' he continued. 'Then we can look to the future. Look, I know it's complicated, but my talent lies in turning the complicated into lots of fucking money for me...I mean, us.'

Rebecca turned her face away and scowled. 'Yes, us. And don't you forget it.'

'Of course, sweet tits.'

The words had only just left his lips when his telephone buzzed.

He checked it. 'Adriana's spending the night with her family. She's not coming home tonight.'

'Hmm. But I still can't stay here. Next time, perhaps.'

'Right. Oh,' he added, 'and I almost forgot to tell you. She said a car was parked across the road today, and she saw a man taking photos.'

'And?'

'I reckon it probably had something to do with that stupid reality show she did last year. You remember that trash, *Brighton Billionaire Babes*. Anyway, the cops came, and he left. Sounds to me like fuckwit paparazzi.'

'Don't worry about it,' said Rebecca. 'She's managed to make something out of nothing yet again. You know Adriana just loves the attention, not to mention the drama.'

'I know, I know. Once it's all done and dusted, we won't have to worry about the divorce payouts: they'll be small change compared to what's going to be coming in. We'll be rolling in it.'

'Well,' she said, checking her watch, 'time for me to go. Let's talk about it another time.' She kissed him hard and grabbed his crotch. 'Miss me, till we fuck again...'

And then she smiled at him and walked towards the door.

CHAPTER SEVENTEEN

Seaview Nursing Home

The stench of ammonia stole Misha's breath, and it transported her to a place in her mind that she had vowed to never revisit. 'This is horrible, Peter,' she whispered. 'It's third-world; it should be pulled down.'

Peter was looking around, trying hard not to wear his disgust on his face. The only reason they had decided to go to the Seaview was to locate the Schneider twins. *We need to find them quick and get out, before the stink etches my nostrils permanently.*

Misha's hand was hovering just under her nose. He understood why. He said, 'A nurse I once knew told me that you can always tell how well a nursing home is run, based on what you first smell at the front door. Piss and shit don't usually bode well.'

'I didn't think such places could exist in a wealthy country like Australia. Where I came from, perhaps, but not here.'

They made their way to the reception desk and waited patiently for the clerk to finish her telephone call and attend to them. After two minutes, it became obvious that she had no intention of doing either. She was doing her best not to notice them at all.

'Come on,' he said to Misha. 'We're wasting our time. Fucking lazy bitch.'

They wandered down the maze of corridors running off the entrance, left and right. Eventually, they came across a nurse scurrying by, balancing metal bed pans in each hand.

'Let's follow her,' he said. 'She may lead us somewhere useful. There's always a recreation room in these establishments. I'd say that's where we might find them.'

The nurse was too preoccupied to realise she was being followed.

Peter heard the music before he saw the sign. Written in bold, multi-coloured Texta with balloons hanging off it, it said *Rec Room*, in a way that screamed more kindergarten than nursing home. It made him feel like running out of the place. *Not fucking Elvis. I hate Elvis.*

With a sweep of his hand, he said to Misha, 'And this is why I'll never go into one of these places. I aim to die ingloriously first. Apart from the smell of effluent and the infantilisation, I'm going to hate the music that's played in the rec room.'

She looked around. There was a conga-line of odd recliners, armchairs and wheelchairs along every wall, mostly occupied. 'But how do we find them if we don't know what the ladies look like?'

'We just ask. Questions are our job. And if we're really lucky, they may be wearing name tags,' he replied. 'Just follow my lead.'

They were already in the recreation room when they heard someone calling out behind them. 'Excuse me, but you can't come in here, without checking in with me and signing in first.'

Peter and Misha spun around. It was the lazy reception clerk. Out from behind her desk, her appearance didn't make for a good impression.

What would you expect in a shithole like this? 'You were too busy to take enquiries,' said Peter, 'and we didn't want to miss our gig, waiting for you to finish chatting on the phone.'

The clerk caught her breath. 'But you can't just walk in here,' she stated with an air of arrogant authority. 'This is a secure facility.'

'What? Like a prison?'

'No, but...'

'My name is Bobby Plant; you have probably heard of me. And this beautiful lady is Jemima Page. Together, we're a famous mus-ical duo—Plant and Page—and we're here to entertain these good folk.'

The clerk was shaking her head. 'No, never heard of you. And what's more, no one told me you were coming.'

'Really? That's surprising; I expected our appearance would have been highly anticipated. We're booked to play from ten until eleven, and it's almost ten now. In thirty-five years as an entertainer, I've never missed a gig yet, and I'm not about to start today.'

The girl's face was blank. 'You'll have to leave,' she growled defiantly, hands on her hips, 'or I'll call security.'

'Look,' he said, 'why don't you clear it with your social director? I believe her name is Caitlin?'

'Yes, that's right,' she said, 'but she didn't tell me anything about a musical duo.'

'Well, I hardly think that these good folk deserve to miss out, just because your social director forgot to put us on your visitors list.'

'All right then. So, if you're musicians, where are you hiding your instruments?'

Misha piped up, 'They are still in our car. But we notice that you have instruments here.' She pointed to an assortment of instruments in a box in one corner of the room. 'We prefer to use what's already here, so that we can get the residents involved.' She handed Peter her bag, went over and picked up a guitar lying on top of the pile, and began to tune it.

'This is easily solved,' said Peter. 'Why don't you just ask Caitlin? We'll sign in, while you go find her, and ask her.'

The girl sighed. Peter had worn her down. 'Just sign in, will you.'

After she left, Misha came over and handed him a tambourine. She whispered, 'How did you know about Caitlin?'

He pointed to a noticeboard, with Caitlin's name and photograph. 'See? I took a punt that the clerk would be too lazy to go look for her.'

An hour later, Misha had exhausted her repertoire of Beatles' favourites. It had been such a long time since she had played guitar, that her fingers ached. She finally replaced the guitar in the box, after two encores of 'Ob-la-di Ob-la-da'.

'There's a career in that for you, if you ever decide against journalism. You didn't tell me you could play guitar and sing,' he commented.

'Well, you never asked,' she replied.

'Aside from the fact that I actually enjoyed it, this has been a complete waste of time,' he continued. 'No sign of the Schneider ladies.'

'The day is still young. Watch and learn.' She walked over to one of the men who had joined in the singing enthusiastically, and she chatted with him for a while, as Peter observed from the other side of the room. She flicked her hair more than once and giggled. A few moments later, the man was wheeling himself out, with Misha in tow. Peter followed them along the corridor.

They stopped outside a room. The door was slightly ajar.

'They're in there,' said the man.

'Thank you, Derek,' she returned with a smile.

'Can I have my kiss now?'

She stooped to kiss him on the cheek, but he turned his head at the last moment, and planted one on her lips. 'Derek,' she said, 'you are very naughty.'

'And you are very beautiful,' he replied. 'I don't suppose you'd like to join me in my room for a quickie?'

'Tempting as your offer might seem, no, I would not.'

'Pity,' he said, moving on. 'I'm a stud, you know; I could have taught you a thing or two. Your loss,' he yelled behind him, as he went.

Peter rapped on the door and peered in. 'Come on,' he said to Misha, swinging the door open and pulling her through. The blind was halfway down, and the room was gloomy. He made out two single beds, two overbed tables, two armchairs, two wheelie-walkers, and two sets of drawers. There was nothing at all that was personal to the occupants. A television hung from the ceiling. The Schneider twins were both sitting in the armchairs, dressed in sweatshirts and pants of different hues. In all other respects, they were identical.

'Hello,' he said brightly. 'Henry Honnery, barrister-at-law. You must be Anastasia and Octavia Schneider. Very pleased to meet you both.'

'Who are you?' asked one of the twins.

'Henry Honnery. I believe you were expecting me.'

'No, no,' she answered. 'Were you expecting him, Octavia?'

'No. Are you here to take us home?' asked Octavia, brightening.

'I'm afraid not. I'm here to check the circumstances of your admission and see how you're doing. This is my assistant, Vera Varcoe. She'll be taking notes of our conversation, won't you, Miss Varcoe.'

'*Guten Tag,*' said Misha, taking a pen and pad out of her bag. '*Wie geht es euch?*'

'*Gut, danke. Aber sie sprechen Deutsch!*'

'*Ja, leide nur ein bisschen. Mein Kollege spricht kein Deutsch.*'

'Then we must continue in English, so your colleague can understand.'

'I was told that you haven't been very well,' Peter began.

'Lies, all lies. We are strong and healthy.' She flexed her forearm. 'See? All our lives we have clean air and good food. At home, we took very good care of each other, didn't we, sister?' said Anastasia.

'That's exactly right, Anna. And now we want to go home.'

'I see,' he said. 'So, how did you come to be here?'

'Well,' Octavia continued, 'it happened like this. Our cousin came to take us out for a drive one day, and we thought, why not? It was most unusual of her, but it was a sunny day, and we were happy to go out for a change.'

'Yes. And then it turned into a nightmare,' said Anastasia. 'We were just going for a nice drive. What right did she have to bring us to this place?'

'I'm sorry,' he said, 'am I to understand that you're not here voluntarily?'

'Voluntarily? Are you joking? Who would come here voluntarily? Anna and I were put here "for our own good". Adriana brought us here to visit, and then she left us to die here, like dogs.'

'Adriana?'

'Adriana Balloch, our cousin Hans's daughter. When we first came here, they gave us pills for this and for that, and all we did was sleep all day. One day, I told Octavia not to swallow them. Now we pretend to take them, and when they're not looking, we spit them out in the toilet.'

'Is this the same Adriana Balloch from the reality show?' Misha asked.

'We don't know about reality shows,' Octavia replied. 'All we know is she's Hans's girl, and that she wears very expensive clothes and drives a very expensive car. I don't think Hans was rich, so I don't know where she gets all the money from.'

Anastasia giggled. 'Maybe she found the money in the same place that she found her new face!'

Misha nodded 'Yes. That would be correct. She thinks she's a celebrity. I believe that she owns this place.'

'Can you get us out of here?'

Peter replied, 'I don't know. Do you have any paperwork? Did you sign anything?'

The twins shook their heads in unison.

His eyebrows shot up. 'I can't promise you anything but let me see what I can do.'

The women exchanged glances. 'You are a prayer answered,' said Octavia.

'Well,' he chuckled, 'I don't know about that. I haven't done anything yet.'

'Yes,' said Anastasia, 'you have. You found us, and you have given us hope. Now, please do everything you can to help us!'

'Of course, I will. But in the meantime, you must keep your eyes open and your wits about you,' he returned. 'It may take some time before you see me or my assistant again, but you must trust that I won't give up on you. Goodbye for now, ladies.'

'Those poor women. They're so nice,' Misha said to him, after they left the room.

'I'm going to see what I can do to get some of the paperwork. I have to warn you, I'm not above paying people for information. So, if you have a problem with that...'

'No, no problem.'

'And now, Miss Misha, you have to explain yourself. German as well? You didn't tell me you could speak German.'

'Well, you never asked.' She smiled. 'Now, you go off and do whatever it is that you need to do. I'll wait for you in the car.'

Peter gestured his goodbye and went back through the entrance. His purpose was to find a carer or a cleaner, perhaps, or someone else who would be prepared to trade information for a little cash. Instead, he glimpsed the surly receptionist on her way back to her desk. She was scowling; she just didn't look like the helpful type, money or no money.

He turned on his heel before she spotted him, and headed in the opposite direction.

The Schneider twins would have to wait.

CHAPTER EIGHTEEN

Husbands and wives

Peter rang Rick Burgess as soon as he and Misha returned home. 'Bloody boffins live in their own time zone,' he complained. 'Rick's on holidays and his minions aren't telling me anything. He'll be away for another week. No concept of time.'

Misha turned away from her computer. 'Why are you always in such a hurry? I always thought it was better to take your time and get it right.'

'That's not how it works. As a journo, you're always under the gun. Believe me, if you've had a hunch about a story, someone else out there has had the very same hunch. You'll soon learn that there are deadlines to meet as well as the pressure to get the story off stone ahead of the next guy. I don't think we'll be scooped, but I want those results. I need those results. Timing is everything in this game. Environmental issues are big. Environmental issues in a tourist hotspot are huge. Summer's coming, and a story on environmental issues in a tourist beachside hotspot during summer will get me national coverage. I want—no, I need—this story to break just before the start of the summer holidays. Before everyone's too preoccupied to read about it.'

She swung herself back again. 'Of course, but I think I may have found you another angle,' she said. 'While you've been on the phone, I've been researching Adriana Balloch. She's married to Brian Goldsmith, of course, the property developer and real estate agent. Apparently, she splits her time between building nursing homes—just like the Seaview—and her celebrity appearances.'

'Yes, and so? I left all that celebrity crap behind when I quit writing for *The Melbourne Truth* and the *Star Gazer* back in London.

Not to mince words, but who cares?'

'No, no, *Brighton Billionaire Babes* threatened to drop her after one season for being too vacuous, boring and annoying. The hardcore fans of the show found her so blah, that they couldn't even be bothered sending her hate-mail in the end. She was a complete failure. Her celebrity status is definitely overstated, but that's not my point.'

'Right, so she's put her elderly relatives in a nursing home against their will. I could make something of that, and make it stick. It's disgraceful, but not entirely unexpected.'

'That's not my point either. Look here. Six months ago, a local man named Nick Sutcliffe died tragically when his car left the Esplanade and he plunged to his death. He was survived by his wife, Katherine and two children.'

'Yes, and?'

'He was a colleague of Brian Goldsmith.'

'Now, that's interesting.' Peter's brain was spinning. He stared at his whiteboard for a moment, stood up and wrote DEADLINE 23 NOVEMBER!!!, underlining it twice. A week before the official start of summer should gain his story the greatest traction. *While the kids are still at school and their parents are planning a beachside break.* Then he added Goldsmith's name to the whiteboard. He drew an arrow linking Sutcliffe's name to Goldsmith's.

Misha enquired, 'You think his death could be suspicious?'

'In this game, all deaths are suspicious. All deaths have a back story. Let me take a look at your research. Can you send me the links?'

Her keyboard clattered. 'Done.'

He sat down again and clicked through the links. 'Look at the photograph taken at a local polo match last summer.'

She looked at the photograph. In the foreground were a man in polo gear, another in a linen suit, and two women in enormous hats. 'What am I looking for?' she asked.

'Balloch and Goldsmith look pretty pally with the mayor and her husband, don't you think?' There was something in Rebecca Harrison's sideways glance at Goldsmith that Peter found especially intriguing. He recognised a few of the people in the background as well. 'Okay,' he continued after a long silence, 'we have lots of work to do, Misha. This widow of Nick Sutcliffe, Katherine Sutcliffe, do we have a contact email or some such?'

'We have better than that. I was about to tell you; she lives on the other side of the village. The home she and her husband built was featured on a real estate show a while ago. I have the address.'

'Good, let's see if she's about tomorrow morning. We won't let her know we're coming. Spontaneity sometimes gets results. Door-step interviews have always been good for me and, even though they're tough to do at first, you soon get used to them. Just remember, charm and bullshit win out over resistance and agitation every time,' he remarked.

'Aren't you afraid that you might get thrown out?'

'It doesn't keep me awake at night, no. In order to get, first you have to try. I didn't take you for the shrinking violet type, Misha.'

'You're right, I'm not. Honestly, I am okay with wedging my foot in the door to get an interview. I didn't get this far without taking many, many risks,' she said with a smile. 'Maybe I'll tell you about it one day.'

'I look forward to that day.'

The Sutcliffe home was located in the most exclusive part of the village, towering over its neighbours on a large, manicured block. Peter drove past it at a crawl. It was a meandering house, and the part of the structure that he could see was clad in steel. The steel had oxidised to a deep, dried blood-red. He immediately disliked it, although he had to acknowledge that the view from the upper storey must have been spectacular.

'This house is even more ugly than the photographs,' Misha remarked. 'Why would anyone want to live in a rusty house?'

'Saves on the paint, I guess.' He overshot the house and parked outside a neighbouring Italianate mansion. 'Why do they build these piles, anyway? Totally soulless. They all look like yet another expensive bunker. Built to impress people they don't know or care about,' he commented as he opened the car door.

'Shall I come with you?' she asked.

'Well, you won't learn anything about interview techniques sitting in a car. Of course you're coming with me.'

They left the car and walked back along the road until they reached the Sutcliffe's gate.

'You want to learn how to interview? You just pick a part and play it—or at least, that's what I do,' he said. 'You won't learn it in a textbook. You need to be fluid. You can change your part according to what you encounter.' He rang the buzzer on the gate.

'Who is it?' a female voice demanded.

'I'm Peter Clancy, here to see Mrs Sutcliffe,' he replied. 'I'm an investigative journalist. I was just wondering if you could spare some time to talk with me?'

'I'm Katherine Sutcliffe. Who did you say you were? And what do you want?'

'I'm a journalist. I specialise in investigative pieces. I'm currently doing a piece for a major publication based here and in the UK.'

'I don't know you.'

'I'm happy to wait while you google me. P-E-T-E-R new word C-L-A-N-C-Y. I was hoping you might have a few minutes to speak to me about your husband's accident.'

There was a long pause.

'Doesn't look good,' said Misha. 'I think she's gone.'

'Just wait. She's wondering why an investigative journalist has turned up, out of the blue, to talk to her about her husband. She's thinking that either I'm here to help her find some answers, or I'm here to sully her late husband's reputation. I'm optimistic she'll think it's the former.'

The silence continued.

'I'm not,' Misha replied.

Then the speaker buzzed. Katherine asked, 'Why would someone like you want to interview someone like me?'

'Because I think you have a lot to contribute to a big, investigative piece I'm working on.'

She said nothing for a while. Finally, she said, 'Okay, come in.' The security gate swung open.

Standing just inside the oversized front door, Katherine Sutcliffe looked tired. Peter guessed she was still in her thirties; she retained traces of worn-out beauty, although she had no makeup on. What struck him was that she was still in her pyjamas. Instead of a morning cuppa, she was holding a glass of white wine.

She's a Stepford wife gone to ruin. She's not playing the stoic widow very well.

She was on her way to alcoholic oblivion. 'You're Peter Clancy? You look older than your headshot. Katherine Sutcliffe,' she said taking a mouthful of wine. 'And who's your friend?'

'A colleague, Misha. She's working on the story with me.'

'Well, you'd better come in, I suppose.' She showed them into a room bare of furniture, except for a couch, a marble-topped coffee table, and a single armchair.

Katherine flopped into the armchair. 'I'm decluttering.' She chuckled as she upended her glass and gulped down the contents. 'I don't know how these things work. Do you want something to drink?' she asked.

'No, we're fine,' Peter replied.

'Good. You're pretty famous, you know, Peter Clancy. I checked you out. You have some pretty impressive credentials.' She began to slur by the end, as if the last glass had tipped her past any connection she might have had with sobriety. Abruptly, she swung around and glared at Misha. 'You're staring at me,' she said. 'I don't like it.'

'Yes, you're right, I'm sorry,' Misha responded.

'Well, thank you for being honest, at least. I know you're judging me. You're both judging me: I can feel it. I'm not a bad person. It's just that I can't really be bothered doing anything these days. I can't be bothered dressing. I can't be bothered washing my hair. I can't even be bothered with my kids. They live with my parents now— did you know that?—and I don't give a fuck. You ever been like that, Peter Clancy? Hmm? Too tired to feel anything for anybody, and especially not for yourself?'

'We all have our moments,' he answered. 'But we're here because we're interested in you and your story.'

'My story?' She poured herself another glass. 'Okay, here's my story. You can take it down in that stupid notepad of yours if you want. A lifetime ago, I married a good-looking-but-fuck-dumb real estate agent. He told me we'd be millionaires before we were thirty and I believed him. We spent a shitload on a big, society wedding. We invited everyone—and I mean everyone—that mattered. Then we had two babies. Mummy, Daddy and the two babies all wore the right clothes, and Mummy pushed the babies around in the right pram. We drove around in the right cars, the babies grew bigger and went to the right schools, and we all lived happily ever after in a big mansion on the hill. Except that my fuckwit of a husband died all of a sudden, leaving me sitting on top of a shit pile, without a brass fucking razoo. Not much of a fairy tale ending, huh?' Her voice faded away.

Misha interjected, 'May I please say something important? I don't judge you, I understand you. I lost my family tragically as well. It is impossible to get over, especially when you are left alone and without money, and you have to find a way to live. It makes you do things you never thought you would. I still grieve for my family every day.'

'Yeah, well, that's fine for someone like you, but I wasn't supposed to have this life. Yeah, bad things happen, and people are dying everywhere every day, I get that, but I should have been the rich widow enjoying the rest of my life in my mansion on the hill.' She uttered a squeak. 'The house is mortgaged to the hilt, and I've got nothing left to sell.'

Peter cleared his throat. 'I really wanted to ask you about the death of your husband,' he began.

'Yes, my husband,' she repeated, 'the fuckwit bastard who kept telling me that we were rich, when we really weren't. Just look at me: I've got less money than a crackhead on welfare. How could he not tell me?' She grabbed a tissue and wiped her eyes. 'Everyone thinks that Nick was a good husband and father, but all he wanted was to live an extravagant life. We bought into this perfect fucking nightmare. And now I have to take pills to help with that.' She blew her nose. 'So, do I get paid for this interview?'

'My publication will arrange a payment,' Peter replied. 'How does five hundred dollars sound to you?'

She thought for a while. 'Make it one thousand all up and advance me five hundred dollars now.'

While he was still thinking, Misha dug him in the ribs. He agreed reluctantly, took five hundred dollars out of his wallet, wrote his phone number out on a piece of paper, and passed it and the notes to Katherine.

She continued, 'One of my friends—ex-friends—said I should become an escort. Funny how you find out who your true friends are, when you're down on your luck. The active-wear bitches at school were the worst. Suddenly they didn't know me. All chattering about me behind my back. That's how they get their thrills. They were never truly my friends.' She tucked the money into the pocket of her gown. 'Cheers. Money makes the world go around, doesn't it? These days, I'm barely clinging onto it with my nails, trying not to let it make me dizzy.' She picked up her glass and drained it again.

Peter chuckled. He glanced at Misha, who was staring down at her hands. 'So, Katherine, can you tell me what happened on the night of the accident?' he asked.

She sank back into the armchair and closed her eyes. 'I was at home...' she began.

'Yes, and?'

'I was at home,' she repeated, as the empty glass dropped out of her hand. She opened her eyes for a moment. 'I'm too tired to talk now. Come back later. After lunch.'

'No, let's talk now,' he insisted, but it was no use, she was already asleep. From the almost empty Valium packet on the coffee table to the discarded wine bottles lying in almost every corner, he wasn't optimistic about an imminent awakening. He signalled to Misha that he wanted to leave. 'We'll come back later.'

He pushed in the snib on every lock as they left and covered the sensor on the gate, just in case she woke up, changed her mind, and decided not to let them back in.

'What are you doing, Peter?' asked Misha, incredulously. 'You're leaving the place unlocked? Do you think that's wise?'

'I get the feeling that she's beyond caring. She's in a drink-and-drug stupor and there's nothing to steal in there anyway,' he said to her.

'If you say so.' She shrugged her shoulders.

They drove into the village to look for coffee and something to eat. It seemed as if the entire town had descended on Serenity Bay with the same thought. After passing by the bistro and the bakery, they eventually settled into the last vacant booth of a café overlooking the beach.

'What would you like?' he asked Misha.

She scoured the menu, searching for inspiration. 'Something light,' she replied. 'A salad. That one.' She pointed to the special of the day.

'Right,' he replied. 'I'll order.'

He slid out of the booth and strode up to the counter to order. By the time he returned, Misha was thumbing through the community paper.

'Have you found anything interesting in that rag yet?' he asked.

'Not really. A bit of local gossip. The articles are advertorials, you know, advertising made to read like an editorial. Uniformly uncritical. And self-congratulatory.'

'Well, only the best and brightest live around here.' He smirked. 'There's nothing bad to see here.'

She sighed, folded the paper in half and stowed it on the seat next to her. 'So it appears.'

Just then, a waitress in black shorts and a t-shirt brought them their meals. 'Enjoy!' she announced with a blank expression.

'And you, too,' Peter returned sarcastically. 'So, what do you make of our merry widow, Misha?' he resumed, as he dived into a bowl of fries.

She picked at her fattoush salad, pushing the pita chips to one side of the plate. 'It was hard to make much sense of what she was saying a lot of the time. She seems to be very damaged. And very angry.'

Which tends to happen when you start drinking before breakfast.

'Yes, well, hopefully she'll have slept some of that off by the time we get back. Although, I have to say, judging by the quantity and quality of her favourite beverage and the half-empty pill packet, I think it's highly unlikely that she'll be compos mentis before tomorrow.'

'Hmm. I was thinking that she's like a lot of the people who live on the coast.'

'What? Drunk, vacuous and self-absorbed?'

'Maybe. But I was thinking more along the lines of they come here for the dream, only to discover that it's a nightmare.'

'How do you mean?' he asked, watching two gulls battling over a discarded sandwich outside.

'Haven't you noticed how stressed a lot of the locals seem? I mean, they're living by the sea. It's beautiful and they should be loving their life. You'd expect that every day should seem like a holiday. Instead, they're worried that their children, their cars and their appearance won't measure up to that of their neighbours. They're in debt up to their necks and they don't know what to do about it.'

'And you?'

'Not me. I get to enjoy the best of the coast without any of the pain. Courtesy of Conni and Silvio. And now you.'

'Well, assuming that none of them possesses a Pulitzer or a Walkley, I couldn't care less about what other people have or don't have. And Eddie Arnold aside, I really don't give a fuck about my neighbours. Except when they annoy me.'

She laughed and began to eat.

They returned to the Sutcliffe house just after two. He pressed the buzzer but didn't wait for anyone to answer. They walked through the still-open gate, and straight to the front door. It had remained closed but unsecured during their absence.

He opened it. 'Hello!' he yelled from the threshold. 'It's Peter Clancy again, Mrs Sutcliffe. I'm back. Hello!'

When there was no answer, he stepped inside and pulled Misha along with him.

They went into the front room first, where they had left Katherine Sutcliffe just a couple of hours earlier. She wasn't there. The few bits of furniture in the room were scattered about, and the wine glass was smashed. Someone far bigger and stronger than Katherine had picked up the coffee table and flung it against the wall, with enough force to cleave the marble top into two pieces. A part of it was still wedged in the plasterboard.

'Katherine?' he called out, his head spinning. 'Katherine?' he bellowed again, as Misha suddenly darted out of the room.

'No! Misha!' yelled Peter. 'Someone might still be here! Come back!'

He tracked the sound of her footsteps down the hallway, towards the rear of the house, until he found himself in the kitchen. The door leading out to the garden was wide open.

'Call an ambulance, Peter,' cried Misha, 'quick!'

He found her kneeling behind the island bench, checking Katherine Sutcliffe's carotid pulse with the tips of her fingers. Katherine was spreadeagled on the floor. She was unconscious and bleeding heavily from a gash to her head.

He took his telephone out of his pocket and began to dial. 'Is she…' he began.

'Yes, she's alive,' said Misha, grabbing a tea towel, 'thank god, she's still alive.'

As soon as he had finished talking to the emergency services operator, quietly, and when Misha wasn't looking, he photographed the scene.

Chapter Nineteen

St Kilda 2002
Who's your daddy

'Hello,' said the girl, with a smile. 'Are you here alone? Do you mind if I sit here?'

She would have been pretty, even without the heavy makeup, but what attracted him most was her accent. He replied, 'My mate's gone off for a smoke, so knock yourself out.'

She wiggled herself onto the vacant stool next to the man and turned her body towards him. Her dress was so tight, that part of it stayed in its original position, until she gave it a tug. As he sipped his beer, his eyes followed her every movement, and the impact of her skewed clothing hadn't been lost on him. Once her bra was covered again, she said, 'My name is Lulu.'

The man grinned, and she wished he hadn't. She'd thought that he wasn't all that bad-looking until he'd grinned—neatly dressed, clean, styled hair—but the illusion was shattered the moment he showed his teeth. He replied, 'G'day, Lulu, the name's Andy. Short for Andrew.'

'Pleased to meet you, Andy.'

He put out his hand—beefy with stumpy fingers—and she placed her delicate, manicured hand briefly in his, only to draw it away again swiftly, before he had a chance to grip it. The sensation of her nails on his fleshy palm sent shivers across his body. He licked his lips. She found the gesture repulsive.

There had been a momentarily lull in the music, perfectly timed for them to introduce themselves. Very soon after they did, the driving bass started up again, and any chance of a meaningful conversation was lost in the thumping sound. A few of the patrons moved towards the dancefloor.

Andy looked around. 'Do you wanna dance?'

Lulu smiled again. 'I'd prefer to have a drink first,' she answered, 'if you don't mind.'

He hesitated, watching her for a while, but Lulu didn't reach for the tiny bag that was slung over her shoulder, so he pulled out his wallet. He withdrew a fifty-dollar note from a roll of notes, and then she nodded at the bartender. In a matter of moments, the bartender took the note and brought her a brightly coloured concoction with an umbrella, together with his change.

Andy looked at the money piled on the counter. 'Jezuz!' he exclaimed, counting it.

She shouted at him over the music, 'How much was it? Was it too much? It's Sex on the Beach. I love it: it's my favourite cocktail, but if it's too much, I could pay you for it, Andy.' She turned away and reached for her bag. 'I think I have enough money...'

'Nah,' he said, blushing, 'it's okay.'

They were still sipping their drinks when Andy's friend returned. He seemed younger than Andy, slender, and much better looking. Lulu swapped stools, so that his friend ended up sitting between her and Andy.

'Are you both here alone?' she enquired loudly.

Andy leaned forward. 'You got a friend for my mate Paul here?' he yelled.

'Sure,' she replied, 'We can pair off if you like. I'm here with my friend. I'll go get her and come right back. Don't you go anywhere, okay?'

She found her friend sitting alone at a table on the opposite side of the room.

As they were returning to the bar, Lulu said, 'Just so you know, Andy is yours, Paul is mine, okay?'

'Okay.'

The two men were still sitting in the same spots. 'This is my friend Didi,' she said. 'Didi, this is Andy. Andy, you'll like Didi, she's great.'

Lulu climbed onto the stool next to Paul, and leaned in. As she did that, she touched the tip of his nose with the pad of her index finger. 'Do you have any more of this?' she asked, showing him the white powder.

When he nodded, she said, 'Fantastic.'

He watched her retract her finger and pass it over her gums. He felt the heat of her body close to his, as she baited him with her smile. Her shoulders moved in time with the thudding bass while she sipped her drink and waited for a break in the music. The moment the song ended, she whispered into his ear, 'Sex on blow is fucking unbelievable. So, would you like to party with me all night for five hundred dollars?'

She saw his pupils dilate. He fumbled for his wallet. He was hooked. And then she reeled him in.

Chapter Twenty

Katherine Sutcliffe remembers

The ambulance took Katherine Sutcliffe straight to the Miami Beach Public Hospital, about ten kilometres further down the coast from Serenity Bay.

Miami Beach wasn't anything like the one in America; it was small, and it had two distinct personalities. To the east, its residents were mostly permanent. They either lived in small fibro beach shacks or in tiny 1960s apartment blocks constructed out of yellow bricks and breeze blocks. They were attracted there by cheap rents and the chance to hide away. They gave Miami Beach its unenviable reputation.

To the west and all along the foreshore, it attracted seasonal visitors from Melbourne. They stayed in cheerful holiday homes and campsites, enjoyed by the same family summer after summer, generation after generation. They gave Miami Beach its bohemian, summer holiday vibe.

Peter had never been to Miami Beach before and he left Misha behind on this outing. He didn't know if he'd be able to speak to Katherine Sutcliffe at all, so bringing her along seemed like a waste of time. It was getting late, she had an assignment to do, and he decided that she would be better taking the rest of the day off.

He drove past endless, neat rows of caravans and tents to the right, lit up with lanterns and festoons of fairy lights, like Christmas trees. The only hospital that serviced the area emerged out of the gloom on the left. It looked miniscule and tired, but he'd heard that it was staffed by a team of devoted locals. As a regional hospital, its reputation was second to none. He thought that was both surprising and comforting.

You never know when you might need a good hospital. Especially, after a health scare like mine. Oh god, when did I get to be this old?

He found the second to last vacant spot in the carpark at the front of the hospital, turned into it and pulled up. He looked around; there was no sign of any police. Then he walked briskly to the main entrance and through the automatic doors.

The woman staffing the front desk told him that Katherine Sutcliffe had been admitted to the Sunshine Ward, and that she was occupying bed two in room twelve. And yes, he could visit. Of course, he did have to say that he was her brother, in order to claim that intel.

The door to room twelve was slightly ajar. He poked his head in.

'Katherine?' he said softly when he entered the room.

Katherine Sutcliffe lay in one of the two beds in the room, and the other bed was unoccupied. Her head was bandaged, and she was propped up on pillows. Her eyes were shut, but her hands fiddled, and she didn't seem to be asleep. She turned to look, as soon as she heard her name, and he was shocked by the extent of bruising and swelling on her face.

'Who?' she asked weakly.

'It's Peter Clancy, the journalist,' he added. 'We were talking earlier today. Before all this happened to you.'

'What?'

'At your home, we were in your living room, remember? I came to your home today with my associate, Misha.'

'Oh.' She drew in a breath. 'I was drinking, wasn't I? I don't remember much when I'm drinking.'

'Nobody does if they do it correctly.' He guffawed. 'We spoke about your husband briefly, and then Misha and I went to have lunch, and you were attacked while we were away.'

'The policeman said I was really drunk, and I fell over. He said that I did this to myself.'

Peter sighed. 'Well, that's his theory about what happened. Do you remember anything? Anything at all?'

She looked especially tiny, swaddled up in the hospital linen, and she seemed far more vulnerable than she did before. 'No. Nothing.

I'm so sorry.' She tried to sit up, but the bedding was making it difficult.

'Don't be sorry,' he said. 'You didn't do anything wrong.'

She gave up struggling and lay back for a while. Suddenly she gazed up at him again. 'That's right; I remember,' she said. 'You have a kind face,' she added, smiling weakly, 'and I think that's why I remember you. Your eyes are so blue, and so sad. It's almost like you've been where I've been. We talked, didn't we? You asked me about Nick and then you were gone. I just wish I could remember what happened after you left.' She started to shake her head, but then stopped abruptly. Her eyes narrowed. 'Wait.' She swallowed hard. 'There was a lot of noise. I remember waking up because of all the noise. Someone was in my house. A man.'

He edged forward. 'Was he someone you know? Did you recognise the man?'

'No.'

'Can you describe him?'

'Uh...' She shut her eyes. 'He was old, and he looked a bit like that used piece of wire you try to flatten out again, but you can never get to go straight.'

Interesting description. But he doubted a man like that could have heaved the coffee table. 'Was anyone else there?'

'I don't know. Maybe. I don't remember.'

'Did the man speak to you?'

'I don't remember. I'm sorry.' She looked exhausted. 'Maybe I'll remember more after a sleep. Can you come back tomorrow?'

'Of course, I can come back tomorrow,' he replied as he began to move away.

'Could you do me a favour, Peter?'

He turned and stood by the visitor's chair. 'What would you like me to do?'

'Could you stay here with me until visiting hours are over? I mean, it's scary being alone all the time, you know. If Nick hadn't died...'

'No problem,' he replied. 'I forgot my phone in my car; I'll go get it. Would it be all right with you if I get myself a coffee on the way back? Would you like one too?'

'No, that's fine.'

'I'll be right back, okay?'

He walked out to his car and retrieved his phone from the centre console. He checked it briefly. He'd missed a call from Conni, but she hadn't left a message. He'd get back to her later. He locked his car, and he was on his way back to the hospital entrance when he heard a familiar rumble, thump and scrape. He turned to see Arnold's Audi TT bottoming out on the carpark speed hump.

What the fuck?

Had Arnold had spotted him? Perhaps he had. As Peter watched him, Arnold turned his head away abruptly, as if that would make him invisible. Instead of taking one of the empty spots, he drove through the carpark, while Peter moved to the end of the parking space and stood with his hands on his hips, glaring. It was impossible for Arnold not to know he'd been seen. Since stealth was no longer his advantage and tossing the last remnants of good judgement to the wind, Arnold accelerated hard out of the exit, without giving way to the oncoming traffic.

Peter watched, stunned.

He singlehandedly takes the prize for the stupidest fuck ever to draw breath. Has he never heard of doing something quietly?

He expected to hear a crash, but instead he heard someone toot and Arnold bellowing out abuse. He was so loud that Peter heard every syllable, even above the thundering engine.

Now that is a very interesting development, he thought. Arnold's appearance at the hospital couldn't have been mere coincidence, but what his exact purpose was, Peter could only speculate. By the time he returned to Katherine Sutcliffe's bedside, she was asleep. The nurse in charge had assured him on his way past that Katherine would be safe during the night, and he debated with himself briefly about the wisdom of shaking her awake. In the end, he waited for eight to roll around and then he simply walked away.

She called him the following morning. She sounded tired but lucid. 'I'm still here: they kept me in overnight for observation,' she told him, as if he didn't already know. 'I look awful: my eyes are all bloodshot and swollen; I've had part of my scalp shaved and twenty stitches put in. Lucky for me, the CT scan was clear. The doctor said that the wound was spectacularly bloody, but superficial. Apparently I'll have a couple of black eyes for a while, a bit of concussion, but no lasting damage, thank goodness.'

'That's great,' he replied. 'Is there anything I can do for you, Katherine?'

'Well, yes. They're going to discharge me this morning. Could you bring me a pair of sunglasses, please? I wouldn't want to shock the cabdriver too much.'

He chuckled. 'I believe I can do even better than that.' He agreed to pick her up from the hospital and she agreed to talk to him about her husband.

'I don't know who to trust anymore,' she told him when he arrived.

They stopped briefly to collect Misha along the way, and the rest of the trip passed in silence. The gate was still open when they arrived at the Sutcliffe house, but the front door was locked. The police had arranged for a locksmith to secure the house, and they'd dropped the new key off at the hospital. That was the only indication that anyone had been to the house after Katherine Sutcliffe left with the ambulance. Inside, there was nothing to suggest that the police had collected any evidence, and the bloody mess in the kitchen remained.

Katherine settled herself on her armchair in the lounge room, while Peter took the broken coffee table and the pieces of marble away, and Misha straightened up the rest of the chaos.

'You don't have to do that,' said Katherine.

'I want to. Please let me,' replied Misha. 'Do you think it would be okay if I threw out all of the empty bottles?'

'Absolutely. And would you mind throwing out any full ones, too? I'm sober now, and I'm intending to stay that way.'

'Of course.'

An hour later, the only sign of the fracas that remained was the ugly gash in the plasterboard. Peter took out his notepad and pen and began to write.

'Let's talk,' he said.

Katherine sighed. 'I was at home the night that Nick died,' she began. 'He was working late, as usual. He called me to say he was on his way home, but he never made it. Apparently he missed one of the corners, plunged over the cliff, and crashed onto the rocks below. The cops said it was a dark night, and it was probably just human error. Or he might have fallen asleep. I went to view Nick, but I couldn't even recognise him: he was a mess. His face was battered beyond recognition. It was lucky the car didn't catch fire, they said.'

'And do you agree? Is that what you think happened?' he asked.

'I think he knew every inch of that road. Do you like motor-sports, Peter?'

'Not especially.'

'Well, I do, as it happens. Just the other day, I watched a film about F1 drivers preparing for the Monaco Grand Prix. As well as driving the course, they practise it in their mind, until they know every twist and every turn. They know exactly which line to take and when to accelerate and decelerate, to get their car to the finish line fast and safe. Well, Nick was exactly like that with the esplanade. He'd driven it, run it and cycled it so many times, he could have done it in his sleep. The dark wouldn't have made one bit of difference.'

'So, what do you think really happened?'

'He didn't slide off the road, he was either pushed or scared off it, I'm sure of it. That's it, really.'

'Do you have any proof of what you're saying?'

'Not exactly.'

He put down his pen. 'Not exactly? Here's the thing, Katherine. The way you tell it, all I'm left with is a horrible accident and a near-bankrupt, depressed widow with lots of theories, but nothing to back them up. Not much of a story.'

'You believe I did this to myself, then?' She pointed to the plaster-board first, and then to the bandage on her head.

'Actually,' he replied, 'I don't. I know there's more to this, but I need you to tell me everything, so I can help you. I want to help you, Katherine, honestly, but I won't be able to unless you're totally open with me.'

'And I think you're just scared that you've done your dough, Peter. But, yes, I have more. I think Nick was having a mid-life crisis—no, I know he was having a mid-life crisis. He had changed his view of life. I don't know how or why, but I think that he painted a target on his back, and possibly on mine as well. Of course, my theories about the accident haven't exactly been popular. No one's come near me for ages, except for you, the debt collectors and whoever did this to me.'

'And Nick couldn't have suicided, perhaps?'

'No. When I say he was having a crisis, I mean he was wanting more out of life, not less. The week before it happened, he said that he wanted to spend more time with us. He sounded happy for the first time in ages. He said he was sick of this place. He began to talk about selling our house, taking the money and buying somewhere else. I can't work out how he thought any of it was possible, given how much I now know we owed on it.'

'Maybe, he was trying to tell you that you weren't doing all that well financially. Do you think that maybe he wanted to sell up first, and then let you down slowly?'

'I don't know. I certainly didn't think so at the time.'

'Nick worked for Brian Goldsmith, didn't he? In what capacity was that?'

'Nick was a real estate agent. He didn't want to sell for Mr and Mrs Average anymore; that bored him. He was always chasing the big stuff, and that's how he landed Brian. He sold Brian's developments almost exclusively. Brian was his biggest client by miles, and Nick regarded him as a friend. I'm just not sure that Brian felt the same way.'

'Why do you say that?'

'There's only room for one true love in Brian's life, and that's money. Brian always looks after Brian,' she continued. 'Of course, Nick couldn't see that. We had a lot of arguments over Brian.'

'So what exactly did you see that led you to this conclusion?'

'Well, to be fair, Nick could see that Brian was ruthless in business, but he preferred not to look too hard, because there was a lot of money to be made in real estate development. Of course, you can make even more, if you know the right people and you do deals with them.'

'So, who does Brian know?'

'You can't possibly be that naïve, can you?' She laughed. 'Take a good look around and then ask yourself, who's in bed with who?'

'You mean Rebecca Harrison?'

She snickered. 'I'm just joining the dots. When I first came here, there were lots of farms. There was open space everywhere; that was one of the beauties of the coast. Nowadays, farmers are an endangered species. Their land is suddenly being rezoned as residential, and when they can't afford the increased rates, they're forced to sell up. And, from what I heard, they're being pressured to sell.'

'So, how did all that sit with Nick?' he asked.

'Pretty well at first, I'm ashamed to say. He said it was to be expected: the same thing was happening everywhere. It was just progress. He always had some integrity deep down, I guess, but he was dazzled by the money until just before he died pretty much. Of course, Brian has no morals or integrity. He would sell his grandmother to the highest bidder.'

'Did Nick ever mention any money changing hands? Any deals between him and members of the council?'

'Nick was a ruthless businessman, but he wasn't a dishonest one. If there was any money changing hands, you can bet that one of those hands belonged to Brian. When I think about it, maybe that was what was worrying Nick,' she replied.

'Did he tell you that?'

'No, never outright. A few months before the accident, he became a changed man; he was moody, stressed, pushing me away and drinking a lot. At the time, I thought that maybe he was having an affair.' She paused. 'I confronted him about it. He wasn't having an affair, and he tried to tell me about his concerns, but I don't think I got it.

'All he said was that he'd found some irregularities, and he was going to do something about it, but he didn't say what. He said he wanted out. I told him that I didn't care about the money or the Tyne Coast. I told him that we could start again somewhere else. I just wanted my husband back, and I said that he should do whatever he needed to, to find his bliss. It was after that, that his mood started to improve, and he began to talk about us selling up and getting away. And then...' She stopped and wiped her nose. 'Well, you know what happened.'

'Did he ever tell you what the irregularities were?'

She shook her head.

He tapped his notebook with his pen. 'Are you part of the business? Do you have access to his computer?'

'I was on the payroll. Plus, I'm a director of the company, and so is Brian. And so is his wife.'

'Meaning you and Nick had shares in the company. Who did Nick leave his shares to?'

'All four of us had the same number of shares, except Nick, who had an extra one. But here's the thing: I'm Nick's beneficiary for everything except the business. He left that to Brian. Not that any of it matters. I thought about contesting the will, but when my lawyer started to look into it, she discovered that there were huge loans owed to Brian's wife anyway. The money—if there ever was any—is all tied up. With more debts than assets, the company's borderline trading while insolvent. She told me to get out before the Securities Commission catches up with us and puts us all in jail.'

'And do you believe her?'

'Well, she's meant to be working for me, so, yes, I have no reason not to.'

Peter scratched his head. 'Did Nick have a computer here, at home?'

Katherine froze, and the blood drained from her face. 'Oh my god! There were two men here the other day, not just one. I remember now; the old man kept yelling at me to give him the fucking computer. When I said I didn't know what he was talking about, the other man lost it, and began throwing the furniture around.' Her eyes shifted about wildly. 'Do you think I should tell the police?'

'Do you think they'll do anything if you do?'

She sat back glumly. 'I don't get it. First the police tell me Nick's death was definitely an accident, and beyond that, there's nothing for them to investigate. Then they label me a crazy drunk, and beyond that, there's nothing for them to investigate. I really don't get it.'

'So, maybe I can help you find some answers. Does the name Eddie Arnold mean anything to you?'

'I don't think so.'

'Well, this other man, the one throwing the furniture, do you remember what he looked like? Can you describe him?'

'Not really. All I remember is he smelled bad, like rotting garbage.'

'Right,' he said, exchanging looks with Misha. 'And did you ever locate Nick's computer?'

Katherine hesitated. She eyed him suspiciously. 'Why do you ask?'

'I'm thinking that the answers we're both looking for might just be on it,' he returned.

'No, no I didn't,' she replied flippantly, and he knew it was a lie.

He really couldn't blame her for being wary, even if he perceived it as an insult to his integrity at first. As he stood up to leave, he reminded himself that she really didn't know anything about him. For all she knew, he could have been just another shyster in a long line of shysters ready to swindle her out of her sole remaining legacy—her story and the truth about her husband's death.

Trust was a gift that always had to be earned.

CHAPTER TWENTY-ONE

Another meet and greet

Armed with the few nuggets of information that Katherine was able to supply, Peter spent the next day driving around the hinterland. He was looking for any new subdivisions, while Misha stayed in the office, scouring the internet for the same. If Goldsmith and Harrison were indeed forcing farmers off the land by means of their dirty tactics, he was determined to expose them.

He turned off the highway and drove down every secondary road he could see, winding his way along the coast slowly. He was looking for any road that was surrounded by pasture. Beyond that, he didn't know what he was looking for, but he knew he'd recognise it once he saw it.

He'd driven over fifty kilometres down the highway like this, turning left and right, headed on roads to nowhere. His head aching, he returned home late that afternoon, empty handed and a little dejected, and Misha's searches hadn't given up much more than they already knew.

'You are on the right track, Peter,' she said, 'I can feel it. I believe there is a lot more to all of this than you think.'

He looked at Misha and frowned. 'I don't know anymore. I'm starting to think that I'm out of sync with everyone else; fairness, truth, and justice are outdated concepts. Give up on your dream, Misha, before it becomes your obsession and destroys you. Just stick with puppies and kittens and big-arsed celebrities. I'm starting to think that there's no room for investigative journalism anymore. Maybe I see conspiracies where there are none.'

'No, don't say that. Don't you dare say that! Remember New Mexico? The Flamekeeper? You never once thought of giving up, even when that cult leader was out to kill you, did you? You, Peter Clancy, are my inspiration.'

In that moment, she was beautiful and passionate and sweet, and if he'd been twenty years younger, he probably would have taken full advantage of the situation. Nowadays, it was enough for him to finally have someone with whom he could share the load. If she wasn't the least perturbed by their lack of progress, then he had no reason to abandon all hope. She reminded him that he needed to see the world through fresh eyes.

Misha had none of his old friend Stella Reimers's vast journalistic experience, yet she was blessed with all of her chutzpah. He had a feeling that mentoring her was going to be mutually beneficial. Before she left to go home, they agreed that she was going to follow up with Katherine Sutcliffe in the morning, while he hit the road again.

The following day, Peter was twenty minutes into his search when he finally spotted Moores Lane and turned down it. It had caught his eye: pasture on both sides, elevated but not too steep, with the potential to have exceptional views to the sea. On the frontage to the highway, just outside the post and wire fence, a huge advertising hoarding told him that Goldsmith Developments were caring for the community.

Perfect.

He crawled along Moores Lane, studying the land on either side carefully, braking every so often to take a closer look. A hundred or so metres down the road, hidden from the highway by a windbreak of poplars, was a mound of garbage. The rubbish was heaped high in the middle of an otherwise pristine paddock. Whoever had dumped it there had gouged out muddy paths across the land and was lucky not to have been bogged. *Very lucky.*

He stopped the car and took out his camera. The perimeter fence had been cut and hastily mended. The wind had caught bits of plasterboard and God-knows-what and strewn them about. Having once been graziers, his family's close relationship to the land had taught him that no farmer would ever do that to their own paddock. He snapped the lot before driving on.

Just before Moores Lane disappeared into bushland, he noticed a driveway leading to a farmhouse. He saw the *Keep Out!* sign and argued with himself about going in. He hadn't ghost-written a Pulitzer Prize winning series by being coy; if bullets couldn't stop him in the past, a mere sign had absolutely no chance. He had barely placed his hand on the chain that kept the driveway gate closed when he heard a shout.

'Oi!' The voice belonged to a wiry man, and Peter's thoughts rushed back to Katherine's description of her attacker. The man's face was shaded by a hat, and it was impossible to gauge his age, but the man's gait suggested he was waging a losing battle with arthritis.

'Hello!' he called back, lifting his hand as a greeting.

'Stop right there, or I'll set the dog onto you!'

Peter stopped dead. 'The name's Peter Clancy. And you are?'

'Never you mind who I am. You can turn yourself around right now, Peter Clancy, and bugger off.'

Peter drew breath, looked around and placed his hands on his hips. 'Yep, and I'd be mad too, if someone had done this to my land.'

The man pushed back his hat. His eyes narrowed. 'Are you a farmer, then?'

'Fourth generation born and bred on a cattle station: "Cornish Downs". My family were North Queensland graziers. Cattle are in my blood. It's a little-known fact that my uncle and his business partner were the first people to bring Charolais to Australia.'

Something he said perked the man up, so he continued, 'I didn't mean to disturb you, sir, but I saw all the rubbish and I was appalled. I just had to take a closer look. I work as a journalist these days, you see, and I'm writing a story on the plight of farmers being pressured to sell up to developers.'

'So, you're not a real estate agent, eh? Not a town planner or surveyor?'

'I bloody well hope not! I'm a freelance reporter these days, and I'd love to talk to you about all the shit you and the other farmers have been going through, just trying to keep going. If you have the time…'

The man grunted, lifted his hat and scratched his head. 'So, your uncle was responsible for introducing Charolais, eh? Just so happens that I ran Charolais, myself, until...' His voice faded away. He scrutinised Peter's face for a while. 'Now, you better not be playing with me, son, because if I find out that you are, you'll soon come to regret it. And it won't just be the dog tearing holes in your nice new clothes that you'll have to be worried about.'

Peter held out his press card. 'Google everything I've said. If I've lied even once, I'll be happy to tear myself a new one, without any help from you or your dog.'

The man sucked his teeth, deep in thought. After an age, he said, 'Jack Cunningham's the name. In that case, I suppose you'd better come inside and meet the missus, Peter.'

Peter spent the next few hours with Jack Cunningham and his wife, Beth.

His notepad wasn't the only thing filling up, as morning tea turned into lunch.

Country people always were the most hospitable people I ever met. These scones with cream and jam are bloody magnificent!

He finally left the Cunninghams' after three, nostalgic for the sounds and smell of the cattle yards after the muster. To a city-dweller's nose, it probably reeked. To Peter, it was the scent of his childhood.

The day eventually turned into a still, balmy evening. The cicadas chirped from every tree deafeningly and persistently, interrupted by an occasional bird call. Peter sat on his deck as the light faded, trying to listen to music. Once the mosquitoes arrived, he felt as if he was at war with nature, and nature was winning. He soon gave up trying and went inside.

Conni called him later that night. She said she was calling to ask his opinion of the Glamour Girls, and whether his garden needed a follow-up. She was scheduling visits for the next month and didn't want him to miss out.

'What's this all about, Conni? Give me the truth please. You're not usually the coy kind; you didn't really call me to discuss your girls or my garden, did you?'

'Well,' she replied, 'possibly not. Okay, you're right, I didn't.' She sighed. 'We've been friends a very long time, Peter, so I won't bullshit you. Misha told me that you're having a rough time at the moment. She was worried about you, and I thought a welfare check was in order.'

'Really? That's very sweet of her, but I'm fine. Yes, I got a bit down this morning, but I've bounced back since.'

'Misha is very insightful. I'll tell you everything about her one day. She's not nearly as young as her age or her looks, and she reads people. She's read you pretty well. I take her opinions very seriously, so when she said she thought you were socially isolated and majorly depressed about the future of journalism, I knew an intervention was called for.'

He snorted. 'Well, everyone knows that journalism's all but fucked, and if I am socially isolated, it's only because life has turned me from a playboy bachelor into a bitter, self-absorbed misanthropist of the worst kind. Other than that, honestly, I'm right as rain.'

'Well, I genuinely hope so. But I've also called you with an invitation. You see, Silvio and I are having another one of our soirees and we wanted you there for comic relief but, after speaking with Misha, I am beginning to have some doubts. Do you think you could put all of that doom and gloom aside, and just enjoy yourself for once? I hate to say it, but celibacy and sobriety really don't suit you.'

'You're probably right, Conni, maybe I have been taking life a bit too seriously. The whole heart attack episode shook me to my core.'

'Right. And now it's behind you. The time for introspection and circumspection has officially ended. I demand the old—no, I demand a new, improved Peter. Do me a favour—drink a little: apparently in moderation it's good for your heart health. And could you please embrace your inner Wham! again, and choose life?'

'I was waiting for it: medical advice and George Michael in the same breath. Stop fussing, Conni, okay? You've worn me down. Just send me the details and I'll be there. You don't need to worry about me.'

'Are you sure? You see, I don't want my baby girl turning up for work at yours, only to discover you hanging in the shed.'

He laughed. 'I've always imagined myself going out on a magnificent high, but nothing like that. The world's longest bender, perhaps...'

'I have one final piece of advice—and this positively cannot include Misha in any way, shape or form—you need to get laid, Peter, and soon.'

'I'm hanging up now.'

He had barely put down his phone when it rang again. 'What is it now, Conni?'

There was a long silence at the other end. He was about to hang up when he heard, 'It's Mimi, actually.'

'Oh, Mimi,' he said. 'I didn't check who was calling before I answered... I was just on the phone to a nosy friend.'

'Oh. Did I call at a bad time?'

'No, no, of course not. Is everything all right? Your dad?'

'No, everything's the same as always. I need to speak to you. Would it be okay if I came over for a few minutes?'

He felt exhausted at the mere thought of Mimi. She was far too intense for an evening visit and yet, in spite of himself, he replied, 'Yes, of course.'

'Thank you,' she responded. 'I'll be over in a minute or two. Don't put on any outside lights.'

She was as good as her word. He opened the door even before she had time to knock twice, and Mimi hurried into the lounge room. She was dressed in her usual pair of pink cropped pants and an oversized floral t-shirt. Her hands were trembling.

'I must tell you something urgently,' she said. 'I hope I'm not disturbing you.'

'Mimi, you're not disturbing me. I'm just sitting here wallowing in my misery,' he replied. 'If it's so important that you couldn't afford to be seen here, you'd better just tell me.'

She cleared her throat. 'First of all I need to tell you that I checked you out. What you do, what you've done; you're all over the internet.'

'Right.'

She eyed him carefully. 'You're okay, aren't you, Peter?' she asked as she sat on the couch.

'I was about to ask you the same question. You look like you've had the fright of your life. Do you want a glass of something to steady your nerves?' he asked.

'No thanks. I gave it up many years ago.'

'Okay.' He sat down and settled back into his chair. 'Give it your best shot.'

'I overheard Arnold, his father-in-law and several men talking just now,' she said. 'The men rode in on motorbikes. Everyone must have heard them. They were pretty loud.'

'Strange that I didn't hear them,' he replied. 'Go on.'

'Well, I don't know exactly what they were doing, but it had something to do with the shipping container in Arnold's yard. They were going in and out and it was quiet for a while. Then I heard Arnold lock up the container and it sounded like he and a couple of the men were arguing, so I opened up my back door and I listened in. One of the men was pretty angry, and he kept saying something about Arnold leaving too many loose ends. He told him he needed to wrap things up and quick. He started asking Arnold what he was going to do about the "crazy bitch", and I thought he was talking about me, of course. That was until Arnold's father-in-law dropped a name.'

'But not yours, then?'

She shook her head. 'He told the others that there was nothing to worry about, he was dealing with that Sutcliffe bitch, and she'd get what she was owed. I think he was talking about that estate agent's widow—you know, the one whose husband drove over the cliff—and I think she may be in big trouble. And I have a really bad feeling he wasn't talking about making arrangements with her to pay back a loan.'

'So, this father-in-law of Arnold, does he have a name?'

'Well, we've never been introduced, but Arnold's wife calls him "Dad", obviously, and from what I've heard Arnold call him, I think his name is Ronny or Ronald.'

'Surname?'

She shook her head. 'I'm not sure. Sometimes I get their mail by mistake. I've seen letters addressed to an R Cooper, but I'd just be guessing.'

'Can you describe him?'

'He's thin, in his seventies, and he always looks like he's just about to disappear down a drainpipe. He never stands square-on, and he never stands up straight.'

'Hmm. And did you hear them say anything else?'

'They were arguing about something that happened at a farm, as well,' she added. 'I heard him complain that a farmer was being a pain in the arse. The men told Arnold and his father-in-law that they had to deal with the farmer, too.'

'Did they mention any names?'

'No, no, they didn't. Arnold has really ramped up his operation lately. You've been out a fair bit, so I don't know if you've noticed. He's started advertising his rubbish removal services on the internet, even though he's really got nowhere to put it, except the creek and his own backyard. Look, I know he's been dumping rubbish on farms at night. A few of them do it. There's a lot of money to be made getting rid of other people's rubbish, especially when you're not paying exorbitant tip fees to do it legally. So, he dumps it wherever he can, whenever he can't dump it here. He hasn't got a licence to do it, even though he's been doing it for a while now. I've tried telling the authorities about it.'

'And nothing happens?'

'Nothing.'

'So are you going to tell the police about what you heard?' he asked.

'I think I'll have to. I don't think I'll have a choice.' She exhaled loudly. 'Look, I wasn't going to say anything, but I've arranged to meet one of the councillors who's been opposing a lot of the development proposals. I don't know much about her, except that she's a greenie by all accounts. I'm seeing her on Friday, the week after next. I have to say that I've lost faith in the system, and I don't know if she'll help.'

'Well, that sounds promising, I guess. Whatever you decide to do, just be careful.' He stood up and poured himself a small whisky. 'Are you sure you won't join me?' he asked her, jiggling the bottle.

She shook her head.

'Okay.' He took a long drink. 'What you've told me tonight is very important, Mimi. No matter what happens at the meeting, please believe me, I'm not going to let this thing lie. It's a scandal just waiting to be uncovered. The reason I've been out a lot lately is that I've been doing my own research. There's a great deal we don't know yet. We already know you're getting no traction from those who should care about this, and I'm out to uncover why that is. When the time is right, I'll strike, but I'll need to scoop everyone else for maximum impact. So it's important that we keep what we do know quiet. Talk to the councillor of course, but do not, whatever you do, do not talk to any other reporters.' He took a sip and for the first time in ages, he felt good in his own skin. 'Please don't mistake this for false vanity, but I happen to be very, very good at what I do. Once I have all the answers, you can be certain that I'll be going for the jugular.' He put down his glass. 'When all hope is lost, the only person you can rely on to expose the truth is an investigative journalist.'

Mimi wiped her eyes and stood up. She said, 'Thank you, Peter. I won't say a word to anyone,' and kissed him on the cheek.

Peter churned the conversation over in his mind. What she had told him only served to reinforce his own observations. Apart from giving a probable name to a villain, none of it was particularly surprising, but even that was help enough.

After Mimi left, he went into his office and wrote *Ronny Cooper* and *bikies* on his whiteboard. He drew lines connecting them to Katherine Sutcliffe and Jack Cunningham, and all of them back to Arnold. Then he stood back and looked at the fast-spreading web.

His deadline was all but shot to pieces. He had a feeling that he would have added many more names and lines to those already on his whiteboard by the time he'd figured it all out.

CHAPTER TWENTY-TWO

Neighbours with benefits

By about eleven, Peter had fallen into a fitful sleep. It was a humid night, too still to blow away the bugs that passed invisibly between the gaps in the flywire on his open windows and tormented him. Between waking and dreaming, he had a sense of being watched, but exhaustion kept him far away from total consciousness. He was simply beyond caring, and it wasn't until he heard a strange noise emanating from the pile of spare pillows that he had pushed to the other side of his bed, that he realised he wasn't alone.

He listened for a while, as he drifted in and out of dreams that made no sense. The noise continued. It wasn't altogether a snore, and it didn't sound altogether human. It was somewhere between a whistle and a wail. He blinked himself fully awake. It was breaking dawn, but not yet six. He removed the uppermost pillows from the pile. Behind them was a head covered by a mass of tangled hair, resting on the crook of a bare, skinny arm. The noise he had been hearing was connected to every exhale from the pinched, designer nostrils belonging to the creature that was sharing his bed.

'Rhiannon?' he said. 'Is that you?'

He heard a brief grunt just before the wailing whistler resumed. He smoothed back the hair to check, and then he shook the skinny arm.

'Rhiannon! What the hell?'

He couldn't tell if her eyelash extensions had simply fused together, but she seemed to be having a very hard time opening her eyes. Eventually she muttered, 'Please let me sleep. Not now, Andre, I'm really, really tired.'

'Rhiannon, it's not Andre, it's Peter. Remember? Your neighbour, Peter.' He snapped on the bedside lamp.

At last, something clicked. She lifted her head and pouted. She peered at him, rubbed the corner of her eyes and focused.

'What are you doing here, in...' she began. She looked around, first at the unfamiliar room and then down at her utterly naked body. 'Oh, my god! I must have been more pissed than I thought.'

He thought she was about to scream. *No, Your Honour, I didn't lure her here...* He was scrambling for a denial that might actually stand up in court. And then she smiled. She reached for the sheet, but she didn't cover herself. He tried not to look, but his eyes travelled from her breasts to the spot where her thighs united, and back again.

'How... What...' he stuttered.

'I was lonely,' she said. 'Andre's taken the kids camping and I was all alone last night, so I thought I'd pop in and see what you were doing, and if you wanted company. I thought you might want to come for a swim at my place. Or we could share a bottle of Veuve. But then I noticed that your door was unlocked, so I walked in.'

'Without any clothes on?'

'Well, I didn't exactly start out that way. You were asleep, and it was so peaceful, and I always sleep in the nude anyway.' She was fully awake now. She leaned across and kissed him on the lips. 'I guess I just forgot myself.'

He pulled back.

'You don't find me attractive,' she said. 'I get it. It's been such a long time since Andre and I fucked, I was thinking... But if you don't like what you see.' She stretched herself out.

'I do but...'

'There's someone else?'

'It's not any of that.' He sighed. 'You're married! And my neighbour! It doesn't sit right with me that I go to bed with you, even if your husband is a certified bastard.'

He thought of some of the married women he had slept with over the years. He had always rationalised that if a married woman wanted an affair, then she wasn't into her husband, and he probably deserved it. If her hubby was having an affair himself or if he was being a plain arsehole, then he definitely deserved it. As long as Peter didn't get caught. And he had been caught on the odd occasion.

'So what that I'm married? You don't exactly seem like the ten commandments type. Look,' she said, 'Andre's mantra has always been a fuck is just a fuck. We've tried monogamy, but I guess he isn't into it. He doesn't give a shit. I'm up for it. So, the real question is, are you?'

He took another long look at her. Laid out over half of his bed like a Swedish smorgasbord, he had to admit, she was in pretty good shape. *Fake tits, lips and bits aside, she's really not all that bad.* Besides, at a few minutes before dawn, her logic seemed impeccable. *She's married, so what?* He was going to be the beneficiary of some tawdry revenge sex, and nobody was about to be hurt by it. *Why the hell not?*

This time, it was Peter who leaned in for a kiss. She laughed and pulled off his boxers.

A second later, her hungry lips were devouring his. His long abstinence ended before the sun peered over the horizon and before Arnold had the opportunity to fire up his excavator.

CHAPTER TWENTY-THREE

Misha meets Moylan

'You look different, somehow,' Misha remarked, as she walked into the office. She placed her hands on her hips and studied Peter's face. 'I know what it is,' she said. 'You're smiling.'

'Am I?' He chuckled.

'Yes, and you look genuinely happy for a change. Whatever the reason for it, it suits you. You should do it more often.' She sat down at her desk and pulled out her laptop.

He cleared his throat. He was glad that they sat back-to-back, in case she spotted his embarrassment. He stood up without saying anything more, went to the kitchen, and brought back two cups of coffee. He put one on her desk and sat down again.

'I had no luck getting through to Katherine Sutcliffe, by the way,' she remarked.

'Never mind.' He took a sip. 'We have a couple of new leads to follow up today,' he said. 'And I'm going to visit Jack Cunningham once again. So, you can either stay here and do more research, or you can come with me.'

'I'd like to come with you,' she replied. 'I can catch up on the research later.'

'Fine.'

He checked his emails while he drank. There was one from Mimi, forwarding details of her upcoming meeting with Councillor Taylor, and inviting him to tag along. He examined his planner for the following week, even though he knew there was nothing in it, and then he declined the invitation. After that, he rinsed out the coffee cups and prepared himself for the day.

He and Misha were at the bottom of the steps, heading for his car, when the Audi TT roared past and disappeared in a cloud of dust.

'So, that's the infamous Titty Man,' she said, her head swivelling.

'That's him, man boobs and all.'

'I can understand why you hate him so much.'

'And you don't even know the half of it.'

Peter turned out of the driveway and headed towards the highway. He was in a good mood. He didn't care about Arnold at that moment. He didn't even care that it was a miserable bastard of a day. He glanced at Misha, messaging furiously on her phone, and he smiled. What would have taken him ten minutes to express, she broadcast to the world in a few seconds. He glanced at her again. She embodied journalism's future.

The future of news reporting is instantaneous. It requires very few details, a restricted vocabulary, and a heap of emojis.

:(*Sad Face.*

And then it began to rain.

The rain dribbled down the windscreen before the wipers could sweep it away. For Peter, there were two immediate benefits to the rain: it settled the dust on the dirt roads, and it kept away the tourists. No tourists meant that he didn't have to play leapfrog with the sun-worshippers meandering along the narrow, winding road towards the beach, or the cyclists wobbling and weaving down those same roads, and often at the same time.

The traffic was light, and he arrived at Moores Lane in under half an hour, just as the rain was clearing. He hadn't travelled very far when he was pulled up by a police cordon.

'You'll have to turn around and go back, sir,' said the constable.

'Why?' he asked, slipping the car out of gear, and letting the engine idle.

'There's been an incident. Please turn your car around.'

'I'm press. I also happen to be a close friend of Mr and Mrs Cunningham.'

The constable rocked on his heels. 'I don't care who you are, I'm telling you to leave.' He lifted his arm and pointed back down Moores Lane. 'Now!'

Peter shook his head. 'I have a duty to report the news, Constable, and that's exactly what I intend to do.'

The constable didn't reply. He turned and signalled to the sergeant further up the lane.

Peter spun the car around and pulled over. 'Stay here!' he said to Misha, as he switched off the ignition, took his camera and climbed out. He walked back a few paces, to where he had been stopped.

The sergeant glimpsed Peter. He came over and snarled, 'You again? You're getting to be a right pain, aren't you? Didn't you hear the constable? Get in your car and drive away!'

'I'm on a public road. I'm the right side of your cordon. I'm a journalist and I'm here to report on a matter of public importance. So, no, I'm going nowhere. I'm staying put.'

'Move, before I take you in.'

'For what? If you're going to threaten me, Sergeant, you'll need to do better than that. I've had the camera running all the while. I'm recording to an external source, so you better mind your language.'

He scowled. 'You with her?' he asked, looking over at Misha.

'None of your business,' Peter replied, standing toe-to-toe with him. 'We never really met the last time, did we? As I recall it, I introduced myself, but you had your head so far up Eddie Arnold for some unknown reason, that you forgot to do the same. So I'll need you to give me your name, for the article I'm writing, as well as for the complaint I'll be making.'

'You cocky bastard!' His face pulsed with rage, but Peter returned his glare and didn't flinch. *I've hit a raw nerve, haven't I, Sergeant?*

After a while, the sergeant broke off staring, looked over at the car and chortled. 'Why am I not surprised at the company you keep?' He sidled over to Misha and tapped on the window, but she turned her head and looked away. Unperturbed, he yelled through the glass at her, 'Long time no see, Lulu. You still on the game?' He spied the momentary shock on Peter's face. 'What? Don't tell me you didn't know? So why don't you go home like I told you to, and on the way, you can ask your girlfriend how she pays her rent.'

Peter settled himself down. He thrust his hand in his pocket and chuckled. Shaking his head, he returned, 'Like all good journos, I know a thing or two about the law of defamation, and if I were you, I'd be keeping an eye out for a summons.' He walked to the driver's side of the car and opened the door. 'So, you reckon you know her, do you? Well, if that's true, then I bet she knows a thing or ten about you. No prizes for guessing which one'll make better reading. The only question I'll be asking her is why you're so eager to get me out of here, Sergeant.'

He placed his camera on the back seat, shook his head and laughed again. He lowered himself into the seat, turned over the engine, opened his window and continued, 'Once again, you've read me totally wrong, Sergeant. You see, she's not my girlfriend, you prat, she's my source.'

Without another glance, he drove beyond view. He turned off onto a narrow track and pulled up behind a thicket. He couldn't tell if Misha was crying.

He asked, 'Are you okay?'

'Uh, of course,' she replied. Her face was still turned away and she made no effort to look at him.

'Look, that man is an arsehole. I have no idea why he picked on you.' He huffed. 'The only thing I'm sorry about is having thrown you to the wolves when I called you my source. If he's as rotten as I think he is, I may have just painted a target on your back.'

'No, please don't worry about that. That's okay.' She took out a tissue and blew her nose.

'I'll take you straight home if you like. We can forget about today.'

She turned to face Peter. If she had been crying, there was no sign of it. 'No, please don't. Can't we go back? Maybe after they leave?'

'There's another way to the Cunninghams, via a bush track. But only if you're sure you're okay.'

'I'm okay, honestly I am.'

'Great. Once we get back to the office, if you wouldn't mind doing some checks, and finding out that bastard's name for me, that would be great.'

She looked down. A frown swept across her face. 'And I would be very happy to do that for you, really I would...' She wrung her hands and sighed. 'Except that I already know his name, Peter. It's Sergeant Michael Moylan.'

CHAPTER TWENTY-FOUR

The Cunninghams revisited

Misha followed Peter silently along the overgrown bush track until they reached a paddock. It was ragged with karamu, and the fence had been cut in several places. Two of the far posts had either fallen or been pushed over, and the wire hung limp over its entire length. He pulled it down with his foot, so that she could step over it easily.

The paddock rose gradually underfoot and then it fell away sharply. The farmhouse revealed itself at its highest point, looking shabbier than it had before under the heavy cloud cover. There were two cars parked in front of it and people in the yard. Peter recognised the older woman as Beth Cunningham. A younger woman held onto her. From afar, he judged the younger woman as Mrs Cunningham's human prop rather than her comfort: the woman seemed to be there for the sole purpose of preventing her collapse. Standing next to the pair was a man in his forties. Peter and Misha were only metres away from them when the trio noticed their approach.

The man confronted Peter at the yard gate. 'If you're not from the police, mate, you can piss off. We don't want any media or them bloody real estate bastards coming anywhere near us.'

Mrs Cunningham raised her eyes. 'Oh, Peter!' she cried. 'It's all right, Graham, Peter's a friend of Dad's.'

Peter said, 'I came over to see Jack, but the police have cordoned off the farm. What on earth is going on?'

Graham replied, 'Dad's got himself in trouble. Big trouble. The mongrels cut the gate as usual, drove in and were dumping the rubbish. My father confronted them this time. He used to ring the police every other time, but they never came. He even got a security camera set up, but when he asked them to look at it, they weren't interested.' He fidgeted with his hands incessantly. Peter found it irritating.

'This morning,' he continued, 'Dad warned them off, and then he fired some shots. His gun wasn't registered because they'd taken all the legit ones off him. He didn't hit no one or nothing, but the cops must have been close by, and they arrived a few minutes later. They've taken him in. They reckon they're charging him with a heap of firearm offences...'

'Sergeant Moylan?'

Mrs Cunningham nodded. 'But that's not the worst of it,' she sobbed. 'He's been charged with attempted murder.' Her knees buckled under the weight of the words she'd just spoken. 'Attempted murder! I just don't know what to do!'

Peter bit his lip. 'Let's not jump to any conclusions: I doubt he's been charged with anything yet, and attempted murder is way above Sergeant Moylan's pay grade. First of all, Jack needs a lawyer.'

'We don't have the money for lawyers and such. And I know we won't get legal aid, because we own the bloody farm.' She sat on her front step as it started to drizzle again, and she began to sob.

'Please don't worry, Mrs Cunningham, I'll make some calls. I'm going to get to the bottom of this. I'll push some parliamentary buttons if I have to.'

Graham thought for a moment. 'Dad's never done nothing wrong before and it's not his fault that it came to a head today. Look, he wasn't out to shoot anybody: he just wanted to scare them away. They've been harassing him for ages.'

'I believe you. I've been working on a major story with your dad. It was going to be about dumping and toxic waste, but I think there's a lot more going on here.'

Mrs Cunningham wiped her eyes. 'That's what Jack said, too. Can you help him? Please, Peter?' she asked.

'I'll do my best,' he returned.

He stepped aside for a minute. For most of his life he'd tried to avoid knowing too many lawyers: in his world, they were generally bad news. Poppy Reynolds had been the only criminal lawyer he'd ever truly known—*although unfortunately for me, I didn't restrict myself to only knowing her in a professional sense.* She'd had an insatiable appetite for crime (alongside a good many other things) but, after she was released from jail a few years ago, she was forbidden from practising law again. So, he called the only other lawyer he knew in Melbourne.

'I'd love to help your friend out, mate,' Shaun Hanrahan replied to his enquiry, 'really, I would, but my practice is strictly limited to wills and conveyancing. I'm afraid I don't do crime, although I do know someone who does—pro bono occasionally, if it's in a really good cause. I'll send you her details.'

'Thank you,' said Peter.

Ten minutes later, Suzanne Spellman returned his call. She told him that she was involved in a contest in the Magistrates Court on the other side of Melbourne, but she promised to go down to the Tyne Police Station and see Jack Cunningham as soon as she was back on the coast.

'I'll pick up the tab for Jack,' he told her. 'Don't bill Mrs Cunning-ham.'

'No problem. Although, I've had so many dealings with the Tyne Council, I'll be happy to call this one as my gift to the good folk of the coast.'

'Thank you,' he replied and hung up.

The weather was setting in. He dashed across the yard and up the verandah steps, where Graham and Misha were sheltering from the downpour.

'Brian Goldsmith,' Graham confided while Peter shook off the rain, 'has been buying up all of the farms here to turn into ugly housing estates. You have heard of Brian Goldsmith, haven't you?'

'I have.' He nodded.

'Goldsmith offered big money, but Dad didn't want to sell. The more he and Mum refused, the more aggressive Goldsmith got. He kept telling my parents the bank was going to sell them up, because their rates and land taxes would go so high, they wouldn't be able to afford to pay them. Then there was that real estate agent… He was here every week. Plus phone calls and emails. Letters, too. He constantly harassed my parents.'

'Do you know his name?' Peter asked.

'Hold on.' Graham fished inside his shirt pocket. 'I have his business card here. Found it stuck to the fridge.' He handed the business card to Peter.

'Nick Sutcliffe, the bloke who died in the car crash.'

'That's him. He got what he deserved, I reckon.'

'Swap,' said Peter, pulling one of his own cards out of his wallet and handing it to him. 'Would you mind if I kept this?'

'I suppose it's okay. As long as Mum doesn't want it.'

Peter tapped his forehead with the corner of the card. 'You mentioned a security camera,' he said. 'You don't happen to have the footage?'

'You're about thirty minutes too late. The cops took it,' Graham replied. 'This time it seems that they actually wanted to look at it.'

'Hmm. Got a backup?'

'Maybe. I don't know. If there's one, I'll bring it over.'

Peter motioned to Misha that they were done. They ran back to the car, dodging the droplets as they fell, and jumping over the puddles. It felt good to breathe. He wasn't recovering from a heart attack anymore. He was done reflecting on his life and all that bullshit. He was back on the hunt. He was going to bring down everyone who had inflicted misery on Jack and Beth Cunningham, one arsehole at a time.

The pity party was over.

Chapter Twenty-Five

Conni's fairy tale

'It's storytime now, Peter,' announced Conni, 'and I want you to get comfortable while I tell you the ultimate tale this idiot's ever told anyone.' She refilled and drained her champagne glass in a single gulp. Then she wiped the corners of her mouth with the edges of her manicured nails and adjusted the diamond rings adorning every finger.

Up until that moment, he had been enjoying yet another soiree at the mansion. Silvio's fritto misto had gone down a treat, washed down with huge amounts of Birra Moretti—the favoured beer of Italian workmen—which was permitted now that Peter had stopped wearing his hypochondria on his sleeve. He was tired from the day's events and feeling too mellow to listen to her and not fall asleep.

'Wake up! I want you to get yourself ready for some sound and fury,' she said.

Peter nodded, his vision blurring. 'I know, it's William Shakespeare, *Macbeth*. You're going to recite the entire play from the witches' perspective,' he quipped. He settled into the feather cushions, although he was struggling to keep his eyes open.

'Absolutely not.' She smacked him on the back of the hand and began, 'Once upon a time, in a land of ice and snow far, far away, a poor but beautiful young girl got herself knocked up.'

'In the old-fashioned way?'

'Shut up and listen, will you?' She scowled. 'The boy was young as well and, boys being boys, he didn't stand by her. The girl couldn't tell her parents of her condition, for the shame it would bring the family. So she went away to give birth to her baby.'

'The girl and the baby, what were their names?'

Conni glared at him. 'For the purposes of this story, we'll call the girl Cindy and the baby Ella. Are you happy now?' She cleared her throat. 'Cindy was so poor that she had no option but to leave her baby with strangers: a couple and their nasty children, while she worked as much as she could in any job she could, earning very little. She sent almost all the money she did earn, regular as clockwork, to the couple to care for Ella. But she was working so much and so hard, that she almost never had enough money, or time or energy to visit her child and check up on them.

'And time passed. Cindy was proud of herself that she hadn't dumped Ella in an orphanage. With every humiliating thing she did, she believed she was doing the best for her child, and that thought was her motivation to keep going. What she didn't know was that the couple were treating Ella very badly.'

'I recognise it now. It's Victor Hugo, *Les Miserables*,' said Peter.

'Right! Now you're just pissing me off.'

'Okay, well get on with it, then. I'll shut up and listen.'

'So, from a very young age, Ella was expected to clean and cook for the couple and their children. In exchange, they fed her just enough to keep her alive and clothed her in rags and hand-me-downs. They didn't even send her to school. Fortunately for her, Ella was very bright and, at night when everyone else was asleep, she used to borrow the children's schoolbooks and teach herself everything she could. She taught herself to read and write, she learned maths and science, history and geography. She even learned English and other foreign languages from listening to the radio and the TV.

'As Ella grew, she began to look more and more like Cindy, only prettier. She had hair like spun flax and enormous green eyes. One day, when Ella was just a teenager, Cindy suddenly disappeared, or so she was told. The money had stopped coming, so they had no use for Ella anymore. But what were they to do with her? She was still legally a child, but she was too old for an adoption agency.

'What they did next was nothing short of shameful. You see, Peter, they took Ella to the nearest big city, and they sold her to someone. The man they sold her to was a pimp.' Conni sighed. 'The pimp was exactly as you might have imagined him to be. In Ella, he saw a unique opportunity, and he took it. He videoed and photographed her and put the images on the internet. Long story short, he auctioned off her innocence to the highest bidder.

'Now, lucky or unlucky for her, the man who bought her was influential and corrupt. He saw her on the internet, and he immediately fell in lust with her. He had deep pockets and he didn't just fill them up with money. He knew things about people that made them vulnerable. Important people. He used all that money and influence and corruption to get Ella a visa and bring her to Australia. But even that wasn't the worst of it.

'He had his fun with her for a few years. Eventually, as beautiful as she was, Ella became familiar, and like all boys with toys, he gradually grew tired of her. The thing was, he had paid a lot for her. Men like him aren't in the business of losing money. This fellow was as ruthless as he was evil, and he did what any ruthless, evil, corrupt businessman would do: he got her hooked on heroin and he pimped her out for sex to anyone who was willing to pay for her. He called it *getting a return on his investment.*

'So, Ella wasn't yet twenty and working a St Kilda nightclub when she came to the attention of her fairy godmother and her fairy godmother's then life partner, an old-fashioned tap dancer with the kindest and gentlest of souls. Her fairy godparents had been a long time coming I suppose, but once they saw Ella and her predicament, their hearts shattered into a million pieces. How could a sweet gem such as her end up whoring in a sleezy nightclub, turning tricks to support her pimp and her drug habit?

'It went on until one day, her fairy godparents staged an intervention. They showed her the way out of the life that this man had imprisoned her in, and they got her clean. They gave her an education and made her safe. They broke the chains that had bound her to him, and she soon realised that there was a wonderful world out there for her to discover.

'So, now to finish the story. Ella may not have found her prince yet, but she has recently found her mentor, and hopefully, with your help, she'll find her vocation.' She refilled her glass, but she didn't drink from it. 'Look, Misha told me what happened with that pig, Moylan, today. She still carries a whole lot of shame around with her, even though none of it was her fault, but she wanted you to know the truth. She couldn't tell you herself, you see, so she asked me to do it. And now I have.' She took a sip. 'So now you're pretty much up to speed on how Ella—I mean, Ludmila Tarachenko— became Misha Harris, and why I know she'll live happily ever after.'

Chapter Twenty-Six

What's in the water?

'Peter Clancy!'

'I hope it's good news, Dr Rick.'

It was scheduled as an office day; Peter had written *Phone Rick Burgess* on his whiteboard, under the heading, *Things To Do Today*. He didn't believe in psychic connections, but, after having heard nothing from him in weeks, Rick's coincidental call first thing in the morning spooked him.

'My mentee, Misha, is here,' said Peter. 'Would you mind if I put you on speaker so that she can listen in?'

'No, not at all. Okay,' he began, 'so we have had some very interesting results. We tested the sample you provided, using a battery of different tests. That's why it's taken so long to analyse. I'd need at least an hour to describe the various tests and tell you all the results now, but you can read about them in the report I'll be sending you.'

'Okay,' said Peter.

'I'll summarise them for you. You said you took the samples from a local creek, right?'

'Right.'

'Well, I've never seen anything like it. Where on earth did you take the sample from? A tributary of the Ganges?' He chuckled. 'There's just about every type of heavy metal in the water, and not just in trace amounts. There are higher than safe concentrations of mercury, lead and arsenic, not to mention the e-coli, diesel, kerosine and other chemical pollutants. There are even huge amounts of asbestos fibres suspended in the water.

'We also detected a high level of dioxins, which are by-products of industrial processes and waste incineration. These things are very,

very dangerous. Short-term exposure to high levels of dioxins can cause skin and liver problems, and long-term exposure can damage the immune, endocrine and reproductive functions. Dioxins affect children far more than adults, and you can imagine the effect that everything else we found has on people's health. In short, your water is a lethal cocktail that nobody should be anywhere near.'

'So, what effect would all this have, for example, if it was draining into a beach?'

'Where people are swimming?'

'Well, yes.'

'Are you kidding me? People would get very, very sick. I mean, of course, once it flows into a greater body of water, assuming the water it flows into is relatively clean, it would dilute down, possibly even to safe levels. The problem is, it will wreak havoc on the way through, and continued run-off of effluent like this will cause immense destruction. Nobody should be exposed to it on the way through, not people, not animals, not fish and not the environment. I can't overstate the importance of stopping this, Peter.'

Rick added, 'And let me tell you, even if it is one of the worst I've seen, this isn't an isolated case. It's happening all over Melbourne. There are illegal operators making huge amounts of money out of dumping waste anywhere and everywhere, because no one knows what to do with it.'

'So why aren't the authorities doing something to stop them?'

'The environmental officers are run off their feet; I get that. I have raised these illegal operators several times because I have done some investigating myself. Maybe it's incompetence. The Environmental Panel is a toothless instrument in my estimation, but don't quote me on that. All I'll say is, if you want to look for greed and corruption as a motivator, you'll always find it.'

'I live three houses away, Rick,' Peter ventured, 'so am I safe where I am?'

'You should be, as long as you don't go near the dump site or get the contaminated material on you. I won't mince words: it needs to be shut down ASAP. I'll send you through the report the moment it's ready.'

'Many thanks, mate, I owe you one. Their attitude's pretty discouraging, but I'm hoping that the investigative piece I'm writing will embarrass the powers-that-be so much, that they'll have no choice but to act.' He sat back and sighed.

'What now?' asked Misha.

'Well, for the first time in a long time, I have to admit, I'm not sure. If it wasn't as dire a situation, I'd contact the council first for their comments, but I'm worried that if I do that, they'll do everything in their power to shut me down. People need to know about this before they get sick. I'm all for balanced reporting, but it's summer, and people are swimming not a hundred metres from where this creek meets the bay. I'm thinking that the greater public good weighs heavily in favour of getting the article out there, and that I should worry about jostling for council's comments later, along with every other dickhead who'll sail in on my coattails.

'So you may as well go home now, Misha, and I'm going to work on it for the rest of the day.' He thought about it for a moment. 'Maybe I'll even sleep on it. Ask me again tomorrow.'

Misha shut down her computer and put on her jacket. She gave him a peck on the cheek as she was leaving.

'What's that for?' he asked.

'For caring,' she replied. 'For caring about this, about the people who'll be affected if nothing is done, and about me.'

He sniggered. 'We're journalists, Misha, it's what we do.'

'No, Peter, it's not what all journalists do: it's what you do, and what I hope I'll do too.'

He hid his emotion under a smile and went on writing.

In the early evening, just as he was starting to unwind, he heard Rhiannon's voice from a distance. 'No, Andre,' he heard her say, 'you cannot come over tonight.'

From the strength of her voice and her breathy resonance, Peter concluded she was climbing the stairs to his front door.

'Why?' she continued. 'What do you mean why? Because I'm busy and you're an arsehole. No. No. No! Don't you dare! I'm hanging up on you now.'

After calling the council's media rep and getting a *no comment* response, Peter had spent the rest of the day preparing his article: 'Tyne in Trouble—Pollution on the Peninsula Exposed'. He'd finished the first draft about twenty minutes earlier but had held off pitching it to the papers: he was still considering whether to contact the mayor for her comments first.

He looked out of the window and saw Rhiannon standing by the front door, silhouetted against the moon: short-skirted, high-heeled and perky, a bottle of Dom Perignon sheltering under her armpit. He had been playing classic rock, loudly but not loudly enough. He turned up the music but it was too late: her knock came first.

'Peter,' she said. She trotted past him into the kitchen, placed the bottle down on the counter and took two glasses out of the overhead cupboard. She cracked open the champagne, filled both glasses and then gulped down one of them.

'Cheers!' she said, refilling hers. 'Sorry, but I needed that.' She turned towards Peter and pressed herself against him. 'I've had an awful day! It's been horrible.'

He didn't ask why.

'And now I need this.' She grabbed at his crotch.

'Ah,' he said, backing away. 'We respect personal boundaries here. How about we exchange pleasantries first, and work our way up to sex?'

'But we're well past that, I think,' she said. 'We've already established our relationship.'

He blanched. He searched for words. *She thinks that what we're having is a relationship?* Rhiannon's face betrayed nothing.

She laughed, but her expression remained frozen. 'Oh, relax, will you? We're just neighbours with benefits. Peter! Lighten up and let's have some fun!'

There he was, snared again by her logic. Before he knew it, they were in his bedroom. She was playing the burlesque queen at the foot of his bed, bumping and grinding to *Paranoid*, still streaming in from the speaker in other room. She had absolutely no inhibitions. Occasionally, he caught her watching herself in the mirror as she danced.

The sex has nothing to do with me; it's obviously the ultimate act of autoeroticism for her. I probably should be worried.

Suddenly she was writhing naked on his bed, while he shoved his bruised ego aside.

Then again, who cares? Maybe I'll just lie back and enjoy the ride!

Chapter Twenty-Seven

Hearts and minds

He first heard the news of Jack Cunningham's death over breakfast radio.

With his Arnold-cancelling headphones on, Peter was making
himself an espresso while listening to a stream of his favourite
program, when the regular crime reporter came on and spoke cryp-
tically about the overnight death in custody of a coastal farmer. No
name was mentioned, but he nearly dropped his cup when he heard
the reporter say that police had taken the farmer in for questioning
over firearms offences just two days earlier.

What the fuck?

How hadn't he heard about this before anyone else? Peter was
pretty sure—night-time diversions aside—that nobody had tried
to call him. His heart thumped. If it really was Jack Cunningham
who had died—and it seemed very unlikely that it could be anyone
else—it should have been him who broke the story. But nobody had
let him know. As far as he knew, Suzanne Spellman was taking care
of Jack, and she had been recommended, so he'd trusted that Jack
would be in good hands. He had been scooped: weeks of his hard
work hijacked by a radio hack. It was totally unacceptable.

He turned up the volume to drown out the parade of trucks past
his house and listened to the rest of the radio segment attentively.
The reporter made no mention of the reasons behind the firearms
charges; perhaps he didn't know. There was no mention of rubbish
dumping or corruption; perhaps Peter could salvage his article and
his reputation after all.

He phoned Graham Cunningham first, but the call went straight
to voicemail. Ditto with Mrs Cunningham. He left messages that

were purposely ambiguous, showing concern for the family's welfare, clear enough to convey what he meant if it was Jack who had passed away, yet absent of any overt mention of death.

When he hadn't heard back from either of them an hour later, he called Suzanne Spellman.

'Right, Peter,' she said, exhaling loudly, 'I saw Mr Cunningham late that evening, after you called me.' The rest of her monologue flowed like a checklist: where, when, how, why, and in particular, why not her fault.

She continued, 'The police interviewed him—it was nothing remarkable—but it really stressed him out. I did try to get him bailed, but he didn't help his cause, yelling at the magistrate. The magistrate deemed him to be too great a threat to the community at large, and his bail application was refused. I have to admit that I was concerned for Mr Cunningham: he was pretty shaken up when I last spoke to him, and he just wouldn't calm down. Remand was packed to the rafters, so he spent the last two nights in the lockup. Apparently the custody officer checked on him in the early hours of this morning, but he'd already passed away. The doctor believes he had a heart attack overnight.'

'A heart attack?'

'I suppose it was hardly surprising, given his age and level of agitation.'

Peter scowled. 'Yet you didn't tell anyone you were concerned about him? You didn't try to get him medically assessed? I mean, if you noticed he was agitated, the police must have as well. So how come no one did anything about it?'

'Agitation might be too strong a word: I meant to say that I noticed he seemed perturbed, but so would most people be in his circumstances. There's nothing unusual in that, but most people don't up and die just because of a little stress.' She paused. 'I'm not taking any blame for this, I'm a lawyer, not a doctor.'

Wow, and not a caring one at that!

It wasn't the response he expected from someone who had been prepared to see Jack Cunningham for free and whose living depended on the ability to choose her words carefully. He sighed.

'I suppose the autopsy will provide some answers.'

'Oh, I don't think there'll be a need for that. He was seventy-six, the cause of death was cardiac infarct, so why put the family through any unnecessary pain?'

'No autopsy, then? But I thought it was mandatory to investigate deaths in custody.'

'Yes, that's right, investigate. And I suppose the coroner will determine the proper extent of those investigations, and whether there is a need to waste all that money, time and emotion on an autopsy when the cause of death is abundantly clear, as it is in Mr Cunningham's case. There was nothing suspicious about his death as far as I could tell. The family doesn't want one, and I won't be pushing for an autopsy.'

'Huh. Right. So, it was a heart attack then?'

'Yes.'

'And you agree with that even though, as you just said, you're a lawyer and not a doctor.'

She hung up. Peter shook his head and returned to his work.

Graham Cunningham called him two hours later. 'They told us that the stress of being in jail killed Dad,' he said.

'Did you know that your dad had a heart condition?' Peter asked.

'Dad? A heart condition? Is that what they reckon?'

'Yep.'

'Nah, mate, Dad's ticker was good; he was as fit as a Mallee bull up till now,' he said. 'Never had a sick day in his life. I thought they said he had a stroke.'

'So does it shock you to hear that he died of a heart attack?'

'Well, like I told that lawyer woman, stress can kill, and he'd had a lot of that recently.' He paused. 'I suppose it's not impossible that we didn't know nothing about his heart, but... A heart attack? So, not a stroke? They know that for a fact?'

'No, they don't know anything for a fact, unless they perform an autopsy. I was told you and your mum didn't want one.'

'Well, I don't remember us being asked. We just want to know what killed him. I mean, they can't tell us one thing and you another, can they? I dunno... Maybe it was the shock. Maybe I was in shock...

Maybe I heard stroke when they actually said heart attack...'

'I'll see what I can find out,' said Peter.

The Police Media Department had nothing further to add, so he typed:

FARMER'S FAMILY FRANTIC
Family Demands Answers After Farmer's Death in Custody

After that, he opened a bottle of Jameson's. He already had five hundred words ready to go in a little over an hour, together with the obligatory photos. The article was good—no, it was great—but now he had to sell it and fast. What he had lost in the scoop, he'd have to make up in style and substance, if he was going to make any money from his hard work. He picked up the phone. Five minutes later he secured himself a very nice deal.

Fortunately for him, he still had his hard-hitting, global reputation as his calling card.

CHAPTER TWENTY-EIGHT

Six kilometres from the Hermit's Hut

For the second time that week, a fox had infiltrated the henhouse. The first thing Sadie Taylor noticed when she went to collect the eggs for breakfast was the feathers. Then she spotted the bits of flesh and gut stuck to the weatherboard siding, from the ground right up to the roof.

It amazed her that although she never saw any evidence of foxes during the daylight hours, it seemed that they rioted unabated through the town by night. The last time it happened, she went directly to one of the council's officers.

'Here's the number for the pest management association,' the officer said, hardly looking at her. He took a card out of his desk and handed it to her.

She glanced at the card and returned it to him. 'And that's the best you can suggest, Mr Killian?' she asked him.

'Absolutely, Councillor Taylor. It's not in our jurisdiction.'

'But tending to the environment is very firmly in our jurisdiction.'

He turned his attention to his computer screen. 'Well, yes and no. But not foxes.'

'So, as a council, we're doing nothing to control these vermin— they're someone else's problem—isn't that what you're really saying?' She sighed. 'Look, I was voted in to protect our precious ecosystem. I promised people change: I said that we were going to care for the coast together. In the meantime, I discover that feral cats and foxes are slaughtering our native wildlife along with my chickens, and we're powerless to fix the problem. What am I supposed to tell my constituents?'

'I really can't advise you on that, but part of my job is to educate the residents of the Tyne Coast. I let them know that they can set traps to catch the feral cats and the ranger will come to their house, collect them, and dispose of them humanely. Other vermin, however, are a different matter.'

'What?'

'We can't be responsible for the foxes and rats and other pests that result from people's general untidiness.'

'Really? Are you insinuating that it's my fault that the foxes attack my chickens, because I'm dirty?'

'Not you personally, Councillor Taylor, but...'

'Fine,' she replied. 'It's my and everybody else's household waste that's the problem. And yet, the moment I mention the words "rubbish" and "dumping" in a council meeting, I'm howled down. Thank you for nothing, Mr Killian.'

She didn't mind if she'd wounded his pride. It was clear that Council was failing the residents in all matters environmental. It felt to her that she was always the lone voice, crying to protect the wilderness. First she'd taken on overdevelopment and then she'd demanded Council look into the rubbish unexpectedly accumulating in open spaces. Now she would have to take on this. The awful truth was that little ever seemed to come of her rants and raves. She was infuriated that no one else cared. In Council, the vermin had the upper hand.

Sadie paused at the door to the henhouse enclosure and listened. She felt like crying. Instead of the usual cackles and squawks she was met with silence; the destruction was absolute this time. Only one chicken had been taken in the last attack; the victim that time had been a grumpy, indifferent layer and although she didn't deserve to die so brutally, Sadie felt ashamed to admit that she had barely noticed her absence. After that attack, Paula had scraped together two precious, hard-won hours away from her counselling practice, to shore up the floor and tack down and bury wire mesh, in an effort to stop the foxes from digging their way into the enclosure. But the foxes were clearly in the ascendancy, and she and Paula were the recipients of a rampage once more.

As she looked around, it became apparent that Paula's time and energy had been wasted. Sadie opened the door to the enclosure and stepped inside. She gasped and raised her hand to her mouth. She wouldn't be able to keep it a secret from Paula, and not just because all the chickens were gone this time. Her prize-winning hen, Princess Lay-a, was stretched out alongside the coop. She had been beheaded. Sadie picked her up and took a closer look. Her head had been removed with surgical precision, beyond the capacity of any animal without opposing thumbs.

As she turned to go, the rest of the wall revealed itself. She squealed and let the chicken fall. To add a full stop to the massacre, someone had daubed a message on the leeside of the coop:

YOU NEXT

DIE BITCH

It was written in blood.

CHAPTER TWENTY-NINE

The passing of an honest man

Jack Cunningham's funeral wasn't a celebration of his life or a requiem for his death. Graham sent Peter a short email—along with anyone else whose name appeared in the exercise book that Jack kept next to his computer—saying that Jack's *rites of passing* were to take place at ten the next day.

It was to happen at the Serene Chapel of Rest by the Sea, located somewhere in the Tyne Coast Memorial Garden. Peter had never heard of the place and didn't know where it was, so he googled it. His eyebrows shot up as he read: *not to be confused with a place of traditional religious worship, the Serene Chapel of Rest by the Sea is a pantheist refuge of peace and contemplation...*

After that, the email mentioned, they were to witness the cremation of Jack's earthly remains. Which turned Peter's mind to mead, flaming Viking longships and Valhalla. He was pretty sure that that was a construct entirely unfamiliar to Jack and Beth Cunningham, so he assumed that Graham must have arranged everything according to his own beliefs.

The next morning, Peter was up by six. He dressed, had two espressos and a mouthful of a stale berry Danish for breakfast and sat behind his computer for a while. On his way out, he cleared the letterbox of the previous day's mail and tossed it on the passenger seat of his car. Then he arrived at Moores Lane early and parked a short distance from the Cunningham farm.

He wasn't a voyeur but, like the celebrated reporter Jimmy Breslin, he was looking for that something extra for the piece he intended to write about Jack Cunningham's life. It was too soon to assign an unnatural cause to Jack's death, so he was hoping to find an angle that would turn a boring bit of local chit-chat into a feature worth reading.

He sat in the driver's seat and watched a half-hearted sun burn the dew off one blade of grass at a time, until the clouds fused together overhead and stopped it dead. After that, boredom compelled him to tear open the envelopes and read his mail. *Bill. Bill. Bill.* And suddenly, *What the fuck!* He frowned. The fourth letter contained a statement of social security benefits. He had never received benefits of any kind. He turned it over and searched for a covering letter. Too late, he realised it wasn't addressed to him.

Mr Edison Arnold.

He reread the letter.

Notification of an Increase to your Disability Support Pension...

But how on earth was Arnold entitled to a disability support pension? He had a business, a million-dollar-plus house, expensive foreign cars and, weight issues aside, seemingly robust health. Something was most definitely wrong there. Yet somehow, it wasn't the right occasion to be thinking about Arnold; all that had to be ammunition for another time. He put the letters aside and turned his attention back to the Cunningham farm. He stepped out of his car and took a short walk.

He thought it would be better to observe the day from its inception and from a respectful distance, rather than knock on the door and bother Beth Cunningham and her family. The kitchen light was already on, and he could hear the kettle whistle. Despite the heavy air and unseasonal chill, it surprised him how clearly the sound carried across the paddock where he stood.

For some time, the only noise he could hear related to the preparation of breakfast. The hum of voices arrived with the smell of burning toast. Then someone opened a window and the voices resonated.

'Mum,' he heard Graham say, 'I've made you a cuppa, but you need to eat something.'

'A cup of tea's enough for me; I'm not hungry, Graham.'

'No, Mum, no it's not. You have to eat. It's going to be a long day and you'll need your strength.'

'I said I'm not hungry.'

'But Mum…'

'My stomach's in knots; I couldn't eat, even if I wanted to.'

'But Mum…'

Her voice rose. 'Listen to me, Graham. Are you listening to me?' she continued. 'I said I am not hungry.' After a pause, she added, 'You can't just bully people into doing what you want them to. I'm not having breakfast, thank you, Graham. And I'm not bloody selling the farm neither.'

'But Mum…'

'Enough! I know what you think about it; you've told me a hundred times already. Your father didn't want the farm sold, and neither do I, and I don't want to talk about it anymore.'

'Right. Well, then don't expect me to help you run it. And I don't know how you're going to pay the loan.'

'None of your business.'

Peter heard the clatter of a cup in the sink, a running tap, sloshing dishwater, and nothing else for a long time.

The hearse transporting Jack to the chapel arrived at the door about twenty minutes later. A limousine followed shortly behind. Peter took some photos of the cortege while the drivers waited for the Cunninghams to appear. Then he returned to his car and drove directly to the memorial gardens.

He and about another fifty or so people turned up on a drizzly, grey, mid-summer's Melbourne morning to witness the event. It was an unexpectedly small crowd, given that the Cunninghams were a popular, generations-old coast family. Since Graham hadn't put an announcement in the paper, possibly the reason for the poor attendance was that few people knew about Jack's funeral. Possibly it was because Jack and Beth Cunningham were Catholics, but Graham wasn't, and he wasn't seen to be doing the right thing by his dad. Or possibly it was just the weather that kept them away.

Beth Cunningham arrived alone in the limousine that followed the hearse. She was a forlorn figure in black. She didn't move when the driver opened the door; she needed to be helped out of the car. She rested on her wheelie-walker, although Peter couldn't remember her using one before. She was unsteady, glassy-eyed and emotionless. She didn't look to Graham for help, and he didn't offer any. Peter glanced around the crowd, but he couldn't recognise anyone else. He took out his phone and pretended to message as he photographed the mourners. If they were good enough, he'd attach some of the photos to a sentimental piece of fluff later.

Someone from the funeral home pegged back the chapel doors at around ten minutes to ten and invited them to enter and find a seat. Instead of following the crowd, Peter dropped back and sheltered from the drizzle beneath a tall acacia. From there, he watched for any stragglers.

Minutes passed. He saw Sergeant Moylan arrive alone and loiter outside the chapel door, his ear pressed to his phone. After him came a parade of local luminaries: Brian Goldsmith and Adriana Balloch, Rebecca Harrison and her husband arrived simultaneously.

Peter snorted. *Well, well, well, who do we have here?* The Cunningham family had farmed the coast for generations, yet it surprised him that any members of the glamour set had bothered to come to the funeral. Possibly the community was tighter than he'd anticipated. Possibly they were hoping to exert some subtle sales pressure on the son and widow by their mere presence. Possibly they were just looking for some positive publicity.

But I don't see any snapperazzi around, guys: perhaps you should have left the diamonds in the vault.

The couples nodded to each other from a distance, upholding the pretence that they were barely acquainted. Moylan looked up from his phone. He caught Goldsmith's eye, and Peter noticed the unspoken exchange. *What was that?* After a purposeful incline of his head in Moylan's direction followed by a glance that lingered too long, Goldsmith followed his wife into the chapel, his hand resting on the small of her back. Then a familiar gurgle in the adjacent carpark announced the arrival of Arnold and his wife. The disability pension would barely cover the cost of petrol. Peter watched them prise themselves out of the car and saunter over to the chapel. It was the first time he had seen Arnold in clothes without tears or stains.

He still wore his long shorts and work boots, and he still looked as if he smelled.

They're not conducting a board meeting, are they?

He took some quick notes of what he'd seen and darted into the chapel just before the doors closed again. He claimed a seat in the back row for himself, near the door, in case he felt the need to escape. The whole affair was mercifully speedy. Some old photos. A short eulogy. Jack's final journey.

After the service, mourners chatted briefly in small groups and then disappeared. Graham drifted past Goldsmith and the others. He mentioned something about refreshments in the adjacent gazebo, and Peter saw a few people shelter there just long enough to gulp a hot drink out of plastic mugs and eat a thin, white-bread sandwich. It wasn't his cup of tea, so he stayed where he was for as long as he could stand the raindrops coursing down his back, and then he left.

But Peter hadn't been the only one watching from the wings and taking notes and photographs. A hundred metres away a tall, well-built man in his late forties seemed particularly interested in the passing parade. Peter tilted his phone, so it appeared that he was reading a text message, and he photographed the stranger. He'd try to attach a name to the face later.

CHAPTER THIRTY

Not the Arnolds again

The rubbish trucks started up especially early the following day. By six-thirty, Peter's kitchen was filled with the aroma of espresso extraction, while outside the road was gusting dust and refuse.

He wondered if anyone else had noticed. *Six fucking thirty. Obscene.*

He caught sight of himself in the bathroom mirror. His eyes were bleary. As he pissed, he was thinking of doing harm to Arnold and his trucks. Maybe he could dig a trench across the road, fill the bottom of it with stakes and then cover it up. *What a pity you can't buy landmines on eBay.* In the time it took him to finish, he had compiled the definitive manual on how to dispose of infuriating neighbours, using only his imagination.

He was sure it would be a best seller. With potential to be turned into a reality show.

Back in the kitchen, he uncurled his dry tongue from the roof of his mouth and downed his first coffee. It was just like the old days: from piss-up to extra strong double espresso. Courtesy of Mr Jameson, he had made himself match-fit in a mere matter of hours.

He was just settling in for his second espresso, when there was a rap on the door. It was Mimi O'Connor. Again. She was sobbing and looking out towards the road.

Surely I'm entitled to get my shit together before I get harassed.

He scrambled into shorts and a t-shirt and opened the door. She swung around to face him, wiped her eyes, and gulped back her tears.

'Hello, Mimi. What's wrong now?' he asked. He tried to mask his irritation, but he'd already had enough commotion in his morning.

'Oh, sorry! It is early, isn't it? I'll go away,' she said without moving. 'It's just that I thought you'd be up. Who could sleep with all that noise going on? I'm so sorry, Peter.'

'It's very early, Mimi.' He stared her down, but she stood fast. 'Oh, what the hell, you may as well come in.'

She managed a faint smile and then followed him inside. He made two cups of coffee and indicated by the wave of a hand that he wouldn't be ready to listen until he had sat down.

He handed her one of the cups. She said, 'I read your article. It was very good.'

'Thanks, Mimi, but you really didn't have to come here at six-thirty in the morning just to tell me that. Later would have been fine. Much, much later.'

'No, that's not why I came. They've pushed over my fence. Did it overnight.' She glanced at the cup in her hand. 'Did they think I wouldn't notice? The rubbish is right up to my boundary now. They're getting more brazen. You should have a look at what they've done and take some photos for a follow-up.' She put down the coffee without drinking it. 'I don't know how much more I can take.'

She was on the edge of crying again. He put both cups in the sink. 'Right, then. Let's go.'

He followed Mimi home. Arnold had uprooted a long length of the fence that separated his yard from Mimi's and tossed it across her yard. With the fence down, there was nothing to obstruct the view of Arnold's Audi TT, the LandCruiser and a bin truck, all parked near the shipping container. There were a half dozen skips full of rubbish dotted around the yard; Peter counted them.

Arnold's father-in-law and a kid with a rat's tail posing as a hairstyle were sorting the rubbish from one of the skips. On Mimi's boundary, they had built themselves a fort out of soiled mattresses, and another out of plastic drums. Peter had to admit that the stinking piles were uncharacteristically neat. Some crows sat in Mimi's trees, waiting for an opportunity to add themselves to the party. Peter expected a pile of rats to be scurrying about, but he couldn't see any. Only the human variety. Maybe the place was too filthy for rats.

'You'd think he'd try to hide his crimes, wouldn't you?' he whispered to Mimi. 'The council must think that a festering, stinking pile of rubbish in a residential area isn't a problem. I'd love to see how the mayor would react if this pile of shit was next door to her house.' He leaned over the boundary and focused his camera.

Suddenly Arnold shouted from nowhere, 'What the fuck are you two cunts doing on my property?'

The men dropped the mattress they were carrying and looked up. The rat-tailed kid darted towards Peter, as Mimi beat a retreat. 'Give me the camera, old prick,' he shouted. He reached down and picked up a large stick.

Peter quickly sized up Rat not to be much of a threat; he looked like he probably lived in the rubbish. He stood his ground while Arnold lumbered towards them, pausing occasionally to catch his breath. 'You'd better not do anything till your boss arrives,' said Peter. 'He'll be here in about half an hour.'

'Give us the camera,' Rat threatened, 'or I'll fucking kill you.' He swung at Peter and missed.

'You look like you need a good feed and worming, son.'

Rat took another swing, but this time Peter grabbed the stick and threw it away. He pushed Rat in the chest. Rat teetered backwards, yelling as he fell, 'I'll fucking sue you.'

'Piss off kid,' countered Peter, 'before I give you a proper flogging.'

Arnold finally arrived. He motioned to Rat to leave, and then turned his attention to Peter. 'Give me that camera, arsehole, or you're dead.'

Peter scoffed, 'Really? You're running a hazardous dump illegally in a residential area. I intend to shut you down, Arnold. This is just some of the evidence that'll do it.'

'Good luck,' Arnold said with a laugh. 'You can't stop me. No one can.'

'Then why are you so worried by me taking photos, if you're sure that nothing will happen?'

'I don't like people snooping around my property. Plus, you're an arsehole and I don't like you. And neither do my friends. So give me the camera.' He reached out to grab the camera, but Peter backed away. 'You don't know who you're dealing with, you old cunt. I fucking kill people for fun.'

'Don't worry,' Peter snapped back, 'I know exactly what I'm dealing with. The thing is, you don't have a clue who you're dealing with, Arnold.'

'Yeah?' he chortled. 'I know where you live, arsehole. You and that bitch of yours who drives that crappy green Corolla. Just you remember that!'

Misha! Peter seethed. He felt his heart pounding. He turned and walked away.

'She's a tasty one, she is,' Arnold continued, simulating a hip thrust. 'She takes it every way you wanna give it to her!'

It took all of his strength to keep walking. He was tempted to return and lay Arnold out on his back, even if he died in the process. He wasn't usually the violent type, but there were always exceptions and, since he wasn't working for anyone at present, he was his own agent. But hit Arnold, and he'd be the one charged by the police. And no doubt, he'd be the next one having the unexpected, deadly heart attack-cum-stroke in the cell.

He returned to Mimi, while Arnold watched them keenly.

'I want justice, Peter,' Mimi cried. 'My nerves can't take this anymore.'

'Listen to me: you have to be patient. These people are far more dangerous than you realise. At the moment, he thinks I'm just another old coot with a camera and an axe to grind. As soon as my next piece comes out, I'll have blown my cover. He may not be able to read, but his associates might. I'll be bloody exposed.'

'I'm so sorry I involved you, Peter,' she wept as she climbed the stairs to her front door. 'You're the only one who can do anything, and you have to do something soon before more people suffer.'

'I already have something in the works. Try to stay calm, Mimi. I won't let you down.' He nodded goodbye and strode back down her driveway. He stopped at the crossover and glanced over at Arnold's place. Arnold reached into his shorts and retrieved his mobile; he couldn't hear the conversation, but he just knew what it would be about.

He had to move quickly and get this story out.

He was on the phone the moment he returned to his office. He had missed a call from a source he didn't recognise, so he shelved that for later. His first call was to Rick Burgess. Rick answered the phone, but Peter's joy turned to despair when he heard that the report was still at least two days away. He really needed those lab results. In writing. Stat! The strength of his piece hinged on them.

He talked at Rick non-stop for at least half a minute, appealing to his rational side. Where reasoning failed, pleading and inducements worked. Rick promised he would devote all his spare time to writing up the report. 'Fine, by tonight. Or tomorrow morning, at the latest,' Peter said. If Rick delivered, Peter owed him big-time.

His next call was to Conni.

'You know it's not yet seven, don't you?' she muttered. 'My girls may do early, but I don't. Never have done. If death isn't imminent, you should hang up now and call me back later.'

'I just had a very unpleasant conversation with the thug across the road.'

'Oh, right. Were you looking for a dawn-buster? Or did you get up on the wrong side of bed again, Peter?'

'I was in a good mood, as it happens, until one neighbour turned up in tears on my doorstep, and the other one threatened me. Which is nothing new, of course, and hardly rates a mention. That's not why I called you. The thing is, in the midst of me trying to restore law and order, the thug across the road made some lewd remarks about Misha. I wanted you to know, because I don't want anything to happen to her on my account. She's had enough shit in her life and she doesn't need this. I know she's poured her heart and soul into working with me, and I don't want to disappoint her, but her safety is my primary concern.'

'Well then, in that case I forgive you for the wake-up call. Does this thug have a name?'

'Eddie Arnold.'

'Hmm,' said Conni. 'The name rings a bell. He wouldn't happen to have a father-in-law who looks like he just crawled out of a sewer, does he?'

'Ronny Cooper?'

Conni gasped. 'Not Ronny Cooper, Peter. I think you'll find it's Renard Cooper. He calls himself Rennie Cooper.'

'You know them?'

'Indeed—and I mean this in the worst, most vilely possible way—I do. I'm surprised you never came across them when you were a crime reporter... On second thoughts, they probably arrived on the scene after you'd left for London.' She sighed. 'How we missed you after you left!'

'So, about this Rennie Cooper...'

She hesitated for a moment. 'Now, what I'm about to ask you to do for me is very, very important. You said earlier that Arnold said something to you about Misha?'

'He did.'

'Did he allude to any of what I told you about her past?'

'Not directly.'

'Has he seen her?'

'I don't know. Possibly. He did mention her car. But I don't know if the rest of his remarks were pointed, or simply intended to degrade women generally.'

'Right. Well, that sounds like Arnold all right. I'm not going to explain myself, but you need to keep Arnold and his father-in-law well away from Misha. Don't let her see them if you possibly can. That's all I'm going to say.'

Peter drew breath, but she interjected with, 'Please don't ask why, Peter, just do it. For once!' She continued, 'Misha really loves what she's doing right now, and I don't want it to end just because of them. She's proud and headstrong and she wouldn't take my inter-ference well, and she'd be heartbroken if you let her go. So I say we ignore his remarks for the time being and you keep on doing what you've been doing.'

'I'll try, but I'm writing a series of articles which places them in the epicentre of something pretty big, and I'm relying on Misha to help with the research. She'll notice if I suddenly freeze her out.'

'Look, Peter, Eddie Arnold and Renard Cooper are unlikely to be in the epicentre of anything other than the world's filthiest shit-storm. They're mean and violent, of course, but in any big operation, they're just bit players. Think of them as the stone in your shoe.'

'So, why...'

'It's personal,' she interrupted. 'Now, how did you say that that garden of yours was going?'

'I didn't.'

'Well, Misha just happened to mention that you need a bit of assistance with it. And you require some home maintenance, too. In fact, she said that the place is falling down around your ears.'

'I don't think it's that dreadful, although, truth be told, I suppose it could do with a little work,' he replied. 'But it very much depends on the hourly rate. Honestly, I don't think I can afford you, Conni. I spent just about everything I had to buy this place. Freelancing doesn't pay that well, and I'm still waiting for my next royalty payment to come in.'

'Let's not talk money: it's so degrading. For you, darling, let's call it a labour of love. You need help and it just so happens that I can provide it. I'm going to send a team over who are simply fabulous at everything. They're the original triple threat—experts in gardening and home maintenance, and they have impeccable fashion sense. Now, can you get that garage door of yours open, so that Misha can park her car and not be seen?'

'I could try.'

'Oh, please don't try, Peter, you're so very bad at it. I'll take your answer as a no, and I'll send my team over to you as a priority.'

Over the next fifty minutes, things began to move quickly. Conni's handy-gals (her words, not his)—two statuesque women in khaki shorts and Doc Martens—arrived in a Winnebago. They pulled up on the far side of the driveway, connected their van to the electricity supply and set up an awning. Within minutes, they had the garage door gliding up and down effortlessly. Shortly after that, Misha turned into Peter's driveway in a black Mercedes Benz with tinted windows. She parked in the garage and entered the house from the back.

'Conni asked me to swap cars with Silvio,' Misha explained. 'She didn't say why.'

He shrugged. 'I must say, it suits you better.'

With Misha having to be smuggled in and out of the house and threats tossed about like confetti, the story was becoming too dangerous and shambolic. What was the point? Who really gave a fuck about a backwater beach town and its inhabitants? And why did he come back to Australia? Perhaps it truly was the arsehole end of the world. He sat back at his desk and stared at the only accolade he had bothered to bring back with him from London. Investigative Journalism Award for 2002. It sat next to his Heart of Melbourne award: his first and possibly his favourite. Together, they represented a potted history of his career, minus the Pulitzer in between that he won for someone else.

Awards were nothing, really. Sometimes they gave him hope. But not today.

If it all fell apart tomorrow, he could just piss off back to England and rent his place on Airbnb. Then he could try to find the love of his life and spend however much time he had left apologising to her and trying to win her back. *I'm going back to Blighty*, he finally decided. *I miss my mates, I miss the work and I miss the good times. The weather is crap, but right now I need to be there. And if the doctor thinks I made a bad decision, I'll get another doctor.*

He was toying with that thought when he decided to return the call he'd missed earlier.

You've reached the voicemail of Councillor Sadie Taylor. I'm either busy out in the community or I'm helping someone else, so please leave me a message...

He was unimpressed; present circumstances were wearing away his patience. The way he was feeling at that time, his personalised voicemail message—if he ever made one—would have to be far more prosaic. *You've reached the voicemail of Peter Clancy. I'm either busy taking a piss or I don't want to talk to you, so please leave me a message...*

He left his name and hung up. Moments later, his phone rang again.

'I read your article on the plight of local farmers,' said Sadie, 'and I think we could be of enormous help to each other. We really need to talk. The environmental committee is meeting tomorrow night. Do you think we could meet up after that?'

'Yes, of course,' he replied. 'But can you tell me what you want from me?'

'No, not right now.' She hesitated. 'There aren't many places open at that time of night, so would you meet me at McDonald's?'

'McDonald's?' Peter had been thinking more Malbec than Big Mac, but he agreed. 'At around ten tomorrow night? Fine.'

Misha said, 'Shall I go too?'

'No, best you stay out of sight for a while.'

She sat with her back to him, clacking at the keyboard. Without turning, she said, 'You can drop the needless worry now; I'm not this precious gem that you and Conni have to protect. I'm much, much harder than you think. And I see things, Peter.'

'What do you see?' he asked.

'I see Eddie Arnold in the company of some very bad men on motorbikes, who think that they can get rid of anyone who could ruin their operation.' She swung around. 'You and Conni think that I don't know who he is, don't you? It's not something I can forget easily. I remember Arnold from when he was a bouncer at the club where I used to work. Back then, he looked very different from the way he looks now. He pumped iron and he liked to push people around. These days, the muscles have turned to flab, but the anger is still there. And so is that evil man, Rennie. What has changed is that they don't frighten me anymore. To be honest, I don't care about them. Look, I want to be an investigative journalist: danger is part of the job, isn't it?'

'It's just that those pricks know where I live,' Peter replied, 'and that puts you as well as me at risk. Most times, the people I write about, they don't know where I live. That's always made me feel safer. And I've never had an intern to worry about before.'

'You did that exposé on the Melbourne underworld; I read the book you wrote about it. They found out where you lived.'

'Yes, and that nearly ended badly for me.'

'I appreciate everything you've done for me, Peter, but I'm responsible for the choices I make. I know how things work. I should have died a thousand times, yet I'm still alive, aren't I? You don't have to worry about me.'

'Fine, but you're still staying home tonight. As to you carving out your future as an investigative journalist, well, I suppose that's up to you,' he said. 'I am going to upgrade my security, anyway. And raise the fence. Maybe even get a man-eating dog...'

But Misha had already checked herself out of the conversation. Her mind was elsewhere, reliving a past trauma perhaps.

He hadn't meant to patronise someone he was so desperate to protect. He smiled softly. Just when he thought there was nothing left for him in Serenity Bay, Sadie Taylor decided to call him.

And depending on what she had to say to him, he might have to stick around for a bit longer.

CHAPTER THIRTY-ONE

Coastal encounters of the worst kind

It was the perfect coast day. Serenity Bay gleamed like a blue-green diamond, and without a breeze there was nothing to ruffle its surface. Barefoot teenagers in skimpy swimwear braved the broken bottles, the cyclists and the speeding drivers to drift along the esplanade towards The Colonnade. It was the summer's favoured spot to be photographed leaping off the rocks and into the bay. It was also stupidly dangerous.

The dew was still fresh on Peter's lawn where the sun hadn't yet reached, and it was quickly burning off the roof of his car, where it had. He'd spent hours the previous evening reading Rick's preliminary report and contacting news agencies. By midnight, he'd written up a sizzling piece of outrage about 'Pests Polluting Peninsula for Profit', backed up by Dr Rick Burgess and his research.

He felt as if his latest article could finally gain him the traction that the others hadn't.

His article on Jack Cunningham had spawned several conspiracy theories. It might have even paved the way for further investigation but, as the coroner had already concluded that there was no need for an autopsy to settle the cause of death, nothing more came of it. Jack's long-time doctor had signed off on a history of heart problems—even though neither Beth nor Graham Cunningham could ever remember him filling a prescription for heart medication let alone taking it. It was possible, they conceded, that he'd kept that to himself to avoid worrying them unnecessarily. As to Graham's recollection that he'd been told it was a stroke, since he couldn't say definitively that his recollection wasn't tainted by stress, it wasn't deemed to be important. Bellavista Farm was staying put for the time being.

Peter needed to put work to one side for a while. He had laboured very hard without a break, and he was determined to reap the rewards. Most of all, he needed to get away from the ear-splitting judder of Arnold's jackhammer that had serenaded him since dawn. Contaminated or not, there was a beach day coming.

He left his car in the driveway and began to stroll down to the beach. After so many hours spent desk-bound, he figured that the exercise would do him good. About halfway down, he began to have second thoughts. By the time he reached the carpark, he knew it was a big mistake. Since he hadn't intended swimming— he knew exactly what was in that water—he hadn't brought a towel. He lifted the front of his t-shirt and mopped his face. The return, uphill journey would undoubtedly be far worse.

He skirted around the public convenience, crowded with children and parents. He avoided the splash of the outdoor shower and passed a sign that told beachgoers what they could and couldn't do. He chuckled at the thought that swimming probably ought to have been on top of the list. From there, he descended a wide, bamboo ramp set between the tea-trees and saltbushes. The sand rose to meet him about a third of the way down, and then it was a gentle descent all the way to the water's edge.

Harmony Creek spilled into the bay not very far from where he stood. It had carved itself a gully through the sand, which became wider and shallower the closer it came to the high-tide mark. Unaware of its hidden toxins, children used the dark, damp sand to build castles as they played in the shallows. A little higher up, an off-lead dog jumped in and out of the creek. Peter was concerned. Should he warn them? Would they listen to him, anyway?

He headed towards the southern end of the beach, past the creek, where the yellow sand gave way to steely granite boulders. He figured he'd be pretty safe paddling up to his knees, as long as the water didn't have the chance to enter an orifice. He gazed at the boats moored in waist-deep water barely metres offshore and thought that he might explore the possibility of buying one, just so he could do the same. He could see himself sipping beer in the sunshine, semi-recumbent on the deck of his boat, bobbing gently in time with the beat of swimmers' legs and the wake of the jet skis.

So deep in thought was he, that he didn't see two things happening.

The first thing he didn't see was a length of rope, knotted to resemble a large bone, flying through the air. In fact, he didn't notice it until it struck him hard in the small of the back, ricocheted and landed in the outlet of the creek. The next thing he didn't see was the dog that was meant to retrieve the rope-bone—the same one he'd seen playing in the creek. In fact, he didn't notice it until it bailed him up, bared its teeth and began to growl at him.

'Hey!' he called to a woman standing a little further along, who was holding a leash in one hand and a tennis ball in the other. From her stance and proximity, she appeared to be the dog's owner. 'Can you do something about your dog?'

She didn't move. 'Here, Brutus,' she yelled half-heartedly.

The dog didn't move. It flattened its ears and stared Peter down. He knew enough of working dogs to take it to be a bad sign. 'Hey! You! Get your fucking dog away from me!' he roared.

The woman scratched her cheek. 'Brutus,' she repeated, 'Come.'

But Brutus was not inclined to come. At this point, Brutus was beginning to snarl. Peter bellowed, 'Come here now and get your fucking dog!'

At last, she moved. Without displaying the least concern, she shuffled along the sand. When she was close enough, she screeched at Peter, 'Stop yelling at me! You go away! Go on, get off the beach!'

'What? You're joking, aren't you? Leash your dog now and get it off the beach!' He was incredulous. 'The sign specifically says that no dogs are allowed on the beach!'

She called the dog once more and distracted it with the ball. 'You're a stupid old bastard,' she spat at Peter. 'Dogs have their human rights, too, you know.'

No, they bloody haven't! He took a long look at the woman, if only to assure himself that she wasn't related to Eddie Arnold in some way. His wife, perhaps? He couldn't be sure. Peter had never met so many uniformly rude people in his life. What was wrong with the locals? Their lives were supposed to be serene. He began to wonder if the heavy metals swirling around the environment had affected their personalities in an adverse way.

He was about to fire a retort when she turned away and hurled the ball straight into the creek. He watched the dog jump into the murk, retrieve the ball and, when she bent down to pick the ball up, the dog licked the woman's face energetically. As he watched, he could only hope that some of the toxins had seeped into both of them.

He was on the climb towards home a few minutes later, past the spot where Nick Sutcliffe had come to grief, and past the double- and triple-storey mansions that lined the esplanade, when a thought suddenly came to mind. He paused and looked around. All these houses had CCTV cameras. Most of the cameras were set up to give a view of a gate or a front door, but a few were pointed towards the road.

Although they probably didn't know it, someone must have recorded the accident. The footage would either confirm the police investigator's theories that it was a single-car accident, or it would blow them out of the water entirely. Either way, it was definitely worth researching further. He had meant to visit Katherine Sutcliffe for a while, but he kept putting it off. Once he'd concluded his own research, there might be a reason for that visit after all.

Rhiannon turned up again in the early hours of the following morning. He felt as if his head had barely scraped the pillowcase, when he became aware of a presence: her perfume had charged through the bedroom door a good ten seconds before she did.

After his last altercation with Arnold, he had given Rhiannon his front-door key as a precaution, but not for her to gain entry every time she felt like making a booty call. He had briefly thought of giving his key to Mimi instead, so she could keep an eye on the place in his absence, and as insurance against a lingering death if he ever needed her. The possibility of her using it other than for its intended purpose, and catching him in a compromising situation, became too frightening a thought, and so he reconsidered. Besides, over the last few weeks, Rhiannon had become far closer to him in all respects.

But he was exhausted. And he was regretting having cut a spare key.

He peered at Rhiannon through the dimness. She had already slipped out of her red Nikes, low-cut socks, action-back top and lycra leggings, and she stood at the end of his bed wearing only her G-string.

'I'm coming, ready or not,' she cried, adding the G-string to the mound of clothes. Then she peeled back the doona, snuggled next to him and felt his crotch. 'Not ready!' she announced and dived down until, eventually, his fatigue dissipated.

They had just assumed her favourite position when someone cleared their throat. Twice. It sounded too baritone to be Rhiannon, and Peter was fairly sure he hadn't said anything. It also sounded very close.

Rhiannon seemed oblivious to the noise, overwhelmed by her own squeals voiced in time with her pitching and rolling. Her eyes were shut, she was savouring the moment. He on the other hand was quickly losing momentum. He peeked around her flying pony-tail in the direction of the noise, just before he sat up and heaved Rhiannon away and off the bed.

'Oh god!' he cried, tugging at the discarded doona.

She turned to look at what he was seeing. 'Andre,' she said, 'is that you?'

'Oh, god, Andre! I'm so sorry, mate!' Peter hadn't just lost the urge, he was sure that his testes had retracted all the way back into his abdomen. He leapt up and covered what was left of his geni-tals with a sheet, while Rhiannon lay unconcerned on the floor. He babbled, 'I was asleep when she barged in and jumped on top of me. I...I...I thought I was just having a wet dream!'

'No, no,' said Andre with a chuckle. 'It's fine. Don't let me stop you.'

'Well past that point, I'm afraid,' Peter replied. 'But how?'

'The door was unlocked; I let myself in.' He read Peter's surprise and added, 'I spotted Rhi-Rhi running, and I thought I'd try to catch up with her. Then... Well, all I'll say about it is that curtains might be a good idea, mate.' He sat at the end of the bed and continued, 'We're not prudes on the coast. I mean, you've heard of Wednesday night's all-you-can-eat buffet at the yacht club, haven't you?'

'No...'

'All right, then. Let me explain. Couples night. Every Wednesday at six-thirty. Keys in the dish. I believe it's been a coastal staple for decades. A bit old-fashioned, but we figured that if it was good enough for the mayor and the coast's premier developer, it was good enough for us.'

Rhiannon was up and dressing. She shook her head. 'But we haven't done that in years, hon, you know that.' She turned to Peter, adding, 'We gave it up years ago, in favour of monogamy. And we all know how that went! These days, we're far more discreet.'

'I guess so. More one-on-one. Although we did keep some candid snaps as—let's say—mementos. Just don't ask us how we got them.' Andre laughed at the thought.

Peter had moved past embarrassment. He was sniffing out a story. 'Anyone in particular?'

'Oh, you know, the local celebs and pollies. But it was before they were really famous.'

'Any chance I could get a hold of those photos?'

'You dirty bastard!'

'Not for my personal use, Andre. I'm thinking as a journo.'

Andre placed his hand on his hip. 'I don't know, mate...'

'Don't tell me you're friends with Harrison and Goldsmith.'

'No, no, not at all.' He paused, deep in thought. 'Look, to be honest, I do have a bit of an axe to grind with Becs and Brian; they may have forgotten about it, but I haven't. Let's say it was a past negotiation gone sour. But I don't understand what the big deal is: the photos are a little dated.'

'Well, if they've crossed you, I bet they've crossed many, many others. You said you have an axe to grind? Surely, you're not beyond shoving a little well-deserved humiliation their way, are you?'

'No, but...' He sucked his teeth.

Peter resumed. 'I'm offering you a generous helping of schadenfreude. An exposé. I can see the splash: "Partner Swapping on the

Coast". Complete with saucy pics, regardless of whether they're dated or not. Call it revenge served icy cold. It sells itself, doesn't it?'

Andre chuckled. 'And I suppose you'd pixelate the faces, to protect the guilt-ridden?'

'Naturally.'

'Hmm. Could be fun. Plus, the publicity might bring in some fresh blood.' He stroked the five o'clock shadow on his chin while he thought. 'It almost makes me hungry for that Wednesday night buffet again. I'll pop around with the memory stick later.'

Rhiannon was lacing up her left shoe when Peter asked her, 'So, what is it with the dawnbusters?'

'Nothing, really,' she replied, slipping on her right shoe, 'except that I thought it would be better for you. It's just that older men find it easier to have sex in the morning,' she said candidly, 'after a good night's sleep.'

His mouth was still agape when Andre added, 'So, you're finding it hard to get hard, eh? Well, I have a tip for you, old mate. Ever since I moved on from Rhi-Rhi, I've been doing some research of my own.'

Rhiannon bristled. 'Is that what you call what you're doing with that little bitch assistant of yours?'

Peter grinned. *For two people who like to sleep around, they still harbour a lot of resentment.*

'Ooh, nasty. So, not quite over the ole Andre yet, hey, Rhi?'

His words smarted. She kept quiet.

He put his hands on his hips and smirked. 'Well, here's my top tip, Pete, and it's better than popping pills: stop fucking middle-aged women like Rhi. Simple as. That's all. That's it.'

Her face darkened. Peter glanced around for anything she could use as a weapon.

Andre continued unabated. 'In my experience,' he said, smiling, 'it's true. Women in their twenties are prime. Don't listen to anything anyone else tells you. You don't need horny goat weed or Viagra; here's my top tip: if you halve the age, you'll more than double the sex.'

With that, Rhiannon let out a blood-curdling shriek and lunged at Andre. He had already side-stepped her and was heading for the door, with her in pursuit. Still swaddled in his doona on the edge of his bed, Peter heard the front door swing open and bang shut so powerfully that it made the bedroom wall shudder.

He shook his head and chuckled. *And people wonder why I've never married!*

That afternoon, he and Misha went doorknocking. They began at opposite ends of the esplanade, their mission being to catch at least one of the householders at home, and somehow persuade them to check their CCTV recordings on the night that Nick Sutcliffe came to grief, and then be willing to share them.

In all likelihood, their cold-calls would lead to more doorstep interviews—every tabloid reporter's stock-in-trade—and a skill Misha needed to hone if she was going to enjoy career longevity.

'Don't take no for an answer,' he told her.

She was unfazed; life had already given her the thick skin that had to go along with it.

Atypically, Peter began at his end by telling the absolute truth— he was an award-winning investigative journalist; he was looking into the supposed suicide of the local real estate agent, with a view to uncovering the incompetency-slash-corruption of the local police.

Can you help Nick Sutcliffe's widow and children, please?

It began badly.

Aside from being disinterested in everything he had to say, nobody seemed concerned in uncovering the truth or exposing injustice on their doorstep. In fact, nobody wanted to get involved.

Then it became worse than that. His persistence provoked a response.

'It's scum like you who ruin it for everyone. One minute we're living in paradise, and the next you've turned it into a warzone with your lies and scaremongering. We're not stupid, you know; bad news sells, fear sells, but there's no money in good news. And what if we need the police one day? Honest, law-abiding people like us rely on the police. Not like you, you don't care whose lives you destroy, as long as you make money off it. So, no, you can bugger off.'

What is wrong with you people? You all live in your own, selfish, fucked-up little paradise.

But there was no use arguing. Some people were beyond logic.

He met up with Misha a little over halfway along the road, outside a much-extended Californian bungalow named 'San Remo'. Set higher than its neighbours, it enjoyed expansive views of the esplanade and had three cameras along its frontage. If they'd been looking, the occupants would have had a perfect view of what happened that night. Hopefully a recording of it still existed, possibly from multiple angles.

They stood outside the gate of the house buzzing the intercom and waiting patiently, but there was no answer. There wasn't even a polite refusal.

'Looks like nobody wants to talk to me today,' Misha remarked. 'Or maybe they're just not home.'

He nodded. 'Maybe. Don't beat yourself up, Misha; I didn't have any luck either.' He looked up at the windows. The curtains were drawn back. What he could see of the grounds appeared tidy, but there was no sign of life.

He added, 'Perhaps, you can try again later.'

He left her to make her own way back to his house—at her insistence—while he paid Katherine Sutcliffe a visit. He found her on her way out, keys in hand, wearing dark glasses and activewear.

'I can see you're off to the gym,' he said, 'so I won't keep you long.'

She seemed confused. 'No, I'm going to the shops, actually.' She glanced at her clothes and smirked. 'Oh, you mean this?' She waved her hand over her outfit. 'Oh no, I wear this cos it's comfortable. It makes me feel cute and sexy.'

Cute and sexy were evidently a matter of opinion. He continued, 'I just wanted to ask you one more thing about the night of Nick's accident.'

She looked abruptly annoyed. 'But I've told you everything I can remember. I'm really, really busy and I'm running late.'

'For the shops? This won't take long, Katherine, I promise.'

'I'm sorry, Peter, I can't talk to you about that night; there's nothing more for me to say.'

'Can't or won't? Someone told you not to speak to me, didn't they? You've been threatened?'

'No, no,' she replied.

He could tell it was a lie. She turned her back to him and walked away.

He followed her. 'But I just wanted to ask you about the CCTV footage of the crash, that's all.'

She spun about and sighed. 'What CCTV footage?'

'Well, there must have been some CCTV footage of that night. It would be pretty compelling evidence of what actually happened. What did the police tell you?'

She scanned the garden, as if to reassure herself that no one else was around. 'Sergeant Moylan said they'd checked it out, but there wasn't any. He said there aren't any cameras along that stretch of road.'

'Right.'

'He said there was nothing: no witnesses, no CCTV, nothing.' She began tapping her foot. 'It was horrible and I'm making peace with my fate. I'm getting professional help to pick up the pieces and start again. Now, I really have to go.'

'Yes, of course, we'll talk again when it's more convenient. Thanks, Katherine.'

'No, we won't. It's better for both of us if you don't come over again, okay? I'm sorry, but I've said all I have to say. The case is closed. I've finally accepted the fact that Nick killed himself and I really don't want to talk to you or anyone else about him ever again.'

He wasn't about to let her slam the door on his investigation. 'Right. But Katherine…'

'You're not hearing me, Peter.'

'But I can help you, Katherine.' His face softened. 'Look, I can see you're frightened. I hear what you're saying but I don't believe you and neither do you. We both know Nick didn't just kill himself. Something drove him off that road and I'm not going to stop asking questions until I find out what happened. Exposing the truth will protect you.'

She exhaled loudly. 'Really? And how will it do that exactly?'

He was still formulating his reply when she bellowed, 'Enough! Please! Enough!' Then she unlocked her car and climbed in.

Chapter Thirty-Two

Meeting Sadie Taylor

Sadie Taylor turned the nose of her Citroen CV2 into the driveway at McDonald's. There being so very little car beyond the nose, the rest of it followed quickly. She pulled up a fair distance from the main door, noting that all the car parking spaces closer to the entrance were already occupied. Even the disabled spaces were taken. Not that it mattered. She always tried not to use her disability as a reason to claim priority parking unless she absolutely had to. She was a little early and courtesy of the balmy weather, her arthritis wasn't crippling her anyway, so she left her walking stick sitting on the passenger seat.

As she shuffled towards the door, she counted the rows—she had left her car on the far right of the carpark, three rows back. The heat had brought the tourists down to the coast, and it seemed that most of the stragglers were enjoying a fast-food meal before heading home. The drive-through lane was choked with cars, and on the other side of the glass, she observed that many of the dine-in tables were occupied by people with salt-matted hair and furious sunburn.

Her hip was starting to sting, not enough to require her stick, but enough to make her wince. Just then, a car began reversing out of one of the disabled spots and she wondered whether she should walk back and move her car into it. She was still wondering when a black BMW pulled into it and screeched to a stop. As she passed the car, she scrutinised the tinted windows. She noticed that the car didn't display a disability sticker. She frowned. The able-bodied claiming parking that they had no right to, was among her pet peeves.

A man climbed out of the BMW, hooded and well-muscled. She turned to glare at him.

'You can't park there,' she said. 'It's a disabled spot.'

He ignored her.

'You need to move your car,' she continued. When he still didn't respond, she added, 'Oi! You! I'm talking to you!'

Finally he looked. 'What's it to you, bitch?'

'Actually, quite a lot. I have a disability, and I often miss out on a park that should be rightfully mine, because of inconsiderate people like you. You should be ashamed of yourself.'

He looked her up and down. She couldn't tell if he was angry or amused. He replied, 'Actually, I'm not. Not that I owe you an explanation, bitch, but so what that you're disabled? Like I fucking care. I identify as disabled, bitch! So, stick that up your ugly cunt!' And then he pushed past her.

Sadie was left open-mouthed. Since when had people become so uncaring and arbitrarily angry? Her mind turned to the obscenity scrawled on her henhouse; she had to steady herself on a pillar outside the entrance. If she hadn't been meeting Peter, she would have skulked back to her car and driven away. But she couldn't. She walked towards a side entrance instead and waited until the man returned to his car. Then she stepped in and looked around for Peter.

She'd googled him when she first read his article, so she knew what he looked like; she hoped he hadn't changed much since the photos were taken. The bright, artificial light and busy decor dazzled her. She noticed a handful of men of a certain age, who might or might not have been him, but none of them seemed to be waiting for her, so she discounted each of them and went to the counter instead.

The light and decor had also affected her appetite. She stood in front of the menu for ages, calculating calories and nutritional values. She would have loved to have ordered a burger, except that Paula was an ovo-vegetarian, and she'd promised to adhere to Paula's ideals as well. She supposed she could cheat, except that Paula would probably smell the meat seeping from her pores. She ordered a frozen diet beverage instead, sat down at an empty table and waited.

At two minutes to ten, Peter arrived. He spotted her immediately—what was the likelihood that there would be two pink-haired, matronly women wearing tie-dyed cheesecloth outfits at that time of night?

'Sadie?' he asked.

'Oh yes, Peter. Thank you for coming. Please sit down. Can I get you something?'

'Perhaps later.'

'I've read all about you,' she began, 'and your legacy is pretty impressive.'

'Well, I'm not dead yet.' He sniggered. 'Although that's not from lack of trying.'

She smiled uncertainly and cleared her throat. 'I wanted to tell you that you've hit a raw nerve with that thing you wrote about farmers and rubbish dumping. The council execs are absolutely livid about your article.'

'Yes, well, I did offer them the chance to comment before it was off stone.'

'And of course they didn't take you up on that. They're not likely to do anything about it anyway, beyond shooting the messenger. You can expect to receive a lot of flak from this. Pollution is a shameful secret most locals refuse to acknowledge, because they're scared it'll drive away the tourist dollars and push down property values, so don't think for a moment that you'll be thanked by anyone for exposing it.'

'I'm not looking for thanks, Sadie: that's not why I do what I do. I'm looking for the truth and I think you can help me find it.'

'I've been rattling on about the dangers of dumping for ages, but I'm a bit too alternative for most people to bother with.'

'So how do you get elected then? If you're seen as a wacko, I mean?'

'I didn't say "wacko", did I? Is that how you see me?'

He blushed. 'No, of course not. I thought you meant...'

'I'm elected because I have a huge local profile: I was a teacher at the local school, and I have a social conscience. My partner has a counselling practice, and she's well-known in the community as well. Plus, I have a big LGBTQ following. In Council, I was always seen as the enforcer: I was the one to keep the others in line. I made people feel like they had an ally in Council.'

'And now?'

'Well, I used to keep the others in line, but sadly not anymore. Something's gone awry. I can't keep up with all the land rezoning, the planning applications and the by-law changes. These days, I never seem to see the planning applications until after they're approved.'

'You think there's a connection between planning approvals and rubbish dumping?'

'I think so. I feel for the farmers forced off the land by thugs whose only motivation is money.'

'You obviously suspect that there's corruption in the ranks. Do you think someone's being paid off?'

'I don't *think* they're paid off, I *know* so. I suspect that this goes higher than anyone realises and involves a lot more people. I'm trying to work out who, how, what for and how much. There has to be a paper trail. Once I have that, I want you to make it public.'

'Not a problem. Are you willing to stand by what you're telling me?'

'I can't be quoted.'

'Okay, but I'll need to see what else you find before I commit not to quote you. I need people to stand up for their ideals in public, and not just espouse them privately. If no one's willing to go on the record, it's a non-story. I'll hold off doing anything until you can give me more; you have my word on that. As long as you bring me some hard evidence to back up what you're telling me, then I won't need to quote you.'

She repeated, 'No matter what, I can't be quoted. You'll have to protect me.'

He nodded. 'I always protect my sources.'

'I hope so.' She checked her watch. 'What with tonight's meeting and everything else the day's brought me, I'm all talked out. I really need to go now.' She stood up abruptly and walked towards the exit without another word. He followed her out a few seconds later.

She waited for him beyond the automatic doors. 'This place was a haven for wildlife and beachcombers once, you know. People were kind and generous. It's changed, and not in a good way. I don't see any of that kindness or generosity anymore.'

He stood next to her, gazed out at the cars and said, 'No. I lived in London and San Francisco, and I found people to be friendlier there than they are here. I thought the reality would be consistent with the name, but I've discovered a lot of discord here but very little serenity. That's been my greatest disappointment.'

'You know why that is, don't you, Peter?'

He shook his head.

'The locals are all tired from treading water. The cheap-as-chips beach shacks are long gone. They work eighteen-hour days and never truly interact with their children. They're up to their eyebrows in debt that they can't service and they're desperate to maintain a lifestyle they can't afford. That would make even the nicest person cranky. And suspicious. And probably prone to corruption. I might understand it, but I don't condone it.'

'Yes, I've been told that about the Tyne Coast before; it plays a bit like a Joni Mitchell song. I just wish I'd met this place and its people thirty years ago.' He sighed. 'Thank you for seeing me tonight, Sadie. I'm hoping that we can help each other out. Even if no one else gives a shit about Serenity Bay, at least we do. I'm confident that the powers-that-be won't be able to bury their heads in the sand once we're done with them.'

'I hope so, Peter. I'll give it my best shot.'

'And so will I. Call me anytime. For anything.'

'Of course. And you, too.' She turned and moved away.

She was gazing at her spearmint CV-2 as she scuffled along the rows of cars. Its duco was chalky after decades by the sea and pock-marked by umpteen dings. All the years she'd owned it, her Citroen had never sparkled but it had served her well. She had to face facts: it didn't have a lot of life left. She'd let the CEO know tomorrow that she was going to take up the offer of a Council vehicle, but that it had to be electric. Paula's relationship with her car had never been smooth, so she would be pleased about that. The change would be a monumental leap forward for them both.

***

Peter watched her as she stepped out to cross the last aisle. He didn't know whether she was distracted by a sudden horn blast at the other end of the carpark (it made him turn his head that way too) but, by the time he looked back, Sadie was lying face down, sprawled across the asphalt. Her body was skewed, not like someone who had fainted or tripped, and she wasn't moving. He scoured the carpark. A girl nearby had already taken out her phone and was calling for an ambulance. He heard her say that she hadn't seen what happened exactly, but she thought the woman had been hit by a car.

When he saw a black BMW driving towards the exit at speed, Peter didn't hesitate. He ran to his car, clambered in, and chased after it.

No matter how hard he pushed, he was never in the race.

Following the pursuit, he arrived home a little after eleven. He had lost sight of the BMW on the highway, but he had managed to record the first four characters of its numberplate and he was going to sleep on whether he should go to the police with them. If all Sadie had suffered was a graze and a bit of a shock, he mightn't bother. It wasn't as if the perpetrator would be likely to face a penalty beyond a wrist slap in that case, so why would he choose to complicate his life for no benefit?

He rang the local hospitals for an update on her condition, but nobody was keen to share information at that time of night. He gleaned that the ambulance had taken her to the district public hospital and that a media statement was pending. He had no luck calling the nurses station to find out how she was ahead of the statement. It wasn't just that he wanted to secure a scoop, he was genuinely concerned about her. She was a funny old chook, but her heart was absolutely in the right place, and he wanted to help her. It distressed him that he didn't know if she was alive or dead.

By midnight the news had broken: the police together with the hospital's liaison officer had updated the media pages on their websites. Tyne Coast Councillor Sadie Taylor was in a critical condition. The police called for witnesses.

He knew that he had to tell the police what he'd seen; the incident had escalated to Crimestoppers. Since it was no longer local, he wouldn't need to deal with the likes of Moylan and his cronies. Plus, there would undoubtedly be CCTV footage of his meeting with Sadie which the police would view, and he figured that it would be far better if he went to the police, rather than the reverse. As tired as he was, he climbed into his car, drove down to the nearest twenty-four-hour station and gave a statement.

On his way home, he went past the hospital but, just as before, no one was talking. When he was leaving, a constable barely out of her teens arrived in the company of an older woman. The older woman, dishevelled and weeping and still dressed in her dressing gown and slippers, leaned heavily on the young constable. On a hunch, Peter followed them back through the main door. He passed them in the lobby unnoticed, ducking into the relatives' waiting room ahead of them. There, he slipped off his shoes, slumped on the sofa with his eyes shut and threw an open magazine on his lap. He wanted to look as if he'd been there most of the night.

The constable and the woman entered the room a couple of minutes later. The constable spoke at the woman continually. It was a very loud, one-sided conversation, as if the woman was both senile and hard of hearing, and not simply crippled by grief and concern. Peter listened. He put it down to the ignorance of youth, bordering on ageism. He heard her call the woman 'Paula' once and 'dear' twice and his skin crawled. He rarely campaigned for political correctness in public, but ageism, it seemed to him, was the last popularly tolerated form of discrimination. The older he became the more it irked him. He bit his lip; he had to work very hard to remain silent.

'I'll ask the nurses to update you on Sadie's condition in a moment,' said the constable. 'In the meantime, shall I get you a nice cup of tea?' She settled Paula on a chair and hurried down the corridor.

A little later, he overheard that Sadie had suffered significant internal injuries. She had been prepped for surgery, and she'd be operated on to stop the bleeding. The doctors couldn't say much; Sadie had been weakened by blood loss and had had to be resuscitated once, but they were still hopeful.

Paula's howls were Peter's cue to get up and go home.

CHAPTER THIRTY-THREE

Sexposed!

Andre de Wold was as good as his word. He left the memory stick on the doorstep in a plastic sleeve for Peter to find when he rose the following morning. Happily, there hadn't been any dawn break-ins by either Rhiannon or Andre.

Peter showered with Sadie on his mind, but a quick check disclosed that there hadn't been an official update on her condition. He towelled off his exhaustion, pulled on shorts and a t-shirt and settled at his desk with a double-strength espresso. He turned the memory stick over between his fingers a few times before he finally inserted it into his laptop. Misha arrived a few minutes later, made herself an espresso and then floated above him as he scrolled through the files. There were so many to view, he hardly knew where to start.

Some of the photos featured people he didn't recognise; he'd lavish more attention on them later. Click after click, Andre's photos were an embarrassment of rich people. Like the proverbial child in the candy shop, Peter's eyes widened: he wanted to glimpse everything at once. Many of the photos featured Goldsmith and Harrison, occasionally full-face and mostly full-frontal. They were a little dated—which was probably to Goldsmith's and Harrison's benefit—and some of them (especially those with props and costumes) were ridiculous enough to make Peter and Misha howl with laughter.

Oh, you two! Naughty, naughty! You really were up for anything, weren't you?

Peter still had contacts in the tabloid press, although nowadays they weren't printing hard copies for sale at the local newsagency.

These days everything was electronic. He'd already checked out the most popular one, the online sleaze-blog *Sexposed and Scandalicious*, but the subscription he had bought when he'd first arrived in Serenity Bay had run out. He renewed it grudgingly.

Thanks to Woody Turnbull, the spirit of the *Truth* lived on in his blog. He dished the dirt on sporting celebrities, television personalities and public figures, mostly (but not exclusively) Australian. Woody had a half million followers, and his scandal stories were regularly picked up by the major celebrity magazines and television networks. Peter was confident that Woody would accept his photos of Goldsmith and Harrison. After all, Woody still owed him money for all the times he had covered his tab when he'd been caught short at the pub.

Peter made the call.

Woody listened intently for a while. 'Don't know mate,' he replied. 'I mean, they're not exactly huge on the celebrity radar, are they? A developer shagging a mayor might not happen often, but is it really *Scandalicious* material?'

'It's not just that though, Woody, is it? It's the coast elite meeting up weekly for a root. That's what makes the developer and mayor participation especially newsworthy.'

'Still not convinced.'

'Not convinced? Give me a break, Woody… You're not as much fun now that you're old and sober.' He thought for a moment. 'Okay, how about this: Goldsmith is married to Adriana Balloch,' he shot back, 'and she was in a trashy reality show set in Brighton.'

Woody didn't reply immediately. 'She was one of the snobby bitches in the *Billionaire Babes: Rich and Bitchy*, wasn't she? Now, you see, I can work with that. You should have mentioned it first, mate. Send it through now and I'll have it online by tomorrow.'

'The photos are a little risqué,' said Peter, 'be warned.'

'The more risqué the better,' Woody said, laughing. 'I don't do demure and well-dressed here. If it's picked up by the mags, they'll pixelate the important bits. I call it pathetic but that's how they work. And I expect it will go nationwide, with Balloch involved. She has a national profile. That bitch lives on publicity but she doesn't like the bad publicity.' He guffawed. 'I'll take whatever you've got.'

'I'm on a roll, Woody,' he replied. 'Just don't use my real name. These people are the vindictive types. Call me "Super Sex Sleuth".'

'Hmm, like the old days, hey? They were the halcyon days. The halcyon days… If you could get some reaction snaps from Bitch-face Balloch, that would be great. I can run it for a few days.'

'You know me,' said Peter, 'I'll be getting in the nuts and guts of it.'

'You were always the best muck-raker in the business.'

'No past tense, Woody,' he snapped back. 'I am the best in the business.' He hung up the phone. 'We've fired the first bullet, and now we wait for the blowback.'

'And the dumping story? Where's that at?' asked Misha. 'That's the real headline, isn't it? This one is just titillating gossip.'

'Of course, it is. We're shaking them up. The dumping story's live.'

'And then there's the twins.'

'Yes, the Schneiders; I haven't forgotten. Balloch and the nursing home. By the time I finish with them, Balloch and the rest of them will wish they were never born.' He turned to face his computer screen again. 'Let's get this to Woody now, and we'll work through the rest of them later.'

Once he was done revising the article to meet Woody Turnbull's requirements, he turned his attention to Rick Burgess's report. He told Misha, 'This is too important for a single, stand-alone piece. I could write an entire book on this.'

'Well then, maybe you should,' she replied.

'Hmm. I think I'll test the waters first. I have a mate who's well connected—an old editor of mine. He's trustworthy and he knows a thing or two about trading words for wealth. I'll have to introduce you to him one day; he's a good pal to have. I'll send him a draft of what I've written so far, and maybe he'll be able to do something with it. Let's see what he thinks.'

'Good luck!' Misha responded, while Peter began to search his contacts list.

The calls began early the following day. Peter rolled over in his bed and answered the phone, 'Yeah, whoever you are, you realise it's only six, don't you?'

He heard an asthmatic chuckle on the other end. It was enough for him to recognise the caller. *Henry Crofter.* 'Crofty!' he exclaimed. 'It's early for you, mate. Did you shit the bed, or has time finally caught up with you? Have you finally got prostate problems?'

'Ha ha, neither actually. Something must be wrong with your clock: it's gone seven. I thought you'd be out of bed already having your three beers and a shag for breakfast,' Henry Crofter replied. 'My word, you've changed.'

'It's called ageing, mate,' Peter retorted. 'Why are you ringing me at this time? Let me guess, it's about the dumping story I sent you. Either good or bad. By the sound of your voice, I detect it's pretty positive.'

'Well, yes, it's good news. And it's good news because I really went out on a limb for you this time. Possibly even great news because I put my fucking reputation on the line for you.'

'You're a bloody saint, Crofty. In fact, you're the patron saint of hacks,' he returned, 'but that's nothing less than I expected. So, it's going into the paper? And I'm hoping not buried in the back pages or I won't be happy.'

'Absolutely not, Clancy. It's going in the weekend edition as a feature. What's not to love about illegal dumping?'

'So, my story will be more than a prelude for others?' he asked.

'You mean as a prelude for someone else to run with? No way, it's *the* story. For fuck's sake,' he continued, 'it's the only piece I've ever read that has clear evidence to back it up and scientific analysis of the toxic waste that's being dumped. It's nothing short of genius, mate. You show how dangerous this dumping is to human health. This story is going to unleash hell. I'd hate to be swimming anywhere near that beach.'

'That's what I wanted to achieve. But it goes a lot further than just dumping and pollution. There's high- and low-level bribery, and strongarm tactics used on vulnerable people. I want you to run another story about the background of the people doing it.'

'What else have you got?' he asked.

Peter glanced at his whiteboard. 'The low-life family running the dump has links to some very shady characters. I'll send you photos of them, as well as the men riding choppers who visit them regularly. I've been away so long that I don't know who the villains are these days, but maybe you'll recognise them. Then there's the developer and the local council. Let's say the developer and the mayor are very cosy. I've already done an exposé for *Scandalicious*. Caught on camera with their pants down. That's a high-profile, very married mayor with aspirations to a lofty political office, by the way.'

'You sent it to Woody Turnbull's virtual rag in the sky? Well, I hope you got him to pay you for it up front.' He tut-tutted. 'Still love those exposés, don't you? I always thought you got your jollies doing that stuff. I certainly miss those days of seeing photos of the rich and famous doing kinky things. And now you're giving me sex and corruption in very low places. Love it. Very tasty, may I say.'

'I'm not doing it just for the jollies. It's all part of my plan. I'm unravelling them one thread at a time.'

'Let's hope they don't decide to turn nasty on you,' he rejoined. 'You've had underworld types baying for your blood in the past. Every time you cross them, the target on your back gets just that little bit bigger and just that little bit brighter. I thought you might have learnt your lesson by now.'

'You know I was never good at remembering my lessons.'

'Yeah, well, I hope you'll be able send me more stuff before they come for you.' Crofty chuckled. 'All jokes aside, this piece has major implications. The public will lose their shit when they read this. The government is going to be highly embarrassed. They can't sit on their hands with their fingers up their arseholes, hoping it will go away. It can't go away if toxic waste is being emptied into the sea near a popular beach.'

'That's exactly what I was aiming for,' Peter returned dryly. 'And maybe I'll get the prize. A Walkley Award wouldn't go astray.'

'You always wanted it and you always missed out. I know you crave recognition from your peers more than anyone else I've ever met. It would be good for you to finish your career on a high.'

'Finish my career? You're joking, right? I'm not retiring anytime soon,' he replied.

'Glad to hear that the rumourmongers got it wrong, then. You just keep digging up that dirt and sending it my way. So long as it's not your own grave you're digging, mate.'

'Not a chance, mate, not a chance. They'd have to get past my bodyguards first.

Crofty didn't reply at first. Eventually he said, 'That's right, Pete, you just keep telling yourself that.'

Peter put down his phone and smiled. For once, bad things were starting to happen to those who deserved it.

CHAPTER THIRTY-FOUR

Not me, not you

Adriana Balloch sat on the deck of her beach mansion enjoying an early-morning mimosa. These days, it was the only thing she found palatable for breakfast. It was part of her daily fruit allowance: freshly squeezed oranges and fermented grapes chilled to perfection. She demanded that Cora put a strawberry on the rim for added fibre. For a while she had grapefruit instead of oranges to make it even healthier, until she discovered that grapefruit interfered with her medication.

She crossed her legs and watched the languid waves roll onto her private beach as she sipped. It was her deck, on her mansion, overlooking her private beach.

Hers. Not Brian's.

By rights, everything was hers. Hers was the exertion behind the empire. Brian was an accessory, a mere handbag she carried to set off her outfit, with very little inside it.

In quiet contemplation, she remembered how she had goaded and guided him, from humble beginnings running a small real estate office in St Kilda, to building a portfolio that included seedy boarding houses, a nightclub and even a brothel. She had the glamour and the guts; at best Brian was the charming fast-talker with old friends in low places. Occasionally she wished she hadn't cut all ties to her past; the brothel had been a licence to print money. Morals didn't make money. Even with the payoffs to the police, the underworld and the local legislators, they had amassed a small fortune before very long.

Several years ago, they cashed themselves out of St Kilda and into major developments in Melbourne and along the coast. They became the power couple in Melbourne real estate. They acquired the accoutrements of wealth and style. They rubbed shoulders with celebrities and politicians. Brian and she looked like they had been born into money. They became the new establishment. St Kilda faded into memory. Their past was a textbook PR exercise in reinvention.

She turned her attention away from the sea and looked at her hands—they betrayed her true age when her face and figure did not. The legacy of coastal living were sunspots and wrinkles that even the best plastic surgeons couldn't fix. And then there were the worries, the sleepless nights, the plans and executions she couldn't share with anyone.

Octavia and Anastasia had become her latest concern. Her research had determined that she was their last remaining relative, but simply waiting for them to die seemed like a monumental waste of time. She'd put the demented old cows away and everything was moving along sweetly. That was until the nursing home manager told her that they'd recently had two visitors. It was lamentable that the manager had lacked the insight to let her know straightaway, but Adriana had learned the visitors' names. They were false, of course, and that was where the trail ended. Unfortunately, the CCTV recordings were only kept for a month. She changed managers and protocols immediately, but she was left with a burning question: who would be interested in the twins and why?

She took the strawberry off the glass and pressed it to her lips, but it was sour, so she threw it away in disgust. Heads would roll over it; how dare Cora serve her substandard fruit! Yes, she was demanding, but so what if she demanded perfection? She deserved no less.

Thinking about the twins always put her in a foul mood. How she despised the Schneiders and the mock *Schwarzwaldhaus* in which they were raised. And what a nuisance having to deal with the useless wilderness dedicated to their long-dead mother. Soon there would be houses there as far as the eye could see. Soon the shoe would be on the other foot, wouldn't it?

Brian retained some of his old associates for the occasional stalled negotiation. According to him, they helped with waste management, union talks and security. Adriana preferred not to acquaint herself with such people, but she knew who they were, their history and what they were capable of. As long as she and the public remained blissfully ignorant of their deeds, she was happy with the arrangement. One day she'd consign them to the past. For the time being it appeared she might need them.

The Schneiders' scrubby bush was hers for the subdividing. Estimated worth once developed, forty million dollars.

At least.

Hers. Not Brian's.

The two visitors, no matter who they were, could never keep her from gaining what was rightfully hers. Brian's associates would see to that.

She picked up a notebook and pen that lay by the side of her chair and opened the book to the first page. She ran her fingers over the smooth white paper, bent the spine back a little, removed the cap from her Meisterstück pen and wrote: *My Glittering Path to Success by Adriana Balloch.* And then she paused.

She owed it to the world to write about herself. She was such a long way from her beginnings. Never in her wildest dreams had she thought that she would star in a reality show or have an eponymous range of lingerie and perfume. She simply had to share a little of the wisdom she'd acquired along the way—but not give away too much—just enough to keep them interested. She'd share how she gloriously traded a Housing Commission house and a hand-to-mouth existence for beluga and Bollinger. How she had climbed so far above the Schneiders and every other relative who had given her family nothing, that they would have needed a Dobosnian telescope just to see her glide past.

She re-read what she had written and added, *A How-To Guide.* Money was power and prestige. The more, the better. She could do whatever she wanted. She could buy anyone and anything. She laughed aloud. They could eat the dust from her Rolls: Adriana Balloch didn't live in the wild western suburbs of Melbourne anymore.

Just then, her mobile rang. She put down her pen, closed the book and answered the phone. It was her agent, Harry Wiseman.

'Oh Harry, I'm busy now,' she lied, 'I'll call you when I'm free.'

'Don't hang up, Adriana, it's important. That prick Turnbull is up to mischief again,' he said. 'I thought he would have backed off after my last threat.'

'Who are you talking about, Harry?' she snapped. 'Talk sense.'

'Our friend, Woody Turnbull. You know, from the *Scandalicious* gossip site? Do I have to spell it out?'

'What now?' She grunted, picking up her glass and drinking. 'More photos of Brian and me arguing? More topless photos of me on my private beach? So what? Why do you think I got that boob job?'

'It's none of that.'

'Well, whatever it is, it's all good, raising-the-profile publicity.'

'This is far worse, Adriana.' He lowered his voice, 'It's Brian...'

She sighed. 'What's he done now?'

'...and you.' He hesitated. 'It's Brian and Rebecca Harrison. And you. You've heard of the Philipson Point Yacht Club? Some tabloid scum's got pics and sold them to Woody Turnbull. Photos of you... having...'

'Having what? A meal at the restaurant? Doing beach yoga? Or were we fucking, Harry?' she snapped back.

'The latter.'

'Impossible. I never... Not with them.'

'Not all of you together. But the two of them, as well as each of you...and others...in very embarrassing circumstances... I'll send a couple through now for you to look at.'

There was a disconcerting silence.

'You still there? You all right, Adriana?' he asked. 'Are you... crying?'

'Of course, I'm not crying, moron. Crying is for children and piss-weak wimps,' she replied angrily. 'Look, I haven't had anything to do with the yacht club set in years. Just tell me where these photos came from and who took them, and I'll fucking kill the prick!'

'No need for that kind of talk, Adriana. You're not killing anyone, okay? Now, calm down.'

'No, Harry, you calm down! Of course I know Brian's still fucking that bitch: I smell her perfume whenever I come home. You're well aware that we have an open marriage—have done for years. We always said, as long as we don't go around broadcasting our conquests, anything goes.'

'So, what sort of denial do you want me to issue when the mags start getting onto it?' he asked. 'You and Brian, you're not calling it quits, are you?'

'Of course not. Or at least, not yet. We'll deny everything. It's not me, say someone's doctored the photos, put my head on someone else's body. Or we'll say there's a certain resemblance, but it's not me. Meanwhile, I'll have a frank discussion with Brian and that bitch. Set things straight. Get our game faces on. Make bloody certain that this is as bad as it gets.' She was thinking aloud, 'Or maybe we can have a photo published of me now and use it as a comparison shot, highlighting all of the differences to prove it's not me, and demanding a retraction and an apology from Turnbull.'

'Is that wise?' he replied, 'I mean, you've had a bit of work done on yourself since the photos were taken years back. Everyone knows it. They won't be fooled. Sometimes the less said, the better.'

'Really? Next you'll be suggesting we release a sex tape.'

'Well, it might not hurt… And what about Brian's starring role in the photos? What do you want to say about that?'

'Deny that, too.'

'Denying everything might make it all the more plausible that the photos really are of the three of you.'

'Then, I don't fucking know. Isn't this why I employ you? Do your job, or is that too much to ask?'

'My job isn't to protect Brian, or to spin your car-crash of a marriage. I manage your career, Adriana. I get you gigs.'

'And I would starve if I had to survive on those gigs alone. I make more money developing property in a week than I earn as a celebrity in a year. What Brian and I do is important business, Harry,' she replied, 'especially at the moment. I'm meeting Brian and Rebecca at twelve at The Brass Monkey for lunch to discuss the land reserve development. This development is the only thing that matters right now. It must go through. We can't afford a scandal.

Your job is to deny everything, and I'll make sure he says nothing and keeps his dick in his daks.'

She smiled at the thought of how he and Rebecca would react at the news. She wasn't going to be the shamed wife. No fucking way. She had the upper hand. She was in control. She was the wife carrying the flame-thrower.

She finished her mimosa and stood up in preparation to go back inside to bathe and dress. She looked out again at the bay and her private beach and exploded. She dropped her glass. It shattered in all directions. She ran to the balcony railing.

'Get the fuck off my private beach, you moron. Can't you read? I'm getting security if you don't get off!' she bellowed at a man standing a few metres below her. The man heard her and responded by raising his middle finger.

'Right,' she growled, 'if that's how you want to play the game.' She barked into the intercom, 'There's a strange man on my beach. Get rid of him. Make sure he never comes back. Break his limbs if you must.'

The man didn't linger a moment longer. He lowered his camera, turned tail, and hurried off while she was still screeching for security.

'Gotcha!' said Peter as he scurried away from Adriana's beach, disassembling his zoom lens and putting away his camera as he ran.

CHAPTER THIRTY-FIVE

It's still not me

The Brass Monkey was dark and cosy, even on the brightest day. It had two rooms, decorated eclectically with all manner of charity shop finds: one in the front by the bar (which was ear-splittingly noisy), and one at the rear by the open fireplace. Adriana had booked the one at the rear. Since it was warm outside, there was no fire and, apart from the three of them, the room was empty.

They were seated around a round table in the corner of the room and Adriana had positioned herself so that she could look straight at Brian and Rebecca simultaneously. She wanted them on the back foot immediately.

She jumped straight to the chase just after the drinks were served. Just after everyone had had their first sip. 'There's a shit-storm coming, and it involves the two of you. You've been caught. Photographed doing things you shouldn't,' she announced.

Rebecca and Brian traded looks. Rebecca turned pale.

'What do you mean? The dumping? I've sorted it,' said Brian, taking a long drink of his scotch and dry.

'You know exactly what I mean. You and she have been outed and, may I say, the photos tell the story very well.'

'I don't know how; we have the dumping covered. Nobody can connect us to that, you know that,' Rebecca declared. 'We pay people not to look. That's how we arranged it. It's working well.' She picked up her glass of Bordeaux and smiled, but Adriana noticed that her hand was shaking. It was very unlike her to be rattled by anything.

Adriana leaned forward, lowering her voice. 'Stop this bullshit. You know this has nothing to do with the dumping. You've been snapped shagging and it's hit the press.'

'What?' Rebecca spilled the wine she was drinking over her jacket and tried to blot it up with a paper napkin.

'Does that make you uncomfortable?' asked Adriana as she handed her more paper napkins. 'It should do; you should see the photos. *Developer's Dirty Deeds and the Pollie's Perversion*, I think that's what they're calling it.'

'Christ sakes, Adriana, stop it,' said Brian. 'Shut up, for goodness' sake. Don't make a scene.'

'Me? Make a scene? Wow, that's rich, coming from you.'

'It's been a stressful time. I turned to Rebecca for a little comfort, so what? We're all close friends, Adriana.' He hardened. 'Besides, if Rebecca and I go down the shitter, so do you. Remember?'

Adriana threw back her head and laughed. 'Well, it wasn't me photographed with my pants down and my cock inside her,' she replied.

'We were emotional. We got a little carried away. It's all finished now.'

She shook her head in disbelief. 'You're so fucking deluded. I know that you two have been having it off for a long time and that you're still at it every chance you get.'

'As if you can talk, Adriana,' he snapped back, 'having it off with a man half your age then pissing off to Mallorca with him so you could film an episode of your reality show there. The gossip rags were onto that too. Give me a break.'

'Okay, enough. I haven't told you everything.' She sighed. 'Look, the truth is that I'm caught up in this scandal too. There are photos of me...well... Wednesday nights at the yacht club. Someone there was indiscrete. The thing is, unlike yours, my photos have plausible deniability.' She pushed her iPad across the table. Rebecca and Brian scrolled through the photographs silently.

'Oh, God. I think I should leave,' said Rebecca eventually, reaching for her handbag.

'No, you don't. You stay,' Adriana replied. 'We all have to stay here and try to work this out.'

Brian took a drink while Adriana leaned across and touched him lightly on the arm. 'We both know that money and ambition have kept us together more than love. We're a business partnership more than anything. You two need to sort this out because there are bigger issues at hand.'

'The reserve development,' said Rebecca.

'It's all that matters. I can put your affair behind me as long as it doesn't stop this development. And these photos are already in several publications. Harry rang me this morning.'

'You think this will cause a problem?' Brian asked.

'Of course, it will,' Adriana snapped back. 'How won't it? The mayor voting in favour of her lover's development? Never mind that if they scratch hard enough, they're sure to discover that our money has been underpinning her political ambitions. Don't you think that will be regarded as a conflict of interest?'

'It will go away,' Brian replied. 'People won't care.'

'Oh, believe me, they will. And if they don't, the government will.'

'It's bloody awful,' Rebecca added. 'It's a disaster. It'll ruin my chances of pre-selection for a state seat in parliament.'

'Spoken like a true politician. What a mess! If we can't fix this, we'll have an anti-corruption investigation coming down on us. The Tyne Council could be sacked. Rebecca could be sacked and charged. We get investigated. We could all end up in jail. Get the bigger picture now, Brian? It starts to look very dark.'

'But we can't stop the photos,' said Rebecca, 'now that they're in circulation.'

Adriana replied, 'We could have a chat with Woody Turnbull. We could persuade him and anyone he's sold them to, to take them down.'

'But now that they're out there...' Rebecca looked as if she'd sucked a lemon. 'Too late, isn't it?'

'We could go to court,' said Brian.

'Court? Really? You really want to go to court over this, and draw even more attention to us?' Adriana shook her head. 'For my part, if anyone asks, I'm denying everything. I'm saying it's not me, I know nothing about it, and the same for the ones of you and Rebecca. I'll say that the photos are obvious fakes intended to discredit us, that it's a vendetta by our business rivals, and if we're pushed into a corner then we'll threaten, but not take, legal action. Meanwhile, Brian is going to ring someone to clean this all up, aren't you, Brian?'

He grabbed his mobile. 'Yes, I suppose I am.'

'Do whatever is necessary. Throw money at them, if need be,' she added. 'And you, Rebecca, you just worry about getting final approval for the reserve. We have six weeks to get everything sorted. That's the deadline. Six weeks. Keep your hands to yourself until then. And that goes for you too, Brian. We don't need any more distractions.'

'For once,' spat Rebecca, 'I happen to agree with you, Adriana. Six weeks and we're done, right? After that, I hope never to hear from you or see you again.'

Adriana sneered and went to the bar for a top-up.

Brian swivelled away from the table and made the call. His old St Kilda connections would straighten everything out for him. He settled the terms of engagement and ended the call just as Adriana returned.

'It's sorted,' he announced. 'For a price I expect you to cover, Adriana.'

'Me?' she scoffed, sipping her wine. 'Why me? She,' she said, gesturing at Rebecca, 'should be the one paying.'

He retorted, 'There's two of us and only one of her caught up in this. I'd pay for it myself, except that you hold the purse-strings. It's not my fault; you know that everything I have is tied up at the moment. Do you really want to argue about this?'

She sighed and scowled.

He took that as a sign of her agreement. After all, it was her idea to use his old mates to *clean this all up*, and if anyone bothered to trace the payment, he wanted to ensure it wouldn't lead to him. Job done, and only six weeks to go. Beyond that, he had designs of his own which he had no intention of sharing with her.

Chapter Thirty-Six

Gatecrashers

Peter was starting to feel like he was spending his life either talking on his phone or checking his phone for messages and missed calls. Where once he'd had an office in the heart of Melbourne's central business district to travel to, the camaraderie of numerous colleagues around him, a cold beer and some respite from work at the end of the day, now there was no professional connection beyond his phone and the computer he had supplied for himself.

Which sat on the desk he had supplied for himself. In the office he had supplied for himself.

News gathering had become a solitary, relentless, twenty-four–seven cycle. That meant calls in and out at all hours. He was attached to his mobile phone via an umbilical cord. It nourished him. It also threatened to wrap itself around his neck and strangle him at any moment. He had no choice in the matter; he needed it to remain a jump ahead of the hack-pack. He was determined to stay number one.

But his phone was only one of many unwelcome necessities.

It had taken him a little over a fortnight to work out that the Winnebago had become a fixture in his yard, and that Conni's glamorous handy-gals were really just six-foot two-inch bejewelled security guards with the unlikely names of Peaches and Cochineal and a wardrobe to match. Their presence around the place was a little intimidating, and the lack of privacy was becoming annoying. No more walking around in his birthday suit with the curtains open. Every visitor was secretly logged in and out, Rhiannon included. He tried to tell Conni that life was settling into a routine and that they weren't really needed, but she didn't agree. At the end of the day, he had to admit that having security around at all hours was as reassuring as it was annoying.

Arnold had ramped up the abuse to fever pitch, mostly hurled through half-open windows at speed. Visits from men on motor-cycles increased along with the noise and the smell. They arrived at all hours and loitered mainly about Arnold's shipping container, conducting conversations that Peter strained to hear. But he could never make out a full sentence. He could never get close enough to make out anything more than a few words—a fleeting sight of Arnold or one of his cohorts was enough to set off a full-blown panic attack.

The passage of trucks and clatter of unloading rubbish hadn't diminished either. He gave up telling the council. The handy-gals tried to increase the height of the perimeter fence, to shut it out but, a week later, he received a notice from Council—in its infinite stupidity—*Your fence contravenes the Building Regulations. You have 28 days to reduce the height to 1 (one) metre or you may be prosecuted.* The reason given: it was unacceptable to cut back the native bushes on the fringe of his yard. His fence simply didn't pass muster.

The only alternative was to unleash hell in print.

As a follow-up to his previous article, he composed a piece expos-ing Arnold openly. There were to be no more subtle references and veiled innuendo, he had all the evidence he needed to back him-self up. It was ironclad; he even went to the trouble of having it legalled before it hit the presses. Very late the following night, a car drove into Peter's driveway, its horn blaring. The driver spun the wheels and flashed the lights long enough to jolt him awake, set off the newly installed sensor floodlights and make the neighbours' dogs bark. The driver reversed out and sped away just as Peaches reached the door of the Winnebago.

The night after that, he awoke to a crystal-shattering shriek. Early the following morning, Peter discovered shards of glass near his front door. The security cameras were all smashed. He followed a trail of dried blood back down the driveway and stopped at the road. The blood drips continued past the crossover, but then ceased abruptly, as if the person had climbed into a car and driven away.

Cochineal was already up and clearing away the debris. She heard the crunch of Peter's shoes as he retraced his steps up the driveway and stood near her.

'It looks like someone tried to break in. Somehow, they must have caught their foot in the threads of the old mat we left at the top of the stairs, just outside your front door,' she explained. 'From there, the intruder must have slipped and fallen onto a large box of old nails and broken glass that we picked up around the yard. Naughty me! I don't know how I forgot to throw the box away.' She didn't seem at all concerned.

'So that accounts for the noise last night and all this blood. Well, that was bad luck for them, good luck for us.'

'So, it seems. I've contacted the security company and they'll be around later today to replace the cameras.'

'Do you know who's responsible? Was anything recorded before they were smashed?' he asked her.

'Not really. Whoever it was avoided the cameras, although there was one shot of someone in a hoodie holding a baseball bat. But it's impossible to make out anything.'

'Hmm. Maybe hoodies should be banned.'

'Maybe attempting to break into people's houses in the dead of night should be banned.'

He went back inside, still shaking his head. He needed an espresso to clear his head. His phone vibrated just as he switched on his coffee machine: *Ur up. Coming over. Rhi.*

For the first time, there was no excitement: all he felt was dread; the whole *thing*—whatever that was—with Rhiannon had begun to wear thin. He began to text a reply, but she beat him to it.

'Come in,' he said, opening the door to her. 'I hope this isn't... We're not...'

'Oh, no. I just wanted to see what the fracas was all about.'

'Did you hear it? Last night?'

'No, not last night. I didn't hear a thing. The house is pretty much soundproof. Why, did something happen last night?'

'An attempted break-in.'

'Hmm. That's bad. No, I meant the other night. The car… The dogs… I was skinny-dipping in the pool, and it sounded like all hell broke loose. I was going to pop around yesterday to ask you about it, but then it got crazy and I simply didn't get the chance.'

'Really.' He sighed. 'Haven't you ever noticed the noise and the smell that comes from the house across the road?'

'Not especially. And even if I did, it doesn't affect us. Sound-proof, remember?'

'Of course. Well, I think the noise you heard the other night was the bloke across the road trying to intimidate me. I think he might have tried to break in here last night.'

'And why would he do that?'

'He's running an illegal dump and I outed him. I told you what I do can be dangerous. Sometimes journos have to step on a few toes to break a story. Sometimes the owners of those toes like to break heads in return.'

Her mouth dropped open. 'An illegal dump here? That's a bit over-the-top though, isn't it? And you think someone would do that to you because of a story?'

'Well, there's a lot of money in rubbish these days. It's a favourite of organised crime.'

'What? Rubbish is?'

He could tell that she didn't believe him.

She took a deep breath and continued, 'I can see that you're okay and in the end nothing bad happened, right? Once you've lived here for a while, you'll come to understand how wonderful this place is, and why there couldn't possibly be an illegal dump here. Everyone looks after each other. There's a reason why the real estate around here is so expensive—and why everyone wants to live here, and that just wouldn't be happening if there really was an illegal dump. So, don't you worry about the neighbour across the road.'

She added, 'I mean, you're not alone in having enemies; influencers get trolled, too, you know. I've been trolled myself, personally, but I don't take everything as seriously as you do. You really need to lighten up.' She brushed his cheek with her lips. 'I'm glad that's all it was.' She glanced at her phone. 'Anyway, I've got to go.'

'Yes,' he replied, 'all right.' He didn't bother to follow her to the door. He called out, 'Be sure to keep away from those trolls.'

'You too.'

She disappeared through the door and the house fell silent. A selfie of Rhiannon in a bikini poolside, glass in hand (*Rocking my new bod on yet another perfect Serenity day*), appeared moments later on her social media.

Peter thought, *I really must stop following her; she is as one-dimensional and self-obsessed as my initial impression suggested.*

But he resolved to keep taking the sex regularly like medication, to trust it was doing him good, and not to look for anything more from her. There was no relationship to be discovered with Rhiannon, no meeting of souls, no potential for growth. It was sex as exercise. It was good for his heart-health. It was a release. Full stop.

He drank his coffee and showered. Misha arrived just over an hour later. The contrast between her and Rhiannon was stark. Misha partially fulfilled his need for a human connection, albeit strictly platonic. He knew it could never go beyond friendship; in his position, anything else would have felt too much like exploitation and it would have almost certainly endangered his relationship with Conni. Perhaps, as friends, he and Misha could still enjoy a bond of sorts. They could visit a few wineries and go to the beach.

After this story is done, I'm turning off the mobile and enjoying life.

For the rest of the day, he concentrated on peddling photos of Adriana Balloch's candid reaction to his invasion of her private beach, while Misha finished a piece she had written on Silvio's restaurant, done as a favour to Conni.

As they worked, Peter barely noticed that something was missing.

The only concession to his dumping article was that Arnold stopped operating his tip for a few days. Misha found out that the by-laws officer had finally caught up with Arnold and that he would have to answer some minor littering charges at the local Magistrates Court, for which he could be fined. A fine that Peter was convinced would remain uncollected, along with the many others he must have received over his lifetime.

'What a waste of time,' said Peter. 'The man releases toxins and heavy metals into the environment, with potential to kill, cause cancer and birth defects, and he gets charged with littering?'

'That's what I heard. I guess it's something, at least,' she replied.

'Hmm. Honestly, I wouldn't care if it was a parking fine, as long as it keeps him quiet,' he responded, although he couldn't help wondering if the silence might have been due to an injury.

On Friday night, Arnold let loose with a DJ machine. It was *doof-doof-doof* at a hundred and twenty decibels. Peter hated doof-doof music at the best of times, but it was past midnight and the noise hadn't abated. If anything, it was louder. He rang the police. The constable laughed when he gave the address, so he wasn't surprised when they didn't come.

Peter knocked on the door of the Winnebago. Cochineal answered immediately.

'You can't sleep either?' she said.

'No,' he replied. 'So, I'm about to pay a neighbourly visit.'

'You want company?'

'Sure.'

While Peaches checked out the cars parked along the street and in Arnold's driveway, Peter and Cochineal made their way towards the creek. They followed it past huge mounds of rotting detritus, all the way to Arnold's boundary. From there they kept to the shadows, running from skip to skip, traversing his yard until they reached the house. They eventually stumbled across the fuse box, and they could have flicked the switch, but that would have been an easy fix. Peter wanted more drama.

The focal point of the party had moved inside the house, but Arnold was still cavorting by the pool on a dancefloor he'd made out of a piece of vinyl flooring that Peter suspected had probably come out of one of his skips. He was dancing to techno blaring out of the DJ machine positioned near the deep end. Arnold evidently believed that bigger was always better, and this machine was enormous, complete with swirling, multicoloured disco lights and a searchlight that spun around randomly, highlighting the clouds. It had some age to it. It was undoubtedly another skip rescue.

For a while, Arnold's shaking was so violent that Peter was convinced that he was convulsing. He was in the groove, his eyes shut, mouth agape, panting heavily. Eventually the track ended, and Arnold opened his eyes and looked around. The last members of his audience had gone inside, and he found himself utterly alone. Leaving the DJ machine to blast away unattended, Arnold shuffled off to join his guests.

After he left, Cochineal moved to one side and tapped out a message on her phone. She whispered to Peter, 'I'll meet you back at the house. You know what to do, right? In ten...nine...eight...'

Peter continued the countdown silently, at the end of which someone close by let off a barrage of fireworks. That was when he moved out of the shadows and with a grunt, he heaved the DJ machine and the table it sat on towards the pool's edge. He watched as the power cord unfurled behind it, relieved to see that it hadn't pulled out of the socket.

The sonofabitch weighed a ton. He was considering abandoning his plan until one of the table legs suddenly buckled and the machine lurched violently to one side. From that point on, all he needed to do was to step out of its way, give it a quick shove and let it complete its journey under its own momentum. The second the machine hit the water, Arnold's power went out. But vengeance was always a lot sweeter when it could be delivered in large doses, and Peter had to fight back a sudden urge to piss.

By the time he and Cochineal returned home, Peaches had finished the pyrotechnic display, gathered up the spent cases and was enjoying a quiet nightcap on the deck. She told them that while they were creeping along the creek, she had found the key in the console of Arnold's Audi TT, and that she had driven it onto the beach and bogged it in the sand. The morning's high tide would take care of the rest.

Satisfied, the three of them sat on the deck in peace, drank a celebratory glass of port and then went back to bed.

CHAPTER THIRTY-SEVEN

Unwanted visitors and other pests

A little later, while Peter was settling down for his well-deserved rest, his phone rang again. He didn't immediately recognise the number or the voice. 'Who is this?' he asked.

The voice was strained and muffled, but a few words later, it didn't sound entirely unfamiliar. He couldn't place it. He said, 'If you're a crank caller I'm hanging up.'

'No, no, don't, Peter. It's…it's Woody.'

'Woody Turnbull?' he replied. 'You sound different. Is something wrong?' He could hear loud breathing and an occasional groan. 'Something wrong, Woody?' he repeated.

'Yes…yes… In hospital. Thugs beat me up.'

'Thugs?' Peter sat up. 'Why? Over what?'

'Two…of…them.' He winced audibly. 'Broke my arm and a few ribs.'

'Was it about the story I sent you? The photos?'

'Of…course…it…fucking was,' he grunted.

'I'm so sorry, Woody.' Obviously, they meant business. 'Were they after me?'

'Yup.'

'Did you say who I was?' he asked nervously.

'Nup,' Woody replied. 'I said…Super Sex Sleuth…was someone else. Someone I've had run-ins with…in the past.'

'But they'll work out pretty fast after they beat him up that it wasn't him, and then they'll come back to you a lot angrier.'

'Well, I wasn't…going to give up my source…to that bitch. And… and…I have a strong desire to live.'

'Have you told the police?'

'The hospital...called them. I just said...I was beaten up... on the street. Didn't see, don't remember.' He added, 'What...are they going to do, anyway? The people who beat me are probably... underworld. Cops do nothing. That's how it works.'

'Thanks for taking the punishment for me, mate. I really appreciate it.'

'I don't know why I did it. I did...think about ratting you out... after they broke my arm and hung me upside down...out of the window.'

'Maybe you remembered that time I—' Peter began.

'I know,' Woody interrupted, 'saved my life. Once. A long, long time ago. I thought you...would have forgotten by now.'

'How could I forget? Rescuing you from a burning building? Almost did my back in, carrying you, and I've never been the same since. I kept that ticket in my back pocket, in case I ever needed a favour. I guess I owe you one now. You know, I've always been amazed that we didn't both spontaneously combust that night from all the booze we'd drunk.'

'Yeah, well... Satanists and their fucking candles everywhere...'

'I miss working at the *Truth* sometimes. Breaking into an abandoned church with you, just to get a story, was kind of fun.'

'The good old days. Just a second.' There was a pause. Woody was moving about. 'There! That's better; I think the medication's finally kicking in.' He sighed and added, 'They said I had to take down the story and issue an apology.'

'The thugs did? And what did you tell them?' asked Peter. 'Are you going to do that? Not that it matters; the internet's proven that you can't put the genie back into the bottle. It's out there and the gossip rags have already picked it up.'

'I said I'd do it, for what it's worth. But once I get out of hospital and out of the country, I'll write a fucking story about how I was assaulted and coerced by thugs sent by Bitch Balloch.'

'That should help fan the fire.'

'Yeah. But I didn't call just to update you. Like you said, you owe me, and I'm going to need you to deliver sooner rather than later. If you could just lend me a few quid so I can get out of the country;

I'll send you the details. The minute I get out of hospital, I'm driving to the airport, mate. I have a place in Bali. I'll lay low there for a few months.'

'Yeah. All right. Of course I'll give you a hand, Woody.'

'And the best thing you could do for yourself is to get out of this place for a while. Those bastards are dangerous. I always believed that Balloch mixed with some shady people, and this confirms it. She and that bloody oily husband of hers.'

'I really can't go anywhere just yet,' Peter replied. 'I have a story to publish. It's too important to the public interest.'

'I suggest you put your life ahead of the public interest, mate, and lay low for a while.'

'I wish I could, but I'm committed.'

'Then I suggest you get yourself a gun. Or hire a few security guards.'

Peter chuckled and glimpsed the Winnebago in his yard. 'Will do, Woody.'

'Sure, you will.' He growled, 'Got to go, now. A nurse wants me to have a bath. I would normally look forward to a woman bathing me, but in these circumstances...' Then he hung up abruptly.

Peter got up and sent Woody Turnbull the money he'd promised, and filed their conversation away as interesting, but not something that was about to happen to him. He wasn't running away anytime soon.

Peaches and Cochineal had improved his quality of life. They not only watched over Misha, but they also proved themselves to be very decent handy-persons. Not that he cared much about his surroundings: a house was just shelter, and aesthetics were wasted on a philistine like him. But the more work that they did, the better the house functioned, and the more settled he felt. And he needed to feel settled. It seemed to him that trouble had been parked bumper to bumper at Hermit's Hut since he'd arrived.

The noise. The smell. The rubbish.

He had to admit, as good as it was, the article he had written about Arnold caused barely a ripple. It was syndicated, read by a few and then lost in the ether. No awards or accolades for him.

So, all he could do was to continue to complain about Arnold to anyone who'd listen, as well as to those who wouldn't. *Littering?* He expected that nothing would happen. Nobody seemed to care. Heavy metals released into the bay wasn't a concern; the truth was quickly sanitised by those with far-reaching interests. *Nothing to see here.*

He pushed the thoughts from his mind, sighed heavily, climbed back into bed and slept in until a little after nine. By mid-afternoon, the mystery of how a floating Audi TT washed up at a neighbouring beach went viral.

Then Arnold replaced it with a newer model, red this time, which was even harder to ignore.

The following week, Peter heard more about Sadie Taylor from Dan Browning, the detective handling the case. He said that she had suffered a stroke in hospital and remained in a coma. He'd already spoken to Peter twice over the phone to clarify his statement, although, to date, there wasn't a suspect. Peter gave him what he could, but as he kept repeating, the hoodie had obscured the assailant's identity.

'We'll be appealing for information again,' said Detective Senior Sergeant Browning, 'so I'm very hopeful. And I'll give you my direct number, in case you remember anything new.'

'Of course,' he replied. He scribbled Browning's number on a slip of paper and promptly buried it under a ream of printing paper. The phone number never made it to the whiteboard. What could he add to what he'd already told the constable that night? *The driver wore a hoodie, for Chrissakes!* He'd already told the police that the driver might have been young, but not too young. Tall, but not too tall. Fast and reckless behind the wheel. Yes, of that he was certain; he was very, very fast.

All Peter was sure of was that he was a he. But then again, maybe not.

He spent most of the next hour researching rubbish, if only to confirm his suspicions that disposing of other people's filth was just another way to launder the proceeds of crime. A cash business. Invoices that were easy to fake, but hard to trace. Drug money made clean. The shipping container and Arnold's mysterious visitors on motorcycles explained.

Later that afternoon, he discovered that he'd overlooked a missed call. The message the caller had left for him was already a few days old. He was always on his phone; how hadn't he seen it earlier? He accessed his voicemail and listened to it.

'Peter, it's Katherine Sutcliffe. I read your latest article. We need to talk.'

He called her back a few minutes later.

'That was last Friday, Peter,' she screeched. 'I left the message on Friday night.'

The Katherine Sutcliffe who had left the message was softly spoken and piteous, but the one he was speaking to was anything but. He replied, 'Yes, I know you did. And,' he continued, as sarcastically as he could, 'I'm so sorry I wasn't able to call you sooner, Katherine, but I'm an investigative journalist, you know, and I WAS BUSY WORKING!'

'Oh, really? Well, in case you've forgotten, I'm very, very important to your career, Peter. Remember that piece you're doing on Nick? You need my co-operation. So, when I call you, I expect you to call me straight back.'

My career has been going fine for decades—way, way before you showed up! Had she been drinking? She was hysterical, but she wasn't slurring. 'Well,' he replied, 'as I recall, the last time we met, you didn't seem all that pleased to see me. In fact, you told me to go away and never come back.'

'I was having a bad day. You should have called me first before just dropping in.'

'Right,' he said. 'So, what did you want to tell me Friday night? What was it that couldn't wait till today?'

'It's too late now,' she replied. 'On Friday night, I wanted you to come over, so we could talk. Today, I have nothing to say to you.'

Little by little, he was discovering that Katherine Sutcliffe could be a bit like the Melbourne weather—transitioning all four seasons in a matter of hours. 'Suit yourself,' he said and hung up.

Was she using reticence as punishment, or was there another

reason Katherine Sutcliffe had nothing to say? Had someone tasked her with the job of luring him to her house, so he could be assaulted too—or possibly worse—perhaps by the same thugs that had done over Woody Turnbull? Until he knew her motivation for sure, he'd be cautious, wary but not worried. He suspected that someone else—someone nasty—was jerking her strings but, for the moment, he'd put it down to run-of-the-mill, arbitrary gameplaying.

He didn't spend too much energy mulling it over; he had somewhere else to go. The only thing he knew for certain was that Arnold and his father-in-law weren't at Katherine Sutcliffe's that night.

CHAPTER THIRTY-EIGHT

Sorry's not enough

Yet another of Conni's soirees was turning into a raging success, but Peter just wasn't in the mood. The tealights flickered with the scent of Mt Macedon roses, everywhere people were laughing and chatting, the pianist was more Elton than Elton, and, except for Peter, everyone was having a ball.

Misha had given up playing the taciturn intellectual and was singing 'Candle in the Wind' while draping herself over the grand piano. Every time Conni sashayed past him in her six-inch heels exuding Joy from every pore, he felt a little worse. Her laugh was a dagger to the heart and the clink of her bracelets a rattling sabre.

He had too many questions to which there were no answers. He wanted to be sad. He demanded isolation.

He tried to mask his feelings behind a large whisky, but Conni noticed, and he noticed her noticing, so he turned away from her and Misha, sat down at the table next to a man who had left his hearing aids at home, and prayed for silence. But it wasn't enough.

While Silvio occupied himself ladling parmesan risotto into bowls, Conni tried to gain Peter's attention and when that failed, she came over, tapped Peter's neighbour on the shoulder and demanded that he swap seats with her. Then she leaned into Peter and said, 'You're quieter than a contemplative order of nuns at an open mike night. Have I done something to offend you?'

He weighed his response. 'Nup.' It was all he could manage.

'You're all right, then? Nothing worrying you?'

He returned with 'Yep' before his energy wasted away. He raised the glass to his mouth and let the smoky peat seep past his lips. It was a salve for an injured soul. *Laphroaig. Brilliant.* He peered at her over the rim and saw that she looked hurt, so he added, 'I'm savouring the moment,' and took another sip.

Conni cleared her throat. 'A little birdie told me that you've been having trouble accessing the owners of San Remo, that gorgeous house on the esplanade. Could the little birdie be right?'

He guffawed. 'And let me guess. That singing canary wouldn't happen to be Misha?'

'I never reveal my sources, Peter, you should know that better than anyone.'

He drew a deep breath. 'Well, yes, it's true. The world seems determined to close all the windows and lock all the doors right now, Conni, so there's no surprise there.'

'Ah,' she replied, nodding, 'tell me more. A problem shared is a problem—'

He interrupted, 'Yes, yes, I know, a problem halved. The trouble is, I've just realised that I'm a lone voice preaching to an audience of arseholes who really don't want to listen. People are sick or dying for reasons they should care about, and yet their only worry seems to be whether my bad news might devalue their properties. I've been told to butt out in so many words. Never mind if their kids are exposed to heavy metals and end up with childhood cancers, as long as they're rich, they look good and wear the right clothes.'

She raised her eyebrows. 'That's a bit cruel, isn't it?'

'Is it?'

She sighed, 'Okay, fine, I'll play your game. The world has moved on. People don't want to hear real news anymore: they want it sanitised and delivered oh-so-gently, preferably by someone with a much prettier, younger face than yours. One which they recognise from some reality show or other.' She poured herself a glass of Bollinger and continued, 'There's a new world order, Peter, like it or lump it. Reporters are as irrelevant as the newspapers they write for. Conspicuous consumerism is everything today. Wealth is everything. Social media is everything. Justice for all is nothing more than an archaic concept, because, nowadays, justice has become a commodity to be bought and sold, exactly like everything else. Right now, you're stuck on the wrong side of the riverbank, and the water's rising. Here's my advice to you: you'd best get building that bridge.'

'And that's meant to make me feel better?'

'No. That's meant to make you feel worse. You know what I've learned about you over the years? You're at your finest when life's at its worst.' She reached into her bra cup, took out a jewel-encrusted memory stick and dropped it on the table.

He looked at it. 'What's that?' he asked. 'The chronicle of your life so far?'

'Cheeky. It's the CCTV footage that you were after. Try saying, *thank you, Conni*. Oh, don't look so surprised. It just so happens that I manage San Remo for the owners. The husband's a banker in Singapore and they're almost never there. My staff calls in twice weekly, to clean the place and make sure everything's in order. I paid a visit last week and managed to get that just before it was erased.'

'Have you looked at it?' he asked.

'What for? That's your job.'

'Thank you,' he mumbled. 'What can I say, Conni? Honestly? Sometimes, I think you were sent from heaven to take care of me as well as Misha.'

She tapped the back of his hand with her painted talon. 'Me? Sent expressly from God to be Peter Clancy's very own guardian angel? Oh, come now! Your fairy godsister perhaps…' She laughed. 'But that's enough of that, okay? Faith, Peter, faith is all you need. And a little patience. And if you could've only shut up long enough for me to finish what I was trying to say before, you wouldn't have heard me tell you that it was a problem halved, but that it was a problem solved.'

He was itching to go home straightaway; the memory stick was burning a hole in his pocket. While they were waiting for Silvio to rustle up a zabaglione for dessert, Misha, who had avoided him all night, came over. She leaned over his shoulder and said, 'You're very quiet. What's eating you tonight?'

'Not much,' he replied in a low voice. 'I have some CCTV footage to go through and I'm dying to watch it.'

'And so you think that gives you the right to act like you can't wait to leave? Typical. You want to go so much, you can't even pretend you're having a good time, not even for Conni's sake. So why don't you go? What's stopping you? You could do what any ungrateful, self-obsessed brat would do, and just go now.'

He searched her face. She was emotionless. 'You're right,' he said. 'I've been very rude. I'm sorry.'

Someone was passing around a vintage muscat, and he poured himself some and pushed the bottle along. Once Misha had returned to her seat he stood up, lifted his glass and said, 'May I propose a toast to Conni and Silvio, who are, hands down, the holy grail of hosts as well as the best friends that an ingrate like me could ever have.'

Conni smiled through gritted teeth, and Peter knew it was too little too late. The moment the hired help began clearing away the dessert plates, he stood up.

'I've been a horrible guest,' he said to Conni, 'for which I can only apologise.'

'You know that I hate apologies, Peter. Most apologies are just a cowardly lie that people use to get themselves out of an uncomfortable situation.'

He was taken aback.

'Now,' she continued, 'I know you're not naturally a liar or a coward, but you are becoming very egocentric. And you've forgotten how to enjoy yourself. You've even forgotten how to laugh. You've sunk yourself so deep into this *thing* you've been working on, that you're in danger of drowning. It seems to me you need to get out of your head and back into the real world.'

He sucked in some air. 'You're right. I've been living and breathing this investigation since I got back. It's starting to haunt me. It's choking me. Arnold is the first thing I hear every morning and the last thing I see every night. It's eating me up.'

She shook her head. 'Oh, Peter. A word of advice: you've already had the heart attack. It didn't kill you, so take it as the shot across the bow. You need to find your bliss before it's too late and, honestly, I'm not sure whether that's something you can find on the coast or not.'

'I'm beginning to suspect not. Please don't worry, Conni, this is where I need to be for now, but not forever. I know I need to loosen up. I know I'm in trouble: lately, I've even stopped listening to music.'

She faked surprise. 'What? Not even a little *Led Purple*?'

He laughed. 'Not even a hint of that exquisite melody "Black Dog Night".' He kissed her on the cheek. 'I'll go home now. I'll get a good night's sleep and I won't look at the stick till the morning. I mean this from my heart: I'm sorry for being such a pain in the arse. You know I'll be forever in your debt for everything you've done for me.'

'Stop it! You call me an angel once more and I might just have to have a fall from grace.' She patted him on the shoulder. 'Just do me a favour and live your best life. Deal?'

'Deal.'

He walked out into the darkness. The night air had the nip of the waning season. He unlocked the car and dropped into the driver's seat, cranked the engine and lowered the window. From the kitchen, Conni heard the strains of 'Highway Star' vibrating through one masonry and two plasterboard walls, until her next-door neighbour bellowed, 'Shut the fuck up!' from his front doorstep, and the music echoed down the street and then faded away.

Very early the next morning, he took the stick out of its Swarovski cover. He pressed it to his lips for luck, took a deep breath and slid it into the port. He clicked on his media player and began to play the video files. The third file contained the view along the esplanade but, aside from the regular traffic, there wasn't much to see.

He made himself a coffee and settled in for the long haul. After five tedious minutes, he began skipping forwarding, stopping randomly every few seconds to check if anything had changed. Aside from a growing white light reflecting off the safety barrier as the daylight faded and colour turned into shades of grey, nothing happened. He was about an hour in when his next skip paid a dividend. From one scene to the next, the landscape had transformed dramatically. Suddenly, the safety barrier was gone, and the road was marked and littered with debris.

He took the video back a few minutes and watched it again. Sure enough, there it was: Nick Sutcliffe's BMW driving down the road, and another car—a four-wheel-drive lit up like a Christmas tree—approaching from the opposite end. Nobody was speeding. Then there was a blinding flash and the BMW careened off the road.

He took it back again, slowed it down and watched the scene over. The approaching car had veered toward the centre of the road just before the flash, but he couldn't discern the cause of the light burst. All he could tell was that it came from that car.

He assumed he would see the driver pull over immediately and try to help, but that didn't happen. Perhaps whoever was driving was hearing-impaired and hadn't realised Nick Sutcliffe had crashed. He kept watching. For a while there was nothing again, and Peter's finger was poised to stop the video, go back, and see if he could identify the other car, but he let it run on. A minute or so later, he watched the other car reverse back to the crash site. He was sure it was the same car: the size, shape, shade and light configuration were identical.

Fortunately for him, the spot the driver chose to pull up was in full sight of the camera and, once its lights were dimmed, he realised that he had a brilliant view of the car. The make, model and purpose were evident. He saw the driver get out and walk calmly to the road's edge for a look. He watched him stand there for a while, not reaching for his phone, no shock or concern registering in his demeanour. As the driver turned to return to his car, Peter also had a brilliant view of the driver's face. Without a care in the world, the driver slipped back into his car and drove away.

Peter sat there for a while, disbelieving what he had seen. He went back and watched it all again, pausing from time to time, to make sure he was right. He sent a copy of the video to himself as an email attachment. Then he went to his whiteboard and drew a new line between two old names.

The car he saw dazzle Nick Sutcliffe over the side of the cliff was unmistakably a police vehicle. The driver he saw leave the police car to survey the scene was unmistakably Sergeant Moylan.

Peter's persistence had been rewarded.

While he considered his next move, he finally did something about Eddie Arnold's disability pension. He sat at his desk, enjoying a new sense of power and the tepid breeze gusting through the open window. Ten minutes later, he'd officially reported Arnold for defrauding the Australian taxpayer by claiming a pension he was clearly not entitled to receive. On a roll, he also reported him for tax fraud. As well as for breaching environmental laws. Then he sat back with his hands supporting his neck and smirked.

He was still daydreaming about Arnold's imminent demise, when a blast of air caught the disorder of papers that always cluttered his desk and strew them across the floor. As he bent to pick them up, the breeze caught one scrap in particular and sent it tumbling onto his shoe. It read *Det Browning*, followed by a phone number. On a whim, Peter called him. Browning wasn't at his desk, so he left him a sketchy message. He ended it with, 'Give me a ring whenever you can.'

As he hung up, Peter checked the time: it was ten-thirteen. He told himself that, if Browning called him back within the hour, he'd share the information he had about Nick Sutcliffe with him. If not, he'd keep it to himself until he was ready to sell it to the highest bidder. That way, he avoided a moral dilemma. It wasn't up to him; he'd let providence decide the course of events.

At ten fifty-nine, his phone rang.

Private number.

'Hello, Peter? You left a message for me.'

He was almost relieved. 'Oh, yes, Detective Senior Sergeant. Thanks for calling back.' He cleared his throat. 'I'm afraid my call wasn't about Sadie Taylor's accident. I don't have anything more to tell you about that since the last time we spoke. I actually called to talk to you about another accident in the area.'

'Right.'

'I wanted to talk to you about Nick Sutcliffe; you remember, the estate agent who went over the cliff at Serenity Bay. Now, I know you're not investigating his accident, but I was thinking that maybe you could point me to whoever is. You see, some very significant information has come my way.'

228

'Is that right?'

'It's pretty explosive, and I don't want it getting into the wrong hands.' He chewed his lip. 'Look, this is so explosive in fact that it might just open up a new line of enquiry.'

'And you've come to me with it...'

'Well, without saying too much, I couldn't exactly take it to the local sergeant.'

'I meant to say, you've come to me with it instead of taking matters into your own hands, breaking the story yourself and scooping the opposition.'

'A reporter's first instinct? That just didn't feel like the right thing to do this time, for some reason. Of course, I'd need some reassurance from VicPol that I'll still get the scoop. And that you'll give me anything else that might come up in relation to it ahead of anyone else.'

'I see.' He paused. 'You're not wasting my time here, Peter, are you? Not on a fishing expedition?'

'No, no, no, I have the evidence right here. And it's big. Huge in fact. So, who should I speak to about Sutcliffe's accident being a potential homicide?'

'You're speaking to him right now.'

'But I thought you'd be busy with Sadie Taylor's accident investigation.'

'Unfortunately, I'm not anymore.'

'Oh? You haven't been sidelined, have you?'

'No, no, nothing like that. I was going to phone you later today to update you anyway, and check if you were around for a quick coffee, perhaps. You see, I'm now heading up a homicide investigation.' He sighed heavily before adding, 'I'm very sorry to have to tell you that Sadie Taylor died this morning.'

Peter was taken aback. 'Oh, no. I'm so sorry to hear that.'

'I know we've spoken over the phone a couple of times, but I wasn't really happy with the statement Constable Burns took from you. So, I'd like you to come in and talk to me this time. I mean, you were the last person to talk to her before she was run over. Let's see if we can't clear up a few things.'

Peter wanted to say, *You don't suspect I had something to do with it, do you? Do I need to bring a lawyer with me?* but he thought that might suggest a guilty mind.

Instead, he replied, 'No worries at all. Just tell me where and when.'

***

While Peter was at police headquarters, Misha stayed in the office. She sat at her desk and finished off an assignment for her course and, once that was done, she decided to pass the time by digging a little deeper into Adriana Balloch's business affairs.

She began with a few simple web searches: surnames, maiden names, company names, known associates, notable locations. Then she focused on the companies and securities register, methodically uncovering a web of companies and family trusts so complex that it took up over half of the clean side of Peter's whiteboard to write them all down.

The owner of the nursing home wasn't Balloch herself. The owner was a company registered to an address in Collins Street in Melbourne. Misha also discovered that the company shared the registered office with fourteen other entities. Eventually, by teasing out the threads, she found that they all linked back to Balloch, although Goldsmith was a co-director of only one of the companies, and beneficiary of only one of the trusts.

After that, she cross-linked the companies to planning applications and nursing homes all along the bay, and up and down the coast. Among them, she found a planning application that linked back to the same Collins Street address, but not to any of the companies or trusts that acted as Balloch's alter-ego. A little more scratching and it seemed to Misha that Harrison and Goldsmith had been securing themselves a nest-egg.

After that, she searched for anything to do with Eddie Arnold.

'So,' she asked Peter when he returned from speaking to Detective Browning, 'how did it go?'

He turned away from her and ruffled through the papers on his desk, while he considered his answer. 'It was okay. I had nothing new to add to his investigation, really,' he said.

'And the CCTV?'

He shrugged. 'Well, he's got a copy of it now. He'll get back to me once he's looked at it, I guess.' He put down the papers and turned towards her. 'What dirt did you uncover while I was away?'

'So, I found out that Balloch owns several companies, including one called BlackSwan Enterprises. It turns out that BlackSwan owns Seaview and three other nursing homes besides.'

'Big money in nursing homes,' he replied, 'especially if you overcharge and underfeed the residents. Anything else?'

'Apart from everything I've written on your whiteboard? Well, yes, there's this.' She pointed to the screen of her laptop, but he struggled to read it over her shoulder. She grunted her disapproval, shrugged him away and said, 'Why don't I just email you the link.'

He flopped down at his desk and read silently. After a while, he said, 'Wow.'

'Right, but where to from here?' Misha asked.

'What I understand from this article is that three years ago, Arnold's wife put up the bail for a bikie in relation to a spate of drugs charges and attempted murder. A two-hundred-thousand-dollar surety. So now I'm asking myself, what's the connection? That's a lot of money for the wife of a disability pensioner to bet on whether someone else turns up to court or not. She was willing to put that much on the line? None of it makes sense to me.'

'I agree.' She pulled out her notepad and added, 'And it gets even more confusing. While you were away, I did some other searches relating to Arnold and his wife and I'm pretty sure that they never owned a house before they bought the one across the road. I also searched their land title. It seems that they bought their house at about the same time you bought this place and there's no mortgage registered on it. Who can afford to buy a house outright these days? And their kids go to a private school. What's that cost? Sixty thousand a year, at least? You're right to wonder where all the money's come from.'

He guffawed. 'An inheritance?'

'I thought about that, but then I asked myself if that was really likely. You've seen how they live, and you've met some of the family. All I can say is that they were involved in a few businesses before the dump, but they were all wound up for insolvency. The reviews on the internet about their business practices are bad; apparently, they never paid their bills. From what I saw, it seems that they still don't.' She tossed her notepad onto his desk. 'I can assure you that Arnold doesn't have many fans out there. His name appears in the Law List on a regular basis—I wouldn't be surprised if he's been in court more times than most lawyers.'

'He's a villain, that much is certain. The thing is,' he returned as he continued reading, 'considering everything that Arnold has done, he probably should have had a stint in prison by now.'

She shook her head. 'If he has, I certainly couldn't find anything about it.'

He continued, 'And yet why am I not surprised by that? I don't understand how nothing ever seems to stick to him.' He flipped the page of her notepad and kept reading. 'Wow, this is good stuff. You've been busy, Misha. Where's all this drive coming from?'

'Do you really want to know?'

'Of course.'

She took a deep breath. 'I suppose I have an axe to grind. You know I met Arnold and Cooper when I was in St Kilda.' She looked away. 'These people are truly scum. St Kilda isn't a million miles from here, you know. When we left there, I had hoped never to see them again, but there you are. I guess you could call it fate. So, if I can play a part in their downfall, then maybe there's a reason for everything we've both been through, and maybe that's the real reason you're here and why I ended up interning with you.'

He stopped dead. Her despair confirmed everything Conni had told him and Arnold's pointed comments about her made sense. 'You knew Eddie Arnold from...'

'My past life. You could say that yes, I did. But not that well. In those days he worked as, ahh, let's call it "security", and he was full of 'roids and rage. These days, his appetite for the steroids may have been replaced by fast food and the muscles may have turned into lots and lots of fat, but the rage I witnessed back then is still there. Look, Peter, I don't want to get into the details right now, but as well as I knew Arnold, I knew his father-in-law a lot better.'

'Rennie Cooper.'

She nodded but didn't speak. She turned away. He could tell even without looking at her that she was crying.

'You can speak to me about what happened with Cooper whenever you feel like it,' he told her quietly. 'Or not.'

CHAPTER THIRTY-NINE

St Kilda 1999
The Velour Lounge

'No! No! No!'

The music stopped abruptly. Ted was so loud that she could hear his shouts while she was sorting boxes in the storage room backstage. Concheetah frowned. What was up with him today?

'Attention girls!' Ted screeched, clapping his hands. 'How many times do I have to show you the steps? You're dancing like a herd of three-legged wildebeest! Remember, you're called the Erotics, not the Chaotics!' The music began again. 'Again, from the top. Five, six, seven, eight... Brush left, brush right, walk two, three, four, shimmy, shimmy, shimmy...'

The ladyboy members of the Erotics were the last vestige of Concheetah's once popular drag show. The other members of her backing band in their silver lederhosen and oiled bare chests were long gone, replaced by a compact disc player.

She put down the oversized fans she was carrying and stood in the wings, watching.

How times had changed! Everyone was older and shabbier—the props, the costumes, she and Ted, and, most importantly, their bank balance. She couldn't tell Ted they were living off an ever-dwindling overdraft secured against her flat; he would worry too much, and it might provoke another of his infamous overdoses. She didn't need that on top of all the money headaches. So she kept the bills paid and she made sure that the girls received their weekly paycheque, no matter what. But something was going to have to give. And soon.

She sighed and left Ted to his choreography and strode over to the bar to view the bookings. Friday night was shaping up to be quite busy—at least by recent standards. She scoured the names, but nothing stood out. There were some people who were definitely persona non grata, and had she seen them on the list, big spenders or not, she would have drawn a line through the booking. She went behind the counter and checked the liquor. There was enough, even for the most enthusiastic drinker.

A few minutes later, someone knocked on the door. She sighed again and sashayed across the floor and opened it a crack. 'Sorry, we're…'

A large man stood outside, his eyes everywhere as he spoke. 'For fuck's sake, open the door!'

She recognised the intruder immediately. He was a near-neighbour, but she had no appetite for men like him. As far as she was concerned, bikies were the scum of the earth. Along with brothel-keepers and drug dealers. Of which there was considerable overlap. 'We're closed for rehearsal,' she said. 'Go away!'

'Open the fucking door now, Concheetah, or I'll break it down.'

She swung the door open and stood aside. The man who entered towered over her, despite her six-foot frame and her four-inch heels. She placed her hands on her hips and glared at him. 'Where do you think you're…' she began.

But she was talking to herself. The man had run across the room, leapt onto the stage, sped past Tapping Ted and disappeared into the bowels of the Velour Lounge.

'Con-CHEET-ah!' Ted bellowed. 'What the…' His tap shoes were clattering furiously.

'Yes, Ted!' Concheetah was in hot pursuit, her shirt hitched up to her hips. She vaulted onto the stage with the grace and agility of an Olympic gymnast and was gone in a flash. She caught up with the intruder in the storage room and rounded him up.

'I need a favour,' he said breathlessly.

'I don't do favours for people like you,' she replied. 'Now get the fuck out!'

'Not even for a quick thousand?'

'Not even for two,' she returned.

'Good thing I brought five with me, then.' From his pocket, he extracted a bundle of notes tied up with a rubber band and waved the bundle at her. She felt the breeze blow back her hair.

She looked at the cash and exhaled loudly. It was a terrible thing, how much she needed that money. She found herself saying, 'What would I have to do for it?'

'You'd have to let me stay here for a bit. And if anyone asks you, you never saw me.'

'How long of a bit? Exactly?'

'I'll leave early just before dawn on Sunday morning, when no one's around. I'll slip out the back and disappear and no one need know anything.'

'But Ted will know. And the girls...'

'You can deal with them, can't you? For a cool five thousand?'

She frowned. 'I suppose so.' She took the notes and crammed them in the back of her knickers. She was glad she'd substituted Spanx for her G-string. 'Stay here. And don't move! I mean it! Don't you so much as fucking breathe!'

She told Ted in front of the girls that the intruder had left through the service entrance. After rehearsal ended, she told Ted the truth.

'And you agreed?'

'I took the money, yes. Subject to your approval, of course.'

'What were you thinking? It's blood money.'

'I know, Teddles. But it's a lot of money that we could use right now. And for what? Two nights' B and B?'

'Yes, but it's two nights that we'll be sheltering a drug dealer who's crossed just about every pimp, junkie and copper in St Kilda, Concheetah.'

'I know, but you have to admit that it's a shitload of dough he's offering us for very little effort.'

'It's not the effort I worry about, love, it's the risk.' He paused to think it over. 'Five thousand, you said?'

She nodded.

'Five thousand.' He thought some more. 'Yes, all right,' he resumed reluctantly. 'Did you really think I didn't know how bad things were?'

She smiled sheepishly and stroked his arm. 'I didn't want to worry you.'

He gave her a peck. 'My dear, darling Concheetah, you're such a soft touch. Fine. All right. You can tell Warryn Ward he can stay till Sunday, but then he has to leave.'

'Yes, of course, Teddles.'

'Till Sunday.' He exhaled loudly. 'And not a minute longer. And while you're at it, you also better tell Warryn that he owes us big time.'

Chapter Forty

Take a number, take a seat

Peter realised that he hadn't seen or heard from Rhiannon for nearly a fortnight; he didn't even know if she was home. It was deathly quiet next door; there was no sign of her or her children. Other than the twilight twinkle of her solar path lights, night-time next door was as dark as a tomb. Perhaps Andre had finally taken the children and murdered her.

The absence of a smell and blowflies covering her windows made that theory unlikely, so Peter figured probably not. Perhaps she was just avoiding him. Not that it bothered him; if it was over, it was over. Whatever *it* was. He found himself missing the physical connection with another human, but more than that, he missed the distraction: he never knew when she'd decide to pop in—that was part of her allure. The coast, with its carefully manicured vistas and its carefully manicured inhabitants, was starting to bore him.

With that thought in mind, he began to look for diversions. Billboards and advertising hoardings promoted every type of water sport. But nothing appealed. He was researching wineries (which were much more in line with his interests) when something stood out.

'Would you go on a horseback winery tour with me, if I asked you nicely?' he asked Misha in the morning.

She eyed him suspiciously. 'A winery horseback ride?'

'Yes.'

'Why?'

'I thought it might be fun.'

'But I don't ride.'

'It doesn't matter. You drink, don't you? The ride is just a slow means to a very pleasant end. The horses are mostly old clumpers anyway. They know where they're going, so you don't have to.'

'And this is not a date, right? You are not asking me out on a date?'

'No, of course not.'

'Because I don't see you in that way. I mean, you are a good-looking older man, for sure. With those blue eyes, I'm thinking you must have been a babe-magnet when you were young.'

Was she taking the piss? He replied, 'Thank you for the backhander. I assure you, you're safe with me. If I so much as looked at you that way, Conni would have me hung, drawn and quartered, and then she'd tan my guts and wear them as garters for her stockings. So, thankfully, no, this is not a date, Misha.'

'Good. Okay. Let me think it over.'

After she drank her customary ten o'clock hibiscus tea she said, 'I guess it might be fun.'

Peter booked two people for the morning Pinot on Ponies tour in a week's time and then forgot about it.

In the late afternoon, just after Misha left for the day, he heard a familiar sound somewhere between the revving of Arnold's Audi TT and the incessant roar of his excavators. It was the sound of five carats of diamonds set in platinum knocking against a wooden door frame, followed by a sultry, 'Hello?'

He almost ran to the front door. 'Well, well, well, if it isn't Serenity's sexiest siren,' he said, swinging it open. 'I was just thinking about you and wondering where you'd got to.'

Rhiannon's hand went straight to his crotch. She tut-tutted and said, 'But apparently not thinking quite hard enough.' She strutted through the door and down the hallway. 'Ibiza.'

'What?'

She turned towards him and pouted. 'Andre took us to Ibiza. Me. And the boys, too.'

'So, you've reconciled?'

'No. Well, possibly he thinks so, but I don't.'

'Ah. Is that going to be a problem…for us?'

'I can't see why it should be. This is just a bit of harmless fun, that's all.'

He couldn't disagree. Again, her logic was impeccable. An hour later, his phone woke him up. Rhiannon was gone, and her side of the bed only barely warm.

'Hello?'

'Peter, it's Conni.'

'Are you all right?'

'Yes, yes. I just rang to let you know that Misha mentioned that you and she were going on a winery tour next week...'

'Correct, the Pissed Up on Ponies tour. But don't worry, it's not a date, Conni.'

'Yes, I know, she told me. I just wanted to tell you that I've booked another two tickets...'

'Really? You and Silvio will be joining us? As chaperones? I didn't think you'd be the type...'

She sighed. 'Do you honestly think I'd take the risk of undoing my surgeon's flawless work by putting my designer tushy on a saddle, and subjecting it to hours of merciless pounding? Not me, love; if I'm going to be pounded, I expect it to have a happy ending. Now, will you shut up and listen?'

'Of course.'

'I've arranged for Peaches and Cochineal to join you. When Misha told me about it, I thought, well, doesn't that sound like a fun treat for the girls. A nice outing for all of you. And if you and Misha happen to let loose with the booze, one of the girls can stay sober and drive you all home.'

'The truth is that you don't really trust me being alone with Misha. In case she sees me on a horse and falls hopelessly in love with me.'

'Stop playing with yourself, Peter, you're alone with her every day. If she had been remotely interested in you, you would have known it by now. The vintage Lothario that was Peter Clancy has well and truly had his day.'

'But she's never seen me on a horse. She might go crazy at the sight of me. Apparently, women find men on horseback very sexy.'

She laughed. 'You mean, very sexy like Vladimir Putin or very sexy like Kim Jong Un? Or was that Kim Jong Il? I think she's safe, either way. No, Peter, I booked it as a treat for the girls, and that's all.'

'Fine. Whatever you say. Just so you know, Conni, I may be in my fifties, but I'm still fit and firing.'

'Fine. Whatever you say.'

The morning of the tour dawned with a brilliance that promised a hot day ahead. They all climbed into Misha's Mercedes and drove twenty minutes into the hinterland, winding past acres and acres of land given over to vines. Between the vineyards, there were paddocks of drowsy cattle and the occasional fruit orchard. They turned into a driveway past a sign that read *Tuckers Trails* and pulled up in the carpark.

Past a row of looseboxes was a paddock, a shed and some benches. The horses were already saddled and tied to the fence rail. Peter went over to look at them. Three of the horses looked like hot bloods well past their prime; the rest were hacks of differing height, age, colour and condition.

What a motley bunch of nags!

He returned to one of the benches, sat down next to the others and filled out the paperwork. *Yes, I realise riding can be dangerous. I agree to do whatever you tell me to do and, no, I won't sue if you kill or maim me.* At the bottom of which, they each signed their name.

Once the benches were full, a woman came out of the shed, collected the forms and glanced through them. After she had finished, she said, 'Hello, I'm Tess. Together with Maddy over there'—she pointed to a horsey girl in jodhpurs—'we'll be your guides for today. So, which one of you is Peter?'

He waved at her half-heartedly.

'And the rest of you are all riding novices?'

No one told her otherwise.

'So, Peter,' she continued, 'you say that you've ridden before, huh?' She looked him up and down. 'I see you've ticked that you're an experienced rider.'

'Yes. My dad rode the shows. Equestrian. He also raced jumps and flat, and he was an expert stock rider. He taught me how to ride when I was four.'

'Well, good for Dad. And when was the last time you rode?'

He pursed his lips. 'Ahh…'

She snorted. 'Well, if it was so long ago that you can't remember, then it doesn't count.' She picked up his form, crossed out *experienced rider* and ticked *novice*.

Misha looked embarrassed for him. Peaches and Cochineal looked bored. Tess proceeded to give them some basic training, then they were each given a helmet and assigned a horse. Tess gave Misha an old, stout pony to ride while Peter scored one of the hot bloods, a chestnut named Erik. Peter patted his neck; Erik stood a bit over sixteen hands and the saddle seemed a lot higher up than he remembered.

'Will you need a mounting block?' asked Tess.

'I should be right,' he replied. He checked the girth and took hold of the rein. He bent his knee and lifted his leg. *No fucking way!* He pulled up his jeans so he could stretch further, but his foot was still nowhere near the stirrup. The others had already mounted and were looking down on him.

Tess watched his struggle and sighed. He thought he saw her mouth, *typical*. She grudgingly brought over the block and helped him mount.

'In my defence, I really can ride,' he told her as Misha looked away. 'I guess I've just stiffened up a little.'

They started off at a walk, back down the driveway and along the road for a few metres before turning onto a dedicated horse trail. It felt good to be back in the saddle. Misha and Peter rode side by side just behind Maddy, who led the group. An older man and his daughter on ponies and four French tourists followed them. Peaches and Cochineal were further back, and Tess brought up the rear.

'So,' he called out to Maddy, 'have you been doing this long?'

'Oh, for about a year.'

'And do we stay at this pace the whole way?'

She swivelled in the saddle so he could hear her reply. 'Pretty much,' she said. 'Although your horse would probably love the chance to stretch his legs from time to time. Life's pretty quiet for him these days. He used to be a racehorse, you know. Weren't you, Erik The Red?'

Erik snorted.

'And was that his racing name?'

'Yep. Won a few country races, but he's not up to much now. He barely keeps up with us most of the time,' she said, turning away again.

The trail crossed a national park. The path had been left to grow wild and much of it was overrun with weeds; the park itself was heavily wooded in parts and less so in others. Erik was sniffing out grass, and Peter was tiring of having to nudge him forward. Other than that, they had settled in. They were enjoying picking their way between a thicket of gums on a gentle descent. The sun was filtered, so it wasn't too hot, but the strobing light streaming through the leaves was making Peter sleepy.

He was somewhere along the path to unconsciousness when suddenly the loud crack of gunfire broke the silence. It brought him back instantly and, for a second, he wondered if he'd dreamed it. The other horses were either mildly amused or stone deaf, but not Peter's horse. Erik threw his head up; his eyes were wild; he whinnied and bolted. Peter barely had time to register what was happening.

Pushing past Misha and Maddy, Erik was soon at full pelt. Maddy galloped after him, but the horse was spooked, and with Maddy in pursuit, he must have thought he was back on the racecourse. The closer Maddy came to him, the faster Erik went. The only problem for Peter was that he was still in the saddle. *Fuuucck!* He had to pull Erik around before he was thrown.

He fought against his initial panic. *Get your shit together, son!* 'Whoa!' he yelled. The branches flew past his shoulders. 'Whoa!' He loosened the reins a little and kept reassuring his mount, as Maddy slowed hers and fell behind.

They weaved through a stand of gums and galloped alongside a fenced field for what felt like a kilometre but was probably far less.

'Whoa, Erik, whoa,' Peter repeated over and over. 'It's all right, son.'

It was pure luck that abundant feed and too little exercise worked to their mutual advantage; the horse soon started to run out of steam. His heart thudding, Peter pulled him back slowly, and the moment that the trail opened out, he brought him about. Erik was still jumpy. Adrenaline surged through them; Peter's hands shook. He leapt off the saddle and walked the rest of the way back to the group.

Misha was still astride her horse, who was munching grass as if nothing had happened. Her face told the story—she was white—and next to her, Tess looked aghast. Peter couldn't tell from their demeanour if the French tourists had registered anything out of the ordinary.

'We'll pause here for a while,' said Tess to the group, dismounting shakily and walking over to him. 'I don't know what happened back there.'

'A car must have backfired or something.' Peter rubbed Erik's muzzle. 'But I have to tell you, Erik here's got you all fooled. Today's ride was a bit more exciting than I'd anticipated. It's very lucky for you and Tucker's Trails that I wasn't a novice after all, hey?'

She was in damage control. 'I was at the rear, so I didn't see what happened. In any event, you signed a disclaimer. We can't be held responsible… We don't recommend riders going off at their own pace…'

You're trying to put the blame on me? Erik The Red's a psycho and, disclaimer or no disclaimer, you should be scared shitless that maybe I'll sue you.

He interrupted her. 'You're kidding, right? Firstly, I had no intention of going off at my own pace: that was a hundred per cent Erik's idea. If your bloody horse hadn't bolted, I probably would have been happily dozing off by about now.' He gathered his thoughts. 'Here's the thing you didn't know: I'm a journalist. I was going to do a puff piece on your business for a tourist magazine, but you've just shot that to shit.' He delighted in watching Tess's expression.

'Right. Okay. Well, I suppose I'll have to look into that,' she floundered. She looked him up and down and feigned concern. 'Are you able to continue?'

'Yes, now that we've reached an understanding. But a final word of advice: before you judge people, maybe you should listen to what they have to say first. There's a lot more to riding than what they teach you at pony club; I may not be able to throw my leg over a saddle without a little help these days, but when I say I can ride, I can still ride.'

On that subject, she didn't look convinced, and Peter didn't care.

Behind Tess's back, Peaches motioned to him. She had already dismounted and was looking agitated. She handed the reins to Maddy, walked over to him and said, 'Just thought you should know that wasn't a car, Peter. Someone fired a gun just as you were going past. Cochineal's got the arsehole who did it in a headlock right down there.' She pointed to a gully to his left. 'Make our excuses, you go enjoy yourselves and we'll meet you back at the car in a couple of hours. I'm off to give her a hand.'

He didn't have a chance to reply before she disappeared down the incline.

He returned to the group and watched Maddy check his horse over. There wasn't a scratch on either of them. Erik was solemn after his gallop, and Peter trusted he'd stay that way. Tess was back on her horse, and they were all ready to move again. Using a fallen log to help him, Peter lifted himself onto Erik's back and walked him over to Misha.

The colour had returned to her cheeks. 'Are you all right? I thought for sure you would die,' she told him.

'Ha! Well, I reckon he probably thought the noise was the starter's pistol, and he was off. Now, I won't say it was fun exactly, but it certainly woke me up. We're both fine and that's all that matters.' He chuckled. 'Trust me, I'm a lot harder to kill than that. I guess I'm going to have to add Erik's name to the very long list of those who have tried and failed.'

She sniffed, wiped her nose and nodded. 'Well, I'm very glad you're all right, Peter.'

He smiled and pushed Erik forward. He didn't want to feel what he felt right then: it had the potential to complicate matters. They had a day of fun in the sun still ahead of them through which he was determined to remain dignified.

The girls were lounging in the shade next to the car when they returned. Cochineal waved to them as they approached.

'How was it?' asked Peaches, without opening her eyes.

'Apart from the car backfiring? It was lovely,' Misha replied, unlocking the car. 'Actually, we had a bit too much of a good time, so I think you'd better drive.'

Peter hadn't told Misha anything more; she didn't need to know why the horse had taken off. He trusted she wouldn't find out from anyone. She seemed happy, so why would he spoil it? Lunch was nice, but the return ride had been a blur for him. He'd hammered the wine a bit too vigorously, and he couldn't remember exactly what he'd drunk. In the end, as good or bad as the wine was, it all tasted much the same.

Ahead of him on the return ride, this time the older man slept almost all of the way while his horse plodded along, and the French tourists made it clear that they weren't impressed with the local product. *Des vins industriels*, they called them, for which Peter didn't need a translation.

But now that they were back, he was eager to find out what had occurred in the interim. He climbed into the rear of the car next to Cochineal, acutely aware of those parts of him that had been in contact with the saddle. The sting magnified as the effects of the wine wore away. The moment Peaches started the engine to begin the drive home, he leaned across. He asked Cochineal discreetly, 'So, what happened with the arsehole?'

She replied in a whisper, 'Well, as it turns out, he was a really good talker. I won't bore you with the details right now, but let's just say, he'll be taking a very clear message back to Adriana Balloch and her cohorts that you and Misha are strictly off-limits.'

'We can talk later,' he said. 'Thank you for that.'

'Sure. It's all in a day's work.'

She sighed, looked away and then turned her attention to her hands. 'Shit,' she said loudly, 'all that time and money wasted! I never get to have nice nails in my job, so I thought I'd get a manicure especially for the weekend. And now I've gone and broken two bloody nails already!'

CHAPTER FORTY-ONE

Meeting Sherman Little

The riding incident had infuriated Peter so much that he made himself a promise to blow the lid off Adriana Balloch's tidy world and scatter its contents to the ends of the earth.

He had always meant to visit the Schneider twins again—and he would have—except that he'd given everything else priority. He intended to look into the development of the Schneider land, and how Adriana had managed to sink her claws into it while they were still alive. Especially since (as far as Peter could tell) they weren't just hanging onto life, they were well.

'We're going for another visit to the nursing home,' he told Misha.

'To see Octavia and Anastasia, you mean? Honestly,' she replied, 'I thought you'd forgotten about them. I assumed it was a non-story.'

'No, it wasn't that. I just had so much going that I needed to put the story down for a while. I'm ready to pick it up again.'

She sniggered. 'Do I need to bring some sheet music and a guitar with me this time?'

'A notepad will do. And maybe a pair of glasses if you have any.' He turned away from her. 'I'll be wearing this,' he said as he turned back.

She glanced at him and put her hand to her mouth. 'Really? A porn moustache?'

'It's part of my new and improved cunning kit, you know, for when I want to go incognito. It's my disguise.'

'It's awful. Take it off. You look ridiculous.'

They drove to the Seaview mid-afternoon, before the traffic peaked, and parked on the street just outside the carpark exit. *In case we need to make a rapid escape.* Undisguised, they approached reception together. Peter sighed with relief; there was no sign of the churlish desk clerk from their last visit. A sweet-faced, middle-aged man in glasses sat at the desk instead. He wore a badge that announced, *Hi! I'm Sherman! Welcome.*

Sherman smiled at them.

'I'm here to see the two Misses Schneider,' said Peter. 'Henry Honnery, barrister-at-law, and this is my PA.'

Still smiling, Sherman turned to his computer. 'Hmm, let me see,' he said, typing. He adjusted his glasses and typed some more. 'No.'

'No?'

'There's no one by that name here.' His smile widened.

'They're twins. Anastasia and Octavia Schneider?'

'No.'

Peter spelled out the names. 'Can you check again?'

He did. 'Still no,' he replied with a grin.

'You wouldn't happen to know where they went?'

'No.'

Peter matched Sherman's smile and leaned in. 'Can you say anything other than no?'

To which Sherman chuckled good-naturedly and responded, 'Not for the moment, sir, no.'

Well, fuck you very much, Sherman, and have a really shitty day!

'I have an idea,' Peter announced when they returned to the car.

Misha opened her door. 'We visit the other nursing homes and look for them there?'

'Exactly. As long as they're not admitted under a pseudonym, we might have a chance of finding them.'

'But how do we know they're not under a pseudonym and still at Seaview?'

'I guess we don't. Although logic dictates that Balloch wouldn't have left them where they were already known. That would be too risky.'

'Hmm. I have an idea,' said Misha. 'Are you averse to bribery?'

'Precisely what I was thinking. Knowing Balloch, it's extremely unlikely she pays her staff a cent more than she absolutely has to. In which case, Mr Happypants might be open to a little graft and corruption.'

'Exactly.'

They waited in the car until the end of the day. From where they sat, they watched Sherman walk to an ancient Magna with weather-worn green duco and get in. It grumbled into life and turned left out of the carpark. Peter pulled out behind him and followed.

'You could afford to put a little distance between us,' said Misha, coughing as they travelled down the highway. 'Even if we lose him, we can simply follow the smoke trail.'

He spluttered. 'True.'

The smoke trail led them to a shopping centre where Sherman bought a few groceries on a credit card, a bottle of rum and a large container of fried rice topped with fried chicken in batter, drowned in a sweet and sour sauce. From there, he travelled less than a kilometre to a block of flats. He parked his car and entered flat two.

'Now, watch and learn!' Peter took a pair of disposable gloves out of the glovebox and put them on. He produced a plastic bag from under his seat. 'Stay here and look out for him. Toot if he does anything.'

A few minutes later, he returned to the car. He tossed the plastic bag into the boot, took off the gloves and climbed into the driver's seat.

'Are we finished?' asked Misha.

'For the moment,' he replied. 'That's all we need for now.' He cranked up the engine. As they moved off, he added, 'Never forget, Misha, that one person's waste is another person's Walkley Award. So, let's go home and go through this lot and see what we've got.'

Chapter Forty-Two

Getting to know you

Sherman Little estimated that he was about a month away from losing his home. He had received notices from his letting agent, but he didn't have enough money to pay the rent anyway, so he tore them up and threw them away without reading them. In a month, he'd probably be sleeping in his car.

His pay was still a day away, but he had a half-tank of petrol, some bread rolls in the freezer and enough coins jangling in his pocket to justify a midday trip to the pub. He couldn't wait for lunchtime; his head wasn't in the job. Ever. And certainly not at that moment.

He was a writer. Stream of consciousness. Joyce. Woolf. Hemingway.

He wasn't afraid of homelessness; if it was to be, he would turn his eviction into a fertile field and plough it for the award-winning book he planned to write. The future was his. To write the greatest novel of the pre-annihilistic era (as he'd coined it) was his destiny. He had outlined it all in his head.

Meanwhile, back in the real world, his immediate superior irritated him by saying, 'Sherman, it's nearly the end of the month. Have you posted the reminder letters yet?'

Old people were old-fashioned—in cosmic terms they were minutes away from Foreverland and they had forgotten how to live in the here and now. Paper mail was an agonising anachronism. Sherman resented having to run errands or mail anything. Today, however, it presented him with an opportunity.

He replied, 'I'll leave for lunch a little early and swing past the post office on my way. I have them all ready.' He patted a box by his feet.

'Well, make sure you do. I shouldn't have to remind you to do it every time.'

His response was an unfelt smile.

At twelve, he prepared to go out. There were two missed calls on his phone—both from private numbers—and there were two messages for him to retrieve. The first was his letting agent enquiring about the rent: *This is your last chance…* But that didn't interest him. The second was from Henry Honnery. He left a number but few details aside from, *I have something to tell you that just might interest you…* It was intriguing, but not enough to justify a speedy return call.

Sherman went to the post office first, left the letters with the clerk, returned to his car and drove straight to the pub. Once there, he bypassed the bar.

The lights and bells beyond the partition held him in a rapture. He took out his money. He was headed for the gaming lounge.

Around three that afternoon, Peter called again. This time, his call was answered.

'Hello, Sherman speaking.'

'Henry Honnery, barrister, here, Mr Little.'

'Hmm.'

Peter could hear Sherman breathing. He continued, 'I was wondering if you had a moment to speak with me: I have something I'd like to discuss with you. Let's say, it's an opportunity of sorts. I'd like to offer you a business proposal.'

Silence, and then, 'Sorry, I'm not interested in direct marketing schemes or pyramid selling.'

'And I'm not touting a direct marketing scheme or pyramid selling. Look, I'll be frank; when we met yesterday, I mentioned the names of my clients, but I didn't explain why I was trying to track them down.' He cleared his throat. 'The truth is, my clients are being held against their will in one of the BlackSwan nursing homes and I need to locate them. You may be able to render the humanitarian aid that I need to help me find them and free them. Naturally, I'm more than happy to fund your humanitarian efforts.'

'Sorry, but I'm not the philanthropic type, Mr Honnery.'

'Maybe not, but pardon me for saying, you seem like the hard-working-for-little-reward type. Surely, you could use a little extra money...'

Sherman terminated the call.

'Shit!'

Misha twirled around in her chair and asked, 'So, what did he say?'

'He hung up in my ear. Now, we both know he has really serious money problems. He gambles away most of his pay—his bank statements prove that. He's about to be evicted, and he's drowning in debt. Then I come along and hand him a lifeline. Anyone would have thought he'd fly at the chance to get himself out of a bind.'

'I suppose. Except it's possible that that's not his motivation.'

'What do you mean, that's not his motivation? It'll be bloody freezing around here in a couple of months or so. You reckon that homelessness and starvation aren't motivation enough? Right then, Mindreader Misha, you tell me, what is?'

'Well, maybe he's a bit more complicated than that.' She sighed. 'While you were going through his rubbish looking for bank statements and compromising information, I was reading some of the stuff he'd printed out and thrown away. It looked like pages from a manuscript.' She pulled out a grubby manila envelope from under her desk. 'I think he believes himself to be a novelist. It's unreadable trash and he doesn't have a clue about syntax or style, but I think that's his dream. I believe that's what gets him up in the morning.'

'And so?'

'And so, I think if we tell him who you really are and what you hope to achieve, he might just help us. He wants to be a writer, Peter.'

'As do millions of other no-hopers. Look, I don't know how we can use that to persuade him to help us. I can't get him a publisher and I'm not about to offer to ghost-write a book for him.'

'No, but you could offer him a shared by-line on the article once it's written.'

'Share my by-line? With a talentless amateur? You have to be fucking joking, Misha!'

'Okay. You don't have to bite my head off. It was only a suggestion.'

And a bloody stupid one. 'Money's one thing, but offering up my
reputation to a complete stranger is something entirely different.
Thank you for the suggestion, Misha, I appreciate it, but it's a step
too far.'

An hour later, her idea was becoming a flea in his ear. He needed
Sherman—or someone else with access to patient details—in order
to move forward. Sherman was vulnerable in a way that few people
were, and the awful truth was that he might not have the same
leverage with anyone else. If Sherman helped him out, maybe it
wouldn't be the end of the world if he weaved in a mention of it in
the article.

After Misha left for the day, Peter headed back to flat two alone,
only stopping briefly to pick up a pizza for his dinner. He arrived
in the evening chill, but he didn't have to knock on the door to
gain Sherman's attention; he saw him the moment he walked up
the driveway. Sherman sat on his doorstep shivering, his head in
his hands. He looked up when Peter approached.

'I've been evicted, Mr Honnery' he said. 'They've changed the
locks and I didn't even get the chance to take my stuff out.'

'So, what are you going to do now?' asked Peter.

'Maybe I should have read all of those letters instead of just
throwing them out. I don't know where I'm going to go. I don't have
anywhere and I'm flat broke.'

'What about your friends? Family?'

Sherman shook his head. 'I'll have to sleep in my car, I guess. I'm
going to die.' He looked up. 'You said something about paying me
for some help?'

'I may have done, but it's a bit late for that now, I think.'

'Why? Did you find someone else?'

'Yes. I'm sorry, it couldn't wait.' Peter paused and gave the impression that he was thinking. 'Look, what if I make some calls for you
and we speak in the morning? It may mean that you'll have to sleep
in your car tonight.'

'Can't I just come home with you, Mr Honnery?'

'Out of the question, I'm afraid. Wait here.' He went back to his car and returned with a blanket and the pizza. 'I bought this for my kids, but you may as well eat it while it's hot. Is your phone charged?'

'Yes.'

'Good. Well, then I'll call you in the morning. Make sure you answer me this time.'

'I will. Thank you, Mr Honnery.'

'Call me Henry.'

In the morning, Peter had Sherman exactly where he wanted him. He told him exactly what he needed from him. He might be able to make use of Sherman's information, provided it was timely and good. He offered him some fully paid accommodation for a month, in exchange for it.

'But I won't be giving you any money, right? And I want to see results before I go any further,' said Peter, 'so it's in your interests to get going soon. How quickly can you start searching?'

'Straight away. I'll start searching the records straight away. I'll find them; I'm good at solving puzzles. I'll ask around too, if I have to.'

'Print out whatever you find—I'll need a paper trail to get things going. Whatever you do, you cannot tell anyone anything. Not a word, not even a hint. This is triple-A top secret. I can't emphasise this enough: you must be discreet. If they work out what we're doing, we'll lose the twins again and I'll guarantee that we'll never ever find them.'

'I'll find them. I won't breathe a word about it. Trust me, I can do this, Henry.'

It took Sherman under two hours to locate the Schneiders in the Bayvista Nursing Home, now using the name of Schmidt. Their documents were all in a separate file and he found them too, and emailed the lot to Peter.

The documents included a report on the Schneider twins from a locum doctor: *Residents orientated to time and place, lucid and distressed. Wanting to go home. Wanting to see their cousin. Keep saying there is nothing wrong with them.*

'This was normal behaviour for them?' Misha asked. 'Not demented, but normal was their normal?'

'According to the locum doctor who wrote this report, yes. He was called in one night because they wanted to leave, and the RN became concerned. It was late at night and the nurse couldn't get hold of their usual doctor.

'Apparently the twins told the locum that they couldn't understand why they were there. They begged to be taken home,' Peter continued, 'but when the locum expressed his doubt that there was anything actually wrong with them and his support for them, someone called in a different doctor. That doctor sedated them with more pills. Then that same doctor reported that they couldn't get out of their chairs and that they could only walk with assistance.

'When you go further back in time, you'll find that he was also the one that got them sectioned in the first place, so they could be removed from their house and put in the nursing home. Balloch must have been paying him off.'

He kept reading; it was like Christmas morning, and every click opened a happy surprise. Adriana Balloch was implicated at every turn: she had changed their names and admitted them to the new home herself. She had falsified their records. She had even arranged government funding for them, even though she had more than enough to pay the fees out of the funds she'd swindled from them. It was gold.

All the money in the world and she's still a bloody cheapskate.

He tore himself away from the screen long enough to arrange a bedsit for Sherman to move into. By lunchtime, he'd reported Adriana Balloch to the Public Advocate's Office. He received a call an hour later.

'I've read your email, Peter,' said Jan Seebold from the Public Advocate's Office. 'We operate under strict privacy laws, so I don't want to overstep the mark. I'm going to choose my words carefully. Without going into specifics, you've described elder abuse, not to mention misuse of authority and misappropriation of funds. If what you've told to me is true, well, it's concerning, to say the least.'

'That's why it's imperative that you help them. I haven't over-stated their case: the Schneiders are in immediate danger,' Peter replied. 'Their case can't sit on the backburner. If they're moved again, we might never locate them. I'm sending over the documents that prove everything I've told you right now.'

'Well,' she responded, 'I'm treating this as my top priority; I'm not going anywhere.' She sat at her desk, her foot tapping, waiting for Peter's email. She opened it the moment it arrived. The attachments made her gasp.

Early afternoon, Jan Seebold entered the Bayvista Nursing Home, armed with an urgent order empowering her to remove the Schneider twins and take them to a secure location, until they could return home.

'Are you here to help us?' asked Anastasia, as she watched one of the carers packing up her belongings.

'I'm here to take you away from this place to somewhere safe where you and Octavia can stay until you can go home.'

'We're going home?' said Octavia. 'Are we really going home?'

'That's the plan.'

'Oh, Anna, thank goodness! Did you hear her? We're going home, Anna, we're going home!'

'Thank you.' Anastasia took Jan Seebold's hand, raised it to her lips and kissed it.

Chapter Forty-Three

The stars start to align

The following day coincided with Adriana's *at-home day*—a day she set aside each week solely for list-ticking. It was the day that she gathered all the things she least wanted to do, and the persons she least wanted to see, and assigned them a time in her schedule: coffee with the producer of *Brighton Babes*, a session with her voice coach, another with her yoga instructor, a third with her astrologer. And so on, and so forth.

But first of all, she was expecting a courier to deliver a parcel from the David Jones eveningwear department—a gift from her fast-diminishing circle of sponsors and admirers. While very few things excited her lately, she was more than a little intrigued to see the Alexander McQueen outfit. She wasn't exactly waiting at the door for the courier, but she was keeping an eye out for him or her.

So, when the doorbell rang at exactly nine that morning, she didn't prevaricate. She didn't send her housekeeper to answer it. She didn't ask Brian to see who it was.

She swung open the door in full expectation of receiving a nice, large, black-and-white herringbone box.

So, then, why was this stupid man handing her a very ugly, enormous, beige envelope instead?

'Adriana Balloch?' he asked.

'Yes?' she replied without thinking.

He caught her unawares. 'I'm an officer of the Public Advocate. I am formally serving you notice of the grant of an immediate stay of the powers of attorney you hold for Octavia Schneider and Anastasia Schneider. Please take the time to read the bundle of documents contained in this envelope carefully. You may also wish to obtain legal advice.' And then he bolted away.

'What?' She looked down at the envelope in her hands. 'What?' She lobbed the documents back through the open door. 'What?'

The officer was already at the gate. She watched him retreat and then she stepped outside to retrieve the bundle from the garden bed where it had landed. She brushed off the soil, went back inside and tore it open. The first page told her that she was required to attend a preliminary hearing in a week's time to answer allegations of financial mismanagement of the twins' estate. A very large compensation claim would follow, the details of which had yet to be finalised. In her absence, the court had also ordered a hold on all her assets, in case she tried to make them disappear.

Brian was the second person to hear her scream. She called the head of her security first. 'Find the cunts who did this to me and kill them!' she shrieked. 'Or better yet, bring them to me and I'll burn their eyes out first and feed them to the crows!'

'You're such an earth-mother, Adriana,' said Brian, sipping his breakfast ristretto. 'So warm and so caring.'

She spun around. 'I have every right to be furious: they've cut off all my money. I have people to pay and no access to my money. My money! We could go to the wall because of this. We're fucked without the Schneider development. You think our life comes free?' She waved her hand around the living room, past the Whiteleys and the Nolans hanging on the walls. 'We've been living beyond our means for years. You must know that. And you and that whore of yours haven't helped matters.'

'Don't you dare! Don't you dare involve me in this! Whatever choices you've made, you've made alone,' he retorted.

'Of course, I should have known you'd run away from any responsibility.' She exhaled loudly. 'You've always been as spineless, useless and limp as your dick.'

'And you've always been as hard and uncaring as yours, you bitch!' He snorted and finished his coffee. He chewed over her words and resumed more gently, 'Listen to me for once in your life, Adriana. I think you're overreacting. I want that development just as much as you do, but, if you ask me, what's happening now is a fight over nothing. It'll soon blow over and the subdivision will go ahead just as we planned. And then we'll go on tormenting each other as always and being our usual selves.'

She paused. 'Really? You think so?'

'Really. First things first: get that freezing order lifted until the case can be heard properly. Let's face it, the twins are old; anything could happen. Court cases have a habit of dragging on and, to be perfectly blunt, time is a luxury old people simply don't have. When they die, the case has to die. At their age, they're bound to die soon, and it will all be yours anyway.'

'Yes, but not soon enough.'

***

At the same time, Peter was sitting at his desk, hammering out a scathing piece about Adriana. Which nobody would touch.

His contacts told him they couldn't do anything with it. Adriana had a reputation; she was litigious.

'She'll sue the fuck out of us,' said Crofty, 'and then she'll get one of her associates to beat the living shit out of us. I don't think I can help you this time, mate.'

'But every word of it's true.'

'Yes, but can you get the Schneiders to say so on the record?'

'No, I can't. Not right now.' Jan Seebold hadn't told him where they were, or when they might be coming home. He needed to be patient. He wanted to be patient. He knew he couldn't afford to wait for any legal entanglements that might stop him publishing his exposé on Balloch and her mates.

Several days dawdled past while he sat on his hands. Nobody contacted him. Progress was painfully slow.

Then Jan Seebold called him. 'The preliminary hearing is set for tomorrow.'

'Can I attend?' he asked.

'No, not this time. At the full hearing in the future, questions may arise we might want you to answer, so you might be asked to attend that. I mean, the documents speak for themselves, really, so you might not be needed at all.'

'What about as a reporter, then?'

'Absolutely not. No press. Everything needs to remain private, at least until the Schneider twins decide to go public.' She explained. 'Look, the twins have engaged a trustee company to manage their affairs in the interim, and they have a solicitor representing their interests at the hearing. Adriana Balloch should do the same. Who knows what might happen?'

'Well, keep me posted, Jan, please.' He hung up. He turned to Misha and asked, 'Do you think you'd like to hang around a court-house in town tomorrow without me, on the off-chance that you might get to speak to the Schneider twins?'

She smiled. 'Would I!' she replied. 'It'll be my chance to do some real investigative reporting at last.'

'I can't afford to be seen in case someone recognises me. Bitch Balloch may be there, so whatever you do, you'll need to be care-ful. Take the rest of the day to familiarise yourself. You may want to look at this.' He handed her a hard copy of his article.

'Of course.' She packed up for the day. As she stood up to leave, she added, 'I can't wait.'

The next day didn't come soon enough and, when it did finally arrive, the hours never seemed to pass. The hearing was scheduled at twelve, but Misha called at ten past, to let Peter know it had been delayed, and they were told to return at two.

'Have you seen the twins?' he asked.

'I'll update you later.'

She called him again from outside the courthouse a little after four.

'Peter,' she said, 'Good news! I was able to get into the hearing.'

His mouth dropped open. 'What? How?'

'Well, the Schneiders recognised me as they were going into the courthouse with their lawyer, and they came over to say hello. We spoke for a while in German, and I'm not sure if the other people there thought I was the interpreter. Anyhow, they asked me if I wanted to go into the hearing with them and of course I said yes.'

260

'That's bloody fantastic! And?'

'And then Adriana showed up.'

'With her lawyer, I suppose.'

'No, that's the thing. She came alone. No lawyer and no Brian. At first, she tried to be nice to Octavia and Anastasia, but they ignored her. Then she tried crying and everyone ignored her. After that, she tried yelling, but they told her to be quiet or she'd have to leave. All the while, she was trying to bully the judge to reinstate her authority over the Schneider twins' estate.'

'And?'

'She lost, of course. There will be another hearing later, but for now, Octavia and Anastasia have regained interim control of their lives.'

Peter punched the air. 'That's great news.'

'But I have even better news. I got them to go on the record. The twins. They've agreed to grant you a no-holds-barred exclusive.'

I fucking love you, Misha!

That became his licence to print.

SEASIDE SOCIALITE CHEATS COUSINS

A little over a fortnight later, after a barrage of tradesmen and gardeners had made the Schneider property borderline habitable, the twins moved back into their gingerbread cottage across the road.

Adriana Balloch was on the descent.

Chapter Forty-Four

New neighbours, old neighbours

'Peter,' said Anastasia Schneider, 'hello. I just saw you drive in, and so I came straight over. I hope you don't mind. Can I please talk to you? Do you have the time?'

'Come in,' he replied, still juggling shopping bags. 'I haven't welcomed you home properly. You may as well talk to me while I put these away and then we can have a drink together.' He led her to the kitchen. 'Of course, you know my protégée, Misha; you saw her at the hearing. I think I introduced her to you before by another name. I'm sorry about that, but now you understand why I had to do it.'

'Of course,' said Anastasia.

'*Guten Tag*,' said Misha with a smile. '*So schön, Sie zu sehen.* It's so nice to see you again. *Kaffee?*'

'*Nein, danke.*' Anastasia sat down at the table. '*Es ist schön, Sie auch wieder zu sehen.*' She watched Misha pour herself a cup of coffee.

'Are you sure you wouldn't like some?' Misha asked her again, pushing the coffee towards her.

'Oh, well, but only if you have enough.' Anastasia accepted the cup and settled herself. 'Here is what I wanted to talk to you about, Peter. Octavia and I went around to see Mimi the other day, to tell her that our new administrator is taking that Eddie Arnold to court for what he's done to us and our land. We're asking for ten million dollars, most of which is needed to make good the damage to the reserve.

'We thought Mimi would be happy to learn about it, but she didn't take our news at all well. She began to say to herself, "No, no, no, you can't," and crazy things, like "he's going to kill me and Dad for sure". Then she started to scream at us, and we left. After that, it was quiet until last night when they took Mimi and her father away. Two ambulances. We still don't know what happened to them.'

Peter replied, 'I didn't hear anything—I suppose I must have slept through it. They were taken by ambulance, you said?'

'That's right.'

'Any police present?'

'No, no, I don't think so.'

'Hmm. Do you want me to try to find out what happened to them for you?'

'Please, Peter.' She paused. 'There's more. Octavia and I walked along our beautiful creek yesterday and we followed it all the way down to the beach. That Arnold man did such terrible things while we were away. He raped our land. He ruined our home. He took away all our fences. How could our cousin allow such a thing to happen?'

Peter drew breath. 'I'm sorry to say I don't think she allowed it to happen, I think she made it happen.'

'No, that's not possible. She is not a good woman, I know. She wanted to steal from us, but she loves this land.'

'Oh, it's possible all right. Do you want to know everything I know?'

Anastasia nodded.

'Well, you already know your cousin's role in having you and Octavia locked up. Everyone knew she was destined to inherit your home as well as the bushland your father preserved in your mother's memory. The problem was that she wanted it sooner rather than later. So, she had her own personal doctor drug you to make it appear that you were demented. After Misha and I found you at Seaview, she hid you away in one of her other nursing homes so we couldn't do anything more to help you.'

'I remember you came and spoke to us once. After that, I don't remember anything until they came and took us away from Adriana.'

'She used the power of attorney you gave her to make all your decisions for you and to take over your property without having to wait for you and Octavia to pass on first.' He saw the sadness in her eyes. 'Awful, I know.'

'Yes, we know all about that. It was despicable. And yet we were always good to her and her family. In the old days, when her family needed money, we always found a way to give them some. I know in my head what Adriana did to us, but my heart still doesn't understand how she could do it. You see how she lives these days: she is already very rich, so why does she need more?'

'No matter how much money rich people have, it's never enough. Money speaks to her. It was always all about your land. Your land is of no use to Adriana as a conservation area. As long as you and Octavia were in charge of your own affairs, your land was never going to be anything other than a home for you and the wildlife. I think her aim was always to damage and degrade your land to the point that there was no value in keeping it.

'She has been turning it into a wasteland, with Arnold's help. They're involved in some high-stakes mutual grooming of sorts: that piece of filth gets the benefit of running his rubbish dump on your land with Adriana's blessing, while he turns it from a habitat for wildlife into a death sentence for anything that happens to stray onto it. Once the land's no longer a sanctuary for the local flora and fauna, the path is clear for your cousin and her snake of a husband to get it rezoned with the mayor's help. Then they're free to develop it for housing. At a gigantic profit. And everyone at every level is paid to turn a blind eye to it.'

Anastasia took out a handkerchief and wiped her nose. 'Yes, of course,' she tutted. 'I understand. It's shocking.'

'And what's worse is, I think that that real estate agent who died—Nick Sutcliffe—was involved, too. He was Adriana and Brian's business partner. I think he started off as part of it, but he developed a conscience somewhere along the way. I think Adriana and Brian found out that he was going to tell the authorities what he knew, and they disposed of him. Him and possibly two other people as well.'

Anastasia put her hand over her mouth and gasped. 'You don't mean…they killed him? But that would be murder! No, Peter, surely not! Not Adriana! She has done some bad things for sure, but I can't believe she is a murderer.'

'I hate to have to tell you this, but Adriana was involved in the deaths, absolutely. To what degree, I'm not sure quite yet.'

'But murder?' She trembled. 'Terrible, terrible! No wonder Mimi is so scared of us. But why don't you tell this to the police?'

'I have. So far, I've told the police what I can prove. I know I'm right about the rest of it, but I won't take it to them until I have the evidence to support it.'

'Oh, Peter! But how do I tell Octavia all of this? She will be so upset. We were raised to know right from wrong. Family or not, if Adriana has done wrong, she will have to pay for it.' She shook her head. 'I am so sorry for the mess she has made.'

'You're not responsible for Adriana; I'm just sorry for you, and everyone else who's caught up in it. I'm going to make sure that she and her mates are exposed, and I won't stop until they get the punishment they deserve.'

'We should never have trusted her. We were so foolish. When she came with the papers for us to sign, we thought better Adriana than a stranger to take care of us. She loves us, she loves the land, she will do the right thing, we thought. And her lawyer seemed such a nice girl. She told us not to worry because we were protected.'

'Do you remember the lawyer's name?'

'Let me think... No. No, it's gone.' She sighed. 'We will do whatever we can to help you. Papa would be turning in his grave if he knew what she's done.'

'I think it's best that you forget thinking of Adriana Balloch as your relative. The cousin you remember doesn't exist. Adriana Balloch is a psychopath, and she doesn't deserve your loyalty.'

'I know deep down that you're right. Octavia and I saw our own lawyer last week; we got an order against Arnold, so he can't hurt us, and we're changing our wills. I don't care if everything goes to strangers, but Adriana won't see a cent of our money.'

'I don't blame you for feeling that way.'

She finished her coffee and said, 'But you must be busy. I won't take up any more of your time with my problems.' She rose and he walked her to the door.

'Spielman,' she said suddenly, pronouncing it with a *sh* at the start. 'I am thinking she must have been German, or something.'

'The lawyer?' Peter stopped in his tracks. 'That was her name?'

'Yes, I think so.'

'You said she was a young woman?'

'Yes. She came to see us with Adriana. She witnessed everything. She told us that she didn't do this kind of work usually, but she did it as a favour to us.'

'Could it have been Spellman, not Spielman?'

'I suppose so. It is possible.' Her brow furrowed.

'Suzanne Spellman? Could her name have been Suzanne Spellman?'

Her face brightening, she replied, 'Yes, yes, that was it. Exactly! Suzanne Spellman. I am sure of it. Do you know her?'

'Not personally. I've heard of her, that's all. What you've told me is very interesting. Leave it with me and I'll let you know what I find.'

'If you would, Peter.'

'And if you're ever worried or you need anything, you can always call on me, day or night.'

'That is a great comfort to me. Thank you.'

'Remember that and tell Octavia, too.'

'I shall.'

He locked the door behind her. He steadied himself.

Bloody hell! I didn't see that coming!

Chapter Forty-Five

Show me your friends, Adriana

She bypassed the Bentley and the Lamborghini, and unlocked the Porsche Cayenne with the touch of her hand and climbed into the driver's seat. The lift had retrieved it from the lower basement and the turntable had pointed the car towards the door, so all she had to do was drive forward.

These were the conveniences Adriana Balloch had no intention of living without.

The meeting had been arranged at Manning Park at nine precisely, an hour prior to opening and well before the tourist buses arrived. They were to meet in the carpark beside the homestead. Just the three of them and nobody else. She wasn't worried about the others: they wouldn't be stupid enough to try anything. Hers was the hand that fed their addictions, after all.

She would have arrived a minute early, except that she took a slight diversion to make sure that the others would reach the carpark first. She was the star of the show; they had to be made to wait. By the time she turned into the driveway, there were two cars in adjacent bays nearest the exit. She parked three bays away from them. Both men stepped out of their cars and she met them in the middle.

'So, what can you tell me?' she asked.

One of the men replied, 'It was Peter Clancy again. He got the information from the receptionist at Seaview, and then he took it to the Public Advocate,' while the other man remained silent.

She said, 'Peter Clancy again? What the fuck! You were meant to take care of him. What do I have to do to get rid of that piece of filth? Shoot him myself?' She stifled a scream and turned it into a groan. 'And what about the receptionist—what was his name—Sherman something?'

'Gone. Dealt with.'

'The neighbour and her old man?'

'Committed. He's rotting in the dementia unit of some crappy nursing home somewhere in Melbourne, and she's holed up in a mental health ward of the one of the public hospitals. They're going nowhere. Their place will be on the market soon.'

'And Clancy?'

The man continued, 'I've got plans for him, too. Look, I've got to watch my back right now: there's a detective investigating Sutcliffe again. It's not been easy.'

'I don't pay you for easy, Mike, I pay you for results. I am sick to death of your pathetic excuses. There are others, you know, who'd be very grateful to receive what I pay you. They'd get the job done.'

'I know, I know.'

'I want Clancy dead. *They* want Clancy dead. We all want Clancy dead. You're only alive and well because of me; you'd be finished without me. I'm the only one holding back the floodgates, you know. I'm protecting you. And it seems that I've had to protect you a lot lately—ask Fatso. If *they* ever found out how truly incompetent you are, you wouldn't just have a stupid detective on your back, you'd have the whole fucking gang gunning for you. You don't want to cross them. They're armed to the teeth, and they don't give a shit about collateral damage.'

'I know, I know. I won't let you down.'

'No,' she spat. 'No. Don't you let yourself down. If there has to be a next time, you won't be meeting with me and Fatso, it'll be the head of the local chapter of the Kommandanz you'll be meeting with and believe me, there won't be much talk involved.'

He looked away, sniffed and wiped his nose with his thumb. 'Are you holding?'

'Wait here.' She went to the Cayenne, opened up the door, leaned in and returned with a bulging plastic ziplock bag. She tossed it at him. 'Here.' He caught it with eager hands.

'It's done,' he said, handling the cocaine. 'Clancy's as good as dead.'

Adriana smiled. 'He'd better be. I'm sick of waiting.' She nodded at the silent man and said, 'You don't mind me calling you Fatso, do you, Eddie? You're not offended by that, are you? It's just my way of showing you how much you mean to me.'

He grunted his approval and smiled at her.

She continued, 'Good. And you'll get your payment as usual. Just keep those wheels turning.' Then she turned away and walked towards her car, calling out behind her as she went, 'No more excuses. I want to hear that Peter Clancy's died before the weekend. Just get it done, will you, Sergeant Moylan.'

Chapter Forty-Six

Manna from heaven

The wall next to Peter's desk shuddered.

'What the fuck?' He leapt to his feet. His mind flashed back to London, to 1996 and the massive explosion at Docklands. He had been two kilometres away, but the explosion was still ear-splitting, even at that distance.

'Get down!' shrieked Misha, falling to her knees and crawling under her desk.

'It's outside. Something's hit the house.' He headed towards the door.

'No! Peter! Don't!'

'I'm not cowering in my bloody office. I'm going outside.'

'Then I'll come too. Wait for me.'

Peaches was already standing past the back door, face upturned, staring at the roof.

'Could it have been a bomb?' Peter asked her. 'I mean, it didn't sound like one to me, but then I haven't heard many go off.'

She replied, 'More like a heavy object falling on the roof or hitting the wall, if you ask me.'

'A Molotov cocktail, perhaps? Did you see anything, or anyone running away?'

'Not a thing. And there's no sign of a fire that I can see. Maybe you were blessed with some space junk falling from the sky.'

Just then Cochineal turned the corner of the house, shaking her head. 'Well, it wasn't exactly Skylab, but it did fall from the sky. There's nothing to worry about. You want to see what it was? Come with me.'

They followed her around the side of the house. The top of the wall that faced the de Wolds' was sprayed with blood, torn flesh and faeces. Misha covered her mouth.

Peter laughed. 'That's it?'

'Yes,' she replied. 'But what a noise! And what a mess! And the rest of it is down there.' Cochineal pointed to a ragged, bloody heap in the garden.

'I thought it was something bad,' said Misha. 'So, it's a bird? But it's so big! What is it?'

'A bin chicken? Really? You've never heard of it before? It's a white ibis,' he explained, 'but they're called that because they like to eat our scraps.'

'Smells like it, too,' she said, returning inside.

'It's looks like the bin chicken swallowed a grenade and then detonated all over the house,' he joked. 'It's like a Jackson Pollock painting.'

Peaches commented, 'You know, I heard that there's been a spate of ibis deaths all over the coast. Something about suspected baiting…'

'Or possibly, poisoned to death by the pollution?' He looked down. The stench had reached his nostrils. 'So, the poor old bin chicken hit the house.'

'I'm not paid enough to clean that up,' said Cochineal.

'Seriously? You're good with roughing up villains, gardening in the company of snakes and doing odd jobs that involve rodents and spiders, and yet you draw the line at exploding fowl?'

'That's right, I do. You'll be cleaning it up because I just had my nails done again.'

'What will I do with the bird? It's too big to put in the bin and I don't feel like burying it.'

His words were still hanging in the air when Arnold sped along in his Audi TT with the roof down and the sound system at full volume, tooting the horn. Concealed by shrubbery, Peter and the girls observed him pull onto the nature strip in front of his house. Two trucks full of rubbish followed close behind. Blasting their horns, they drove past the Audi TT and up Arnold's driveway.

'More shit for the shit to bury,' Peter said angrily. 'How the hell does he keep getting away with it?'

They watched Arnold prise himself out the car and lurch towards his house.

'He'll get stuck in there one day with the roof shut. With any luck and all the methane he exudes, he'll end up gassing himself,' remarked Cochineal.

'That's given me an idea: I think I know what to do with the bin chicken.' Peaches smiled. 'A few bits shoved under the seats should add a special something to the atmosphere. The trucks too, if I get a chance.'

Peter chuckled. 'Yes, an Aussie icon needs a decent burial.'

Later that day, he made a few calls. Rick Burgess was high on the list, but he couldn't be disturbed. Katherine Sutcliffe didn't answer. Mimi's phone went straight to voicemail. Woody Turnbull said he'd call back later. He was having no joy. Conni was the lone name left at the end of a long list.

'It's been a while since we've talked,' he told her, 'and I mean really talked. I'd love to catch up with you. How about you and Silvio come here for dinner on Wednesday?'

'Will you be cooking?' asked Conni.

He chuckled. 'I know you're not a fan. I have improved over the years, honestly I have, but I could arrange some catering, I suppose.'

'No, don't do that. Silvio's away for the rest of the week. He's visiting his cousin in Mildura; it's salami and sausage-making time. He'll be elbow deep in pork and garlic and who-knows-what-else for days, and much as I love-love-love a spicy sausage, I don't feel the need to watch them being made. It's the mystery that does it for me every time. Besides, I just don't have the wardrobe for it.'

'Right. So, you're at a loose end?'

'Yes and no. I'm not being rude, but how about I come over for breakfast instead? You still make a reasonable coffee, and I'll bring some pastries. I'll tell Misha too, if you like.'

'Why not? The more the merrier. I'll get the bubbles to go with the coffee.'

'No, don't bother. I can't start the day the way I used to. I'll admit this to you because we've been friends forever and you and my surgeon are the only people on earth who know my approximate real age, but I'm beginning to think I'm too old for breakfast bellinis.'

'Ha! We're all headed in the same direction, Conni. No one lives backwards—although my problem's the reverse of yours: the older I grow, the earlier my need to get smashed.'

'In which case, I'm truly sorry I reintroduced you to your old mate booze. It's just that you were so tedious and pious without it.'

'Shall we say Wednesday at nine?'

'Let's make it eight. I still don't rise at dawn, mind you, but sleeping in has recently become the other casualty of growing older.'

He laughed. 'Fine. Eight it is.'

'See you then. And no more discussion of age ever again once I hang up,' she said.

On Wednesday, Conni floated in for breakfast on a perfumed cloud, wearing a full face of makeup and a pigtailed wig, with a woven basket hanging off each arm. She was a little late. 'I had to wait for the sfogliatelle to cook,' she explained. 'I bought the croissants and the Danish from a bakery, but Sergio makes his own sfogliatelle and then he freezes them. They're nothing short of orgasmic! I baked them fresh this morning. You should have seen me, with my apron and my baking trays and my timer. You should call me Australia's Martha Stewart. Who knew I could be such a domestic goddess?'

Peter replied, 'I happen to own an apron and baking trays and a timer, too. In which case, you should probably call me Australia's Sara Lee. Although lighting an oven and putting something in it does not constitute baking, you know.'

'Buzzkill.' She put down the baskets and kissed him on both cheeks. 'Is Misha here?'

'Not yet.'

'Good.'

He switched on his coffee machine while she unpacked her pastries. He glanced at her. 'You brought your own plates? I have plates, Conni. Look. They're not even chipped yet.'

'Don't sound so offended, Peter. Pardon me, if I prefer to eat my breakfast off Gianni Versace, may the gods of design heaven rest his soul. I've always thought food tastes better when it's served on fine gilded porcelain.' She sat next to him at the table and continued, 'Make sure you make enough for an extra cup. I've invited someone else to our collation; I hope you don't mind.' She had just finished speaking when someone knocked. 'Ah, there you go!'

Peter went to the front door and opened it. 'Detective Senior Sergeant? To what do I owe the pleasure?' He counted down his misdemeanours mentally from most recent to the distant past, but none of them justified a visit from the police.

Dan Browning replied, 'I believe I'm owed a coffee. You've got the pot on, I hope?'

Peter pointed him towards the kitchen. 'I have something much better than that. Come through. I hope you don't mind, I have a friend here...'

Conni was all smiles. She leapt to her feet. 'Hello, Dan,' she said, planting a kiss on his cheek. 'It's been far too long.'

'Conni,' said Browning. 'You're looking exceptionally well.'

Peter frowned. 'You two know each other?'

'We go back a long way,' she began, 'to the glory days of St Kilda and the Velour Lounge.'

'So how come I never met you back then?' Peter asked.

She laughed. 'Back then, he was a mere slip of a boy—but weren't we all? Dan here was a true bumfluff constable. You probably met him, Peter, but you may have considered him inconsequential, whereas I recognised his potential early on. You see, Peter, Dan couldn't be bought. He was and is a rare commodity: an officer who is honest to a fault, fair, smart and ambitious. I knew he'd go places.'

Browning shook his head. 'I vaguely remember you, when you wrote for that scandal rag—long gone, thankfully,' he said to Peter. 'I was still wet behind the ears back then—a pup—all energy and very little brain. I remember you were most hated among the hierarchy; you always asked questions that made them uncomfortable. I was around when you sank your teeth into some very bad coppers and one Dale McCracken in particular.'

'Yeah, well, close to thirty years may have passed since I last saw him, but Detective Senior Sergeant McCracken still haunts my nightmares from time to time.'

'I'm not surprised,' Browning replied. 'I heard what happened to you.'

'Dale McCracken. Now there's a name I haven't heard in decades,' said Conni, 'and very happily so. Dan is hands-down one of VicPol's finest, and McCracken was one of VicPol's filthiest. You were lucky to survive 1989, Peter.'

'I almost didn't.'

Browning resumed, 'McCracken thought he got away with being filthy, although he never figured on the Cobra inquiry. That, and Operation Bart, all meant to clean up the force, and it worked for a while, but the reality is that inquiries and operations drive the corruption underground. There will always be coppers and criminals, as well as criminal coppers. McCracken had a profound effect on me. He changed my life, really. He became my standard: I was determined not to do anything that he would do. He was the reason I wanted to do my bit to clean up Victoria Police.'

Conni piped up, 'I heard that McCracken's murder rap never stuck, but the corruption, intimidating witnesses and trafficking charges did.'

Browning nodded. 'Someone told me he was out a while ago. Apparently, he had a tough time out at Barwon. Prison's never a holiday for ex-coppers but he had it especially bad.'

'He deserved his sentence as far as I'm concerned, plus some,' said Peter. 'He escaped trial in exchange for a shitty sweetheart deal he didn't deserve. He pleaded to the lesser charges and sentencing allowed for his co-operation and apparent remorse. You do a few years and you get your life back? How easy is that?'

'Except he never got his life back, did he? He ended up with brain damage after an altercation with another inmate. These days, he can barely tie his own shoelaces.'

'Excuse me if I don't give a shit,' said Peter.

'And in a nutshell, that's how we all ended up here, today,' Conni remarked.

'I don't get it.'

'Okay, I'll explain,' said Browning. 'Conni's helped me a lot over the years. She's been my eyes and ears over the decades. There was very little that went down in the Velour Lounge that I didn't hear about because of her. She knew everyone in St Kilda in her day, and she knows a lot of people here, good and bad. Peter, you and I made an agreement that, in exchange for giving me that CCTV file, I'd give you whatever I could. It's time for me to honour that agreement. I need your help to flush out a piece of filth, a police informant, who's been using his immunity as carte blanche to do whatever he feels like.

'Police informants aren't supposed to break the law, but this one does nothing but. I made an application to the Chief Commissioner to have his name removed from the register. I cited many grounds for his name to be removed,' he continued, 'but I haven't heard anything yet.'

'Good luck with that,' Peter returned.

'I'm starting to believe this informant is protected at every level, although I can't work out why. Yes, he outed some bigwigs in the Kommandanz bikie gang a few years ago, but he's been a lot more reserved lately. I think he's decided he's protected for life, and he doesn't need to give the police any more information. He's definitely in cahoots with a certain Sergeant Moylan. That CCTV file you gave me is golden as far as Moylan's concerned.'

'It links Moylan with Sutcliffe's death. It's undeniable.'

'And there's more to Moylan than just that. I won't mention a scorched black hoodie recovered from a skip, or all the taped conversations that implicate him not just in the death of Sadie Taylor, but others as well.'

'You just did, although I'm guessing it's off the record?'

'Of course.' He paused. 'I believe you know Renard Cooper,' Browning resumed.

'Yes, he's Eddie Arnold's father in-law. Is he the informant?'

'Cooper? Hardly. He's evil through and through, that one: he would never dog.'

'He ran the brothel—' Conni began.

Peter interjected. 'Misha. Yes, I know.'

'I was working at St Kilda during an investigation into the criminal activities of Cooper and Balloch. Goldsmith came on the scene a bit later,' Browning explained.

'They were into the usual, I guess,' said Peter, 'extortion, drugs, prostitutes?'

Browning replied, 'That, and the rest. I was doing traffic back then, so I knew about the investigation, but I had very little to do with it. Mick Moylan had just been appointed a Detective Constable, and that was his entrée into the slime and grime of St Kilda. Balloch, Cooper and then Goldsmith: altogether a bad lot for a copper to get involved with. Seems that the connections Moylan made there have stayed with him for life.'

Peter guffawed. 'Well, you're not going to get any help from the local constabulary. I learned that after a lot of futile exertions. They're all in cahoots with each other.'

'The whole station's corrupt, you mean?' added Browning. 'Yeah, well, you may be right. Moylan's not exactly the helping kind, especially now that I'm the detective and he's more middle management. He's pretty influential as far as his constables are concerned. Moylan knows what's going on as much as I do, except that he's happy to be paid to look the other way. Him and his cronies. What he may not know is that, because of my local knowledge, I've been able to link the past with the present. I'm aware of at least three cold case murders with strong links to Cooper and Goldsmith and several others.'

'May I ask whose? Off the record of course.'

'They're implicated in the murder of a known drug dealer and a prostitute, and...' he paused.

'And?'

Conni blew her nose.

'Are you okay?' Browning asked her. 'Do you want me tell him?'

'He's family,' she sniffed.

He took a deep breath. 'There's evidence that Cooper and an associate may have murdered Ted.'

'Ted? You mean our Ted? Tapping Ted? What? He was murdered? But you told me Ted died of a stroke.' Peter reeled.

'I did, I know. I just couldn't...' Conni cried. 'When it happened, I wanted to tell you, but you'd already left. All I could find out was that you had buggered off to London.'

'But why Ted?' he asked painfully. 'He was the gentlest man I've ever met.'

'Well, we think he was murdered because Cooper was trying to get back at him. Cooper tried to extort money from the Velour Lounge and failed. It all became very messy after that. You know Ted, he may have been gentle, but he was never one for rolling over.'

Conni stared at her hands. 'Yes, Cooper tried the stand-over thing and failed, but I think he was bent on destruction when he found out that we had rescued some of his girls from the brothel. His and Adriana Balloch's brothel. Four of their best earners, including Misha. I was going to be a witness.' She took a deep breath and steadied herself. 'But it never transpired, and, in the end, Ted died. Ted died, and I lived. We should have both lived or both died. No in-between. It's never been the same without him...'

'What happened?'

She continued, 'We were locking up one night. Ted was in a hurry to get home and I had to go back inside as I forgot something. I heard the shots and rushed outside to see him lying on the ground bleeding everywhere. I ran after them but couldn't catch them. I saw Cooper and another man as plain as day. Arrogant bastards weren't even wearing masks. I went straight to Moylan, and we expected Cooper to be arrested, but he wasn't. So, then I told Dan, but he was shut out of it.' She took out a tissue and wiped her eyes.

Peter snapped, 'Another police fuck-up. Let me guess, Dan, you've spent all these years feeling guilty about it, and now you think you can make amends to Conni.'

'Quiet. It wasn't his fault, Peter,' she shot back, 'he did everything he could. It was a corrupt system. You know how the police worked back then.'

'Sure do. Sometimes it's hard not to think they still work that way. The Lawyer X stuff- up proves it. A corrupt lawyer playing both sides—the cops and the crims—and she was in bed with them, too. I heard all about it when I was in London.'

'Can I speak?' Browning interrupted irritably. 'I didn't bury the investigation of Ted's murder; I tried to escalate it. I pleaded for Cooper to be brought in for questioning. I was told in no uncertain terms it wasn't my call and to let it go.'

'Don't tell me. He knew people.'

'The investigation was deliberately botched, and no one was ever charged. I wanted to blow the whistle, but it was made very clear to me that if I continued, I'd be destroyed. I'd be lucky to have a career if I proceeded. There were many times I wanted to leave. The job's hard enough when you feel supported. But when you don't…'

'It nearly destroyed both of us, Dan,' said Conni. 'I sold the Velour Lounge and moved down here hoping to get away from it. Of course, the pain was always there. I started again. Prayed every night that Cooper would get his just deserts. Even thought of hiring someone to kill him. I still maintained my old contacts. Then I just tried to put it behind me, until Dan knocked on my door a few months ago.'

'This is my final hurrah,' said Browning. 'My health's suffering. I'm going to be retiring from the police. I've finally had enough. Anyway, I've been keeping copies of stuff that's come across my desk over the years. Stuff I thought might come in handy one day. Stuff that implicates people. I've always tried not to arouse suspicion, I kept my head down and my nose clean. Nothing can be traced back to me, there are no computer trails, no searches attached to me, nothing. Sometimes you just have to be patient and wait until the time is right to pounce. I know what I'm doing contravenes any number of laws, but it's right in the court of public opinion. I want you to dish the dirt. You didn't get this from me.'

He dropped a file on the table.

Browning continued, 'I'm done here. Read this file, Peter, and do your worst. Which I understand from Conni is likely to be your best.'

'Thank you, Dan.'

He finished his coffee and made for the door. Misha arrived just as Browning was leaving. 'Was that…?' she asked.

'Yes, dear. He's retiring.'

'Shame. Except for him, I would have been dead.'

'Chances are, except for him, we all would have been,' replied Conni.

CHAPTER FORTY-SEVEN

All things must pass

It took Peter the rest of the morning to read the file Dan Browning had left for him. Then he hammered out a thousand words before he'd lifted his eyes from the screen once. Another thousand, and he heard a rap on the door.

Who the fuck is it now? Don't you people know that I'm working and I'm on a roll—do I have to put up a sign to keep everyone out?

He was in the zone, and he wasn't leaving it anytime soon. He kept going.

New paragraph...

He heard the door open: had he really forgotten to lock it again?

...the Commissioner was asked to comment...

He heard footsteps down the hallway, but they were too light to be those of an assassin. *Assassins don't wear high heels, do they?* Besides, Peaches and Cochineal were around, and they would have weeded out anyone with bad intentions. He continued typing:

...it was part of an ongoing investigation...

'Misha?' he called out.

'No,' was the reply. 'It's not Misha.'

More footsteps, and then a face appeared. 'Oh, so that's where you've been hiding.'

The face at the doorway was both familiar and unfamiliar, cheeks newly inflated with fillers, and the lips doughy and irregular.

'Rhiannon?' It was absolutely a question. His eyes travelled down; he couldn't help staring at her oddly engorged nipples— one pointing a bit too far east and the other too far to the west. He couldn't remember them looking like that before. Her breasts had grown asymmetrically, too. He was convinced that they would have spilled out of her skin-tight tank top and run away from all the abuse, had they been capable of it.

'Rhiannon?' he repeated, if only to reassure himself that it really was her.

'Yes, Peter, it's me. I'm back from the Caymans, all fit and fresh.'

First Ibiza and now the Caymans: I'd call that cosmetic surgery with a side order of sightseeing. He turned away and resumed typing.

'I can see that you're busy, but we need to talk.'

'Do we? What? Now?'

'Oh, yes, we do.' She sat down at Misha's desk, crossed her sun-tanned legs, and swung around to face him.

He scowled. At that moment, he really wasn't interested in speech. Or sex if that was what she was after.

She muttered under her breath, 'Come on, Rhi; it's now or never,' and cleared her throat. 'There's no nice way to do this, so I'll just say it. It's over, Peter. Us. You and me. It was fun while it lasted and I'm really sorry to have to tell you this, but we're through.'

He didn't look up. He replied, 'Never mind.'

'No, no, of course you're right to wonder why. Andre and I have decided to give it another go. We owe each other that much after all these years. For the sake of the boys.'

'That's good. I hope you'll all be blissfully happy.'

'It's okay, don't feel that you have to hold back. I knew you'd be heartbroken, but I wanted to talk it through with you.'

'It's fine. I get it.'

'It hurts, I know. You'll get over the pain in time. I don't want you to have suicidal ideations, because of losing me.'

What the fuck! Did she have a delusion implant, too?

'No need to worry about that.'

She kept going. 'And I wouldn't want you to have any feelings of inadequacy. What we had was wonderful. You were wonderful. Honestly, it's me, it's not you.'

'I know.'

'You did nothing wrong. I know it aches now, but you'll come to see that this is the right thing for you. A chance for you to find someone'—she wrung her hands—'more age appropriate.'

Oh no, you did not just say that!

He turned to face her and studied her for a while, and confirmed to himself yet again that his very first impression of her had been right after all. All doubt vanished—she was genuinely as egocentric and as vacuous as she looked.

Time to rein in her galloping ego. For what I am about to say I am truly sorry, Misha!

He smiled sheepishly and said, 'I've been avoiding this conversation for a while now, because I didn't want to hurt your feelings, Rhiannon, but since you've brought it up, I may as well tell you.'

'Tell me what?'

'I must admit that your timing could not have been better.' He stifled a laugh and continued, 'I have a confession of my own. I think you've met Misha, my colleague?'

'The girl who works here?'

'My colleague.'

'The pretty young blonde thing, yes, I've seen her. What about her?'

He put on his well-practised guilt-ridden face. 'Well, she's told me that she has deep emotional and sexual feelings for me.'

'What, like a daddy thing?'

A daddy thing? Who the hell was your daddy? Jeffrey Epstein?

'No, not like a daddy thing. Like a lover thing. A relationship thing. Maybe even a marriage thing. I've been putting her off because I wanted to talk to you first. But now that you've explained to me that you and I are over, she and I are finally free to explore a wonderful future together. So, thank you for making it so easy for me...to uncouple...'

Rhiannon was gulping air. 'What are you trying to say? You and her?'

'Yes, me and her. It turns out that Andre was right about moving on from...'

'From?'

'Middle-aged women. To someone younger. To maintain erectile power.'

'But she's... But she's... And you're so....'

'But she's what? Mature? Discerning? Unbelievably beautiful? Yes, she is all that and more, wrapped up in a young woman's bod. And she's all mine. So, I genuinely wish you and Andre every success for the future because, well, aren't I the lucky one!'

Seconds later, he heard the door slam as she walked out.

He laughed as he turned back to his computer.

What? Not even a goodbye kiss?

CHAPTER FORTY-EIGHT

The winds of change

The weather turned foul the following day. Summer had held on for as long as it could, even as the calendar approached autumn. The cockatoos that had been pecking chunks out of Peter's eaves and windows for months abruptly disappeared and the wind picked up. It had been windy from time to time—that was to be expected on the coast—but overnight it blew itself into a furious gale that wouldn't ease. The tap-tap-tap of something loose in his roof was driving him mad, despite his efforts to ignore it. The sound cut through his attempt to meditate. It worsened when he tried to sleep.

His mind kept ticking over while he lay in bed. He had worked all day on the series of articles that would tie up the loose threads and out the informant. In the dark, the chatter was unwanted and uncontrollable: he couldn't turn off his brain. He needed there to be a conclusion, a satisfying end to the saga, which there wasn't yet.

The notes that Browning had given him along with the file indicated that he had brought Moylan to the attention of the Anti-Corruption Commission as well as the Office of Public Prosecutions, but so far there had been no changes to Moylan's police registration and there were no charges pending as far as he knew. Moylan was being investigated. The evidence against Moylan was so compelling, Peter knew it had to be a matter of when and not if.

He stopped fighting his restlessness at around two, went back into his office and wrote down everything, both fact and speculation. Moylan worked for the unholy trinity: Balloch, Harrison and Goldsmith. He handled and protected Cooper as well as Arnold. He facilitated payments to bureaucrats, politicians, and other police officers. He had murdered Nick Sutcliffe, Sadie Taylor and

Jack Cunningham. And that was just the start. It was all there; he would get exactly what he deserved.

Peter typed until sunrise and then he backed it all up. He looked outside. The wind had drawn the rain, but the gale persisted, as did the tapping in his roof. He was utterly exhausted. This time he messaged Misha not to come in, checked that the front door was secure, closed the curtains and went to bed. Purged of all thought, he fell asleep in seconds and stayed asleep until the early afternoon.

He awoke to frantic shaking and someone calling his name.

'Fuck off Rhiannon,' he mumbled, his eyes still shut.

'It's me, Misha! Are you all right, Peter? Can you tell me what you have taken?'

'What? Why?' He rubbed his eyes.

'I've been trying to wake you up for ages. I was just about to call an ambulance. What did you take?'

'What? Nothing.'

'Then what are these?' She pointed to an empty hip flask and a trail of capsules spilled all over the bedside table.

'What, those? But they're nothing. Valerian, that's all. I took one with a sip or ten of whisky when I couldn't sleep last night. One. It didn't do a thing. I must have knocked the bottle over when I went to bed this morning. I was up all night writing and I went to bed after six. That's all. That's it.'

'So why the weird message?' She turned her phone towards him.

No need to come in the morning again. I'm finished.

'I was trying to tell you that you could sleep in.'

'Well, you should have said so. I knocked but you didn't answer, and the door was locked, so I used my key to let myself in and when I couldn't wake you, I thought…'

'Was I snoring?'

'Like a freight train.'

'Good chance I wasn't dead, then, hey?'

She sat on the edge of his bed. 'Well, since I'm here now, I may as well do some work.'

'If you like. You know, Misha, I keep meaning to ask you when your placement ends. I mean, it's been lovely mentoring you, don't get me wrong, and I gave you a glowing appraisal last semester. But how long are you meant to stay here?'

She smiled. 'Can I let you into a little secret? My work experience ended weeks ago.'

'And you're staying because...?'

'Because I'm as invested in this thing as you are. Plus, you're the subject of a piece I'm writing.'

'Well, I'm flattered.' After a pause, he added, 'I think.'

'How about I make us a coffee and I'll see you in the office whenever you're ready,' she said.

'Sounds pretty good to me.'

***

While Peter and Misha were sipping double espressos and watching the churning sea below them, in an office high above Collins Street, Adriana Balloch was consulting her solicitor.

'What I want from you,' she began, even before she sat down, 'is to get the freezing orders lifted.'

George Hatzimanolis was an experienced lawyer. It was no secret in the office that Adriana Balloch was not his favourite client. He had drawn the short straw; when she'd called to say she would be coming in and that she demanded to see someone, everyone else was suddenly busy. He had a hole in his monthly billing target that he needed to fill, so he reluctantly agreed.

He said, 'Do sit down, Adriana, and let's talk. May I get you a coffee? A tea?'

She sat down and crossed her legs. 'No, you may not get me a coffee or a tea, George. You may get me my money. Go to court and get the freezing orders lifted. That's all I want. They are my instructions to you.'

He sat down at his desk and drew breath. 'The freezing orders were granted to preserve your assets, and to stop you moving them offshore and so on. Now that you're facing a multi-million-dollar lawsuit from your cousins, I must tell you that it's unlikely a challenge to the orders would succeed.'

'But I need money right now,' she screeched, 'so, don't you dare tell me it's not possible!'

He shuffled the papers on his desk and leaned forward. 'I'm not saying it's impossible, Adriana, I'm simply advising you against it, because you're unlikely to succeed. All you'll be doing is wasting the little you have left in legal costs.'

'What don't you understand? I need the money. Suzanne Spellman. Can't you get her? She owes me. She'd do it for nothing.'

'Suzanne Spellman is a criminal lawyer. She doesn't work here. You're free to consult her if you want, but asset preservation matters aren't her thing. Besides, she's under a cloud at the moment. You must have heard the allegations that she's linked to organised crime. There's an ethics investigation pending, so I'm not sure she's taking on any clients.'

Adriana huffed and squirmed in her chair. 'Well, regardless, I think you're wrong. I own several nursing homes and two houses I live in, as well as fourteen that I don't. I have a subdivision planned that stands to net me millions. How dare you suggest I have no hope getting my money.'

'But it's not your money, is it? You can't confuse the companies with yourself. Or your cousins' assets with yours, for that matter. Look, Adriana, I've given you my advice; you're free to take it or not, but if you decide to proceed against my advice, I'll have to ask you to make a sizable payment to us upfront, on account of costs and barrister's fees.'

'From where? The money I can't access?' She stood up. 'I can't even pay the cook this week. You lawyers are all the same: nothing's impossible when you have lots of money and nothing's possible when you don't. You know what? You can stick your advice.' She walked towards the door and opened it. 'And I still say you're wrong. I think all you are is a really crappy lawyer.'

She stormed out of the office, down the elevator and onto Collins Street.

Outside, it was blowing a gale. The wind lifted the sand and dust out of the tram rails and smacked her in her face with it. She turned away and glanced around for the many paparazzi she was sure would be stalking her, but she found that that there was only one. To be accurate, there was none, but a staff reporter dashing past on his way to *The Age* office spotted her and took out his phone. She raised her Louis Vuitton as a shield to him and the wind, yelled out 'No photographs dickhead!' and hurried towards her Lamborghini.

For her own convenience, she had parked it as close as possible, in a loading zone, as she often did. Parking meters and carparks were for losers—she wasn't constrained by petty bureaucracy. She expected to find a parking fine, but so what? What she didn't expect to find was the car shackled and a notice from the sheriff plastered right across its windscreen, telling her not to attempt to drive it, as it had been seized for unpaid fines.

She stopped dead and stared at her car for a while. It seemed the world was conspiring against her. 'Fuuuuuuck!' she screamed, as the reporter chuckled and videoed the scene. 'Cunt fuuuckerrr!' she bellowed at him, raising her middle finger, and running into a nearby arcade for shelter.

She took out her phone. When her housekeeper and her security guards failed to answer her calls or respond to her frantic messages, she arranged a rideshare car back home. By the time she arrived there, everyone had left.

'One day, you bunch of pathetic arsehole losers! I miss paying your wages by one day and you all fuck off on me?'

She wasn't destitute. The cars were leased but, aside from her jewellery, she kept a stash of gold and cash in the safe in her study, as well as a private bank account with a six-figure balance. She'd pay the staff what she owed them, but they could all go whistle if they thought they could ever return to their jobs.

She went into the room and pulled back the television that shielded the safe. She punched in the code on the keypad. She opened the door. She looked inside.

'Brian! You mother-fucking, cock-sucking asswipe!'

She reeled and clutched at her pounding heart. The safe was empty. Gone. Everything.

Well, perhaps not everything. She placed her hand into the bowels of the safe and felt around. Then a receipt fluttered out; it had been caught in the door. She picked it up and looked at it. The receipt was for her private account. As of this afternoon.

While she'd been out seeing her lawyer, Brian had gone to the bank. The receipt read: *Closing Balance $5.00.*

But Brian was nowhere to be seen. Gone. With everything. Even the Whiteleys and the Nolans.

She phoned Harry Wiseman. 'Do you understand I'm broke? Get me some fucking work!' she shrieked. 'Now! I'll do anything!'

'I don't know what you expect me to get for you, Adriana. You've done this to yourself, you know. You're poison right now. I mean, have you googled yourself recently?'

She terminated the call, and she tried Sergeant Moylan next. He never picked up.

***

Elsewhere, Misha had googled Adriana. 'Oh, my lord!' she gasped.

'What?' asked Peter.

She began to laugh. 'Come here! You have to see this!'

The video of Adriana and her Lambo was everywhere, but that wasn't all. There was another video of Adriana, one she had taken herself, that had provoked a multitude of comments.

Adriana was standing in front of the empty safe. Her face was streaked black where her makeup had run. 'The Government is conspiring to destroy me. They've taken everything from me, everything. I have nothing left. I can't pay my staff,' she cried, dabbing her eyes. 'I can't feed all the old people who rely on me. Many, many old people's lives are at risk because of this…this…vendetta against me!'

She had started a Billionaire Babes Gofundme page to help her out of the bind.

Her site had received thousands of hits almost immediately. She expected to see the funds rolling in. Unfortunately, popular opinion in answer to her efforts to raise money seemed to be *Gofuckyou*.

Misha googled Brian Goldsmith and Rebecca Harrison as well, but there was nothing new there, as far as she could tell.

The following morning, Conni rose at eight. She showered, put on a face of makeup and her favourite pantsuit. Then she took her Audi Q7 out for a spin into the hills that towered over Miami Beach.

She followed the road for about eight kilometres to a turnoff from the tourist drive, then along a dirt road that ran for nearly a kilometre, which ended abruptly at a steel gate. The sign on the gate was unambiguous. Trespassers weren't welcome.

There was an inconspicuous intercom recessed into a pole by the side of the gate. She leaned out of the car window, pressed the buzzer and waited.

A man's voice said, 'Yeah?'

'I'm here to see Warryn Ward,' Conni announced.

'Is he expecting you?'

'You can tell him it's Concheetah. He and I go back a long way; he'll know who I am.'

'Right.'

She waited by the intercom for a few minutes, until a buzzer sounded and the gate began to open automatically. She took a deep breath, engaged gear, and drove through. She followed the narrow road for another hundred metres or so, past a brush fence and into a gravelled clearing where a handful of cars and a dozen or so motorcycles stood.

She parked nearby and switched off the engine.

The sign on the façade of the building fifty metres ahead of her said that she'd arrived at the Kommandanz Clubhouse.

CHAPTER FORTY-NINE

Nature avenged

'It's on!' Misha called out. She was curled up on the sofa in front of the television in Conni's family room.

Conni had invited a select group of friends to hers, to watch the news unfold on live TV. 'A nod to the past,' she called it, 'before we had news on tap. When watching the evening report at six pm was a family ritual.'

'Fine,' said Peter. 'I'll be there.'

There were five of them present: Peter, Misha, Dan, Silvio and Conni. They were all still in the kitchen, except for Misha.

'Hurry up!' she yelled.

'Coming!' Conni replied. She turned to Peter and Dan Browning, 'Have you got your drinks? Yes? Well then, what are you waiting for?'

She grabbed her glass of champagne and led them over to the sofa, while Silvio put his finishing touches to the bruschetta and followed.

'Be quiet,' said Misha. 'It's on next.'

They immediately fell silent, glued to the screen.

The newsreader spoke to camera, next to a still of Harrison and Goldsmith. 'Tyne Coast's mayor and a leading property developer are set to answer charges of corruption and deception, following a story broken by Melbourne investigative reporter Peter Clancy.

'In a sting that stunned the Tyne Coast, Victoria Police raided the homes of Rebecca Harrison and her property developer lover, Brian Goldsmith, this afternoon, seizing computers and over fifty boxes of evidence. Police are also allegedly investigating Harrison and Goldsmith, along with Goldsmith's *Brighton Billionaire Babe* wife, Adriana Balloch, for links to the underworld, as well as in relation to several suspicious deaths.'

After an establishing shot of the Balloch mansion, it cut to footage of the raid, of police carrying boxes and then to an interview with Detective Browning.

'There you are!' cried Conni gleefully. 'I have to say, you look good in person but even better on the telly, Dan.'

They watched the interview in silence. 'It all came to a head this morning,' they heard him say, 'when Goldsmith and Harrison were arrested at Tullamarine Airport attempting to board a flight to Phuket. They were taken into custody, charged and they've been denied bail.'

'Yep,' said Browning. 'They're cooling their heels in the lock-up, as we speak. They're helping police with their enquiries, as they say.'

Conni cheered. 'Well done, Dan! And well done, Peter!'

Browning shook his head, chuckled and sipped his drink.

'Thank you, all of you,' said Peter, 'but don't forget that this was a concerted effort. None of this would have happened without everyone chipping in.'

'It takes a village,' said Conni.

Peter resumed, 'So, I've heard. I'm just a little sad that Arsehole Arnold has gotten away with it again.' He took a gulp of his beer and lowered his eyes.

Conni exchanged glances with Browning. 'I wouldn't be too sure of that,' she replied with a smile.

'Meaning?'

'Meaning nothing, dear boy. What goes around comes around eventually. Hasn't life taught you that yet?'

'Karma? I don't know about karma, but I'm not going to let that prick ruin one more minute of my life. Just hearing that Balloch, Harrison and Goldsmith are in custody, and that Spellman and Moylan are under investigation, is good enough for me.' He paused. 'I'm grateful for the opportunity we've had to do some good here. The Schneider twins are back where they belong, and here's hoping that Mimi and her dad will get to go home soon too. Once

Katherine Sutcliffe stops playing the victim, she'll find her feet, I'm sure.'

'And maybe our dear, sweet Ted will finally enjoy the justice that has eluded him thus far,' said Conni, glancing at Misha. 'Not to mention everyone else they've harmed over the years. That'll be a good dose of well-deserved karma for you.'

***

Back on Helga Lane, Arnold was busy. He had fired up the Audi TT and he and Cooper were preparing to go for an evening drive.

Warryn Ward had summoned them. He told Arnold, 'You'll need to do the drop at the clubhouse tonight. I can't spare anyone to come to your place, so you'll need to shift the gear yourself. Get Rennie to come with you; tell him I said it's time we let bygones be bygones. He'll know where to go.'

Cooper was excited. 'Wardie asked for me to come, too?'

'Yep,' Arnold replied. 'He wants us to take everything that's left out of the container and bring it over. He says the clubhouse isn't on any map but he reckoned you'd know how to get there.'

Cooper responded, 'It makes sense: you probably wouldn't have a hope of finding it in the dark without me. I haven't been down to the clubhouse in years. They've got the best bar and all the grog's free.'

Arnold wasn't as enthusiastic; he didn't like acting as a mule. He hated it, in fact. There were lots of unscrupulous people who'd gladly commit murder for less than what they'd be hauling. The load was worth at least high six figures on the street. If his wife had been home, he would have taken her LandCruiser and driven there in comfort, but, as it was, he had no option but to drive the Audi TT.

He unlocked the shipping container; it was almost entirely empty. Nevertheless, he needed every spare inch of the car to carry the large bundles of crystal meth and heroin that were still there. Cooper even had bricks of it on his lap. Arnold didn't care: he didn't need to hide it from the police; he was untouchable. He never doubted it. Passing information to the coppers was inherently dangerous and he deserved every inch of his immunity. No copper worth his salt would look at him or his Audi TT twice, no matter what.

He helped Cooper pass his seat belt under the drugs and buckle it, not because he gave a shit about Cooper's safety, but because the sound of the alarm would have driven him mad. They took off down the road at breakneck speed and turned onto the esplanade heading south.

From there, they followed the turnoff from the tourist drive, onto a dirt road that ran for nearly a kilometre, which ended at an open steel gate. Arnold revved the car over a grate and, a little further on, he screeched to a halt in the carpark, showering two of the Harleys with gravel.

'What the fuck did you do that for, idiot?' asked Cooper.

'Why the fuck do you care, old man?' Arnold replied.

They reached the Kommandanz Clubhouse a little after eight. One of the lieutenants helped them unload and then they all sat together at the bar and drank a beer. Warryn Ward was nowhere to be seen. Cooper asked after him.

'Nah mate,' said one of Ward's lieutenants, 'you missed him. He's really sorry, mate, but he had to go out.'

'Good on ya, mate,' he said to the lieutenant.

He replied, 'Yeah, he had something on, but he's sent you his warmest.' He turned to Arnold, 'So, that's the lot now, hey? You're not holding anything else, right? The shipping container?'

Arnold responded, 'Nah, it's all there. The container's empty.' He noticed that the lieutenant appeared distracted. He drained his glass and nudged his father-in-law. 'We better go,' he said.

Cooper pushed his empty pot away. 'Yeah, all right, all right. Keep your hair on.' He turned to the lieutenant. 'Tell Wardie, never mind; we'll have a beer together next time.'

'Yeah, right.'

They climbed back into the TT and took the same route back. The sky overhead was lumpy and before too long it began to drizzle. They were almost home when Arnold started to feel weird, like he wanted to vomit and defecate simultaneously. His heart was well and truly racing before he noticed the flashing headlights from the car behind him. He figured it must have been because he'd slowed down and they wanted to pass. It was dark and the road was slimy, but no one overtook the Audi TT. No one. Ever.

The engine roared as he pushed the accelerator hard to the floor and continued along the esplanade. Then he felt the car lurch abruptly to the left before he righted it again.

'Hey, mate,' said Cooper, 'steady on!'

But his words fell on deaf ears.

Arnold's shirt was wet with sweat. He'd filled his pants. He had to keep going. As fast as he could. Get medical attention. Tell his wife.

He grabbed his phone.

He misjudged the bend not far from the turnoff to Helga Lane. He tried to pull back, but he'd already lost traction. The Audi TT was full throttle. It sped over the edge of the road, crashed through tea-trees and black wattle and landed heavily on a rocky ledge below. The windscreen was shattered, and the cabin littered with branches and broken foliage. Arnold was dazed but aware of what had happened.

He shook the fog from his head and tried to refocus, but something wasn't right. He glanced across at Cooper. 'You okay?' His voice sounded like treacle.

There was no response.

'You okay?' he repeated, slurring badly. 'Rennie?'

Again, nothing. Cooper was either dead or unconscious. Arnold gave him a shake. When Cooper slumped over, Arnold noticed a torn branch sticking out of the old man's left temple.

He yelped and wiped the muck off his own face. Then he attempted to open the door, but it was jammed. His phone was still in his hand. He was trying to dial emergency when an SMS interrupted him. The screen lit up.

TIME FOR DOGS TO DIE.

Then there was a loud bang, and the cabin began to fill with smoke.

He had to get out. His hands had become two ham hocks—all sensation had abandoned them. In desperation, he tried to work the door, over and over, again and again. Eventually, the mechanism clicked. He pushed his considerable weight against the door and was able to open it far enough to fit his right calf through. He pushed again but he was hard up against a rock. He tried to squeeze himself through the gap, but it was pointless.

The only thing he'd achieved by opening the door was to add oxygen to the fire.

Above him, he heard people yelling and he wanted to shout out, but his throat had closed from the fumes. A man was shining a torch on the car and attempting a descent on foot, when flames engulfed the Audi TT, and he was beaten back. There was no hope.

A fisherman in a boat on the bay heard the noise, looked across and wondered what the flaming beacon was for.

In the morning, the accident investigator arrived to survey the scene. He measured the length of the skid marks on the road, surveyed the crumpled undergrowth and took photographs of everything. He scraped samples of some residue he found on the asphalt as well as on the bushes.

On the rocky ledge below, he found the charred remains of two men in a luxury sportscar and made a note that it wasn't far from where Nick Sutcliffe had died.

CHAPTER FIFTY

After the storm

The wind and the rain persisted for a further six days, scouring out the drains and washing most of the dirt road down the hill and over the esplanade. The downpour flooded Harmony Creek and swept the detritus that Arnold had left behind onto the beach and out to sea. Peter's house was battered by winds that had launched the de Wold children's trampoline into the air and sent it skidding across the road.

Since the accident, the police had been all over the Arnold's residence. The neighbours were asked if they'd seen anything suspicious, but Peter was given especial attention, on account of the articles he had written.

A detective constable came to speak to him.

'As it happens, I was enjoying an evening with some friends. You may have heard of one of them, Detective Senior Sergeant Browning?'

Fortunately for him, his alibi the night of Arnold's accident was watertight, and he was quickly eliminated as a suspect.

With Moylan suspended from duties pending the outcome of the investigation, the local police station fell into disarray. New officers were scrambled to take over until a permanent solution could be found, and Browning was asked to delay his retirement plans and head an investigation into corruption in the lower ranks. He told the Commissioner that he needed to think about it.

On eve of the seventh day, the wind blew itself out overnight. The following morning dawned in blinding sunshine.

Peter woke up early, showered and made himself a double espresso as he listened to the radio.

'Today's forecast is for sunshine and light northerly winds. An unseasonably warm top temperature today of twenty-five degrees is expected. There's a contamination alert for coastal waters, with an extreme e-coli count as a result of the recent storms, and a warning against swimming or other water sports in the bay.'

What everyone else found off-putting, Peter found enticing.

Perfect! Not even the dogs and their pesky owners would risk dousing themselves in that shit.

He'd have part of the coast to himself. He'd always promised himself another beach day.

Just after midday, he turned off his phone and left it on the kitchen bench. He took a hat, a towel and an esky full of beer, and put them in the boot of his car. He locked up the Hermit's Hut, climbed into his car and drove to the beach. Aside from the council van belonging to the cleaner scrubbing out the toilets, Peter's was the only vehicle in the carpark.

Just as he'd predicted: except for the seagulls, the beach was deserted.

He picked a spot well away from the creek and above the high-tide mark, where the sand was golden and free of all debris. He spread out his towel, lay on top of it, put his hat over his face, shut his eyes and let the sun kiss his aching body.

He had found his serenity at last.

THE END

www.ingramcontent.com/pod-product-compliance
Lightning Source LLC
Chambersburg PA
CBHW030602120726
47904CB00006B/1739